ROBIN
and KING
the

▸▸▸▸▸▸▸▸▸▸▸▸

By Parke Godwin

Limbo Search

Robin and the King

Sherwood

The Snake Oil Wars

Waiting for the Galactic Bus

A Truce with Time

The Last Rainbow

Beloved Exile

Firelord

A Memory of Lions

Darker Places

With Marvin Kaye

A Cold Blue Light

Wintermind

The Masters of Solitude

Collected Short Stories

The Fire When It Comes

Anthology (Editor)

Invitation to Camelot

Play

Cold Journey in the Dark (One Act)

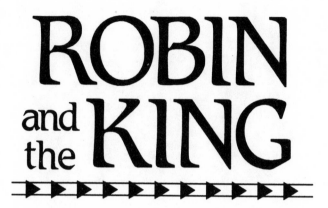

ROBIN
and the KING
the

Parke Godwin

William Morrow and Company, Inc.
New York

Library of Congress Cataloging-in-Publication Data

Godwin, Parke.
    Robin and the king: a novel / by Parke Godwin.
      p. cm.
    Sequel to: Sherwood.
    ISBN 0-688-05274-6
    1. Robin Hood (Legendary character)—Fiction. 2. Great Britain—
History—William I, 1066–1087–Fiction. I. Title.
    PS3557.0316R48 1993
    813'.54—dc20   92-42216
                                                       CIP

Fic

Printed in the United States of America

First Edition

1 2 3 4 5 6 7 8 9 10

BOOK DESIGN BY RHEA BRAUNSTEIN

Foreword

▰▶▶▶▶▰

A Note on Names, People, and Politics

Britain was already known as Englaland by A.D. 1000, and its Anglo-Saxon inhabitants as either Saxons or English. I have used the terms interchangeably as they were used then. Native Celts like Will, Angharad, and Morgan were known as Welsh (*wealsc*), an English word meaning "foreigners." One imagines the British Celts regarded the term with some irony.

While Saxons like Robin and Marian would always lump Normans and Franks together, they were quite different peoples though bound, in the eleventh century, by a common Frankish tongue. The Franks, a northern-Germanic people, overran Gaul in the fifth century with the weakening of the Roman Empire. The Normans began as raiding Norse pirates who settled in northwestern France in the early tenth century. While still characterized by their Viking energy, they very quickly absorbed the language and Christian culture of their nominal overlords, the French.

In feudal theory and custom, William I held his duchy from the French crown in return for fealty. In practice, Normandy was independent and treated with Isle-de-France as an equal power, usually hostile.

King Edward the Confessor was kin to William through his mother, Emma, daughter to Richard I, Duke of Normandy. In 1051, Edward, half Norman himself, promised the English crown to William in right of blood despite strong native opposition, but on his deathbed apparently changed his mind and gave his voice to Harold, Earl of Wessex. William crossed the Channel in 1066 and defeated the English at Hastings. Killed in that battle, Harold was always considered a usurper by the Normans, while most of the English accorded that title to the foreign William. How either felt in his heart in an age when kings were believed to derive their rights directly from God is impossible to tell. Both were intelligent and capable and with great respect for each other. Very likely neither felt the crown settle on his brow without some secret doubts.

However, no one could argue with military conquest. As king in England and duke in Normandy, William became a power bestriding the Channel. The traditional enmity between medieval England and France began with this fact, William's successors an Anglo-Norman spearhead always aimed at the heart of France.

For those readers unfamiliar with *Sherwood,* Robin of Denby (Edward Aelredson) was sixteen when William became King of England and only twenty when, on the death of his father, he became Thane of Denby. A short time later, the knight Ralf Fitz-Gerald was made Sheriff of Nottingham. When Robin actively resisted the foreign king's will, he and several of his followers became outlaws, taking refuge in Sherwood Forest. His lands and hall were confiscated by the sheriff. His wife, Lady Marian, his mother, Lady Maud, and his cousin, Lady Judith, were all sent to serve Queen Matilda at Grantham.

While Robin remained an elusive outlaw and common folk began to swell and sing his legend, Matilda came to hold an affection for the three women, particularly Marian, whose child by Robin she delivered with her own hands. Later, Judith was given in marriage to Ralf Fitz-Gerald, an arrangement she very much wanted. Ralf, who had loved Marian, came to see that reality is more lasting than a dream. Maud was convicted of conveying secret messages to Robin and sent to a dungeon at Hough Castle.

Wounded almost to death by Ralf Fitz-Gerald, Robin was taught to read by Brother Mauger, a monk who joined his band, and Robin's own priest, Father Beorn. The purpose was farsighted: The only English defense against these conquerors was to know and use the law, to remember the history and traditions of their own people. To this end, Mauger had preserved a manuscript of the Anglo-Saxon Chronicle which Robin delivered to Abingdon Abbey.

Earl Waltheof, one of the last Saxon nobles to retain power under William, planned massive revolt in 1075. Knowing the uprising to be a naked bid for personal power rather than restoration of an English crown, Robin sided with the king. He and Ralf Fitz-Gerald became unlikely allies and fought side by side at Norwich Castle in the battle that crushed the rebellion in England.

Winning his pardon, Robin was restored to his lands as a vassal of Ralf, whom the king created Vicomte of Nottingham.

Robin and the King begins eight years later.

Acknowledgments

As the song goes, "... with a little help from my friends." Deepest thanks to—

My agent Merrilee Heifetz for her encouragement and practical support in the preparation of this book, and to Susan Shwartz, author of *Grail of Hearts*, for much of the same.

Jean-Daniel Breque of Paris, professional translator and personal friend, for rapid emergency translations into French whenever needed. Fabienne Rose, kind hostess and supersonic driver, who whizzed us through a whirlwind tour of Rouen and Gisors in a single day. My thanks.

Charles T. Wood, professor of history, Dartmouth College, for a copy of the coronation charter of Henry I, one of the foundation stones of the later Magna Charta.

Again to Cheryl Kedwards for contemporary orthodox medical treatments and insights into the medical thinking of the time.

Persia Woolley, author and medievalist, for patiently critiquing this manuscript line by line and providing voluminous notes, corrections, and suggestions, and above all for her abiding trust.

Jinski, a friend early and late.

Contents

Book I Sherwood—May 1083   15

Book II When Strong Dies   131

Book III Conscience of the King   269

Afterword   363

Book I

Sherwood—May 1083

1

━▶▶▶▶▶▶━

THE forest held its breath. Tranquil summer silence tensed,
crouched in defense as the danger flowed like shadow out from
Lincoln toward west and south.

*The king sends men to raze villages in the lands of Bishop Osmund.
Enclosed for the king's hunting, they say, and who will be homeless
next?*

From Nottingham to Lincoln, men high and low worried the news
between them. Surely such a measure required law and would need
deliberation before the Forest Assize at Papplewick—

*Oh, indeed, the king's case will be put before the court like a gutting
knife before the fatted hog, but while they're at it, the Normans will be
driving the folk out of Linby.*

Men tried to tell themselves that such was not so. Sheriff of Nottingham Ralf Fitz-Gerald was also magistrate at Papplewick Assize.
He wouldn't stand for such plain theft, king or no. Bishop Osmund
would not.

*That's as may be, but I know one who won't for a certainty, and
that's Robin of Denby. Robin's a good lord, Alan of Linby Dale another.
They've mulled and stirred it between 'em, and they'll not just sit by.
We're to wait for the word.*

*Wait? Whatever they do, let it be now. The king's men are on the
road and coming south.*

"Wulf! Wulf Edricson!"

The mail-coated rider, helmet tied to his pommel, sword banging against his thigh, galloped across the meadow toward the sheepcote, jumped a narrow rill, and brought up short before the dozen half-naked men shearing dirty brown fleece from Edricson's sheep. Wulf had snatched for his tunic when Alan called out. He wrestled into it, took the padded surcoat his churl passed him, then buckled on the mail coat and the sword belt over it. Past forty now and thickening through the waist, Wulf had been chief freeman to Thane Alan—when thanes still bore that title—and his father the same to Alan's sire. His saddled horse waited. Wulf mounted with a grunt, waving to his men.

"You know where to meet with us. Let every man bring his arms. Lord Alan, how close are the Normans?"

Alan wiped the sweat from ruddy cheeks and brow. He'd forgotten how hot iron mail could be even so early in summer. "Last word, they'd passed Edwinstowe, by now west of Denby somewhere. Robin will know. Come on."

"Get those stupid sheep back in the cote before anything else," Wulf barked to his men. "And don't be late at Linby. It's Robin who calls you."

The two horsemen trotted their mounts across the rill into the meadow, breaking into a headlong run.

On an open heath north of Linby village, the tall man with the spare farmer's frame watched his friends approach. Since the morning was already warm, Robin of Denby had waited with no armor on but his mail drawers. Reluctantly now, he drew on the padded coat and heavy mail hauberk, buckling the coat of scale armor over all, and belted on his sword. He mounted the sand-hued gelding and paced forward as Alan and Wulf trotted up to him.

"Robin, how much time have we?"

"Not that much. Put on your helms."

"They're hot," Wulf complained.

"Just to see how well you're covered. If we're to be seen in Papplewick court this afternoon, I don't want to be known by the king's men this morning." Robin slipped the old-fashioned helmet over his head. The device had belonged to his grandfather Brihtnoth, of the old design with wide loops forming a mask around the eyes, a hanging skirt of mail fore and aft covering face and neck completely. Alan's helm had a complete face-piece, the gold-worked helm boasting a boar-crest. Wulf's was almost identical. Not many of the type had been commonly seen since the days of King Ethelred.

"This helm was worn at Maldon." Alan swung his visor up, grinning toothily at Robin. "How do I look?"

"Like flamin' old Beowulf himself. Wouldn't know you if you sang out your name thrice over."

Wulf swung his horse about, eager to be at the adventure. "What's the plan?"

Robin swept his arm out to the morning sun. "You go east, Alan west, I'll to the south. Bring every good man you can find. Let them arm and meet us at Linby church."

A pardoned rebel and touchy on the subject of lost causes, Alan was still careful enough now to be troubled by a consideration. "This is the bishop's land and south is the sheriff's. Do they know what we're doing?"

"It was your land first, Alan," Robin reminded him. "Osmund and Ralf will be in court today. Until then, I was given to understand they'll be looking the other way. Now *run* those horses, we've not much time."

West as far as Annersley the call spread, south and east across the fields to the serfs of the vicomte-sheriff Fitz-Gerald: Arm and meet Robin at Linby. Hurry!

Men and boys ran from the fields, leaving the work to wives and daughters. From under the eaves of their crofts, out of old chests, they brought the heirloom fyrd weapons handed down from fathers and grandfathers. A spatha sword carried at Hastings, a round shield, battered but unsplit, old spears and scramasaxes, the leather war shirts dark and cracked with age and their iron rings rusted. The foresters like Will Scatloch and Morgan of Powys laid their best arrows in the quivers and braced their bows.

The motley band began to flow at a trot from all directions toward Linby church.

King William had referred the matter of land enclosure to the Forest Assize, indicating to Robin's legal turn of mind that the men moving on Linby now were not dispatched by the king's personal order. So much was Robin's gamble; his strategy, based on that hazard, was to discourage the men from Lincoln with overwhelming numbers and pray the issue wouldn't come to open fight.

That would depend on the man leading the king's party, Ranulf of Bayeux.

* * *

19

Though an ordained priest, Father Ranulf was as secular a soul as labored in the king's service, the youngest, most capable, and by far most ambitious among William's clerical servants. Keeper of the Chancery seal at Winchester, Ranulf maintained a house and a wife in Lincoln. Any royal business transacted there was done in French. Like all Norman masters, Ranulf underestimated the abilities of his English servants to comprehend the tongue of their conquerors. Certain of these overheard the intent to enclose large portions of Sherwood Forest for royal hunting preserve, and one of them cared enough for a particular name and its memory to hurry the intelligence beyond the doors of Ranulf's house in Steep Hill.

The word traveled south along Ermine Street and the old road to Leicester, whispered in a rush through Newark-upon-Trent and west into Sherwood, seeking the name that still meant *pride* to a defeated people, common folk who storied and sang that name with those of Hereward and King Alfred. Few north of Thoresby knew the man's real name, fewer would care. As legends went, real or fantastical, the songs held the larger truth they wanted to hear, and the larger-writ name which even Ranulf of Bayeux recalled hearing in Ermine Street and Wigford market. In an idle moment he inquired of his pretty young English wife, Elfled: "Did such a man actually live once or was he pure fancy, this . . . Ro-*bin*?"

Elfled corrected the pronunciation. "*Ro*bin. Robin Hood."

"He was quite real?"

"Oh yes," Elfled smiled. "An outlaw, but not like a common criminal." More pragmatist than patriot, Elfled could still take pride in a regional hero. "Our people loved him."

"Indeed?" Ranulf yawned, nimble mind already turning to more important matters. "When did he live?"

His wife could not say precisely. To Elfled, just nineteen, all of the past drew together into a vague Long Ago. She'd first heard of Robin Hood when she was a child of seven or eight, as close as she could remember. "He might be living yet, but I suppose he would be quite old now. If you meet him in Sherwood, you can be honored to shake his hand."

The venerable outlaw of Sherwood was no more than thirty-three that year, a lawyer in the Forest Assize at Papplewick. Ranulf would meet him twice that week, Elfled later, both unforgettably.

* * *

The party of thirty men rode at a walk along the narrow cart track through Sherwood toward Linby: an unusual detail, a gaggle of monk clerks plodding along on mules in the rear; ten men at arms following after a half dozen knights and their squires. At the head, Father Ranulf. No one would have taken him for a priest. He eschewed priestly garb most of the time for a blaze of colors. He intended to make an impression on the forest court this afternoon, but a more lasting one in Linby beforehand, evacuating the village by force and presenting that as a *fait accompli* to which loyal lords such as Osmund and the sheriff could only submit, lesser men following in line. Much of the old forest of Ytena had been so enclosed without serious resistance; Ranulf expected no sharper defiance in Sherwood. His order from King William was simply to lay the crown demand before the Assize; to clear Linby first was Ranulf's own inspiration, the product of a mind yet young enough to stumble now and then over its own precocity. As he rode toward a bend in the cart track, his mood was supremely confident.

The knights and men at arms trailing out behind him were not as sanguine. Battle veterans, they saw how close the thickets pressed in on both sides of the path, how little visibility there was beyond the bramble and hazel. Sharp ears and sharper instincts disliked what they felt and perhaps heard: the sense of being watched and stalked. A fine place to be ambushed with a priest in charge and a useless lot of monks panicking and running about in headlong confusion.

One of the older men, Ranulf's knight-commander for the journey, rode forward to range by the priest's palfrey. He didn't like Bayeux: too sure of himself, too arrogant for his green years, but the man had power to make and break and so must be borne. The knight addressed him with measured respect, one wary eye on the forest around them. "How far to Linby, Father?"

"I would say no more than a mile."

They were almost to the bend in the cart track. Ranulf's palfrey snorted and shied nervously, causing the knight to peer even closer at their surroundings. "Don't rein her too tight, *bon prêtre*. In some matters, one can trust a horse before men."

"What means that?"

"I'll hazard my best armor to your oldest pair of shoes we are not alone."

Occupied bringing the nervous mare into manage, Ranulf shot one cursory glance at the forest around them. "I've seen nothing untoward."

"That's my point," his knight muttered as they rounded the bend. "You won't. These Saxons—"

He reined sharply to a halt. Startled, Ranulf did the same. Not twenty paces before them, three mailed and helmeted riders blocked the narrow way completely. Behind them, a dozen ranks deep, loomed a prickly show of spears and shields. The veteran knight-commander concluded laconically, "That was my point."

"Are they knights?"

"Perhaps, but not Normans." Not in such ancient armor or riding hard-worked mares and geldings. The commander stood erect in his stirrups as the column behind shuffled to a ragged halt. "Whose men are you?"

The rider in the middle, completely masked by the mail fringe beneath his helm, walked his horse forward to a point midway between the opposed groups. He ignored the knight's challenge, addressing Ranulf in educated French. "You are Father Ranulf of the Chancery?"

The priest responded in English with open irritation. "I am. What means—?"

"Bound for the Assize at Papplewick?"

"We are, but first to Linby."

"Oh, I think not," one of the other helmed riders said in English, trotting his mare forward to the side of his comrade.

"You've missed the path to Papplewick," the leader said. "Go back a mile to the first east turning."

"We are on the king's service. Stand aside," Ranulf demanded as the rest of his knights pressed forward around him. Not a military man, he could yet see how close-crowded and disadvantaged they were if the situation turned ugly, aware of the tension in the men around him and those blocking his way. He conferred with the knight-commander in a low voice. "What think you?"

"I tried to tell you. There are more about than we can see. We're outnumbered and in poor position."

Ranulf warned again. "Whosever men you are, to hinder us is to defy your sovereign lord William."

"Eh, then, we've done that before." The third English rider, masked as his companions, ambled his past-prime horse forward to flank his two friends. The remark was mostly lost on Ranulf, whose English was spotty, but the leader spoke again in French, the voice slightly muffled behind mail cowling.

"The king's business is in Papplewick, not Linby, and will be heard

22

there. We are merely concerned that you might be so eager in loyalty that you'd do the king's will before it became the king's law.''

"Listen to me, *Anglais*. I don't know who you are," the knight-commander lashed out. "I don't care. For the last time, stand *aside*."

"Flight!"

While the sound of the word still shivered on the air, two arrows buried themselves in the dirt before Ranulf. Several of his younger vavasors reached for swords, only to be stayed by their commander. "Hold."

Not loud but firm, the decision of a tempered man who knew the difference between courage and virtual suicide. "Father Ranulf, we don't know how many there are or how many archers. This is no time for a foolish test of wills."

"True. Honor makes a cold epitaph for any man." Yet it enraged Ranulf to be checked so, snared like a rabbit because he underestimated his opposition. He raised his voice to the English leader, carefully squelching the anger. "Whoever you are, Saxon, I mark you."

The man paced his horse forward to rein athwart Ranulf's way, almost close enough to touch. He stripped the gauntlet from his left hand. Of peasant birth himself, the Chancery priest knew the look of a hand used to manual work, callused and sun-darkened, a thin white scar running between thumb and forefinger to the heel of the palm. The Saxon raised it as in making a vow.

"Ranulf of Bayeux, by this hand I mark you."

At closer range, behind the helm's broad eye-loops, Ranulf noted placid blue eyes that he would have described as arrogant but for the sleepy good humor he seemed to read there. "You are no knight, fellow."

"Better far!" one of the English riders roared at him. "Nay, have you never heard of Robin Hood?"

Ranulf caught only the name, but that with something of a shock. The Saxon leader grumbled at his companion, "Boyo, you could have gone all your life without saying that."

"Robin Hood?" said Ranulf evenly. "I have heard of you."

"And I of you. You'll be turning back now."

The statement was soft but implacable. Ranulf had swallowed greater humiliations in his rise to power; that was the tax paid by men of ambition without high birth to help them rise. He banked his fires now to conserve them for Papplewick. "Come," he ordered all within hearing. "For the Assize at Papplewick."

Behind them the Englishmen made no move as Ranulf's party re-formed, knights jostling their horses back through men at arms and frightened monks.

"I could see them all around us," one clerk gabbled nervously as Ranulf passed him. "God defend! Dozens of them. A hundred."

The numbers were academic to Ranulf as he rode morosely back along the way to the Papplewick turning. There was even sour amusement in the matter. *This* was Robin Hood, the old man from years gone by? Ranulf had it in mind to advise Elfled that her sense of time was appallingly vague.

2

THERE we stood—stopped, my lords, checked by a hundred armed men, forbidden to proceed on the lawful business of my king by this *ambush*. A flagrant uprising and more than that, for I dare call it rebellion to equal the Earls' Revolt of eight years past. Shameful and all the more so because, though we knew not their leaders, most of the serfs and villeins must have come from Your Grace of Nottingham's lands—and yours, Lord Sheriff. What is the king to gauge of your constancy from this?"

Planted between lords on benches to one side and commoners on the other, Ranulf paused effectively, letting eyes and challenge sweep over them all. "What is he to think? Words fail me."

Vicomte Ralf Fitz-Gerald, Sheriff of Nottingham and presiding magistrate for the Forest Assize at Papplewick, was dryly impressed by the speaker. If words failed Ranulf, it would be the first time in a long half hour of rhetoric. For the authority that belied the priest's youth, for slashing eloquence, Ranulf of Bayeux was a very blazon to paint on a shield. Appearance, dress, and carriage conjoined to set off the man's natural gifts: a commanding height and fine head with fair hair swept back from a high, sloping brow, eyes that riveted whomever they fell upon. Higher-born men would give much for these physical endowments and the ready tongue of this young man.

The court usually met under a tall ash tree just beyond the village square, but a rain shower decided them to use the old Danish mead hall commonly employed for folk-meet. Outside the ancient timber hall, sheltering under trees or crowded into the tavern, the armed retainers of every lord present were idle, waiting for the session to close. For this day little Papplewick strained to bursting with men and horses. Osmund, Bishop of Nottingham, Sire Henri Chailliard, and a scattering of knights lounged on the lords' benches, plainer-dressed Saxons on the other opposite: former thanes such as Edward of Denby and Alan of Linby Dale, former freemen like Wulf Edricson. What the sheriff might know about the "flagrant uprising" he would keep to himself. King William's new demand for land enclosure affected all of them. The preventive measures of that morning were taken *in extremis* and would not stop William or the incendiary Ranulf without legal strategy shrewd as it was bold, and for that Ralf Fitz-Gerald would trust in Edward of Denby. *Marian's bonny sweet Robin. How will he manage this fire eater?*

At thirty-seven Ralf had matured, mellowed by time and contentment, from an early instinct for leadership to a deeper understanding of what motivated men. Ranulf presented no coil there. Risen out of obscurity in Bayeux, son of a minor priest, his abilities were early recognized by Bishop Odo, half-brother to the king. For all the precocious competence, there was a flamboyant streak in the man laboring too hard to look the noble in his fine linen and blue samite pelisse—but striking for one no more than twenty-three, already able to command any hearing with voice, eyes, and manner. A player born to perform; if not as subtle as Robin, perhaps more imposing.

Ralf measured the man before him. *I know you. I was you before titles and a good marriage came to sate the sharp hungers, a bastard brat needing to get on, fortunate in getting my chance, sufficiently sure of myself to make the most of it. Like you, I was the king's hound to snap at his enemies because he fed me. Now I am full of life and can lift my snout from the bowl and ask questions as Robin always has. This is not Normandy; peers like Osmund and myself are not quite what we were. If you think any of us, Norman or English, will meekly surrender large portions of our lands and livings, think again.*

Ranulf had addressed most of his remarks to Bishop Osmund and the knights on the lords' side of the hall. They were studiously casual even to the appearance of boredom, but none ventured to interrupt the royal attorney. Ralf leaned forward in his chair on the dais. "Does the Chancery accuse this court of complicity in the regrettable incident at Linby?"

"My lord, I do not," said Ranulf.

26

"Then do you rest the crown's case in merely decrying the laxity of order in Sherwood?"

"Rest?" By his emphasis and skillful use of pauses, Ranulf drew all attention to himself again. "By the court's leave, I do not. My heart is in my cause and that cause is not only just but self-evident. What do I stand upon but *jus sanguinis,* the king's right of blood; what custom but those always granted him without dispute? The king will have these lands. He rules by the will of God—and what vassal lord, lay *or* clerical"—this last jabbed at Bishop Osmund with such power that Osmund's scribbling clerk looked up, startled—"what holder of a mere knight's fee will speak the twentieth part of denial?"

Ranulf's vocal power dropped to a persuasive purr. "Who will, in justice, duty, or even prudence gainsay that all forests belong to the anointed king? You, Your Grace?"

Bishop Osmund, like Ralf, had ridden with William the day he won England at Hastings. A stolid, courageous man, his valor was yet mixed with a vassal's caution. He liked this priest no more than the sheriff did. Priest? The man spent ten hours on secular business for every one grudged to God. Osmund responded noncommitally. "I do not dispute the principle."

"Of course not," Ranulf affirmed with satisfaction. "However—"

"I might have a thought or two on the matter."

"Who speaks?" Ranulf whirled about to scan the commoners' benches; someone had addressed him in English. "Who?"

"I do." The shire-accented words sounded like *ah dew* to Ranulf. A beefy, fit-looking man in his prime with long hair and beard the color of new straw rose from his place. Clad in a worn and much-mended linen gown, the Englishman looked like a farmer in holiday best. "Me. Alan of Linby Dale."

"Indeed," Ranulf conceded in mock astonishment for the benefit of the Norman lords. He'd actually hoped for such an interruption. Before coming to Sherwood, he had troubled to familiarize himself with the names of known troublemakers over the years. Besides the near-legendary name of Robin Hood were those of one Edricson and Alan of Linby Dale. Ranulf repeated the name as if it were badly in need of laundering. "The former Thane Alan, my lords, who holds his hides yet by the clemency of our king and the tolerance of Bishop Osmund. Are we now to be honored with that noblest of human utterances, the voice of the English commons?"

27

Knowing Ranulf fortunate that Alan spoke no French, Ralf interceded quickly. "The court recognizes Alan of Linby Dale."

"Aye, tell 'im good," Wulf Edricson grumbled from his bench.

"So I will. If the king's to take our land, what means of payment, hide for hide, can we expect from him?"

The question was translated for Ranulf, who had caught some of its drift. His brows arched high, as if the blunt farmer had inquired of compensation due Adam for the expulsion from Eden. Ranulf swung about to address the lords; the samite pelisse swirled elegantly about his long legs. "*Messires,* let us consider the source of this impertinent question. This rebel, this traitor—no, he cannot deny it—this false subject who made one with Waltheof in that rebellion which still smokes and smolders in the king's dominions oversea. This was one of them, this felon whose head, but for royal clemency, would have been stricken off with Waltheof's."

Ralf shaded his eyes with a grimace. By all he'd heard of Ranulf, the man was in his usual predatory form, prosecuting any man who opposed him like a criminal in the dock.

"You proven outlaw. How *dare* you raise the question of payment when all you possess should long ago have been forfeited for treason?"

"Because the question is quite valid," Ralf answered for Alan from the dais. "Father Ranulf, we consider a civil matter, not felony. Alan is not on trial. Will you answer the question or shall I call for discussion?"

The king's *causidicus* stalked to a place among the nobles but turned back to the court before sitting. "I remind you all, my lords, that I have presented not a request but royal right. You all know what burdens our king carries. His beloved queen will not live out the year, and even now his heir, Robert, rebels in Maine, Absolom adding to the grief of David. But do not think that sorrow will blunt the royal will. Let him contend who will—the king *will* have his due."

The rain had ceased; the hall's warped wooden casements dripped. Ralf spoke to Bishop Osmund. "As our chief peer and prelate, will Your Grace debate the case?"

Osmund whispered briefly with the knights around him and rose to say what Ralf knew full well he would. "Please the court, the peers defer to Edward of Denby to speak our part."

Ranulf settled on the bench next to a young knight as a lank-limbed Englishman rose from the common benches; a man tall as himself, wearing a gilt ax in his broad belt. Before conferring with the court clerk, Ranulf saw the shaggy-headed fellow wink at Alan.

"Your pardon." The Chancery priest touched the sleeve of the friendly-looking knight scarcely older in appearance than himself. "You are called—?"

"Sire Henri Chailliard." He inclined his head to the dais. "I hold a knight's fee from the vicomte."

"Ah, *oui*. And this English lawyer? Why does he come armed into court?"

"Armed?"

"The ax."

"Tradition, one hears. The gilt ax signified the rank of thane—as Robin once was."

Ranulf sat straighter as his mind closed like a sprung snare. "What did you call him?"

"Oh, he's properly Edward of Denby but called Robin. His folk called him Robin Hood in the old days." Henri Chailliard chuckled with tender reminiscence. "Ralf and I fought at his side at Norwich."

"Please the court, Your Grace, lords and commons of Sherwood."

The tall Saxon began to speak, lapsing easily as needed between fluent French and his native English. He might have framed his first remarks in Gaelic for all Ranulf heard them. Yes . . . the set of the shoulders, the timbre of the voice. His partner in the ambush naming him. *Robin Hood. I do indeed mark you and so will the king, I promise.*

Now Ranulf studied the speaker more closely: beyond the unusual height, the thick chestnut hair and beard spiderwebbed with grey here and there, a manner that might be taken for arrogance but for the mild humor lurking about his eyes and the corners of his mouth.

"The king, my lords, who already holds in desmesne one fifth of all the lands in England, sends his clerk to demand more. An able and eloquent *causidicus,* to be sure." Robin bowed courteously to Ranulf. "One who lends pathos to his cause by reminding us of the king's personal burdens and losses. Since many of us sustained similar loss in the famine of a twelvemonth past, I held my tears in check. For all of that, the court will recall the enclosure of the Forest of Ytena four years ago."

"Fact in point," Ranulf interjected. "My ax-bearing colleague argues for my own cause. The clearance of New Forest is precedent for my case. I ask the court scribe to so note."

"By all means," Robin conceded pleasantly. "Put it in writing."

Sire Ralf hid a smile behind his hand. In all his years of friendship

29

and old enmity with Robin, the man had never pronounced the word *writing* without squashing the *i* to *ah* like Alan, with an audible split between syllables. The shire drawl was thicker when Robin first appeared before him with a heart full of law and an illiterate passion for justice. *Oh, we were young then; has it been so long?* Robin had the words now, skilled in them as in his bow, the passion concentrated and controlled.

"Let my lords recall that enclosure now called New Forest."

"For which due compensation was rendered," Ranulf reminded them sharply.

"Compensation." Robin tasted the word carefully for the English benches. "There's a fine French term for you. Value returned for value taken. In that enclosure, the thane of Brockenhurst lost three out of four manors, the thane of Ringwood, over fifteen hides. Let the king's request appear modest as it may when we consider one hundred and forty hides taken out of cultivation. Seventeen *thousand* acres, one hundred and forty families dispossessed—"

"My English colleague is well informed," Ranulf put in.

"Thank you," Robin acknowledged. "We have long memories for hunger. Most men are familiar with these numbers, and what compensation to them, sir? Twenty-eight villages of folk. God knows where they went or how they survived, cast out to steal or starve. But what of that? The king will have his hunting land in *jus sanguinis*— by which the blood in his royal veins washes that from his Chancery's hands."

Ralf Fitz-Gerald sat a little straighter. Robin's tongue could bludgeon or slice like a razor. *Careful, friend.*

Robin paced between the benches, hands clasped behind him, head bent in contemplation. "And this upheaval, this disregard of vassal lords and commons alike was all so that one man—deserving certainly, but no less demanding—might enjoy his chase without let—yes, Sire Henri?"

The young knight had risen to gain Robin's attention. "Fairly said, but what recourse have we in fealty and law?"

"None!" Ranulf's voice was a knife cutting off any question. "What the king sends as request could and will return as demand if this Assize refuses him. Take care, *mes seigneurs*. Grudge this little, you may lose much. I warn you."

Robin turned to him—turned *on* him; his glance lashed Ranulf like a whip. "You warn? Well."

30

Ralf Fitz-Gerald heard the subtler warning in the few soft-spoken words and stepped in smoothly. "The court commends the speaker from Denby to that prudence for which he has always—or at least of late—been known."

Through the ripple of knowing laughter from both sides of the hall, Robin acceded to the admonishment. "My good lord of Nottingham schools me. To answer Sire Henri who questions for us all, I move that the king's demand—I cry you mercy, Father Ranulf—his request, be continued to the next meeting of Hundred Court at Mansfield. Those in favor?"

The *ayes* roared to the rafters from all throats but one.

"Opposed?"

"No," said Ranulf for all the good it did him.

"So moved." Ralf ruled quickly, with considerable relief.

Ranulf shot to his feet, furious. "You cannot. This court cannot. This only increases the penalties you will pay later."

Perhaps—but Ranulf and every man present knew what Robin had done in a few seconds. By continuing the case to Hundred Court, Robin had opened the way of appeals to Shire Court as well; in short, a legal delay of months or even a year.

"If you want bread, boyo," Robin told him genially, "you must wait on the grinding of the mill. The king knows more of England than when he came. He will not abuse loyal lords out of hand for the sake of a few deer."

Amid the buzz from the benches, Ranulf moved to confront Robin, speaking with muted venom no others heard. "Yes, it was you. You were the one in the forest."

Placid blue eyes reflected only a mild lack of comprehension. "Don't follow you there."

Ranulf did not flinch from that gaze. "I think you do, *bonhomme* Robin. Your companion named you so."

"Robin's a common nickname in these parts. You would need witnesses, Father."

"Some of whom are here, I would venture to say." Ranulf's eye slid to Alan and Wulf sprawled on the bench. *"Prenez garde, Anglais.* I have never lost a case of this kind."

"Impressive—but like getting drunk or making love. There's always the first time."

"You insult the king!"

"As you insulted Alan." Robin's voice slid up on a sharper note.

31

"You're a foreigner, you wouldn't know, but we've had a gutful of defeat without you into the bargain. That man you called rebel and felon was a landowner when you were trotting at some bishop's heel, learning to be a lickspittle lackey. I've heard how you bully honest men in court when they ask only plain rights. Don't come the king's loyal servant to me. You're a jumped-up villein yourself, and you damned well love having the whip in your hand for a change."

Ranulf did not color or sputter his fury. He had not risen so rapidly by giving vent to spleen at the wrong moment. Rage in him stayed cold, the better to keep. He knew the weapons and the tactics of law. He could allege but hardly prove Robin's complicity in the ambush. In any case, this was not the time or place. No, his answer would speed to William. "You will not impede the king's will, nor his servant whose charge it is."

"You heard the court; your suit's appealed." Robin turned away. "Go say a Mass, Father. If you remember the words."

Some precepts of caution Robin had yet to learn. An idealistic Greek once postulated that power was deserved only by those with no need of it, though the hungrier men most often sought it out, and when the whip was in their hand, they usually layed about liberally and presented a large bill for injuries inflicted on them while climbing.

Robin returned to his bench as Ralf rose to adjourn the session. There was a general sigh and stir of approval from lords and commons alike eager to get home or at least to horse and open air.

Ralf descended from the dais, staying Robin as he took his leave with Alan and Wulf. "You were bound home?"

"There's the sheep. My folk have been shearing all week and need me there."

"Wait a little," Ralf requested of his friend. "I think you've made an enemy."

"He did leave that impression."

"Men walk carefully about Bayeux. His voice is nearest to the king's ear."

"He angered me, Ralf. A little green, ent he, to be scoring good men like Alan?"

"I rose like him, remember? Men like Ranulf were never boys, never young. Tread warily, *mon ami*."

Robin threw an arm around the smaller man's shoulder. "Old worrier."

"I am serious, Robin. You tilt with Ranulf, learn more of him first."

"Oh . . . perhaps I will. Come drink with me before I leave."

Ralf declined, having duties in Nottingham. "But remember you of this. He's new in his office. A baby adder, if you will, just out of the egg. But such are born knowing how to strike."

3

ROBIN rode home to Denby with Will Scatloch, Morgan of Powys, and his steward Mauger through late afternoon sunlight dappling the forest floor. He spoke little, his mind turning on many things at once, giving the black mare her head as she ambled along the forest track.

"You did well," Mauger assessed. "This Ranulf is a man-eater in the courts."

"A walking plague," said Will Scatloch, who had awaited his lord with Morgan in the tavern. "A winter wolf among lambs so the soldiers said."

"Lord Robin drew his fangs," Morgan humphed. "And grand sport it was to turn him back."

And dangerous as Ralf warned. He'd not drawn Ranulf's teeth, just gained time, jammed into the priest's ravening legal craw too much for William's *causidicus* to chew all at once.

The king stood on rights but no reason or justice. The boy wonder from Bayeux would fume to William, who would roar in Normandy and even send more peremptory demands to Ralf and Osmund—who, in return, would promise to consider closely the royal rights in Hundred and Shire courts, some English subtlety having rubbed off on both men in the last decade. William could not now exercise his "rights" without damage to loyalties on which he depended. They would also remind their sovereign of last year's bitter famine.

We missed the worst of it, Robin reflected gratefully. But after young Edward, three more boys had come, one stillborn, the others dead soon after birth, until Marian begged of Father Beorn and God: What was she punished for, what sin, that her children wasted and died?

Marian almost died herself last summer with the famine and then another babe, the wee, frail girl born when none of us had enough to eat and I prayed by her bed for God to take the child rather than my lady, sin or not. I could stand the loss of the bairn, but not her who's always been the best part of me.

A miserable, hungry year, barley blighted on the stalk, turnips in the ground. Folk crowded into churches with prayers first sincere and then desperate. Weeks of fear for Marian with himself hardly leaving the bower where mother and child lay closer to death than life, and Will's wife Angharad nursing both, shining what light she could on her haggard lord. Though Father Beorn baptized the babe even as his sexton dug the small grave, they'd not named her yet since she was not like to live.

"It is a wheel, this life," Angharad sighed to Robin in her Welsh lilt, "and if her *moira* is not to come in our day, the wee one will come round again. Souls are not wasted ever."

"*Moira?*" Will Scatloch defined for Robin. "Your word would be *wyrd*. Fate and destiny; what is writ out for each of us."

God heard Robin's prayers. Marian and her baby lingered, rain filled the waiting grave. With his wife's cheek hot against his palm, Robin promised anything to a God who would save her. *And if the child survives, we will call her Moira.*

The infant strengthened, Marian healed, but both slow enough to drive Robin to despair. He let Mauger direct the work of the steading. The sheriff's knight Henri Chailliard clattered up to Denby gate with news Robin barely marked in his misery. Earl Odo of Kent had been seized by King William for attempting to lure away high men to follow him in his bid for Rome and the papacy. Robin was distracted but courteous to his friend. He thanked Ralf for the news, but for the ambitions of Odo, the man could go to Rome or to hell, Robin cared not. His cousin Judith, Ralf's vicomtess, sent letters almost daily.

My very dear Robin, I will come to Marian as soon as I can. Ralf and I pray for her each day, though my husband is so burdened now. There could be war with the southern counties, not to mention the king's son Robert. One hears he is called the perfect knight. Alas, in wit or statecraft, the man should solicit the counsel of his more intelligent horse. It is out of all compass for so strong a king to suffer so disastrous an heir, and a

sore wound to subjects. No, I promise again, cousin: Tell Marian I will
be there this week and stay as long as she needs me.

A burden to all men, such misrule, and those royal ''rights'' of which
Ranulf brayed as self-evident were not at all obvious to Robin of Denby.
Common men fought the king's incessant wars and incessantly died in
them, and were now commanded to cut off pieces of their own narrow
livings so William—*oh, I can bleed for his sick queen who was kind*
to Marian, for mine's that close to dying—could have the best of hunting.

That had stuck in Robin's English craw since the day he swore fealty
to William at the age of twenty. Thirteen years later, the lump was still
there, unswallowed.

''Nay, is it so bad?'' Marian posed when they saw little Moira thrive
where they looked to bury her. ''You ungrateful man, we live! We lost
three babes, but two will live. Leave worrying at the king. Denby's
whole and hale. Look at the men who serve you. Friends, Robin. Like
Ralf, who says you're plain sick with the business of the king, and even
Mauger says you ponder too much on things you can't change.''

''Do I, Marian? Then Mauger should not have taught me the way to
change them.''

Will Scatloch and Mauger of Peterborough—one Welsh, the other
born of an English mother ''and a passing Norman knight who could
not tarry,'' as Mauger lightheartedly recounted. Each man in his time
had been Robin's tutor and none better. Long before Mauger taught
him to read, Will spread Sherwood before his master's son, showing
what was writ there toward the day when Robin would be thane. After
their pardon and return from Norwich, Brother Mauger abandoned his
monk's robe and continued Robin's education as Denby's steward. Polished his English and French, both spoken and written. Robin discovered
his own facility for words and uncanny ear for dialect. No sheep went
to Denby's table but the skin was stretched, treated, and folio-cut for
parchment; no kid was eaten by any tenant without first rendering the
vellum to bind what Robin wrote. No goose but surrendered her share
of quills for writing.

When Robin's old steward Ethelwold passed to God and a preferably
English afterlife, young Mauger readily assumed the office and helped
restore Denby's prosperity.

Mauger and Will. Will with his black curls gone grey but yet no
slackening of the small, spare forester's body that could still match
Robin or Morgan with a longbow. Will, who went into outlawry with

his master, a slave to Robin's father, who bought his freedom from the son. There was a lesson Robin would never forget.

His father, Aelred, had been concerned with justice and good laws as he knew them, Robin the same. Yet Aelred put a slave collar on Will, Angharad, and their sons. Robin, seething against Norman tyranny, never saw his own until it mocked him to his face, showed him clear-sighted in one eye but blind in the other.

"There's the nut of it, Mauger. Aye, and you, Marian."

That was the year Marian was carrying their second child and quite content with what had been given back to her. "Nut of what, love?"

"Why, the case of Will and me. The same with the king's politics."

"Ah, God, are we on that again? A good harvest, one healthy son, and pray God another coming, a full table, and you scribbling away at a notion."

"No, woman, but do you see what I mean?" How even the fairest-minded men were as hard to lift from deep-worn habit as a plough mired in mud. Robin had been shocked, shaken even in outlawry when Will insisted on buying his freedom and that of his family, and flat, unthinking furious when Father Beorn argued passionately for Will.

Those days in the forest seem so simple now, an adventure, a dream. We'd just robbed Bishop Osmund of his rents. Fine sport, and all of us with more money than we'd ever seen. I was a hotheaded boy then.

A boy cocksure of his own rights and place, and no man dare tell Robin of Denby he didn't know the lot. Yes, he could devine some little of what drove a pup like Ranulf. Get angry first, think later. Not that Robin wanted Will a slave, mind, just he'd never thought the matter to clear conclusion. So with most men, high or low. You had to push them uphill and devil if they didn't roll back down to old habit the moment you let go.

"Do you see, Marian?"

She kissed him, thinking about the child to come and a hundred more important things to do within that busy hour than argue with thick Robin. "I love you, but be off with your parchments and pothooks, I've work."

He read and committed to memory the Laws of Alfred, noting his own questions as he went and in time codifying these into an inquiry. When he burned late candles in the hall, sometimes Marian would come from their bower where she woke and missed him beside her, to peer over his shoulder at the scratchings he made on parchment. Robin had once tried to teach her to read, but Marian reckoned there were more pressing matters to get on with.

" 'In' . . . what's this word?''

"Inquiry."

She slipped her cheek down beside his to let him kiss her unbound hair just washed and softened in rainwater. "You'd sleep better without all this learning. Come to bed.''

"Anon, love."

"Now, Robin."

"Can't you sleep?''

"If sleep were my wish. I want you with me.''

"I'll be in. This is mickle matter; it's important.''

Over the years Marian saw this concern grow in him, a part of Robin she never married and would never understand.

Mauger did, at least, knowing Robin let go of convictions no easier than the oak parted from its roots. "You write well, even if you write blasphemy.''

That seemed excessive to Robin, who thought his reason lucid and nary word against God.

"Was it not blasphemy to the Welsh when our fathers fought for room to live in this island?'' Mauger explained. "Not blasphemy when our own ancients preferred to argue law rather than accept it from the lips of some god-king? When Romans told us Caesar was divine and we were not impressed, did they not think that blasphemy? And this?'' Mauger took up Robin's half-written page: " 'INQUIRY INTO THE NATURAL RIGHTS OF SUBJECTS.' More subjects than not will call this as great a sin. You found yourself that men are lazy and fearful. Blasphemy is any idea that frightens them.''

More afraid of losing than what they might attain, and so have I been more than once.

Denby had much to lose. Once an enemy, Ralf Fitz-Gerald had given him back his lands after his royal pardon. Much was risked, lost, and won in the years of the intricate game. There were scars on Robin's body, scars on Denby itself. His mother rarely left Denby now. Lady Maud had survived over a year in an earthen dungeon at Hough Castle. Maud refused to die conveniently for a foreign king, but she came from the pit with its shadow a stain on her mind. On dark days or in unlit rooms she would fall to the old dry-scrubbing at her hands, or stand motionless in the courtyard, her face lifted up to the sun's warmth and clean air. She never forgave Ralf Fitz-Gerald for denouncing her to William as Robin's spy, even when her son argued that Ralf, through his position and his marriage to Judith, was the best friend Denby could wish. "You hold too much with what's gone, Mum."

Her dark eyes, shadowed with something elusive and darker, fixed Robin. "And you do not remember your father?"

"The best of him, yes. The best of what was, what we can save. The rest is gone and won't come back."

"You say that so easily."

"Never easily," Robin assured her. "But I can say it."

With education Robin developed some perspective, but Maud yet flew a tattered and fallen flag. Earl Waltheof did the same in his self-seeking way. Maud stood on a way of life, Waltheof dreamed of its power. The people loved him; he was the last of Old England to them and he looked a king. Cynical Normans like Breteuil would have used him for a standard raised in their revolt against William. More clever than wise, Waltheof allowed himself to be used, saw himself a ruler, not the puppet they would have made of him.

To the end he couldn't understand why I chose the king's side against him. That last day in Winchester Castle, he thought it was all vengeance for my father, could not conceive the larger cause.

A summer day much like this, nigh on a year after the battle of Norwich. His rebellion failed, Waltheof fled to Flanders. The king made light of his treason in letters and embassies, allowing Waltheof to trip over his own cleverness, believe himself forgiven, and return to England. He was arrested as he set foot on shore, conveyed to Winchester, where he was convicted of treason and dungeoned to wait the king's sentence. Harried, badly defeated by the rebels in Brittany, William delayed a year before sending the death warrant.

The new keep at Winchester was of stone, grey and square. More and more of these granite warts were appearing on the face of England to tell the Saxons their conquerors were come to stay. Robin shivered entering the keep, even though the evening was balmy. He handed his written authorization to the castellan. "From the sheriff of Nottingham to see your prisoner."

The order was called to a turnkey. An iron grating was lifted, a ladder lowered into darkness. Winchester's dungeon had only two walls of stone, a mere excavation in the castle foundation. Robin was given a horn lantern before descending.

The cell's occupant sat on his bedshelf, a blanket about his shoulders, sipping from a wooden cup by the light of a small candle end. Condemned or in his own hall, Waltheof never forgot courtesy, rising to greet his visitor cordially.

"Ah, Robin. Here, the castellan sent me wine. Sorry there's only the one cup."

Waltheof squinted against the added light. The once glittering earl was grimy and disheveled, glossy black hair and beard once meticulously curled with hot tongs now matted and overgrown. Waltheof, Earl of Huntingdon, who aspired to a crown. During the tournament at Grantham, the English had cheered the man and hailed him as their choice of king. But he was not hard enough, relied too much on charisma and his power to persuade, far too little on facts. At Norwich in 'seventy-five, Robin and Ralf and a single company of bowmen had snatched the dream from Waltheof's hands and dashed it to pieces.

Robin drank from the cup and returned it. Waltheof swirled and sniffed the contents with a schooled distaste. "Miserable wine."

"I wouldn't know the difference."

"I daresay not," Waltheof agreed with his old superiority. "But the castellan was kind to send it. One might lay many sins to his soul, but not a poor vintage. Well, Robin—why am I not surprised to see you?"

"I've come from Ralf Fitz-Gerald. Mansfield is forfeit to the crown."

Waltheof shrugged and drank. "And the countess, my wife?"

"Safe conduct to Flanders, save she send no letters to de Gael in Brittany."

Waltheof smiled thinly. "I thank the king for that."

Robin took a purse from his belt and set it on the rough stool that served as a table. "From my cousin Judith. For the poor, tomorrow."

"That they bless me on my way?"

"Many have come to do that. You're their martyr."

"And you, Robin, will you bless me?"

Robin could only answer with a silence Waltheof accepted, The earl shifted his glance and the subject. "Vicomtess Judith is kind as she is comely. I would have raised her husband high and you with him. You chose otherwise. My God, but you're vindictive. You've come to gloat."

For an educated man, Waltheof was thick as bread, raised in a time when the earls were still more powerful than their king and always a threat. Power was a habit of his kind, too seldom a talent.

"Why, Robin?" Waltheof asked the question as if it had been swelling inside him and no longer containable. "Was it all for York and your father?"

Robin said evenly, "Some of it. The part that ends tomorrow."

"And the rest? Tell me. I want to know."

If Robin were still twenty as when he watched Normans dump his father's body into a common grave at fallen York sold out by Waltheof, he would have scathed the man with enough righteous contempt to leave the headsman little to finish. That was past. Let him burn down his last candle, then see him to his death. "We have to live with Normans, like rats and fleas. But you, my lord—we can't afford you anymore."

Waltheof toasted Robin with his cup. "Denby as philosopher. York was a sacrifice."

"Weeping Jesus." Robin gaped at the man in cold disbelief. "You really believe that?"

"No other earls of our blood were left, and who with more right than myself? I say *right,*" Waltheof flared with a ghost of the old arrogance. "The decision at York was a strategic withdrawal to better ground. What could I do for the people dead?"

"I don't know. You did nowt alive."

"What I had to do," Waltheof snapped, stung. "You . . . you farmer's grandson, what do you know of sacrifice?"

Robin took up his lantern and moved to the ladder. "Enough to make one of you. Willy Bastard could hold England together; you couldn't. Guard!"

"Wait, please." The burst of anger had burned off; the old, genial Waltheof held out the cup to Robin. "I see only foreign faces here. One last cup with a countryman?"

You were never one of us. You were never anything but power. Robin raised the parting libation to Waltheof. "Good forthfaring to my lord." They drank together. "Alan of Linby sent word."

"Oh, good Alan," Waltheof mused into the depths of the cup, possibly finding the dregs of a lost future. "He did not judge me, only came when I called. What did he say?"

"That though you kneel to die, let the ghost warrior find you standing."

Waltheof settled on his bedshelf. "Alan is an old-fashioned man of high values. I will not shame him. I well understand dying, Robin; it is men like you who elude comprehension." He emptied his cup as the rusty grating overhead groaned open. "You will ride with me in the morning?"

"I will," Robin promised. "Good rest, my lord."

At sunrise next morning, Waltheof was allowed a bath and a razor. He told the Norman barber to leave his long-grown mustache. "It is my country's fashion. I want them to see I was ever one of them.''

Fresh clothes had been provided. Waltheof thanked the castellan for his many considerations, while Robin held his horse. A groom spread the earl's rich cloak over the bay's crupper.

"Good day, Robin."

Robin bowed. *"Hoch, Eorl."*

"Yes, ride at my knee and remember you might have done so in a baron's coronet." Waltheof's coolly amused appraisal took in Robin's plain dun linen and old cloak. "You might have looked less of a farmer."

Well, Robin thought, that's what he was. Waltheof at least looked a king. Balding William with his jowls and pot belly simply was one, did the work, took the risks and the blows, made the hard and often brutal decisions. But Waltheof now, erect in the saddle, what a royal icon he would have made. No more than the hollow image, but one men would worship like a magnificently carved crucifix.

The way to St. Giles Hill grew narrow, with commons crowding forward to see him. Men cried, "God save Waltheof!" and women wept as he passed. To the most destitute, Waltheof passed silver pennies. The English strained forward to touch the false, foolish figure of a dream, the king who might have been; to brush his stirrup or the horse, the mere hem of his cloak, before they were pushed away by the soldiers. Through Market Lane to Eastgate and up St. Giles Hill, where the block waited. Waltheof dismounted and passed his mantle to the priest who had shriven him. "For the poor."

The earl had reserved a portion of his alms for the headsman, a brawny young man who knelt before Waltheof to crave pardon in a Somerset drawl.

"My lord, forgive me my duty."

Waltheof granted the absolution negligently, as if the man had no more than jostled his elbow at table. "But of course. There's for your office. I pray you be proficient. I hate to pay for less than the best."

The Saxon, with tears in his eyes, presented the broad blade for inspection. Waltheof scraped a judicious thumb across the keen edge. "Good."

Before kneeling, he looked down at Winchester spread before him in the morning sun. "This was great Alfred's capital, Robin. It might have been mine."

He turned without another word or glance to the others, and knelt before the block. The headsman was worth his fee. One stroke sufficed. Waiting assistants bore the head to impale it on a pole.

"Wait." Robin turned the pole until Waltheof's half-open eyes stared north. Toward York.

So much for his father's *wergild*. Robin rode away from Winchester.

"And are you done with vengeance now?" Father Beorn asked him later when Robin made confession.

"Mine, yes." England's he would work on.

And did. Three years ago, after studying with Mauger and Judith until he felt one more memorized precedent, fact, or maxim of law would burst his skull, Robin waited to present himself at the Forest Assize in Papplewick. Judith came for the occasion, and Marian with her, proudly choosing to seat themselves with the English landowners.

"For the peers, His Grace the bishop of Nottingham."

"For the commons, Edward of Denby."

Judith said afterward that it was a victory. Marian ventured no sentiment at all, only glad to take Robin's arm and get home to the world she knew, that this place of lords and lawyers and her husband's own obsession threatened.

"AN INQUIRY INTO THE NATURAL RIGHTS OF SUBJECTS."

"Such big words." Marian admired the letters over Robin's shoulder, teasing at his ear with her lips. "Save the candle, come to bed."

"Presently."

"Leave it, love." Behind him, Marian stared like a rival at the words she couldn't read, and felt afraid. "Aren't you happy enough, then?"

4

APPY? Who could not be, just returning to Denby? Their horses splashed across the rill that ran along the low wall of the steading. Catching sight of them as they emerged from the forest, a dark youth loped across the courtyard, sprang up onto the gate where the ancient horn hung, and blew a welcoming call.

Will's eldest son, Eddain, was nineteen now, with a deeper voice than his father's, but as sweet in song; even Morgan of Powys admitted to that. He jumped down lightly to swing the gate open as the folk of Denby appeared from hall, kitchen, and bowers to greet their lord.

"There's loyal he is!" Will crowed as blind Wystan came from the latrine, hitching up his trousers, calling impatiently for his wife Minna to stand with him. "Eddain, take the horses; you and Gwaun give them a good rub."

The men swung down. Mauger made for the well to splash himself off, but Will held out his arms to Angharad and stocky young Gwaun, seventeen now and eager to be his father's image in all.

"Da!" Robin's son Edward came bounding across the western meadow, only ten, but already shedding the baby fat of childhood. He leaped the rill clean, vaulted the low steading wall and ran to hug his father fiercely. "I was to the shearing down the cote when I heard the horn. How went the court, then?"

"How, boy? Like Caesar, we came, we saw—"

"And we conquered," Mauger finished, offering the dipper for Robin to drink. "The king will not pinch off a foot of Sherwood ground this year."

44

"Not an inch!" Will vowed with arms full of wife and sons.

"Not without throwing out the law entire," said Robin. "Edward, did you do the lessons Mauger left for you?"

The boy's exuberance faltered a shade. *"Ach, Da . . ."*

"Well?"

"There was that much else need doing."

"Edward, I'll not have a lout for a son." For sure now Robin was home, he'd oversee the sheep himself and back to lessons for Edward. "See to it, Mauger. With a good birch rod if that's all will salt the learning into him." Robin sent the boy off with a playful swat on his rump and went to greet his mother, a small figure in the door of her bower, delicate hands writhing at each other before embracing her son.

"There now, Puck-Robin, a welcome home. Have you denied the Bastard his claim?"

"Appealed it, Mum. Tangled it in Shire and Hundred, given us more time. Now then, where's Marian and my sweeting?"

"Just coming." Maud's eyes directed him to the hall entrance—then, as Robin had seen more and more over the years and always with a pang, they clouded under a private shadow. Maud raised her head to sunlight like one long denied it. Robin did not want to look at her then. He hurried to Marian.

"Home, love." He kissed Marian and took the child from her arms. "Let me. Has she been well today?"

Robin pushed back Moira's blanket and put his lips to the small forehead and silky first hair. "Have you been good while your da was away? Hm?"

"Here, give her back," Marian said. "I'm that worried. She's so small and grows so slowly."

"The hunger last year. You did not have the strength."

Moira might never attain the constitution or stature of her parents after so spindling a start. She would be late in walking, late in all things, but like the folk she came from and given half a chance, Moira would endure.

"Did you miss me, love?" Robin teased his wife.

"Almost as much as the men and the fields. Both've been wanting you."

Content? Strolling with Marian, baby Moira in his arms, through the tranquil west meadow, Robin wondered how a man could feel more fulfilled in his portion. Except that there were things to be fought against.

Happy? Yes, and a thousand times over he could show that much of it to Marian, but not the rest.

Because he was deeply frightened; because a foreign king with a darkening mind could take it all away at whim, from Robin or any man, and there was no right in that, only unworkable wrong. Because someday, if Robin rose too far off his knees, William might nod to Ralf Fitz-Gerald, and that honorable man would have to put aside friendship and the ties of marriage to be William's broom again and sweep away what little Robin had. Often he argued with himself that such need not be if a man were careful.

Why can't I just bend my knee and be content? Marian worries when I argue against the king's will, and more than a little common sense on her side.

Then those like Ranulf came to flay them with a whip of braided royal rights, and *someone* had to oppose such if only for the danger in avoiding it. Complacency was a French word but an English failing. Friends like Alan and Wulf would rebel only if someone led them like Waltheof or himself this morning, mostly grumbling, moved to action only when their own portion was threatened. William claimed the right of blood to walk over their lives; bald way of putting the case, but the matter came down to that. Perhaps, but if no one argued or tried the question mind to mind, then such became right, first by custom and then by precedent in law—which, Robin learned in the years of Mauger's teaching, was only something agreed to often enough for men to accept it eventually as unquestioned law. To change that, you had to attack the root like a weed. Furrow by furrow, farmers must fight weeds each year; if not, the damned things choked out good crop. So much was also true in law. Ferrets like Ranulf with his fine clothes and finer tongue and William's seal swinging about his neck—*he* didn't just grumble and turn aside. He was out each day doing and getting, so sure his end justified the means.

Caution, Ralf urged him. Cautious or not, someone had to slow the Chancery priest down, stop him cold if he could. But if threat came to fight, Robin wondered gravely, would he hazard his own portion and family against the king's will, or would he heed wisdom and leave well enough alone?

He'd put a pawn in the way of the crown for a move or two, no more, and made an enemy. So much couldn't be helped.

"Of course, to be an enemy of Ranulf may be considered a social distinction," Mauger said. "Albeit a dangerous one. Lives in Lincoln, civil married to the daughter of a rich wool merchant. Bullies the Chancery as he did Alan in the court. And in daily communication with Rouen.''

From a blithe young scholar with a serious understrain, Mauger had grown less flippant over the years. Entering the Church through the back door as a lay brother, he'd seen all too many monks and ordained priests with more ambition than conscience or honest calling.

''You must do what you think right, Lord Robin, and there's the nut. When it comes to right, you and Ranulf spell it differently. Such men take up the world like merchandise in their hands. They may see its beauty, more often only the value and the price they can get. If there is anything missing in such men, it is never audacity or readiness. Walk softly, then.''

Fancy that: a house in Lincoln and an English wife. Interesting.

5

THE English scribe, busy collating royal manor accounts, kept his scorn to himself as Ranulf gusted into the tiny, three-sided stall off the Chancery's main aisle. He did not like or approve of the keeper of the seal. A priest should look and conduct himself with the humility of his calling, not as a fashionable fop. Just now and then, by the by, he should show as much courtesy to subordinates as he fawningly lavished on superiors.

Ranulf glowered impatiently at the work laid out on the scribe's writing desk. "Fetch me fresh parchment."

"You wish a letter written?"

"No, just your desk. Get out."

The plump scribe gave place and vacated the stall, wrinkling his nose at Ranulf's heavy perfume. *All is vanity after all,* he sighed inwardly. If vanity had weight, this Norman priest could sink the Church by himself.

Only hours returned to Winchester from the north, Ranulf needed to kick the very world out of his way like a cur underfoot. A double-edged thorn lodged in the flesh of his self-esteem. Edward of Denby, the beloved Robin Hood of Elfled's memory, not only unseated royal purpose but vented on Ranulf's origins and motives a contempt so scalding as to leave a permanent scar.

He wrote rapidly, jabbing the quill at the inkpot as at an enemy, the rapid scratching sharp against tranquil summer sounds beyond the casement.

WILLIAM, BY THE GRACE OF GOD KING OF THE ENGLISH, DUKE OF NORMANDY, FROM HIS SERVANT RANULF AT WINCHESTER IN DUTY AND GREETING—

My royal lord, I must report that your just demand for the enclosure of certain lands in Sherwood Forest has been delayed by obstacles that will cost only time but I fear much of that.

The quill hissed across the page with Ranulf's acrimony, accusing those men who opposed the king's will. Ranulf had marked each of them even to the precise spelling of their names: Bishop Osmund; Vicomte of Nottingham, magistrate of the Assize. Knights like Sire Henri Chailliard, the Saxon malcontents.

Legal recourse may expend the rest of this year if not overleaped. The Assize voted to a man to appeal my lord's cause, shameless and ingrate since their livings were created by his munificence. Most injurious and suspect of all was Edward of Denby, author of the appeal, once pardoned by the royal will but ever perfidious. I wait on the king's pleasure in this.

Ranulf poured wax over the folds of the missive and pressed his seal to the cooling puddle. The report traveled to Normandy that evening on the first courier boat out of Solent bound across the Channel.

King William plodded up and down between the heavy columns of his palace at Rouen, through spear shafts of light into shadow again as the clerk at his elbow read the dispatch a second time. Grown more florid of late, swollen in girth to where no tailor's art could disguise his protruding belly, William of Normandy looked far less a king than a frustrated merchant in an unstable market. A realist, he regarded his world without fondness or prejudice, but with growing suspicion: a powerful, square countenance with a strength that might have waxed gentle if peace and not continual war had been his lot. At fifty-five, the king of England had the aspect of a fighting mastiff turned mean.

William listened to the bald little clerk with only half of his attention. He had attached the Sherwood manor of Mansfield to his personal holdings after Waltheof's defection; these further enclosures were no more than claiming his own property, this opposition a predictable annoyance. Norman lords in England guarded their own as jealously as any native, and often resisted him in the matter of hunting lands. For all that, William could be sourly amused that the little terrier from Bayeux had been outbarked for once.

And by whom? Edward of where?

"Denby, *mon roi.*"

The name plucked a faint chord in memory.

"Will my lord make answer to the Chancery?"

"Later. Who is waiting?"

The clerk consulted his tablet for the rest of the day's audiences. "The embassy from King Philip. And Prince William, just returned from Count Robert."

William would see Rossel first. He turned toward a stone stairway. "Send Prince William to me. The French can wait."

He dismissed the clerk and started laboriously up the stairs. All he could manage were ten before stopping for breath, looking about in hope no one observed his weakness. *Pardi,* he was coming apart at the seams like an old shirt, still serviceable, but with frays and widening rents here and there. The messengers from the young king of France would tell him nothing of import or even truth. Of an age with his own son Robert, Philip was by far the craftier statesman. *Before God, I wish Robert had more of his ability and less of his company.*

William had sent Rossel to his older brother to bring him to Rouen at Matilda's express desire. He hoped Robert would rise above his usual mien of injured sulking and come to his mother.

"I will be a son when you use me as one."

While his mother wasted in agony, desiring only him. Damn the boy.

William looked up as a short-gowned physician's apprentice hurried down the stairs on some errand, bobbing his head in deference. The king caught his arm. "Wait. How does the queen?"

"Through my master's skill, sire, the queen has no pain and rests well. By your leave, sire." The boy hurried away down the stairs.

Another rent in his heart and the worst. *When Mora goes, I will be terribly alone, always was alone save for her. . . .*

She dotes on Robert. What physic will ease that pain in her, seeing him grown into a fool with a false sense of honor and no more foresight than a fly? A spoiled boy become a selfish man who must be cajoled to her last sickbed.

The fool my brother, the fool my son. There is nothing beneath Odo's miter but ambition and conceit. And Robert, God help him, could be cozened by any village witch selling love-philters. Mora knows, much as she loves him. Crown him king in England and duke here, we build on sand. Divide between Robert and Rossel, I leave them only to battle each other, and weaken both against France.

Robert simply will not *see!* Oh, I don't understand these younger men now. Suddenly, I and the men who made the kingdom, we are *les ancêtres,* tedious old bores at whom Robert and those of his generation smirk behind their courtesy. Robert rides by and these upstart knights cry, *"Regardez!* The image of honor!" Image without spirit, too easily flattered, swayed and bent by every breeze to pass over him.

For young William—our rumpled, profane Rossel—with his whores and catamites, he is loyal, but is there any more of a king in him when I doubt he thinks beyond his next meal or rutting bed? What I did, I fear is badly done, sowing tares amid my intended harvest. We set too much store by Robert, gave him too much too early, while I worked Rossel hard in my service. The boy never seemed to mind, never complained of hardship or too little pay, never looked to be more than he is. But Richard's dead, and Rossel is now a second son who knows the first as much danger as disappointment.

But Matilda always had her hierarchy of affections. Richard was her darling before he died, then Robert, perhaps the girls. Little Henry she barely knows, but Rossel she never could bring herself to love; he was always shadowed, jostled aside by the others, Mora's whipping boy and catch-all basket for her irritation. She could be sharp. No word of praise for the boy without one of detraction: "Yes, he is well favored. He has your semblance, Gilly . . . but his mouth is coarse and lacking the firmness of yours. But of course, we should see to a good marriage for Rossel, one that won't trouble us later . . . if he only had better taste in companions and pastimes."

For the latter, William screened Mora from as much as he could, having a stubborn affection for Rossel and understanding, within limits, how it often went with royal boys raised in the field among knights and camp followers; unnatural practices were unavoidable in some. Matilda frowned on the boy and rejected the man, while William met the facts with resignation. Unannounced early morning visits to Rossel at Gisors would usually flush some nondescript creature of either sex from the prince's bed. Rossel, hardly abashed, would rub the wine fog from his eyes and observe regretfully, "If they only looked as good the morning after as they did the night before. *Bonjour, mon père.*"

At twenty-three, William's namesake had a soul profane as a brothel and tough as boiled oxhide, once taking a wound to save his father's life in battle at Gerberoi. At least Rossel was what he was, while Robert lacked even simple constancy, vacillating and always making the wrong decision. *Simple* was the term. In the guise of sworn friendship, Philip danced the heir to Normandy like a stringed puppet. Unless some healing angel lifted the blindness from his eyes, Robert could lose all that William and Matilda had built over a lifetime. Were Rossel not so frivolous, so openly contemptuous of the Church and despised by them in return, William might easily prefer him. The boy could apply himself when needed, but as readily swaggered off afterward to slap a back or a backside and rut or drink the night away. There was no surety in the world that kings would beget kings. . . .

"Father!"

A younger, fairer copy of William bounded up the stairs to bow his blond head before the king. "Just came from Robert."

Obviously. Rossel's boots and riding cloak were splashed with mud. He reeked pungently of his horse. "How is my mother?"

"Well, they said. I was just going to her. Is Robert with you?"

"No, Father."

"But he is coming?"

"He—had conditions. Very difficult to get his undivided attention. I found him in his stable cooing over a sick mare and fondling the infernal thing as if to bed her when she recovered."

"Did you tell him how ill his mother is? How little time—?"

"And her own wish for him to improve her state by coming." Rossel raked a hand through the blond bangs hanging over his brow. "He felt he might or he might not, he couldn't say. By Lucca, Father—I reminded him that his horse already had an arse and he need not be one; to come home, embrace you and mother and be family again." More, as Rossel delivered his brother's mind, William was unjust in doubting Philip's friendship, and in any case, Robert was long out of leading strings, was he not?

The king listened with aggrieved impatience. "Well, what conditions? Will he *come*?"

The prince's sardonic grin faded, revealing the seriousness underneath. "Only under safe conduct from you, forty knights to escort him for surety."

"Surety! Does he—?" William dropped his tone to an angry whisper.

They were near Matilda's chamber. She need not hear this. "Does he think I'd take him like a common felon?"

"Father, he—" Rossel shifted under his scrutiny, clearly embarrassed. "He cited the safe conduct you gave Waltheof before arresting him."

As if there were no difference between a treacherous Saxon and his own blood. When would sons learn how much they could hurt a father? "So. He does not trust me."

Rossel drew a short breath and delivered the last. "He declares Philip has always dealt more fairly with him than you have."

"To hell with Philip. What about his mother, has he no feeling?"

The young man could only shake his head in bewilderment. "I don't understand him. If it were me . . ."

"Yes. I see," said William. "I will tell your mother. Go rest and change, Rossel. Pay your respects later to the queen. I want to be alone with her for a time."

When William entered his wife's chamber, Matilda was propped up on pillows, a frail, tiny craft on the oceanic expanse of the great bed, stroking a brush through her faded red hair and conversing with her physician, John of Tours, who bowed to the king and withdrew. William stretched himself across the bed, one arm around his wife's emaciated shoulders. A knife went through him to feel how wasted she was, plumpness melted away with the last of her stubborn constitution. She nestled into the crook of his arm like a kitten who trusted the haven implicitly.

"Oh, yes, I always feel good in the morning," Matilda chirped in a sprightly tone with no strength to it. "No trouble at all today. Well . . . it comes and goes, like this, like so. I heard you outside. Is Robert come?"

"That was Rossel."

"Oh."

He heard the bare disappointment. "He will attend you later."

"Bathed, one hopes."

"You don't show him enough affection, Mora."

"I can't help that. I do not like the manner of his life, and he always smells of horses or whores. It shames me to have a dissolute son."

"Be kind." He kissed her cheek. "That is more like you."

"Did you see Robert? Is he coming?"

William lied gallantly for her sake. "As soon as possible." He decided then and there to send a safe conduct to Robert, who might come with an army of knights if he wished, so long as he was here.

Matilda was not deceived. "Gilly, I am not a child to be fobbed off with—" She sat up, trying to mask the sudden spasm of pain in her ruined uterus, but her husband saw the constriction and pressed her gently back onto the pillows. "I can well imagine what Robert said; he's said it for six years . . . *parlons d'autre chose*. Have the dispatches come from Lanfranc?"

"Nothing important. The archbishop prays daily for you."

"What a dear man he is. I vow I could learn to love all Italians if they are like Lanfranc. Gilly? Why don't we go there when I am well?"

"We could do that. Yes, we will."

"It is time you met this Gregory and set him to rights. He is such an unreasonable man for a pope." Matilda savored the prospect a moment before the old habit of royal detail reclaimed her. "What from Winchester?"

Relieved to see the pain washed away from her eyes, William recounted Ranulf's news. "Just annoyance and delay. Don't trouble yourself now."

Matilda stroked his hand where it lay against her cheek. "It is not as if you have no hunting land at all."

"The principle, Mora. Give in on one point, they press for two more. Ranulf says Ralf and Osmund backed the opposing *causidicus*. Some insolent commoner. Den . . . Denby? Somehow familiar, that name."

"Bon Dieu!" Matilda vented a little gasp of exasperation. "Not *him*."

"You know the man?"

"Oh, honestly, Gilly! Of course, and so do you. I delivered his wife of her son in Grantham. That charming fair girl? One of the few English I ever liked. You outlawed Denby and then pardoned him after his service at Norwich. What was it they called him?"

"Robin Hood." Recollection dawned without joy. The troublesome outlaw. The mother who refused to die in a dungeon. The silent young wife stiff with pride. "Not Denby," the king groaned. "Not again. He was a farmer who could barely read his own name."

"Apparently he has learned—*oh*." Matilda's small body clenched suddenly; a strangled sound escaped her. "Gilly . . . dear God, it hurts so."

This was the moment William feared to face, frightened and helpless before her pain. "Why didn't you tell—? I'll fetch Tours."

"No, don't leave me. It will pass. It always does."

54

"But—" *Don't do this to her,* William begged of God. *Don't let this happen.* "Surgeon! Tours! Damn you, get in here!"

He held Mora and hoped she couldn't feel his arms shaking as the physician hurried to attend her.

When William finally left her to find what ease she could, he felt utterly savage. Servants and chamberlains scurried aside as he stumped toward his scriptorium like an approaching storm. Heaven and hell leagued against him, and this day he feared neither. Mora was dying, France planted its banner too close to his door, Robert proved apt only to defection and betrayal—and an English commoner who should have hanged years ago was underfoot again to do him out of his forest rights. He was curt with his scribe, dictating faster than the monk could write. His instructions to Ranulf crackled with malice.

We well remember him wily in argument and enamored of law even while defying it. Denby exudes treason as other men sweat. Give none of them any further pretext for delay. Proceed with good heed to legality, but swiftly as possible. Isolate Denby from his support and you need not seek far for cause to apprehend him.

The letter reached Ranulf at Winchester before he rode north for a brief midsummer holiday in Lincoln.

The king's response vindicated and unleashed Ranulf against Robin. Quite superior in his own youthful estimation, he always measured that height of ability in others. Far too many men of inferior gifts were born above him; Ranulf early decided to vault high through natural talent, if with a servant's discretion. The son of a poor priest, he quickly perceived acutely how the high-born regarded the common humanity beneath them through the "natural" order of things. Growing to uncommon physical height, Ranulf employed every inch in dealing with lords that they must always look up to him. At the table of the world, the drab condition of his birth taught him the best portion went to the longest reach and fastest grab.

That table exacted its price; he had spent much time in the inhospitable antechambers of the great and powerful. Possessed of talent and ambition, the first brought him early to the notice of Bishop Odo, the second advanced him steadily through the scriptorium of Bishop Maurice of London to William's Chancery, intellectually amused at how easy the passage was. As his enemy Robin discovered in a different key,

Ranulf saw the highest men and even his king mired in mediocre thinking. Sorting through blizzards of writing daily, Ranulf often noted the marginal scribblings of copyists: comments on text, doggerel verse, literacy taking a stretch and yawn before bending to work again. In their marginalia, these scribes begged a ride on the page of history; so with King William in building cathedrals. Like the clerks, the king scribbled his name on eternity, the upthrust cathedral spires like fingers poked in God's rib to remind Him of His good servant. *Look at me!* Their tower bells clamored for their patron. *I live. I built these edifices to heaven.* Yes indeed, for the king was an old man who feared death.

Kings rose and were torn down as were their churches, their foundations used to build better. Ranulf saw himself as such a deep-struck base on which there would rise a towering conclusion. In this, though with far less humility, he was not unlike Robin.

Ranulf would not waste time raging at or threatening his enemy, simply determined to pay him back with interest. He began a careful study of the man he would destroy. Paid informants dispatched to Sherwood reported some peasant nonsense about a witch grandmother. Not much there, even questionable taste, since William's own grandam was rumored to have been a witch who changed into a wolf and leapt through a church window rather than suffer the Mass. Or was that the countess of Anjou? Spectacular but puerile. Another fact yielded more promise. Denby wrote commentaries on English law. Ranulf determined to avail himself of them.

The man stung him in his pride and showed him to the back door through which he had squeezed with such difficulty in seeking a better life. The time was nigh when no man could do that with impunity.

En route to Lincoln, Ranulf rode with a party of knights returning to Cambridge and so enjoyed the hospitality of Richard de Guilbert, Baron of Buckden. The baron was only too willing to vent his opinion of Denby *and* Fitz-Gerald. Fat now, middle-aged and wheezing, de Guilbert was one of those older men whom Ranulf found it necessary to suffer with patient grace if profit lay therein. Like most battle commanders of limited ability, the baron would have penned his memoirs of the Earls' Revolt, if that monkish occupation were not beneath him, and especially of the decisive battle at Norwich in 'seventy-five, showing himself to be a tragically misunderstood hero. Ranulf forbade himself to yawn while de Guilbert refought the campaign in superfluous detail over dinner. He was an honorable knight, Bayeux must appreciate that;

56

a man bred to the strict courtesies of warfare, one who despised the use of common archers against mounted vavasors.

"Inhuman! Dishonorable! The most shameful day, the best blood of Normandy, the noblest destriers all cut down like scythed grass by those pigs. Fitz-Gerald disobeyed my express orders, sent in Denby with his butchering peasants. Yes, they were my men. Yes, they won for the king. But, my God, that last charge . . . Raimond de Beaumont was a rebel, the king's enemy, but I would not countenance such slaughter, tried to stop it. By my faith, I *did*. Have you seen the arrows the English use? A cloth yard in length. Nothing will stop them."

Overcome with emotion—rather practiced, as Ranulf thought, the rendition of a speaker in a tale too often told—de Guilbert choked and took more wine to clear his throat. "When I rode up, they were done with Raimond's men. Denby was blood from head to foot. I thought him wounded to death, and good riddance. But it was not his blood. He'd cut off Raimond's head—cut it off with a knife and battered and torn the rest away with his bare hands. He dropped it in front of my horse, calm as saying grace, but it was the calm of a madman who has called demons to aid him and then in sheer fatigue sent them hence. A lunatic, Father Ranulf. A devil who infected all around him with his evil."

And those around him, Ranulf took pains to remember, were Vicomte Fitz-Gerald and Sire Henri Chailliard. Well and well: All of them in one cozy little forest den.

As he rode home toward Lincoln, Ranulf reviewed what he had learned—young but far more formidable than Robin yet guessed. As Ralf Fitz-Gerald observed from his own bleak beginnings, such men had the briefest childhoods and the longest memories.

6

> > > >

ILLIAM's charge that he proceed "swiftly as possible,"
Ranulf interpreted as the speed of lightning. Another show
of force as at Linby would be stupid. He conceived a subtler
method to the same result, a party of knights merely to observe and
survey a portion of Sherwood for future enclosure. This would more
gently test the waters, while not really stirring them. The men detailed
should use no violence toward the people, a royal commission on legitimate service. Better conceived than his earlier plan; nevertheless,
Ranulf chose his target with malice aforethought. Papplewick: held in
fief by Ralf Fitz-Gerald and the scene of Ranulf's humiliation by Denby.
If the village cooperated sensibly, other surveys would be dispatched.
Eventually the Shire and Hundred courts might more readily back down
in adjudicating the appeal. Ranulf could present his king with the enclosures in half the estimated time. Slower than outright force, but surer.
William would rarely overleap the law so far as to make enemies of his
landowners.

Ranulf's error was in appointing Sire Guy de Gavrillac to head the
survey; dependable, but not too swift on his own initiative. As for the
attitude of English peasants toward property, Ranulf considered them
not at all. Thus the incident which ever after Judith, Vicomtess of
Nottingham, with tongue *couchant* in cheek dubbed the Great Turnip
War of Sherwood Forest.

The week before Saint John's Eve in June, there came languorous,
flower-scented days when the lightest mantle was too heavy, ladies
donned something light and bright, and even the dullest soul paused

in garden or field to breathe deep of summer. Robin and Marian, Ralf and Judith and Henri Chailliard took an outing a mile or so from Papplewick in a green meadow bordered by oaks. They ate and drank and lazed in the sun, the horses grazing loose. For Judith the day was respite from children and servants; for Marian, an escape from the smell of the wool room which she'd overseen since coming to Denby. Still a bachelor, Henri beguiled the time playing with his Lise, a small black-and-tan bitch lazy as her master today. She flushed a hare or two from habit, but her chase was uninspired. In loose linen shirts and trousers, Robin and Ralf practiced with sword until they worked up a fine sweat, Henri swigging from his wineskin and shouting the fencers on.

"Good, Ralf! *Formidable,* Robin!"

Robin was pupil, Ralf the master with an arm like a catapult. Over the years, he'd schooled Robin to proficiency with the Norman sword, longer than its English counterpart, though Robin would never equal him. Ralf's wrist was supple steel, the right arm an inch longer than the left from years of swing and thrust. The meadow rang with their parries punctuated by grunts until Robin, panting, held up his hand.

"Enough, you're too good."

Ralf spun the heavy blade like a toy. "Cry quarter, do you?"

"Cry thirsty. Marian! Pour me some beer."

The combatants collapsed in a welter of sweat and laughter by their wives. They drank, unwrapped the broken meats and boiled eggs to eat, gradually aware they were being shyly watched by men and women back among the trees, villeins of Ralf's from Papplewick. He hallooed them in idle curiosity: What did they do in the wood today? He couldn't make out their answer. "Something about Saint John?"

"Gathering mistletoe," Marian guessed. "For the dreaming."

Henri and Ralf had seen young English couples go midsummering every year. Those with a mind to marry brought blankets and beer to the wood, as had some of these today, clearly intending to stay the night in the long twilight that lasted until dawn this time of year. Some of the young men clambered into the high oak branches now, where the mistletoe clustered. They cut it with care as wives and children ran whooping and squealing to catch the white sprigs in aprons before they touched earth and lost their magic. The women all seemed to be pregnant. The children raced about shrieking for pure excitement. One little girl no more than six caught a large bunch of the berries and darted out into the meadow to show her prize to Marian, ignoring her mother's sharp summons and the fact that she was charmingly bare as a peeled willow wand. The child went without hesitation to Marian and held out the mistletoe. "Look, *Hlaefdige.*"

Marian gravely inspected the catch and pronounced it the finest ever seen—as the expectant mother waddled up with a red face and profuse apologies; her child knew better manners than that. They waved her cheerfully on her way.

"Every year this mad dash for mistletoe," Ralf mused. "Whatever do they do with it?"

"For tucking 'neath their pillow on Saint John's Eve," Marian told him. "You saw how that woman's carrying. The mistletoe will tell her in a dream if she's to bear boy or girl."

Judith shifted lazily to lay her head in Ralf's lap. "Silly old midwives' nonsense. I've had two boys and each time my women swore't would be a girl."

Robin noted the fleeting strain in his wife's smile. Marian set great store by mistletoe and ash leaves, among a myriad of other heart-fond country beliefs. Often he'd found a sprig of something or other under her pillow during pregnancy. His Marian was devoutly Christian, yet to draw a clear line between her holy and pagan practices would be a coil for scholars and perhaps an orthodox embarrassment. Some years on May Eve, less often now than when Maud and Aelred were young, the folk of Blidworth held a mock marriage between a horned boy and a flower-crowned girl as Lord of the Animals and Mother Earth. Father Beorn was always invited to bless them that the occasion be thought not blasphemous. In Northumbria, folk still made a doll of the last sheaf cut at harvesting and proclaimed it Barley Maid. A local woman presided over the fashioning of the new doll and burning of the old and the feast that followed. Some priests ranted passionately against these rituals which were, to Robin's folk, as natural as crossing themselves in prayer. Robin's own grandmother Guntrada was seldom seen in church in her time, or so his father said, and there were still ancient *wicca* women such as Wytha who followed the old ways, regarding the world ill-balanced under a father god alone with no goddess for harmony. Remembering the bargain he and Marian made over the young oak after their wedding night, Robin sometimes wondered how much of his own faith was purely Christian, how much something older. His heart, like an arable field wrested from the forest, was bordered yet by Sherwood, wrapped in lush green. Whatever futures he dreamed, the verdant past rustled and whispered against it, and in the midst of memory was his blood oath to the land, the scar on his palm and Marian's like signatures to the promise.

But this was no day for deep thinking. They ate and drank the warm, thick beer and drowsed in the summer-buzzing meadow, watching the young couples gather their harvest of magic and drift away. The wind had been a soft whisper out of the west; now it shifted. Ralf noted how the grazing mares lifted their heads nervously to test what the new air wafted to them. As he read them, they scented stallions from the direction of Papplewick, where the only riding animal was the priest's mule.

Judith raised her head from his lap. "Ralf? What is it?"

His head tilted up in that same sifting of the air as the horses. "Robin? Henri?"

The knight was in a light, sun-warmed doze, Robin drifting that way. He opened one eye. "What then?"

Old instincts tweaked Ralf now as the small boy came running out of the trees, calling for the sheriff. By the time he skidded to a stop, they were all alert.

"My lord, coom! There's king's men all over the place. Knights and them men in black that writes things down."

"Clerks." Robin reached for his sword belt. "Why, lad?"

"Don't know." The boy rubbed at his sooty nose. "They're into houses and the hall, even Father Ayulf's church."

Ralf caught the boy by the shoulder. "How many?"

"Six, seven knights, as many of the others and God knows what. They just coom in t'our house, pushed my da out'n the way. Lord Robin, Father Ayulf's dreadful mad. Some folk in the wood said you was here. "Y'must come help us."

Buckling on his sword belt, Robin asked, "Think Willy Bastard's jumped our appeal then?"

"I don't know," Ralf replied in a tone fraught with doubt. "He may have. Henri, please fetch the horses."

The knight got up, rubbing the drowsiness from his eyes. "What do we do?"

"Whatever we must," Ralf returned on a note Judith had heard for years when he was deeply angered. "That's *my* village." He spoke again to the Saxon boy—gently, knowing the child already shaken. "Think now: What did these men say? Why are they come?"

"Said it's to prepare for turning us out. All legal, they said. Can they do that, my lord?"

No, the boy would never understand. He'd been born in the same hut that most like saw the birth of his grandsire. Ralf gave him a reassuring squeeze at the shoulder with the promise. "Not today they can't. What is your name?"

"Cawlwin, sir."

"Well, Cawlwin, you're to stay out of the village until we've seen to this, understood?"

Cawlwin looked down at his bare feet, uncertain for his parents. Marian knelt so that she was eye to eye with the boy. "Are you a good tree climber, Cawlwin?"

He nodded shyly.

"Those oaks yonder bear a fine lot of mistletoe in the high branches. Bring me an armful, mind none of it touches earth, and you shall have a silver half penny."

"Ja, Hlaefdige." Obediently the boy started away on his commission as Henri returned leading the horses. Robin touched his wife's arm in gentle command. "You and Judith will stay out of this."

"Oh, for sure." Marian curtsied respectfully. "Well we know that nowt of importance can be done but by men."

"Damn," Robin grumbled as the three men mounted. "The mouth on her. Curse me if I haven't spoiled that woman loving her so much."

A blessed fermenting, Ralf thought. In the same vein Judith could show a deal of her intractable Aunt Maud when he took a notion to be bullheaded.

Judith and Marian waved as the men galloped away toward Papplewick. "That's my village, too," Judith asserted as they collected the cloth and baskets. "I've heard Mass in Ayulf's church and embroidered the altar cloth myself."

"Yes." Marian had been present often in the village tithing barn on Saint Michael's Day; the women of Papplewick she regarded as neighbors. A gleam of purpose passed between the two wives; each found the same impulse in the other, winged with mischief. "I'm thinking this is the doing of that Chancery priest Rob can't abide. I'd give those men a bit of my mind."

"And I," said Judith, leading the way to their horses.

His business in Papplewick was going well, Guy de Gavrillac estimated, and no serious trouble from the Saxon folk huddled about their priest to one side of the village square. He was to ruffle as many peasant feathers as he could without real damage, and throw a fright into Sherwood. His knights and scribes ferreted about, noting the extent of the hamlet, the number of dwellings and outbuildings to be razed, including the church.

Regarding that homely place of worship, Ranulf had given express orders to examine any records there and to confiscate anything of interest in the king's name. Father Ayulf fumed at the profanation: "This church has stood since Alfred's time and *never* disturbed until this day!"

But that was a pity. One of the survey clerks busily tucked a cache of parchment leaves into his pouch. "Very interesting. The Chancery must see this."

Emerging from the church, de Gavrillac saw the three riders plunge out of the forest at full gallop. He thought at first they were of his own detail. He mounted, signaling his knights to join him, wondering why the sullen English peasants broke out in sudden cheers. The farmer just driving a wagon load of turnips onto the south side of the square?

They weren't looking at the carter, nor were the three riders of his party. Resolution faltered as he recognized one of them: the sheriff of Nottingham. Though not a timorous man, he did not relish crossing Ralf Fitz-Gerald. Actually, de Gavrillac felt most secure when following orders to the letter. Those instructions issued from Ranulf, not the king, and did not cover a confrontation with the rightful lord of this village, a man who stood in some favor with William.

Ralf reined short in front of him, sword already drawn, flanked by a young Norman vavasor and a bearded Englishman. "So it is you, de Gavrillac."

"Vicomte." The knight tried to respond in the same unyielding tone, grateful that his own men closed ranks about him. Ralf pointed at them with his sword.

"Whatever lackeys you have in these houses and in my church, call them out. By whose order do you dare trespass my holdings. *Speak!*"

The command rang out like a brazen gong. In the charged silence following, the hiss of Henri's sword sliding from its scabbard was comment in itself.

"The sheriff asks a simple question," Robin prompted easily, "and I am curious myself."

"By order of the king," de Gavrillac attempted. "To survey—"

"The king is in Rouen," Ralf cut him off. "You are of Lincoln. This is Ranulf's doing, not so? Answer me!"

Robin moved his horse a little forward of Ralf's hearing the danger in his voice, seeing it in his friend's taut body. The man had a ferocity equal to William's when provoked, and these intruders violated his personal rights. As far as Robin could see, no looting had taken place or bodily harm to Ayulf's folk beyond their fear and outrage.

"Easy on, Ralf," he murmured, hooking his thumb close to the throwing ax in his sword belt. In these next seconds, the danger could pass or burst into flame. The squat knight from Lincoln did not seem all that sure of himself or his authority in confronting Ralf. That was to the good—

Oh, weeping Jesus, no.

Considerations of diplomacy snapped short as Marian and Judith rode briskly into the village, waving graciously to their husbands and Father Ayulf's folk. They trotted their high-tailed mares to the turnip cart on the other side of the square.

Henri Chailliard said, "This could be trou—"

He was still speaking when one of de Gavrillac's younger knights drew his sword and drove at Robin with a cry. As quickly, Ralf kneed his horse forward to intercept. No need; Robin's hand went by instinct to ax rather than sword; his arm snapped back. The missile flew, catching the attacker's stallion squarely between the eyes. The animal convulsed with a strangled shriek and dropped like a stone, half pinning the rider under it. The dishonor momentarily confused the knights from Lincoln.

"*Honteux!*" one sputtered.

"*Déshonorant!*"

Hearing the outcries of shame and foul play from his men, de Gavrillac knew he had to regain control of the moment. Matters were never intended to go so far. "Hold, I say. All of you. Hold in the name of the king!"

"Hold for knights, yes." One of his men started forward, drawing his sword. "But no Saxon who slays a fine stallion."

"I say hold," Ralf challenged them. "Who wants to try me?"

"Or us?" Henri hurled at them in support as he and Robin ranged their mounts to flank the sheriff.

"Look at Robin," Marian worried to Judith. "He's not half of Ralf with a sword. He'll be hurt. There's so many of them." Desperate and protective, she reached from the saddle into the farmer's wagon for the nearest weapon, snaked down from her saddle, tearing the green tops from her missile as she ran forward. "Here, you—"

She wound up and let fly with a wiry arm. Beautiful it was, as Judith later recalled, fine as Robin's shot at Grantham that won the golden arrow. The turnip whizzed like a stone from a sling, hit de Gavrillac square in the helmet with a dull *clong*.

"Well struck!" one Saxon cried from the sidelines as the villagers shifted like a tide toward the ladies. "Give'm another."

De Gavrillac turned his horse about, feeling more ridiculous than hurt. "Who . . . who threw?—"

"Who indeed," Marian jeered.

The Lincoln men were between Robin and his wife. He suffered through a horrible moment, but then the villagers saved the day.

"Who?" Father Ayulf took up the call and then the folk about him. *Who? Who? Who?* like a chorus of drunken owls. The carter was inspired to emulate Marian and hurl a good one of his own; in a few seconds the air was full of turnips pelting the Norman vavasors who covered themselves as best they could, looking to their leader for what to do.

"Ralf, Henri: to the wagons quick." Robin was already moving. For all the danger and tension, he felt like laughing. There was the wrathful Ayulf praying in Latin as he lobbed turnips with the lustiest of his flock while Marian and even sedate Judith tossed fresh missiles to the hurlers and winged a few on their own. Robin jumped from his saddle into the cart, caught up in their manic spirit.

From taut fury, Ralf and Henry descended to puzzled anticlimax as Robin hefted a turnip. "Go, lads," he bellowed at the folk of Papplewick. "Go, Saxons! Remember Hastings and Norwich. Remember Denby!"

Henri asked innocently, "Why Denby?"

"Why not?" Robin grinned. "That's *my* house."

Ralf had a sense of humor, but it was not English. Through a hail of outgoing turnips and curses, the embarrassed men from Lincoln moved back out of range. Ralf looked sternly at his wife. "Judith! Put down that ridiculous vegetable this instant."

She tossed one to him. "Don't be a spoilsport. Lend a hand."

Ralf stared at it. "What . . . what am I to do with this?"

"Good God," Marian giggled, "think you'd never thrown a turnip before."

De Gavrillac's clerks on their mules got the worst of it, scuttling this way and that, more often hit than dodging clear. De Gavrillac called across the square, "Fitz-Gerald, this is unknightly. You tell them to *stop* this!"

The sight of him, florid and flustered, shattered Ralf's anger into unrecoverable shards. With a hoot he hefted the turnip, roaring to his folk, "Right. All together now—for Papplewick and England!"

"Sherwood and Saint Dunstan!"

Another storm of vegetables lofted high. Shoulder to shoulder with Marian, Robin called encouragement. "On, you Spartans. Out on Lincoln. Out!"

Gradually through his confusion and embarrassment, de Gavrillac began to function like a leader. He outnumbered the sheriff; if the matter had come to sword, he could have ended it quickly, but to unleash his men thus exceeded his orders. Then there were his survey clerks, no more help in a fight than a gaggle of terrified geese. He cursed Ranulf of Bayeux for this misconceived mission. To hell with him. Orders had been followed. They had their survey, valuable papers from the church, and nothing bruised but pride. Much as he longed to hang the lot of these people and Fitz-Gerald first among them, it was clearly time to minimize humiliation and depart.

"Allons!" He took the unhorsed and incoherent knight up behind his saddle, waving the others to follow him out of Papplewick. Seeing them retreat, a huge shout of victory went up from the folk of the village. Marian collapsed amid the remaining turnips, flushed and joyous, while the carter ruefully estimated half his load had been pressed into war. "But in a good cause."

"Noble carter," Judith sputtered, trying to arrange both hair and dignity. "You shall be paid twofold."

"Three," Robin vowed. "Oh, ladies, you were glorious. Homeric."

Marian unwound her veil to wipe at damp neck and cheeks. "We were that."

Now that any real peril was past and he need not fear for Judith, Ralf vented his tension on her. "You were damned lucky, that is all I can say. Just fool's luck this wasn't serious. *Bon Dieu,* woman, you are a vicomtess. What were you thinking of?"

"That it was a grand day for justice and sport," Judith said with a disarming smile. "Bless me, I've not had such fun since school, when I put a worm in the abbess's soup."

Robin leaned over the side of the wagon. "It's a hot day for the work of heroes, Father Ayulf. Who's got some beer?"

Drink appeared from a half dozen houses in an impromptu celebration, squashed turnips underfoot everywhere. Mellowed with good beer, Henri reflected he'd won often enough in battle and tournament, but never with a vegetable, and Ralf admitted Judith was a fine but unusual sight hurling with the vigor and occasionally the vocabulary of a crofter's wife.

"The world needs to fall on its arse once in a while," Robin philosophized, lying back with Marian amid the trampled produce. "Things get far too serious."

Marian wriggled about, feeling under her for something hard in just the wrong place for comfort. She brought forth a small pulp of red, white, and green. "It's a good thing we'd plenty of turnips. Who could I rout with a radish?"

Robin drew her to him, stretching luxuriously. "I haven't felt this outrageous good in years. I swear that's what ails me."

"That's God's truth." Marian nipped playfully at his ear. "After all that reading and writing to set your eyes a-squint, it's marvelous good for you. You should do it more often."

"That I will, love." Robin gazed contentedly up at the summer sky over Papplewick. "I think I will."

7

━▶━▶━▶━▶━

A measure of Ranulf's power was that those men invited to celebrate the Feast of Saint John at his house knew it unwise not to attend. As Mauger held all the reins of Denby in Robin's absence, so the keeper of the Chancery seal minded William's English house. All the major business of the crown in England passed under Ranulf's scrutiny and stewardship. If one wanted the king's ear on any matter, first approach Father Ranulf. Despised or not, he must be courted to profit, and men did.

On the morning of the twentieth of June, entourages from the south could be seen on Ermine Street, passing through the little village of Wigford and old St. Mary's church, turning off toward Ranulf's town house in Steep Hill below Lincoln Castle and the new cathedral under construction. Ranulf chose the two-storied stone house for its spaciousness. There were ample kitchens, larder and pantry, private chambers above, and a ground-floor hall that would have accommodated the household of a minor baron. Until a few years past, the house had belonged to a prosperous merchant who left England for his political health, as Ranulf was fond of pointing out. A little too fond, his wife Elfled reflected of late.

She rose early that morning to supervise the final preparations for the feast. Through the day her slight frown was not entirely preoccupation. There were, even at nineteen, the beginnings of marital disenchantment. Ranulf liked the light Saxon coloring in women and flattered her with his attentions at first. Her hair was one of the honey shades, tending to darken in winter. In summer she bound it up in the intricate Continental fashion rather than cover it with a veil. Her full mouth had that slightly overripe pouting aspect many men found attractive. Elfled made careful and continual inventory of her best features as complimented by men, and always put them forth in the best light.

She was the only surviving child of a Huntingdon merchant who had doted on her. Before marrying Ranulf, there was not much Elfled wanted that Elfled could not have. When her eye fell on the dashing priest already a power under William, sophisticated beyond his years and utterly fascinating, Elfled complacently assumed that he and the world were her oyster.

Ranulf was forceful and completely sure of himself. When she met him, Elfled was considering the marriage suit of a disenfranchised thane's son with eight or nine scraggly hides and no money. Ranulf was infinitely more exciting. More to the point, his star was on the rise and he loved her. Passion and practicality formed an invincible alliance. The thane's son cursed her for a Norman's whore and went away. Elfled married the fiery young meteor from Bayeux.

When their first daughter was born the following year, Ranulf had dropped a remark that at first warmed Elfled as the tenderness of a husband newly become a father.

"I will always make provision for you and the child."

Lately, the promise began to nag at Elfled under bleaker interpretation. Was he planning to leave her? She dealt with the insecurity in feminine fashion, by a straight-on view of her situation. Ranulf was a priest; his advancement would be within the Church, no matter how secular his leaning. She had no real hold on him if—when—he chose to put her aside, which he must someday. Early on, when she was surer of him, the fact had been remote. Now Ranulf became more detached from her, spoke absently and with some condescension. Irritation waxed to pain. Elfled felt uneasy in her place, her oyster lost its pearl. She felt increasingly vulnerable and yearned vaguely for *something,* though unable to name it.

While consulting with her astrologer, her first recourse in all serious matters, she began as well to see every former point of favor in her husband as one of pain and then criticism. Charismatic and handsome, yes, but calculating as well, with a hound's nose for being in the right place at the best time, above all for the right men: whom to cultivate, whom to discard. He spent lavishly. Raised with money, Elfled excused it as the sheer pleasure of having enough after a penurious childhood, even thought him dear when he preened in a new tunic and cloak for which he always paid too much. Nothing at a bargain could be any good. His instinct for men and opportunity went blind in his luxuries.

"Really, you could have had it for much less if you'd shopped about."

Wisdom in deaf ears. It must be expensive and proclaim its cost. Elfled compared her husband to her shrewd-dealing father, who was ever a genial and generous host but able to spy a shaved penny among a hundred and a bad credit risk over the first drink.

Elfled suspected that the men Ranulf dealt with had no great regard for him, but trod warily within his sphere of influence, most of them needing his favors. For all of that, nowadays, she felt Ranulf absent when he was with her, and more critical than before. Want of affection became resentment. Ready to be a good wife, yet she was raised to expect some consideration and felt he took her for granted. *He* had reached up to marry her, when it came to that, and today Elfled was expected not only to oversee the feast faultlessly, but to beam at the right men, see to their every comfort and wish, then retire modestly with no acknowledgment of her efforts. These were not only taken for granted but—salt in the wound—curtly criticized.

This morning, for a start, Elfled had first conferred with the child's nurse and then the cooks preparing the dinner. Of course nothing was quite right, one could never trust competence from scullions. She deftly prevented several culinary disasters, saw that fresh rushes were laid down in the hall and adequately strewn with rosemary, then at last went to bathe and dress. Her hair was cunningly done up in gold wire, the green kirtle trimmed in gold and daringly cut to show that Elfled still retained (almost) the dainty waist of maidenhood. Her mirror's judgment was more than complimentary: admirable, even stunning. Rich, but understated. To set off the whole, a Celtic cross of Irish goldwork about her throat. She would definitely turn a few male heads. That would help in her present mood. If vanity was sin, a little warmed a woman like a glass of good wine.

Ranulf entered their bedchamber with the distracted air of a man late for something more important elsewhere. Elfled turned from her mirror to be admired. Her husband ran his eyes over her like a column of suspect figures. "Is that—? Oh, you must have something better than that to wear." Before she could speak, he vanished again. Crushed, Elfled turned back to the admiration of the mirror, seeding her own mutiny. "Well, I like it and I will wear it."

His brusqueness hurt her. Well enough. He'd come home out of sorts from Chancery business in Sherwood, then there was trouble reported by de Gavrillac in some forest village. Elfled made dutiful allowance for Ranulf, but enough was enough. His rejection of her gown set the tone of her day. She would wear what she damned well pleased. At least *she* knew something of taste.

She gave her mirror one last hopeful glance and descended to the crowded hall, smiling dutifully at this or that Important Figure. There was Ranulf, basking, ringed about with men of power, relishing the assurance that he could check the greatest among them and ruin the lesser. There were Taillebois, Sheriff of Lincoln, and other king's reeves from all corners of England. Valognes of Essex and Haimo of Kent, the latter no doubt glad to have escaped the fate of Earl Odo and anxious to demonstrate his loyalty to the king. There were Urse d'Abetot from distant Worcester and Picot of Suffolk and more like them, each man with his specific need to be here, all with their satellite knights and clerks. Not to mention those Ranulf termed the "debris," office- and favor-seekers, ingratiating and overpolite when he deigned to address them. According to their rank and need, they all deferred to her husband while Elfled passionately wished for his head on a plate. She worked her way cordially through the male guests toward the kitchen, where her eye and judgment would certainly be needed, since anything cooks could botch, they would.

Part of every feast was provision for the poor of Lincoln. Elfled had ordered extra loaves baked, knowing the beggars would gather like sparrows by the kitchen door well beforehand to collect the leavings and used bread trenchers. She never grudged this charity and, frankly, wanted to be out of the hall just now.

No need, she found. In her absence, the alms were already being distributed by a rangy priest. A Father Brand from Abingdon, the butler informed her. As Elfled approached him, the priest gave out the last warm loaf, turned, and smiled at her. Depressed and vulnerable, that smile went through Elfled like a shaft of sunlight through shadow. Father Brand took up a stout briarwood walking stick. Leaning on it diminished his height, which was at least equal to Ranulf's. His dark chestnut hair glinted with hints of red in a freshly shaved tonsure. His eyes were gentle and humorous.

"Forgive me, *Hlaefdige,* but the folk were here and the loaves ready. . . . "

"Of course." Elfled flushed under his openly admiring gaze. "But

I am not of that rank, merely mistress of the house."

"A natural mistake. But what a splendid gown for your coloring. You look fresh as May."

She blurted, "You really like it?"

Father Brand's critical inspection was punctuated with a firm nod of approval. "Does one like perfection? One recognizes it."

Elfled covered the frisson of pleasure with a polite question: Was he here to see her husband?

"Just passing through, dear lady. I thought to ask hospitality at your lower table."

"You are most welcome, Father."

"And you most gracious."

To Elfled's thirsting ear, the adjective carried many other meanings. That this meticulously kempt, clean-shaven priest was handsome in a craggy way was secondary to her. What impressed Elfled most in three years of dealing with an ambitious husband and other men too long accustomed to power, was that there was nothing overbearing about him, nothing predatory. He did not plant his masculinity like a banner demanding obeisance, merely . . . was. Not self-important at all, Father Brand saw clearly what he looked at, more than mere reflection of himself. Elfled listened closely to him. His accent hinted of the south. London, she guessed, but softened with a kind of music that seemed to come more from his inner life than travel. They were standing now in one corner of the crowded hall raucous with male laughter and assertion. The priest looked about inquiringly. "Your husband is . . . ?"

"There," Elfled indicated too casually. "The one in scarlet and too much jewelry."

That came out too hard and flat; she wondered if the priest noticed. He answered her with a conspiratorial glint. "Yes, he does shine a bit. Those about him?"

"Royal business. My husband is Ranulf of Bayeux, keeper of the Chancery seal."

"Of course." Father Brand reproved his ignorance. "And you, Lady?"

"Elfled, Father."

"Elfled. What a lovely name."

She loved the way he pronounced it, delicately tasting the sound.

"You were educated in Lincoln?"

"No," she scoffed, blushing—fetchingly, she hoped, but it felt good to laugh a little. She hadn't enjoyed herself or felt so at ease for a long time. "My father was a merchant, not a lord. He would've turned blue at the thought of his daughter bending over books. My husband is learned. Perhaps too much so." There, again: She couldn't help the snappishness. "It might be best to avoid him, Father. He loves to play jokes on the clergy."

"And a priest himself?"

"Rather cruel jokes sometimes. His humor can be very raw."

"Then tell me of yourself, Elfled."

That too was unusual in Elfled's experience with men, more that he actually listened intently. Before she had much time to reflect, she found herself telling of her life in Lincoln before Ranulf came. Father Brand nodded now and then at some familiar family recollection. At length out of feminine habit and some wile, Elfled managed to turn the conversation to himself.

"Nothing much," he shrugged it off. "I was a bit raw myself before Dol." Wounded there, he told her, a common soldier serving the king through that disastrous battle against the rebels in Brittany. He always wanted the Church, but there was life to be tasted first. Brand accompanied some knights home to Poitiers and there he found men who wrote verse in the warm, lazy sunlight. "I think men's souls respond to light and dark as flowers do, don't you, Elfled? The Acquitaine warms poets, the soul throws off prohibition like a winter cloak worn too late into spring, stretches and breathes." Brand smiled with the gentle confession. "And then of course, there was a woman. Altogether, I got round to God rather late, but with nothing undone."

In the natural gesture of explanation, he spread his hands to her, the strong capable hands of a soldier. Elfled longed to touch them.

Across the hall, Ranulf was in conversation with Haimo of Kent, dominating his audience as always. Her husband glanced at her—proprietarily, making sure his property was still on the premises, so to speak, barely flicked his glance over Father Brand, and then appeared to forget them both.

Yes, husband, I am here, and at least one man finds me worth looking at.

Elfled stopped a servant passing with a tray of wine and goblets and offered some to the priest. "So a woman delayed you from holy vows."

"To my profit, Elfled. She taught me how to love, really love. How to care. I can't think of a better reason."

"Nor I. Your health, Father. This fascinating woman, did she marry someone else?"

"No."

Wrong to ask. Elfled heard the muted sadness in the word.

"No, Marie did not marry. There was illness in her village. She died. All those years I mucked along with no destiny at all, then suddenly, there was this girl. I first saw her in a forest. She had a quality that made her seem as if she belonged there among growing things. She shimmered in the light like a faerie girl come from under her enchanted hill to sing a little time across my life like wind through chimes, and then melt away. In the matter of loving, who could follow her but God?"

Father Brand came back from memory to the present, swirling the contents of his goblet. "Excellent wine."

"What?" Elfled realized her eyes had not left his face while he spoke. "Oh. Thank you. I chose it myself. In the matter of vintages, my father did school me somewhat. I am not totally a fishwife."

"Nor without excellence of your own."

Elfled felt a flush of heat surge through her. If this priest set his mind to win a woman even now—but no, he was not bent that way, merely gentle and candid, appreciating her as a woman, with no ulterior motive she could sense. Were it otherwise, chastity might find itself under mortal siege.

Dinner was about to get under way. A discreet signal from her steward summoned Elfled to the high table to bracket her glittering husband with Remigius, Bishop of Lincoln, on his other side. Festive dinners were always a strain on Elfled. Her husband was flamboyantly on display; in a more subdued capacity, so was she. Elfled had to listen politely to her guests, keep an eye on the smooth serving of courses, and hope Ranulf's questionable humor did not run away with him. No luck there this night. He left the table often to confer with this man or that, growing more acerbic with each goblet of wine—not drunk, more like a vicious blade emerging inch by inch from a jeweled sheath. His crowning jest today was in cruelly bad taste. Dessert was served by specially chosen young girls in ridiculously tight kirtles. Those lustier clerics who followed the girls with their eyes or comments, Ranulf loudly denounced in mock piety as false to the vows of celibacy—as if he were not himself, his wife thought grimly—and those who pointedly averted their eyes from the women he called hypocrites.

"Like our good Remigius here! Impure thought with downcast eyes. Suffer no ambivalence, Your Grace. Marry by all means, or go blindfold."

All of which pained Elfled. She honestly liked the bishop, who was well up in years. She had loved Ranulf to distraction when they married, loved him still, she supposed dutifully, but no longer so dazzled by glamor she could not see the flawed seams that knit the magic together. Courage he had, ability and wit, a mind like a thousand candles ablaze, a husband not without the tenderness that meant so much to a woman . . . but something ugly as well that she could not deal with. The world was his debtor and delinquent. *Not enough that you rose, not enough to hold power over men better born. No, you have to rub their noses in it.*

Once she caught Father Brand's eye far down at the lower table. He raised his cup to her; otherwise, he followed the actions of her husband. Then something diverted Elfled's attention. When she looked again, Father Brand was pegging unobtrusively out of the hall on his cane.

In her chamber that night, brushing out her hair before bed, Elfled tried to remember exactly how he looked and what he said. Impression and appearance all blurred together in a roseate excitement. Too soon: Clearer memory would return with time. She tucked the prospect away to age like wine.

When at last Ranulf came to undress for bed, Elfled knew almost to the cup how much he'd drunk. Not too much, not ever. There was that in him unable to relinquish control. He had created and presented to the world one face and would allow no one, not even her, to see anything else.

"Fine sport with old Remigius, eh?" Ranulf pulled off one shoe and dropped it. "Did you see his face when that girl waggled her dugs under his long nose?"

Elfled plied her brush. "You shouldn't. You go too far."

He removed the other shoe. "My clerical brothers amuse me, dearest. Randy as goats, but they'll expire before admitting it. Speaking of clergy, who was that priest you spent so much time with before dinner?"

"Oh—Father Brand. From Abingdon, I believe he said. Interesting fellow."

"So I gathered from your rapt attention."

Elfled heard the veiled comment. "Most of your guests are such dullards."

"He dyes his hair."

"I thought he might."

"Must be going gray," Ranulf said. "A good job, almost indiscernable at a distance, but not entirely convincing. Good to see a man of

God retain a vanity or two. Restores one's faith in human verities. I can always tell. Very little escapes me, Elfled. You should learn to *see* what you look on.''

Oh, I did. ''Yes, Husband.''

Another brief silence as Ranulf removed his rings. ''What did he say that was so fascinating?''

Everything. Be thankful I am not a light woman. You don't see as much as you boast. ''Nothing much. I enjoyed his company. He listens well; that's a rare quality in men. Oh, he *did* say something touching de Gavrillac. Odd.''

''Speak of dullards.'' Ranulf slipped into his nightshirt. ''There is one you might cast in bronze.''

''Just a remark in passing. He said he loved turnips spiced with basil.''

Ranulf stretched out on the large bed, yawning. ''I fail to discern the cryptic in that.''

''No, that de Gavrillac will tell you the most valiant turnips come from Papplewick.'' Elfled went on brushing. The bristles hissed and crackled through her hair. ''I mean, valiant? Well, he had an unusual gift for words. What's valiant about a turnip?''

''Oh—God!''

''What?'' Elfled swiveled about on the bench. Her husband was sitting bolt upright, glaring at her.

''Ask de Gavrillac,'' he bit off too precisely.

''What in the world—?''

Ranulf sprang off the bed like an insulted lion. ''I don't believe the *cheek.*''

''Ranulf, what are you talking about?''

''This 'priest.' Did you notice his left hand?''

''Very strong hands. Capable. Well, he'd been a soldier.''

''He was, dear heart. He has been a great many things. A long thin scar on the palm of the left hand?''

Elfled was not sure; there might have been . . . yes. ''You know him?''

''Quite,'' said Ranulf, livid. ''He is not a priest.''

''Oh, but he is, as gentle and wise as ever I made shrift to.''

''Spare me.'' Ranulf sagged down on the bed under a black cloud of fury. ''In my own house. At my own table.''

''I don't understand.''

Ranulf smiled at her with honeyed acid. ''I daresay not. That would ask too much. Some days ago, de Gavrillac and a party of equally stupid vavasors were driven out of Papplewick by farmers hurling turnips.

76

They were led by the sheriff of Nottingham and the former brigand you call Robin Hood.''

"No, impossible," she scoffed. "I remember Robin Hood when I was a lit—"

"Shut—up."

"Don't speak to me that way." Elfled was affronted by his tone. "I am your wife, not your steward or lackey. An equal and perhaps a bit more, if truth be told. If Robin Hood came into your house, I must say he has better manners than all the rest of your ponderous Norman bores put together."

Robin Hood. He was Robin, that *Robin?* Not old at all, but of a perfect age to complement hers. Robin Hood . . . Elfled never gauged the moment, but it was precisely then, between one breath and the next, that she fell in love with glamor for the second time.

Ranulf stared at her. "What did you tell him, what of me?''

He might have been questioning a minor clerk who'd committed an unpardonable blunder; Elfled returned his tone with interest. "Only that you wear too much jewelry and have a crude sense of humor.''

Ranulf hunched forward, arms on his knees. Deliberate, the mask in place again. "If I am a peasant, dear wife, you are not above me. Your father had money, that's all. Every jewel, every stitch you wear was given to you. What I wear I earned.''

There would be no intimacy tonight, Elfled decided without regret. He was being impossible, and she far from the right mood. Ranulf lay back across the bed, still brooding. Long after Elfled had extinguished the lamps and gotten into bed herself, when she thought Ranulf asleep, he thrashed over on his back. "But this time, Denby . . . ''

"This time what?''

"Nothing.''

De Gavrillac's humiliation in Sherwood was not a complete failure. Among the papers confiscated from the church at Papplewick was a treatise on the rights of subjects written by Edward of Denby.

Ranulf carefully studied and absorbed Denby's Inquiry. The man was clever, his arguments proceeding from facts and questions the king himself revolved upon—and Ranulf himself, to be honest, though Denby's course was dangerously direct. If Ranulf questioned the quality of the grain in the tree he climbed, he would not chop down the means by which he ascended. Robin Hood . . . how curious, the enduring English affection for rebels and outlaws. William once remarked of these people that they carried treason in the blood like Original Sin. Certainly that stain was in Denby—

We are told kings rule by the grace of God. Was Ethelbert of Kent less of a king before he accepted Christ? And if he became sacred at that point, what has Pope Gregory wrought when he stated in his *Dictatus* of 1075 that kings are totally subordinate to the Vicar of Christ and even to his bishops, in effect ruling by the tolerance of and as the vassals of Rome? Gregory declared the Church the only infallible arm on Earth. If this is so, then infallibly has he declared kings mere subordinate and secular heads of state as they were in this island under English law, chosen by the Witan, which implied the common consent of the realm and only after the fact by the consent of God and Rome. How this stands between the crown and the See of Peter is for them to debate. For secular men a time has come wherein rights of kings must no longer be taken for granted but examined, redefined and, if need be, challenged.

For Ranulf's purposes a vein of seditious gold. Denby challenged the unquestionable right of majesty with a boldness the Chancery priest could not but admire. Like himself, the man groped intuitively toward a *state,* not the prolongation of a quasi-religious institution, and saw rights as secular and divisible. Yet Ranulf could not dare so far; the implications frightened him and angered him all the more for recognizing fear in the citadel of his own self-esteem. He quelled admiration and dwelt on the danger. The king must see this poisonous work. As for Sherwood, no more testing of the opposition. That only stirred up the hive with no honey gleaned for his trouble. His men would continue to infiltrate Sherwood; personable, sociable men ready to stand a drink here and there, listening. . . .

8

▶▶▶▶▶

FOR his part, Robin learned much of Ranulf in his own house, even more from the elliptical remarks of the man's wife. The key to his character: self-conceit and strutting pride in his power, especially in his dexterous mind. If Robin risked a good deal in entering the house, the whole adventure was profitable and a lark in the playing. He *did* miss the brazen daring of the old days sometimes. There were children to think of now and the less flattering truth that he was—well, not old, not even middle-aged, but no longer one-and-twenty. Still, Robin would have loved to relieve Ranulf of his stuffed purse in the company of Tuck, Much, and Little John, God rest them gentle.

"That's been and gone," Marian stressed sharply more than once. "You hazarded too much then, you take too much on yourself now writing so, and for what?"

And Ralf seconded the sentiment from experience. "The secret of combining valor and reputation with a long life, *mon vieux,* is never taking a needless risk."

"I needed to see the wee man on his home ground."

"And let him know you'd been there and got to him through his woman." Judith shook her head over her cousin. "You fool. Your arrogance is the obverse of his. He won't forget or forgive."

Oh, no more of that. For this moment in warm July, he went off to drink with Alan at the Cross and Crown in Linby.

Alan of Linby Dale shared much in common with Robin. They were of an age and boyhood friends, both inherited their lands and titles, both were outlawed and pardoned by the king, though in different cir-

79

cumstances. Alan at thirty-three was a typical Saxon countryman, waxing beefier and more florid with years and ale and a lost war he couldn't swallow. Sometimes Robin jokingly called him a professional rebel, which Alan could take in good humor up to a point—if he was drinking ale, that is. On Welsh whiskey, that point was early reached and dangerous to pass.

Such as today. Alan had downed his second whiskey, his weather clear but clouding over. Into the third, he began extolling Waltheof, who would have made a great king. Not that Robin wasn't a friend, mark, nor Alan forgetting who saved him from eviction once at risk to his own life, nor that Waltheof didn't owe something for Aelred's death, but . . .

Robin flinched inwardly. *Here it comes. The same sad song.*

But how could he turn against England and his own kind to ride with William when it came to a fight?

Summer drowsed beyond the open tavern door; even the flies buzzing within and without were not taking business seriously today, nor could Robin. He looked about at farmers he knew, the two peddlers at a corner table minding their own affairs, while Alan finished the third drink and poured a fourth.

"Easy on," Robin advised. "You can't hold that stuff like Will Scatloch."

"Never mind that." Alan scowled at him. "I know we've been friends, but you're a goddamned whore."

"Now, that hurts."

"Let it hurt. You're a political whore." Through a thickening tongue, Alan labored to qualify his judgment. He should be fair, after all— Robin had proved a wizard in the Assize and certainly stopped Ranulf from wreaking havoc in Linby, but if he and a few more like him had fought for Waltheof instead of running to inform on him—"At least we'd have an English king, the best since Alfred, and no need to fight for our rightful lands."

"An English king, but the same Norman overlords, harder on you than Osmund's been. Nay, you'd have no land at all."

Alan glared truculently at Robin. "You think not?"

"I do that. If you had a head left on your shoulders, there'd be a price on it. Don't play martyr to a lost cause, there's no pay in it. You want to fight William, fight as I do, through the law." After eight years of the same nagging complaint, Robin's patience with Alan wore thin at times over this one-note resentment. "It's too fair a day to quarrel with an old friend. The hay's safe and dry in your barn and mine alike. Let's drink to a good year."

"If nothing else." They touched cups and drank. Alan's head drooped lower over his drink. "No, I'll never forgive you that."

"Ah, leave off."

"Proper hero," Alan mumbled. "Voice of the common man."

Robin saw where Alan's mood was leading him: to scathing insults, then tears and a need to be forgiven because they were friends, then incoherence and sleep. "Alan, let it go."

"Why?" The shaggy head came up in challenge, reddened eyes unfocused but hostile. "You informed on my good lord."

"Call the dice as they fall. Talk of fools? Waltheof would promise anything to anyone. The Normans would've eaten him alive."

"Traitor."

"Will you let be?"

"Traitor!" Drunk, Alan didn't measure the force of the word or his voice. It came out too hard and loud. Heads turned from the other tables, conversations suspended. Oblivious to everything, Alan jammed his dagger into the scarred tabletop and used it to wobble more or less erect. "Tha's the word, Aelredson. Bloody rutting traitor."

"Alan, peace. Sit down as a friend, or I'll leave you for Algive to fetch on her own."

"I've a mind to carve your liver."

"Aye, and eat it, too. Proper bear sark we are."

The knife leveled at Robin. "Get up, traitor."

Christ, not again. He rose reluctantly, aware that they were the center of taut attention from all parts of the tavern. He kept his voice calm. "Far enough, Alan. Peace, I say."

"Robin?"

He turned to see Henri Chailliard enter the tavern with two Norman soldiers. Robin flung out one hand, warning Henri back. Alan focused muzzily on the knight and his men, growling. "Your liver and any Norman's who tries to stop me."

Alan took an unsteady step around the table toward Robin, slashing at him clumsily. Robin dodged easily as Henri and his men moved in purposefully. They were armed. Alan was no match for them, barely able to stand up, but he'd try. Robin stepped in and swung from the shoulder at Alan's thick jaw. His aim was off; the blow struck Alan on the nose, propelling him backward over the table in a spray of blood.

Henri snapped to the soldiers: "Pin his arms."

For Alan's sake the blow should have knocked sense into him, or consciousness out, but it only infuriated Waltheof's lost rebel. He struggled against the men restraining him. Robin tucked the dagger out of reach while Henri tried to quiet the drunken man. Alan would have none of that, bleeding from the nose, mad as a wounded bull.

"Bastards, all of you!" he raged through the blood. "May God strike you down, every blighted one and the bastard king you serve who stole my lord's place. And you, Robin, you—"

"For the love of reason, man. For the love of your family, shut up," Henri warned him in a rough whisper. "We're king's men. I can't listen to treason like this."

"And there," Alan mumbled at Robin through sudden tears, "there's the man who went to Winchester just to see my good lord die. Death to William of Nor—"

Robin upended the thick whiskey jug; before Alan could damn himself further, he brought it down on his friend's head with a terminal thud. Alan sagged. The soldiers lowered him back onto the table.

Robin knelt beside him. "He's drunk. Always this way when he drinks. Me and the king, we're the cause of all his troubles."

Henri nodded. "I know. Let him be careful of his language."

"He's a good man sober, just too much he can't forget." That was Alan and all of the man. Take away his cause and his anger, there wasn't much left to hold the rest of him together. *O lost and lost . . .*

Henri instructed his men quietly, "This goes no further than us, *compris?*"

The matter was already beyond them. The peddlers at a corner table quietly returned to their ale and conversation as tension relaxed in the Cross and Crown. Paid by Ranulf, and more efficient informers than any Alan might curse, their business was to listen and not be noticed. In the Queen's Rest at Blidworth, they drank health and long life to Denby and all its folk, buying drinks for Robin's churl farmers and listening to tales of the region.

"Ah, Lord Robin—he'll always be a lord to us—why, he's close to the earth as any of us, close as a radish. Put his own blood and Lady Marian's in the tree. Good a Christian as any man, but sometimes the old ways, well, they're like old songs, right? New ones come along, but some tunes stay in your head."

Oh, do they not? the amiable peddlers agreed, buying another round.

A week later, Guy de Gavrillac rode into Nottingham with a Chancery order to the sheriff, a copy to Bishop Osmund, and forty knights to enforce the peremptory command. They were to arrest Alan of Linby Dale for treason against the king's person and majesty. The large armed escort made it abundantly clear that Ranulf would not be checked this time. Ralf rode immediately to Alan's hall, his own men augmented with a detail from Osmund, as much for Alan's safety as anything else.

Too late. Ranulf took no chances this time, left no margin for bold action or legal maneuver. Even as the orders were delivered to sheriff and bishop, Alan had been dragged from his house in chains and rapidly spirited away.

Overnight the mood in Sherwood changed; from Nottingham to Denby a shadow lay over the forest and its folk. Before fear could turn people to panic or the frozen helplessness of terror, Osmund and Robin were urgently requested to join Ralf at his home. A silent sign of the times, Robin observed, that they met in a small privy chamber off the hall. Ralf could not even trust his own servants in this. Anyone could be reached and bought by the serpentine Bayeux. Nor were Ralf and Osmund that free in speaking before him. Their hesitant silences said as much as their weighed words.

"Alan is held in Lincoln," was all Osmund could learn. No word of any trial.

Ralf had found better luck through old friends in Lincoln. Several of them owed considerable favors and redeemed them with information at some personal risk. "There's been no trial at all, but much talk of making an example of Alan."

Grey, portly Osmund paced about the small chamber, hands behind his back. Robin sat across the table from Ralf, fingers steepled before his lips. In what the two Normans said he could detect more than regret; there was an unspoken fear and perhaps a shamefaced apology to Robin as well.

"I would have had to deliver him anyway," Ralf admitted. "Ranulf's message is clear. Bow to the king's will in this—and through this the land enclosures—or be called rebels."

Robin agreed. Bayeux would love nothing better. "Alan made it easy for them. He always cursed me drunk. This time he included the king, and the wrong ears heard him."

Studying his listeners, Robin read their ambivalence. Strong men both, but teetering now on the narrow ledge between loyalty and what might be construed by William, certainly by Bayeux, as palpable treason on their own part. Something must be done quickly and in cool-headed legality. "My lords, it's not Alan we must protect now. He's dug his grave with his mouth. It is the principle we must fight for. Hold Alan and perhaps execute him without trial, and then which of us can't be taken on his own hearth?"

Osmund nodded thoughtfully. "One whisper of resistance."

Ralf was firmer. "Whatever we do, the whole shire must be with us."

Osmund lowered his episcopal bulk into a chair at the head of the battered refectory table that filled much of the small chamber's space. "Of all times for this sort of trouble."

"Your Grace," Robin contradicted, "all times are alike in that. Such trouble is always coming when men seek to avoid it. We must not."

"Damn you, Denby," Osmund flared back, stung by the implication of timidity—in fact the very emotion he felt—"are *we* to blame? You had to twit Ranulf in his own house, had to be Robin Hood once more."

"No, that was not well considered," Robin admitted. "Just the malice and conceit of him . . . "

"His Grace is right," Ralf put in. "But right or not, we must act quickly and in concert."

"Then I'll stop thinking like the ass I've been and more like a lawyer." Robin laid before them the thoughts firming in his mind. "We have one possible vantage. The order bore the small seal, not William's. The king may not know what his wee manny's taken on himself. If that's true—"

"Yes, I see," Osmund took up the thought. "And this as well. I have some influence in Rouen. My family has always been loyal to William and his father before him, as I am now. Troubled but loyal. I say we go round Bayeux directly to the king and Lanfranc at Canterbury."

"Sue for indulgence? No," Robin declined vigorously. "My lord, that ent what we're after."

"Then in Heaven's name, what *are* we after? Total revolt?"

"What Ralf named. The shire behind us in a written statement of grievance. A petition to bind the king on oath so that this can never happen again."

"Bind?" Osmund stared at the Saxon in disbelief. "You mean *force* a curb on royal power?"

"A legal balance. His coronation oath vaguely implies as much, but then it wasn't thought out by a good lawyer."

Osmund sent an imploring glance to the sheriff: *Can you believe this man?* "Am I dim, Vicomte? We speak of healing one treason, and as remedy he prescribes another. Very astute, Denby.''

"That or else." Robin impaled them both on the point of his argument. "One day that unhappy old man or his heir will be snapping at Your Grace's own heels. At yours, Ralf. Or your sons' and nowt to stop him but us, here and now. My lords, trust me so far. You are from Normandy where there is no law but the duke's power and the arms of his vassals. For English law, there's more room within it than without.''

There was a soft tapping at the door. Judith entered carrying a sealed letter. "Pardon, my lords. This," she placed the letter before her husband, "from Lincoln. The courier said it was urgent.''

"Thank you, my dear." Ralf broke the seal and scanned the contents. Robin watched his friend; Ralf held the letter above the tabletop. As his eyes went down the sheet, the hand drooped until it rested on the table surface. "Alan has been hanged.''

Judith gave a soft little cry. "No, they cou—''

The glance her husband gave her was subtle but easily read by Judith after years of marriage. *Later. You will hear it all, I promise.*

She took the hint, curtsied to the bishop, and quietly withdrew.

Silence lengthened among the three men. Robin broke it. "And the trial? Who defended him?''

Ralf said flatly, "There was no trial.''

"Then Ranulf murdered him.''

"Robin—''

"That's the word. *Murdered!*''

"Peace, listen to the letter. This is from a close friend I trust. For his own safety, I won't name him. He writes, 'The man was hanged a day after arriving at Lincoln Castle. There cannot have been more than the most summary proceeding, if any. Men go in fear of Bayeux and inform on one another for their own safety. What I owe you has been paid twice over in sending this letter, which I entreat you to destroy.' '' Ralf deliberately tore the parchment into a pile of tiny scraps. "Robin, you were Alan's friend.''

Sadly: "When he was sober and didn't curse me for a traitor.''

"I know. Will you take the news to . . . ''

"To Algive, yes." Robin heaved up from the table and moved to the door. "It should be a friend. Your Grace, Alan was your man and you are God's. His lands revert to you. Please, I ask you to be generous to Algive and the children.''

Osmund was still appalled by the brazen fact of the hanging. "What? Oh. Yes, of a certainty."

"Robin," Ralf said soberly, "I am sorry for this."

"But now you see what I must impress on you. Men go in fear today, in chains tomorrow. By all means write to Rouen, Your Grace, and perhaps to Lanfranc, but think as you write. William is distant, an old man with a bad stomach and a dying queen. Ranulf is young, hungry, and here. We fight him now or not at all."

The closing door punctuated his point. There was another thoughtful silence. Eventually Osmund made a sound between a grunt of resignation and a sigh. "May as well say it now, Ralf. Whatever Denby proposes, we hold most of Sherwood in fief. You know where that puts us in this."

"Clearly. In the middle."

"Denby speaks for our interests, of course."

Ralf heard the qualifying pause. "But?"

"*Ma foi,* man! He is more dangerous now than when he was robbing us."

"About Alan's widow—"

Osmund's heavy rings flashed in the light with his gesture of assurance. "No fear. I will provide for her. But you are ambitious for your sons. How far will you go in this? How far with Denby?"

No reminder was needed of the danger to Ralf's future or that of his sons, nor how perilous was what Robin proposed. Ralf took up a pinch of the letter fragments and let them fall like snow to the tabletop. Osmund leaned forward in his chair, earnest. "I ask in confidence, Ralf."

"There is no more confidence, only fear. You heard the letter. You are not seriously thinking that I would betray you to save my own, nor I you, but the thought is here in the room. Men inform to hold what they have because they are greedy or afraid. I have coerced such people myself. And I am very afraid now."

They parted on that, both glad to be out of the chamber, away from the shadowy presence of Robin like a bad conscience and what neither wanted to say. All they had came through loyalty to William; they and their forebears knew no other way, and neither could detect the clear line between that fealty and treason this summer, except that the crime was now being defined for them by a razor-minded young priest in Lincoln who had just shown them how far he would go.

How far will I? Ralf echoed Osmund's question to himself.

He scooped up the pieces of the letter and burned them to ash.

86

9

▶▶▶▶▶

WILLIAM's rule was always personal and increasingly severe as he aged, like a husband jealous of a wife he needed but could never fathom or trust. After Waltheof's revolt, earls were rare, the lesson of King Edward always vivid in William's mind. Under Edward and his predecessors, the old earldoms, once kingdoms, were still virtually independent of any monarch not strong enough to impose his will. On the eve of William's conquest, his cousin Edward reigned, but Harold ruled as Earl of Wessex, his brothers Tostig, Gyrth, and Leofwine equally powerful earls in their own right, a filial siege about the king. William swept that away at Hastings. After Waltheof's defection, he determined never to make the same mistake again, ruling England through sheriffs directly responsible to him.

He went a step further, never granting his nobles too much land in one place, but scattering their fiefs throughout England. Prelates like Osmund and Ralf who held only local honors in Nottinghamshire could draw on no other livings or power, and answered directly to the king for everything they had. The increasingly suspicious William bulwarked this policy by relying more and more on his Chancery in lieu of his regent, the diligent but ailing old Lanfranc, Archbishop of Canterbury.

No one was more acutely aware than Ralf Fitz-Gerald how entirely his fortunes leaned on his loyalty or how swiftly they could fall in dereliction. He had been seventeen years in England, more in armor than out for the first ten. Noticed by William at the age of twenty, he rose early to the post of Lord High Sheriff of Nottingham, later created vicomte and given Judith of Denby to wife. With his relatively small holdings, he still had ample power and the ease of modest wealth. He was wiser than ambitious now. He loved Sherwood, settled down with Judith, and over the years found himself astonished by contentment.

They were wed in the autumn of 1075. On Ralf's investiture as vicomte, they went on the customary progress about his lands. On Robin's advice, Ralf visited his people often.

"Like the horses you raise yourself. So with your folk. Whenever possible, go yourself. Let them know you don't just hold the land, you're part of it."

Through last year's famine, Ralf relieved his folk out of his own pocket by way of deferred rents. Presiding over the Forest Assize, he found the experience a fascinating key to the complex, litigious English mind. Yet in some ways he would always be Norman. Their first son, Jean, was born in 'seventy-seven, named for Ralf's father. The second would have been William in deference to the king, but Judith's small English foot came down firmly on that.

"Really, aren't there enough Willys already? Let me name him for my father Hakon."

"Hakon? Unusual."

"No, just Danish."

"But you hate Danes. Your whole family hates them."

"Especially Robin," Judith laughed, "and all the more for there's that much Dane in us. But there it is."

Well enough, but firstborn Jean would inherit any lands and title. Hakon would go into the Church. To that end, Jean would be fostered out at the proper age to the most advantageous noble house they could find. Hakon would be tutored at home by Judith, his clerical future a virtual certainty through her close friendship with Lanfranc. Jean was dark as his father and promised to resemble him later. Judith herself had the ebony hair and delicately sculpted features and form one occasionally found among Danes, with hints of violet in her eyes that went darker in passion or anger, smoky in candlelight. Queen Matilda once said of her with open envy that there was simply not a bad or unflattering angle to the girl's face. Ralf took a husband's secret delight in studying her. Like a deep river that showed no ripple on the surface to hint of the currents surging beneath, very few men would guess at the fire in Judith. Her contempt was ice, but her love was as savage in its sudden hunger as it soothed in giving. Ralf always looked back with erotic pleasure on the painfully delicious discomfort of her nail marks raked down his back and buttocks in their first months together. Convent-schooled in Caen, Judith might have become a nun. Ralf gave frequent thanks the outcome was otherwise. Judith in the Church would have been—if not a waste of love, God pardon the thought—certainly a misdirection.

Hakon bore out the old Mercian strain in Judith, belying the dark coloring of both parents, big-boned, blond, and placid, less energetic than Jean, but sturdier.

Year by year Ralf's interests became more narrowly bound by Nottingham and his beloved Sherwood. Like Robin, he perceived the unnatural strain in a single monarchy divided by the Channel. Norman or English, all landlords were in grumbling agreement on this point.

"If William rules in England, let him *be* in England."

The grip of the aging king was not yet weakened; they were all held fast in it.

"The font from whom all blessings flow," Robin wrote once to Judith, "and the font never lets you forget where you drink."

William considered lords like Ralf and Osmund members of his old guard, tempered and tested reliables who had helped him carve a Norman throne from English oak. That old guard was now settled in England while the swaggering, riotous younger generation in Normandy flocked to Count Robert or to Philip I of France for profit and fame. Time exacted its toll; as Osmund's joints stiffened and his health declined, as the grey crept through Ralf's hair, they were genuinely shocked to hear themselves derided by Robert and his callow contemporaries as *"les ancêtres,"* silly old farts.

"Old?" Ralf fretted to his lady. "Not yet forty, not a stone heavier than when I jumped from the boat onto the beach at Pevensey."

"And yet the handsomest man I have ever known," Judith attested affectionately. "Only a little—*un peu*—larger in the waist, as I am. You fit marvelously to me, my sweet. But old? It is to laugh."

They visited Denby often. Both loved the morning's ride through Sherwood to the warmth of the hall with its feel and smell of the life lived under its low, thatched roof. Both houses were one blood in marriage now, which sat well enough with the younger folk, but Maud was a problem. Ralf had put her in a dungeon. By no persuasion would she break bread with him or remain in his presence, marriage and fealty be damned. Only when Robin, Marian, and Judith wore her down with, "See here, Mum!" and, "Aunt, for the sake of my son!" did Maud soften, and only when Hakon was born did she journey with Robin to Nottingham with gifts for the child and the kiss of peace for Ralf.

As for Robin, the growth and deepening of his mind awed Ralf and Judith alike. At twenty-four he could read or write little more than his name. Ralf observed him over the passing years. An attentive listener in the Forest Court, consistently voting for royal law in Sherwood but never unchecked royal power, never an *aye* given without urging some concession from William in return, *quid pro quo*—rising at last to plant his colors before the Assize as openly as the flag he unfurled at Norwich Castle.

"For us in Sherwood, lord and vassal are one in interest. I say *one*—else we're no more than William's chattels."

Quite true. Lords like Ralf and Osmund were no longer a conquering guard set down about their king's new-wrested possessions, but land-owners in a country whose colors seeped year by year deeper into their very grain. William must be more tractable, give some thought to England, see this shadow from Lincoln lengthening between crown and feudal lords.

What Robin presented to sheriff and bishop smacked less of treason than radical revolution.

TO WILLIAM, KING OF THE ENGLISH, DUKE OF NORMANDY, AND TO HIS REGENT LANFRANC, ARCHBISHOP OF CANTERBURY, THE LORDS AND LIEGE-MEN UNDERSIGNED IN THEIR FEALTY SUBMIT AND PETITION—

I. That the execution of Alan of Linby Dale, for whatever offense, went forth without due process of law. That in this one man's end, all men of good faith can see their own. That this miscarriage was too hastily enacted by the keeper of the Chancery seal, Ranulf of Bayeux.

"Plain enough and no less than truth," Robin attested.

"Beyond plain," the bishop averred. "It is a gauntlet thrown."

"Your Grace, plain or blunt, the rope around Alan's neck is long enough for ours."

Osmund had ascertained that the order did not come directly from the king. "My source in Rouen would know. No such writ was issued from the palace."

II. For the good of the realm, we argue that no man of any condition be henceforth imprisoned without trial within the venue of the shire wherein he be accused.

III. That this assurance of common right be sworn in the coronation oath as binding upon the king and his successors forever.

To Normans such as Ralf and Osmund, the implications of the third article alone were staggering. "In the oath itself? Binding in perpetuity? That means . . ."

Osmund could not bring himself to voice the logical conclusion.

"That the king is accountable to common law," Ralf finished for him.

"Impossible."

"Utterly, but Robin also means we speak out for these rights now or stand in peril someday of dangling like Alan."

"And will you stand so, Ralf? I asked this before; you gave no answer."

"I don't know. There is no simple answer." Ralf would not hastily put his name to a course that cast Judith and his sons into hazard for an ideal. "I am as afraid of Robin as I am for him. When you greeted me today, I kissed the episcopal ring. If we do not stand with him in this—all of us—I think we will kiss whatever Ranulf tells us to."

What they held they should hold in safety, none denied that, but proceeding must be cautious. They all danced on eggs now. They must win support throughout the shire. Commit the strongest men first, the commons would follow. Only then send a copy to Lanfranc and to the king. If possible, let Ranulf hear of it last. Difficult when his eyes and ears were everywhere.

Ralf feared more than he showed. Judith could sense the shadow over her husband. "Why?" she beseeched him. "Why won't you tell me what is happening?"

Ralf drew her to him under the covers of their wide bed. "I cannot, Judith. Not yet."

"You have never been secretive or apart from me. It's this business of Alan and Bayeux."

Ralf wound her hair about his fingers where it spilled in a dark burst over the pillow, and tried to frame his heart toward an answer. "Fear of dying has been with me so long, it is accustomed, like the sword I wear. But fear for you and the boys, *jamais*. Never. There's too much I can't afford to lose."

"Nor I." Judith pressed her mouth to the warmth of his scarred shoulder. "Is it what Robin has written?"

He raised up over her, stern with his fear. "Where did you—?"

"Now then, don't come the sheriff with me. I can read, you know."

"You should not have."

"Forgive me?"

Ralf lowered his forehead against hers, whispering and earnest. "Judith, forget what you read. Discuss it with no one, I beg you."

Most alarming to Ralf was the silence from Normandy which might betoken William's ignorance of the matter or tacit consent to Alan's execution. If the latter, even bolder license would follow from Ranulf. This summer courage came down to which frightened men would find within fear the fortitude to move against him.

When he arose next morning, Ralf rode alone through Nottingham to the bishop's house, found Osmund at breakfast with his chantry priests, and placed the articles before him without comment. Osmund dismissed his priests, beckoning Ralf to the scriptorium before opening the rolled and tied parchment. Ralf's signature and seal were boldly affixed, but space had been left above it for Osmund to sign first as prelate and ranking peer.

With a significant heave of his shoulders, Osmund chose a quill and signed as first subscriber and pressed his signet into the wax. Done, come what may. The bishop settled back in his chair, folding jeweled fingers over his ample girth. "I remember when courage was as inexpensive as charging a shield wall."

"True." Ralf tied up the petition. "Now the price goes up."

Lanfranc, Archbishop of Canterbury, was now well over seventy and in declining health, traveling much less between Winchester, London, and his own metropolitan see. The tolerant, very human nature that Judith always loved in her old teacher at Caen was deeply worn with the concerns of state and the growing schism between the king he served and a Church which could no longer be subservient to temporal crowns if it were to survive and flourish. The tawny hair of his Lombard ancestry had gone white; these days there came a time when Lanfranc needed a nap between morning and afternoon audiences. This Lammas Day, fresh from his rest and clad in the lightest of vestments, Lanfranc walked slowly through the soaring nave of his cathedral, genuflected to the altar, and turned into the transept toward the consistory chamber he used for audiences.

"Excellency?"

A chubby, cherub-faced young priest bustled after him, brandishing a schedule. "I am remiss for not meeting you earlier. Here are the audiences before Vespers."

"The fault is mine, Peter. I overslept. Who is first?"

Severely nearsighted, Father Peter brought the schedule close to his nose. "Edward of Denby."

"Ah. Yes."

"A defrocked priest, Your Excellency?"

The notion amused Lanfranc. "Denby? I hardly think so."

Not of a clerical caste, Father Peter would have said, but with a tonsure or the remains of one now growing out.

"Denby is a number of things, Father Peter. Coming from Picardy, you would not know him. Former thane, former outlaw—"

Father Peter gasped. "Good God!"

"Quite. All of those, and an unending annoyance. We will see him."

The old archbishop had just settled himself in the audience chair, specially cushioned for his ease, when Robin entered in mud-spattered linen and knelt to kiss the episcopal ring. From one source or another, Lanfranc heard most of what transpired in the Chancery. He always reserved his opinion of Father Ranulf—which was more than Ranulf had done in the matter of "Father Brand."

"Welcome, my son. I fear one day Robin Hood will tweak the wrong nose."

The mild blue eyes reflected nothing but bland inquiry. "Excellency?"

"You portray innocence well, but spare me. Take care you do not become the mirror of what you mock. This business at Lincoln—"

"He frightens me," Robin blurted. "He frightens us all; that's why I've come."

Lanfranc dismissed the subject. "Father Peter says you are delegated from the lords of your shire."

And well chosen in that, he reflected with some surprise. The shire accent that once made Denby's new-learned French an ordeal to the ear when they first met, was wholly submerged in fluency now, evident only occasionally in flattened vowel sounds. The man must have an uncanny ear.

Robin handed him a rolled parchment. Undoing the strings, Lanfranc recognized the seals of Nottingham see and the sheriff-vicomte of that city as leading signatories. Denby's name followed, then the marks of unlettered men beside their neatly printed names: Chailliard, vavasor; Ayulf of Papplewick; at least two score others.

The three brief articles were penned in French and English. They took only moments to read but, Lanfranc estimated, would need perhaps centuries for kings to accept. Without comment, he asked, "Has the king seen this?"

"We ask you to send it under your seal," Robin said. "As in the salutation, we humbly submit a request for redress and change."

Lanfranc inquired delicately, "And the Chancery?"

"Good my lord, the Chancery has its own channels of information, I think."

Meaning its own network of spies. "I would imagine they have already perused this."

There was the meat, Robin urged eagerly; that was why he and the lords and men of his shire came to the king's regent. Ranulf would view this petition as treason or worse, as might William hearing it from the wrong quarter and in the worst light. By appealing to the crown through the most respected minister of the realm and God, they earnestly and honestly sought to avoid the taint of rebellion. "Which we do not intend, sir. We know to a man how dangerous a path we take."

"Do you?" Lanfranc challenged with surprising sharpness. "A nice distinction between two sides of a hairline. Revolution of a process may not be the same as revolt—"

"But revolution is a *turning*," Robin jumped in, respectful but headlong. "A wheel turns without breaking the cart."

"Very nimble but disingenuous." Lanfranc scanned the third article again. Neither Osmund nor Fitz-Gerald had the sort of mind to shape such a concept. "Who conceived this?"

"Our common need, Your Excellency."

"Nimble again. You evade my meaning."

"I wrote the articles."

Lanfranc's delicate Italian ear caught the overtone of pride. "One guessed at it. You are an unusual man, my son." *And may have the same failing as that other vaulting intellect in the Chancery.* "Very well, tell the lords of your shire I will convey this to the king."

"Our thanks to Your Excellency." Robin bowed his head in leave-taking. "Without delay, we beg you."

"At our discretion," Lanfranc reproved mildly.

"We entreat your earliest opportunity. Ranulf rode over bishop and sheriff and hanged a man."

"For outright treason, we hear."

"Aye, Alan was guilty, I was there. But hanged without trial! They violated hearth-right, stove in his door, and took him." Robin pointed to the petition. "The common men like me who have put their names and mayhap their lives to that page know that no English king or earl—not Harold, Siward, or even foolish Waltheof—would dare so flout common rights. And every man whose name the king finds there is agreed. There is no substance in the king's peace while Bayeux or any man can do this."

"Denby, subside." The archbishop stirred restlessly in his hard chair. The cushion did not help much over a protracted audience. "It is possible that William consented to the execution."

"Pray he didn't. Please, Your Excellency express in clearest terms to the king that we have written and signed for the common good of his realm, for we truly believe so."

Good of the realm. The thought struck Lanfranc, used to dealing with the most sinuous minds in Europe, that Denby uttered the phrase with no awareness of presumption—but now Father Peter's head was in at the door, the next audience awaited him, the aldermen of Canterbury. Lanfranc invited Denby to take supper in the monks' frater and his night's rest in the adjoining hospice. He offered the ring to be kissed.

Yet when Denby's hand was on the door latch, Lanfranc stayed him with a cautionary thought. "You are aware of what you ask in this? That an absolute ruler be less than absolute. Go and pray for me."

He let the aldermen wait his pleasure a little longer after the Englishman departed, reading again the articles signed by lords but penned by a farmer.

III. That this assurance of common right be sworn in the coronation oath as binding upon the king and his successors forever.

There were volcanoes in his native Italy that had buried whole towns in their fury. The petition in Lanfranc's hand was no less volatile, a rumbling in the deep human soul, no less, attested by straggling X's and squiggles beside the names of priests, bowyers, fletchers, butchers, and blacksmiths who respectfully asked in the witness of God that anointed kings relinquish some part of heretofore unquestioned power for the good of the realm.

Send it now or wait? Better to forward it with softening comments; certainly Ranulf would do so directly his hands were upon it. For the king's sake, Lanfranc hated to add one more care to the man's load now.

He is by Matilda's bed every moment now unless they tear him away. Old Flanders' child, my good friend. Let God take her in swift mercy, not suffering. Let the sin be on me in seeking to hasten His will. Let it be a single caress of an angel's wing sweeping her from pain to peace.

He would send the petition in the normal course of couriers to Rouen. Pity Denby had no more humility than Ranulf. Neither saw William as a man who grubbed at an unforgiving task with the tools given him. Ranulf brandished the tools like a juggler. Denby broke them outright and called for new.

10

▶▶▶▶▶

THE sturdiest parents often produced deformed children, the fairest intent misshapen results. The shire nobles supported Robin in intelligent self-interest, the commons in the same vein with no true understanding. In the churches, taverns, crofts, and fields, men idealized Robin's petition, enlarging its three lean articles with their own grievances and hopes.

"Nay, it should give us this as well, give us that, land reforms and lower taxes." Should ultimately promise a good life, easy death, and guaranteed paradise for every poor, honest, worked-to-early-death soul in England. What Robin shaped as a simple bowl, men's need made into a Grail and into it poured all their hopes.

Early in August, Father Ayulf of Papplewick, still outraged by the ransacking of his church, preached a sermon of pure brimstone from the pulpit. Intended or not, his folk took it as an open declaration against all Norman overlords. Sent to the village on the sheriff's business, Henri Chailliard and two of his soldiers were caught in the local fever and stoned. No serious injury, but ominous undertones. Ralf swept down on Papplewick with an armed escort, dragged Ayulf from his house, and selected ten men for flogging in the square. Ayulf was spared this, but forced to watch the punishment. Stubborn, defiant, his scraggly tonsure standing up like the hair on a spitting cat, Ayulf *would* not see how his lord could do this when he himself had signed the petition.

"Wrong to stone your knight, my lord, but are you with us in this or not?"

"It is not that simple," Ralf fumed, caught between the folk he cared for and the king he owed. "We are putting our necks in the noose for all of you, and you kick the ladder out from under us."

Ayulf's reaction was no more than the "brick wall" look Ralf knew early on from a much younger Robin. "Lord Robin would not think so."

"Then you don't know him or what he works to accomplish." At the moment, Ralf wondered if he clearly knew himself either the man or his elusive intent. But these folk were still putting the image of Robin to music.

Many swore to have witnessed deeds Robin Hood never did nor ever could. As his image, so his words blossomed in their need from plain, healthy stem to full-blown flower. To keep them all from disaster, Ralf conferred with Bishop Osmund early on the tenth of August, then took a fresh horse from his stable and rode through Sherwood alone to Denby gate, sounding the horn. At the call, Minna poked her head out of the kitchen-house door.

"Give you good day, Minna. Where is Robin?"

"*Lord* Robin?" Minna corrected him with righteous emphasis, swinging a bared red arm in a wide arc to the west. "Where's he like to be, sir, but in the barley while there's light."

Ralf turned his horse and jumped the narrow rill that meandered along the steading's west wall, then urged the swift little mare into a canter toward Denby's barley stands. The day was hot; the sweating men worked in no more than a breechclout about their loins, the women with skirts tucked up high into wide aprons, bare and dust-stained to their thighs. Ralf had learned to respect the rhythms and needs of the land. While barley grew, you prayed for enough rain and not too much. Come Lammas Day, everyone worked at the harvesting until the yield was safe in the barns. Rain in spring was a blessing, last month at haying time it would have been disaster. The folk of Denby and Blidworth moved steadily through the uncut grain, every movement and task organized. First came the sheaver to twist the stalks into sheaves of uniform size in the hand. Behind came the cutter with his sickle, slicing off the sheaf, then a woman gathering the sheaves and laying them flat across readied strips of linen lyngel. Finally, the banders tied them securely and set them upright in stooks.

Ralf walked the mare through the fresh-cut stubble to where Robin, bare as his workers, carefully greased a wooden strickle and then plunged it into a bag of sand to make a fresh whet stick. The sharpening of sickles was done by a village woman seated on the ground and working around a child slung to her front and placidly feeding at one breast.

Ralf dismounted and looped the reins lightly around one hand. "Walk with me, Robin. We need to talk."

Robin looked off toward his harvesters, wiping sweat from his forehead. "If it's extra reapers for boonwork, I can't spare a one."

"No, it is not for that." They walked slowly across the cut furrows, the mare clopping behind them through the hot, dusty field. "You heard what happened in Papplewick?"

"I did." Father Ayulf should have considered his words and their effect. "I don't blame you for what you had to do."

"That is gracious of you," Ralf acknowledged dryly, "considering I signed a petition for change, not a peasant revolt. These villains don't understand what you're trying to do, only that somehow right now we seem to be with them against the king, and ought to be. I've just come from Osmund."

Robin took a few long strides ahead of Ralf and swung about to him. The crossbolt scar from Ralf's weapon was a pale white circle over his left hip against the glistening, sun-bronzed skin. They had fought twice almost to the death. Shorter and heavier-muscled, Ralf knew Robin's slenderness deceptive. The man had the wiry endurance of those unbreakable pulley cords the peasants fashioned from bulls' testicles.

"And what from His Grace?"

"He heard from Winchester. Ranulf has seen our petition, and why was it not sent first to the Chancery? The little weasel accuses us of working in secret. Osmund said we took it properly to the king's regent— an evasion and Ranulf knows as much."

"Are y'worried, then? Lanfranc sent it on to Rouen."

"Not so speedily as Ranulf."

In the sunlight Robin felt the chill of a shadow not really there. "But why? I urged him to put wings on his courier."

Ralf shrugged. "Who knows? Delayed, simply put aside. It's *how* this comes to William that makes all the difference. Sent by my wife's old teacher and friend is one thing. From Ranulf is quite another." Ralf paused, hands on his hips, squinting through the sun's glare at Robin. "Osmund says we must modify the articles."

"Modify? How?"

"Strike out the coronation guarantee."

Robin regarded him steadily. "And?"

"Possibly reword the other articles."

"I see."

"I hope so."

"You were never a timid man, Ralf."

"Damn it, I have sons!"

"And I've none?"

"A fine son and the best of wives. Pray you remember them."

Yes, you loved her once, Robin thought, regarding his friend. *I loved her always.* Marian and the children were stations on the way of the particular cross he bore, but how to say this to Ralf when he could not even voice it to Marian. "Well, then. Weaken this, water that, you say. Until we have no point or purpose, just a begging. 'If the king would be so kind as to try us before hanging, we promise to stay on our knees.' Is that what you ask?"

"Sangre du Christ!" Ralf exploded, stamping about, raising dust in his frustration. "This is my country, too. I am committed as you and still not enough. No, you must push, push, *push!* We have never bothered that much with ceremony, Robin, but remember I am your lord."

Robin regarded him evenly. "You would silence me?"

"No, I would only—"

"Go back on your signed word?"

Ralf turned away from that damned inexorable thing in Robin, trying to quell his anger, knowing it based in fear. "I urge you to common sense. Another draft of the petition. More stress on our loyalty, more diplomacy in our requests."

"A little danger now is safety later."

Fool, Ralf despaired: *What could he say to the serene ignorance of an educated man able to appreciate the nobility of a lion-king and not see the feral cat William was at heart?* "You don't know the king or what forged him. He trusts one way: Be strongest. He knows one rule and that is absolute."

Over Ralf's shoulder, Robin saw Marian ambling a mule toward them from the steading, bringing his dinner that he need not leave the barley while the light held. "And so? One day that absolute or his Chancery peacock could hang your Jean or my Edward at a whim. No, Ralf. For their sakes we must dare now or not at all."

"Then think what you would weaken," Ralf countered soberly. "How inconsistent you are. What other man of Normandy or England could have so held it all together? For that very reason you fought for him against Waltheof."

Robin couldn't deny that; such was not his point, though hinged to it. You secured the foundation of a house before expanding and improving it. "Absolute and strong, yes, but how when strong dies, Ralf? Will strong follow? Will strong give us a few rights, let us live like men without taxing the food out of our children's mouths? If the king's hard, you think his sons will be flamin' angels of benevolence?"

"Robin, none of us go back on our word or intent, but we must be cautious. Caution can win. What in hell do you *want*?"

"I want it in writing," Robin shot back. "Sworn before God, but in *writing.*"

"Like a merchant, penny for penny."

"Damned right."

"You—" Ralf wheeled about, imploring of God and the sane world in the face of this impossible man. He saw Marian coming on her mule and remembered the day he gave Robin the scar in his side; how, even in raising his sword to kill the man he paused for love of her to swear to Robin that she would never come to harm. Ralf had wanted her then, and in the years since, he'd come to love her exasperating husband as much. *"Par ma foi, tu es emmerdant! Tu es—"* Ralf's own tongue was inadequate; only earthy English would serve for this frustration. "Robin, you are a large wound in the arse!"

And wouldn't you know the maddening man just laughed and agreed with him. "I know."

Marian's mule halted. She jumped down with a small sack and a skin of ale, greeting Ralf merrily. "Lord love me, but this Emily's a slow creature. Give you good day, Ralf. Cutting barley with us?"

"No." Ralf threw a sour glance at Robin placidly gulping and chewing. "I am dealing with your other mule."

"Robin, love, have you seen Mum?"

"Been out here since Matins bell, why?" With a mouthful of bread and chicken, Robin ruminated on the cause of Marian's concern. *Mum's wandered off again.* "Most like gone to the church to see Father Beorn."

Few words were needed between husband and wife for understanding. Ralf was trusted, but some family matters did not go beyond Denby gate. *Go seek her,* Marian's eyes asked of him. *You know well how it is with her.*

Robin offered his meal to Ralf. "Here, settle your stomach with a good farmer's meal. Marian, see the folk don't idle too long at dinner."

He set off across the fields at a trot toward the hall. Ralf handed the ale skin and food back to Marian. "I must be back in Nottingham."

"Wait." She held his arm. "You were arguing. What is it, then?"

"Nothing, my dear."

"This writing Robin's made?"

He did not answer directly, gazing off at the reapers gathering into family groups to rest and eat. "Name of God but I love this country, Marian. Robin says sometimes I even sound like an Englishman."

"I do think he's right."

"How has it gone with you and the children? Is Moira well?"

"God's been good to her—and I did ask a question of you, my lord. This writing, it's the one thing Robin won't speak of or share with me. Don't lie to be kind, Ralf. Tell me straight."

Her wide-set brown eyes held him. He read affection there, but strength and concern as well. "No, a man does not lie to you, Marian. There is trouble from this writing. For what will come out of it, what the king will call it, reason or treason, we can only wait to know."

11

I
N the bad old days of their enmity, Ralf had so severely wounded Robin that the man would have died had not Will Scatloch and Morgan of Powys carried him to Wytha, the *wicca* woman who healed him. Robin never forgot his debt. When he was restored to Denby after Norwich, Wytha sued for a modest living on his lands, no more than she had enjoyed under his grandfather, the first thane. Robin could hardly refuse her.

Wytha's needs were few. She asked for a new hut near Holy Pool in a part of Sherwood Denby never allowed its folk to encroach for bookland. Guntrada, before she became Robin's grandmother, had lived near the pool, and it was well known that she had prayed there to deities and powers other than the little stone saint by the pool's edge. Wytha the same, living all her life in the forest, heard more in silence than most folk in sound or speech. She was ancient when Will and Morgan brought Robin to be healed. No one then or now knew just how old, though Wytha herself kept careful count. If her limbs grew stiff, her mind remained sharp. She could not always get about as nimbly now and sometimes needed to squint at the rune sticks cast on her earthen floor. Most days she needed an afternoon nap, but she forgot nothing. Never as beautiful as Guntrada but born with the same gifts that went far beyond mere craft. When Harthacnut passed her in state on the road after claiming Canute's crown, Wytha saw the queerly colored nimbus about the violent king's hulking frame and knew he would not live long no matter how he roared, bellowed, and guzzled at his mead board.

With the Sight came natural pride but a curse as well to keep her humble. Thirty years ago, her hair began to thin. So much for vanity, Wytha consoled herself, too proud to wear a wig and having no idea where to buy or steal one in any event. Guntrada never lost her hair but died after fifty-five harvests. A ripe span, but having now lasted two decades beyond that, Wytha could feel in spite of infirmity a certain vindictive satisfaction. When the two of them were born, being of an age, the north of England was still mostly Dane. Guntrada's kin were only two generations out of Jutland, where the cross of the White Christ was so new no one was sure how much of their religion was Christian and how much of the old ways. More like a mixture. Blidworth then was part of the royal manor of Mansfield. One spring, the news spread that a new holding was to be carved out of northern Sherwood, and a husky young thane was coming to be lord. By name, Brihtnoth, son of a free farmer but favored by King Canute and nature herself, Guntrada vowed. She fell in love with him when they first met in the forest. Though young then, Guntrada was already respected as a *wicca*-adept, but with a wild streak, more of the forest in her than Wytha, more given to worshiping in the old way on May Night: on the heath under the moon, free and sky-clad. Wytha tried to tell her that the way of craft was honored but lonely, the path to mastery always so.

Guntrada reasoned the matter otherwise. "I am not made to be lonely, Wytha."

Though married in Blidworth church, Guntrada did not abandon the old ways, and persuaded Brihtnoth to make the blood bargain with her after their wedding night. They poured their mingled blood over a tiny seedling oak in a clearing by Holy Pool. Nigh to sixty years ago, that was. The seedling was a tall tree now, and twice again Denby blood had been offered to it. In the old days, folk thought the ritual was necessary for growing. Not even Wytha believed that now, but the custom was a good one for all the frowning disapproval of priests like Beorn. Lord and lady affirmed their responsibility to the land, showed their folk and Goddess Freya by the scars on their hands that they took up the eternal vow. The blood of Aelred and Maud nourished the tree in its time; later, that of Robin and Marian.

When Guntrada's son Aelred was born, Wytha presided as midwife and preserved the birthstring as part of the protective magic she would weave. She set wards about the hall, the steading, and fields, and when the years had passed, Aelred brought his own woman to Denby.

A proper court lady Maud was then, Wytha remembered. *Manners delicate as her figure and a way of letting you know she was above you.*

Polite enough, but keep your distance. But she loved Aelred with all her soul, which was strong from her aura then. The forest grew up around Maud like ivy until you couldn't tell in spirit where land left off and Maud began. No one kept the bargain better. Never liked the woman, but I can't deny that. She was Denby, the land was her.

A year or so after Maud came to Sherwood, Wytha was banished from Denby for one of the commoner reasons. A young Blidworth widow became inconveniently pregnant. She had three children already, and the lot of them poor enough. She came to Wytha who spared her that, but the widow was guilt-ridden and confessed all to Father Beorn.

Beorn was still more soldier than priest in those days, not very tolerant. He drove Wytha from the village. They were both wiser now and knew more of the world from rubbing up against it. Beorn had his ways, Wytha her own. By these ways, she knew there would be a visitor soon. On this hot day after Lammas with barely a breath stirring Sherwood, Wytha heard the soft clop of hooves along the footpath leading to Holy Pool. She was not surprised when the woman came into view, leading the mare behind her. Wytha hobbled out to meet Maud, bowing her head in careful respect. Maud's aura had changed much. Wytha had seen its like perhaps once before, a condition totally beyond her power to understand, much less heal. The eerie nimbus bathed the woman from head to foot.

"Welcome, Bread-Server," Wytha greeted her formally, thinking, *she's much too old before her time. The dirty Norman dungeon did that.*

Something else. Maud always had a direct gaze. The strength was still there, but no longer focused. Remote now, vacant. She produced two silver pennies from the purse at her girdle. "I would have you cast for me. There is that I must see."

Wytha's experience urged caution. Women like herself always trod a thin line between tolerance and persecution anywhere, and Maud had supported Beorn in her expulsion from Denby all those years past. "Lady is of the Church."

"And older ways." Maud held up her left hand with the faded scar. "I have need of them now."

"What need that your priest cannot fill?"

"There is something . . . coming to me. Coming over me. My mind. Sometimes it is like thinking through cloud or cobwebs. Is it my death, Wytha? I would know."

The woman asked it with her old directness, but Wytha ignored the proffered silver. "No. Not your death."

"That is not worth money."

"That much is free. For old times' sake." Wytha started to enter her hut again with the air of a person concluding matters. She turned in the doorway and caught her breath. Maud had not moved. The mare's reins dropped unheeded from her hands. The woman might have forgotten where she was, simply gone away within herself. The strangely corrupted aura writhed about her like pale green flame in ashwood fire. The strength had washed completely out of her features.

I am the last person she would come to. A last resort beside Beorn and his prayers. If it is what I think, there is no help for her beyond kindness. She beckoned Maud to follow her inside. "Come, we will read what is shown to us."

Her new dwelling had been built and furnished with Robin's generous assistance, with serviceable cast-off chairs and a rough table from the house of John Littlerede, who died at Norwich. Robin would have laid in a plank floor, but Wytha preferred packed earth as more comfortable and better for casting a circle.

The *wicca* woman did not forget place or manners, nor the value of what was now asked of her. She knew the look of physical health or the lack of it. No element in Maud's natural humors wasted her. Wytha's arts must hunt a more elusive condition, grasp and define a shadow, and should be fairly compensated. She would be remiss not to bargain, but first she settled Lady Maud in the hut's best chair.

"What you seek is worth more than you offer."

"Old woman, you are a bordar on my son's holding. You want for nothing," Maud pointed out like a practical steading wife. "Consider it boonwork."

"Fourpence. I ask only what is fair."

Nothing vague about Maud on the subject of money. "Fair and Wytha in one breath? That is blasphemy."

"You are cruel—but as you wish. Threepence. That is more than reasonable."

"Tuppence ha'pny."

"Oh, so little?" Wytha mourned for glories flown. "I can recall when Denby would not dicker a halfpenny with an old woman poor and ill herself."

Maud folded her hands primly in her lap. "Speak of memory, mine is as clear. When you stopped the coming of a child, Aelred might have hanged you, yet you haggle now like an ingrate. You have lived lordless too long, Wytha. You forget your place."

"My place?" Wytha seated herself on the floor before the woman, but looked directly at her in the manner of an equal. "When Guntrada's time came to deliver the man child who became your husband, who set wards about the babe and all Brihtnoth called his own? Who grasped the coming child and lifted him into life? I have done no ill to Denby nor ever stopped a wanted child."

As casually as she might comment on the weather, Maud said, "You are a liar."

"Am I? Look at me." Wytha's gaze did not waver. "We are women. In the way of this world, have we not always had to lie a little or much to men? To tell the husband, the lover, the child, or even the priest what they wanted to hear? That is not magic but experience. I have more of that than you. I do not lie now, nor can you afford to lie to me. I am worth fourpence, the mere fifth part of a single cow because even now I guess what possesses you. You spoke of memory. Memory troubles you in its absence or its treachery, not so? If I cast for you, I am worth my full price. But"—Wytha relented magnanimously—"because your son and I have been friends through good and bad times alike, three silver pence."

Maud's hands, which had returned as always to their compulsive scrubbing at each other, paused, then moved to purpose. She put three silver pence in Wytha's hand. The wise woman went straight to the business for which she was engaged. "Have your courses stopped?"

"Two years ago and little enough discomfort," Maud dismissed that aspect. "But you are correct. I forget things."

Wytha began to trace a circle in the earthen floor with a black-handled knife. "Tell me all. When I ask for silence, give me that. How does this come on you?"

"Sometimes . . . " Maud sounded less certain now than when she bargained. "Sometimes I know a thing is true and now. But then Marian or Minna will say it was yesterday or long ago. They look at me sometimes as though I were touched."

From a doeskin bag, Wytha took the four smooth-worn rune sticks of rowan wood, purified them with salt and water. "I have seen this only once before. Some call it the Soft Demon, others the Gentle Mocker." Not the worst of troubles to Wytha, who had lived through six kings and losses of her own. Her charburner husband hadn't been much company before he died of drink and his own meanness. Before it ripened into solitude, loneliness had been an ache in her. She would go into the dark with natural human fear, but with her full senses. For

Maud the dark was coming early, like winter twilight in mid-afternoon.

Within her circle, Wytha drew two smaller ones. At the precise center she placed her quartz seeing-stone. "Now I will ask you to be very still and not speak until I ask."

The stone must gather and concentrate her powers, for she must be stilled and focused herself. Maud's eyes were closed. Something in the woman seemed to have simply gone away, like the sun behind a cloud. When Wytha felt herself prepared, she threw the rune sticks across her circles.

Mocker, you are well named, Maud chided the demon behind her eyes. *Though you came so kindly at first, softly as an angel would. You made darkness a friend to me.*

Ten years ago in the dungeon at Hough, Maud had wished often for death, but was too strong to let go and just slip away. She had wished as time went on for the benefice of madness to soften cruel reality. God would not give her death but sent the angel to reconcile her to darkness. Made it her reality so that light became alien and painful when she was summoned into it. Allowed her more and more easily, like a devout nun choosing the cloister over the profane, to slip into a world of her own. Later her mind was never as bright again. The wits were there, but *stained,* like shadow across sunlight.

The angel had been kind but did his mischief in the dark. After Maud returned to Denby, the friendly darkness which had become her light became solace as well. *Then* was always sweeter, anodyne to *now.* The angel seduced Maud until she could never be sure if one was the other. When he left her and her faculties dealt clearly with now, Maud felt a horror at how easily she could be cozened. Her mind was dying piece by piece, snatching a memory from here, hiding it there to make her stumble on *then* in the middle of today. . . .

Edward must not give our crown to a foreign king. Aelred has said as much.

No. That is the Demon mocking me in the guise of an angel, as he always does. That was years ago. I must remember where and when I am. Ralf Fitz-Gerald is now. If I cannot reach William, I will cut off his right arm in Sherwood. Ralf is solid and near to hand and hate. I will keep his image in front of me.

Black and gold. He wore black and gold the day he first came to Denby. Be careful, he is clever. He found you out once and sent you to the dungeon. Find the right time for the knife. We are a practical folk. We do not admire treachery but can employ it to purpose as did Rowena, the daughter of Hengist on the Night of the Long Knives when Vortigern, even after the slaughter of all his Welshmen at Hengist's board, yet could not believe his love had married him only to work him like wax to her father's will. So I put my hand in Fitz-Gerald's, gave him the kiss of peace, and called him kinsman when he married Judith.

Soft Demon, well named in the hell you bring, that between Prime and Terce rung from Blidworth church, I can hate the man who served his usurper king by stealing my home—and then, passing from my bower to the hall, forget that Aelred is dead. Years vanish, never happened, not yet passed, and I wait to hear his footstep on the threshold, turn and expect to see him, my arms already reaching. . . .

Like her royal husband, Queen Edith is a sheep-witted fool. Last week the king asked Aelred as his liege man if he supported the succession of William. We've known this was coming, seen men dividing into two camps on the question. Give the crown to Edward's Norman cousin William, or stand by Harold and the English party.

Aelred could not avail himself of tact any longer when it came too near a lie. "My lord king, you are of our own royal family. William is a foreigner. The nation will not countenance him on your throne."

Poor shocked Edward. Docile, bewildered Edith. Two obedient children of Mother Church, and Edward sharply angry with my husband. "Thane Aelred, there is only one nation and it is God's. In our person *we* are England. You verge on heresy as well as treason."

Well, that is Edward for you: raised among Normans and mostly on his knees in prayer. He hasn't seen our nation maturing, growing to awareness of itself in these long years of peace. Only last night before we went to sleep, I told Aelred he'd been right to tell the truth, "But I fear there's the last of royal favor for us."

No. *No.* Edward is years dead and Edith dust beside him in Westminster. Demon, you give me ghosts, a shadow husband to dance me through a vanished time. My mind is clear. Not last week; I remember last week. Robin was harvesting the barley and Marian asked me who would be in the hall for dinner, when I distinctly remember having told her. Yet she swore I didn't.

What is happening to me?

"What? Wytha, what did you say?"

There, she'd drifted off again and had to ask the old crone to repeat herself. She must be on guard, catch herself when she slipped so. "Don't mumble at me, woman. What do the runes say?"

"They are clear." The ridiculous old woman studied the runes and the patterns formed by their painted symbols. "Clear, but one part gives the lie to the other. Dragon's tail, dragon's head. Something begins. Something ends."

"But you said not my death."

The *wicca* woman shook her head definitely over the runes. "No."

"What begins? What ends? Why can I not . . . tell time clearly anymore? Why can I not—"

"Remember?"

"Why?"

12

I N time Elfled might have relegated Robin to a small rear closet of
memory and then forgotten him altogether, but the man was constantly thrust before her by Ranulf's personal enmity. Natural curiosity did the rest. She was no Judith; she could not read Robin's
writings that so inflamed her husband's malice. They would have meant
little to her in any case. Her father never had much to do with the thane
class, who were mostly poor and did little business in cash. Most of
those old country warriors were dead now or had left England to seek
better fortune abroad. His standing with men like Taillebois, Sheriff of
Lincoln, was worth far more in business and political connections.

Elfled had never really known any overlords but the Normans, a child
when she first heard of Robin Hood. Somehow, he was a central concern
to her husband now, something to do with politics, a foreign tongue to
Elfled. Her fascinating memory of the man was constantly restimulated
by hearsay, more and more of which she sought out: former lord, outlaw,
eluding the king's men for years while lightheartedly relieving Norman
lords and prelates of their money. Visiting his imprisoned wife in disguise and winning the golden arrow at Grantham under their very noses.
Then the lightning strokes at Norwich, praised in dispatches to the king,
hysterically damned in others. Elfled had been used to male deference
all her life and found them simple to manipulate. Given less than her
due attention, she tended to sulk. At a certain time, Ranulf neglected
her, Robin did not. Whatever ills one could lay to such a man, he
was far from ordinary, his life riding the very comet of legend. Most

young women could fall in love with the mere dream of such a man, and Elfled did.

He did mean his attentions to me, I know he did. What matter if he dissembled as a priest? Disguise was as much a part of his glamor as the unjust disgrace. Elfled's imagination discarded the clerical subterfuge and clothed him as a lord and far more opulently than Robin would ever have donned. She imagined his hall and himself in it, tried to picture his wife. He'd misled her about that as part of necessary disguise. Still, a man of such sensitivity would cleave to a woman of equal feelings. Or perhaps not, Elfled reasoned in defense of her dreams. Perhaps his was an arranged alliance, those were common enough. The dull daughter of a landowner packed off with her dowry, big feet and thick ankles, sturdy as a barrel and as plain. In a word, Elfled was halfway to her own seduction. Always indulged, indulgence came easily. Convincing herself that such arrangement must have been the case, she already took Robin's part against the gross, plodding wife, convinced that he yearned out from the cage of convention toward a woman closer to his soul.

Elfled recalled their meeting and tried to fix in memory everything Robin said to her. The soothing, lulling sound of his voice, how his head inclined just so when he listened, which he did with flattering intensity, and day by day invested each moment with pregnant meaning. Ranulf sloughed off her questions when Elfled tried to comprehend just what made the man so dangerous. As for Remigius, Bishop of Lincoln, he only patted her on the head benevolently and considered such things far beyond her limited womanly ken.

So seeds put forth sprouts and work up through the soil, sweet or poisonous, to flower.

Two copies of the "Sherwood Heresy" went to William. Lanfranc forwarded his while urging moderation and a reasoned dialogue with the lords of Nottinghamshire as well as some curb on Ranulf. However valuable to the king, young Bayeux was hardly a royal justiciar *yet* and should not have assumed such powers—

...this precipitate act, in hanging one of their vassals out of hand, gives the lords of Sherwood legitimate grievance.

Lanfranc's copy and comments were delayed. Ranulf's reached William first, still seething—

My lord king, this Denby writes treason more virulent than any man ever uttered. Submit royal will to interpretation and a king relinquishes the authority bequeathed with anointment by God.

Which William grimly translated: Submit royal prerogative to any lay court, then by implication kings were accountable by law for their actions. He had to suffer such *ex cathedra* rot from Gregory in Rome, but only an Englishman would have the bald, godless guts to maintain that a king must account to his subjects. Yet that was exactly what Denby's Inquiry argued in two languages, no ambiguity in either. Could any king *not* see the danger?

"Here, read this again," William directed his counselors. "When I see an adder coil, shall I doubt the creature will strike?"

In the preface to Alfred's written laws, he admits to gathering what statutes existed, keeping some and discarding others, but making allowance for the circumstances and revisions of those to come after him. In this effort Alfred said he sought the advice of his counsellors, the custom of which led to our nation's Witan and to the experience that law, proceeding from custom as the barley from the stalk, must grow and change, its benefits harvested and the stubble turned under to make way for new planting.

As the alien words were read again to the already troubled king, one digression lodged in his consciousness. Robin had described the control of currency, the efficient system of land assessment under English kings, and the building blocks of English government from folkmoot through the higher courts to the defunct Witan whose restoration he deemed vital to his "nation."

That word again, peculiar to Saxons as the Covenant of the ancient Hebrews. On the one hand, William's seasoned mind tucked away valuable insights for future need; on the other, he experienced a chill of the oldest and deepest of his fears, his right to England in the sight of God. Small comfort that Edward promised him the succession in 1051. Edward was a changeable man, triumphant that year with Godwine and his sons banished abroad, expansive and apt to promise anything. Many said he specifically passed the throne to Harold on his deathbed. Certainly Harold was crowned quickly enough with that god-damned Witan crowing for joy. William had to take the land by conquest from a rebellious people who would not break under his bridle for four years and ever after answered his rein sullenly. Young Denby was one of those who saw William's rule as a rape. As for God?

What say you, Lord? I have paid Peter's Pence to Rome. I have built cathedrals to reflect your splendor, yet must I still burn eternally? This is the world I was given, and not a good one, nor any balm in a cold crown. All men know power is a prize to be won. My son Robert is no different. I have the prize and he covets it. If heaven is eternal, in this fighting pit of a world, all I have to love is dying upstairs.

William's fear of hell was feverish and literal, but included no mortal born. If Ranulf proved overzealous, he was nevertheless useful now when the king suspected enemies everywhere and generally found them. Great mortifications could grow from small wounds. This matter in Sherwood could foment another Earl's Revolt. A letter sped from Rouen to Nottingham with a copy to Winchester.

TO RALF, VICOMTE OF NOTTINGHAM AND SHERWOOD AND OUR REEVE IN THOSE PARTS—YOU WERE ONCE AMONG MY MOST LOYAL. ARE YOU STILL? REMEMBER HOW AT CHESTER I CAUTIONED YOU AGAINST TOO MUCH AM-BITION? I CREATED YOU. REMEMBER THAT, FITZ-GERALD. YOU WILL AT-TEND US ON SAINT MICHAEL'S DAY AT WINCHESTER WITH YOUR VASSAL EDWARD OF DENBY, WHO WILL ANSWER TO US FOR PUBLISHING ABROAD WRITINGS PERNICIOUS TO THE WELFARE OF THE REALM.

A similar summons went to Bishop Osmund. William's business at Winchester would be brief. He dared not leave Normandy for long with Philip and Robert at his back, and would not be one hour more than needed away from Matilda. In William's present frame of mind, the matter of Denby would require no more time than that.

13

L AST year had been grim in all respects. As if to make up for that, God lavished soft sunlight and gentle rain on Denby in perfect balance toward a splendid harvest and added the benefice of balmy weather through the first three weeks of September. Now there was the sowing of rye to oversee, repair to tenant crofts with fresh willow for wattling. Most important, Mauger presented his accounts against the quarterly rents due to Robin and payable in turn to Ralf on Saint Michael's Day. Mauger's accounts were precise. On the one hand such thoroughness served as a model for William's great survey three years later; on the other they included personal notations which that survey lacked.

This quarter, Ulf the new beekeeper makes up in need work what he was short last quarter . . . Sven Fletcher is in arrears because of sickness . . . Lady Maud has not given any instructions on the arable hides of her personal maintenance, bring to Robin's attention.

"And when I reminded the lady, she nigh bit my head off," Mauger reported in confusion to Robin. "I merely said she might have forgotten. Lady Maud tartly answered that she *never* forgot, she'd merely been occupied—and then forgot again."

Robin dipped his quill in the inkpot and pricked the item. "She is distracted these days. I can't tell how."

The king's summons was delivered to Robin on September 15. Of all Denby, Marian had the keenest and darkest fear of its implication.

Only the family knew the nature and degree of Robin's trouble with William, though all Blidworth guessed from Father Beorn's request for their specific prayers, that their lord was once again in royal disfavor.

"When was he ever out of it?" Will Scatloch despaired to Marian. "I told you years gone, the man's as thick as bread."

Marian, fermenting in private frustration and pain, looked to house and children and pressed down harder on the lid of a pot fast coming to a seething boil.

Robin must leave in time to join Ralf for the long journey to Winchester. Since the quarterly rents were about to fall due, Mauger announced to all tenants that Denby would hold hall moot and rent collection a mite earlier this autumn. To augment the customary feast for all, Will Scatloch and Morgan of Powys planned to take two great bucks.

In his forties and still more fit than younger city men, Will secretly felt himself slowing, the habits of his life more firmly molded to home and comfort. He barely understood Robin's political troubles, but hoped they would not mean outlawry again. More and more Will appreciated returning at evening to his bower and family. Morgan lived a bachelor, set in his ways, content as ever to love by moonlight and leave by morning. Not as nimble since the wound taken at Norwich, but neither he nor Will had lost one jot of eye or arm in shooting. When Eddain, Gwaun, and little Edward suggested accompanying the hunt, the older men refused them with a resounding *no*.

"*Och,* Father, you'll be needing us," Eddain argued. "If only for the carrying home."

"Will I?" Will's lip curled at his older son, who now stood somewhat taller than himself. "Will we, Morgan?"

"We will not."

On the eve of hall moot, they took their stand at a point near the rill and waited for the red bucks to come to drink. There was a dispute of years' standing between them. Morgan always maintained he was the better bowman and sometimes included Robin in that boast.

Will punctured him deftly as always. "Were you so with the golden arrow at hazard?"

Both men shot well today and congratulated each other sportingly before attempting to shoulder their kills homeward. The bucks were heavier than either thought: must be, for they'd never had such difficulty in the task before. After several labored attempts, they paused and rested under a tree.

"In our time," Will reminisced, "and that not long past, we were dashing men. Were we not in the front rank at Norwich?"

"And left our blood to prove it," Morgan attested stoutly. "But never unreasonable. Was it not yourself said, when you were helpless drunk on Beltane Eve, 'Moderation in all things makes for a good life'?"

"Look you, I included moderation. A man must do too much of something from time to time."

"I remembered as much carrying you to bed."

Will eyed the carcass of his buck. "We are still every bit the men we were."

"Gwylm, I will fight the man who says we are not."

"But in the matter of these bucks," Will's pride surrendered to common sense, "perhaps a cart would help."

But the afternoon was that fair, certainly no hurry for two good men who'd waited on their feet for hours. A moment more and they'd be about it. "I am uneasy on this feast," Will admitted. "Like the Last Supper."

He didn't enlarge on the thought. There had always been enough of the Sight in Will to see things coming. What he'd glimpsed for Robin, he would not share even with Angharad. Now he seriously considered getting up to cut his arrow from the buck, and was halfway to his feet when Edward came bounding out of the trees toward them, shouting their discovery over his shoulder. "Here they are!"

In a moment, Edward, Eddain, and Gwaun stood admiring the fresh-killed bucks and the masterfully placed shots that brought them down. Will looked to Morgan and then at his sons in their vigorous youth. He hated to admit he needed a cart for what he once hefted with ease. Edward saved him the shame, skipping about with spirit to spare, counting the bucks' points, then lordly appointing Eddain and Gwaun to carry home the kills. Not rude the boy was, but already with a kind of confidence Scatloch knew all too well, the stamp of that English dogma bred into and through the father. As Denby went, so went the world, beyond argument unto Everlasting, Amen. The good-natured Welsh boys bent to their work with ease like an insolence to the older men and perhaps a secret sadness, and started home toward Denby, singing together. Edward sprinted ahead and back like a playful puppy, hurrying them on, finally dashed away to tell the kitchen of their coming, a bottomless well of impossible energy.

Will and Morgan strolled after the singing boys, allowing for youth and only fair they should be the porters now.

"To each his time and gift," said Morgan. "What man could have equaled your shot?"

"Or yours. We are all we were and no need to prove it."

Said Will Scatloch, frowning with the private worry of a future imperfectly seen, but like an importunate stranger prodding him from behind.

At the feast preceding hall moot, Father Beorn gave the benediction and read the Bible verse. Marian drew and presented the first cup to her husband. He gave the traditional cheer to his folk.

"May it well become you."

Marian's three-legged cat Perdu, a feline ancient now, curled contentedly under the high table. She had never been quick enough for mousing nor needed to be, well-fed and bonded to Marian since kittenhood. Perdu licked her one forepaw and benignly observed the feast from her cat's-eye view, assured as Robin once was of her unassailable place in the cosmos. Generations of her kittens had come and gone. Perdu drowsed out her latter days in the sun or by the fire. She might terrify a passing mouse for a moment's sport or harry a low-flying moth, but nowadays, Perdu was too old and slow even for that. Her territory was marked by long custom as the boundary stones of Denby: the hall and the bower. In winter she slept beneath the covers between Robin and Marian; in early spring, with her old body stretched along Marian's, her head on the same pillow. These summer days Perdu napped at the foot of the bed and knew in her way that life was good. She was one of two instinctive creatures who sensed that Marian was miserable this feast day. In this Perdu had some advantage over Robin in not wondering why.

Marian's husband, knowing the colors of her happiness, knew their lack in small absences. The open smile of a woman in harmony with her life was forced at this supper. As he complimented his lady on sauces and seasonings and received her measured thanks, Robin felt a widening distance between them. He might have said, "Right then, what is it?" but already sensed some of the matter and a subtly pervading guilt made him draw back.

He must depart early in the morning for Winchester. Since the summons came, he'd gone out of his way to be close to Marian. At this evening's feast, she was a faultless *hlaefdige,* but not near to him. Gone twice to confession in as many days, troubled but sharing none of it with him. No, she only looked to the feast, dealt with Mum, who was more querulous than usual this week, placating her, standing properly this night with Robin and her son through the farewells as the folk left the hall—then gone without so much as a word or nod to husband or son, to supervise the putting up of leftovers for tomorrow. Robin said goodnight to his steward and son, then went unhappily to his bower.

Marian came silently to bed and lay unmoving on her back by Robin's side, but with a palpable distance and a tension between them. In this intimate place shared year in and out, the silence became an acute third presence. Robin needed to be close to Marian, not knowing how the king would dispose of him.

He turned on his side and put an arm over Marian's breast. In the feeble light from the open casement, he couldn't tell if her eyes were open but knew she was far from sleep. "You managed splendid tonight."

She moved a little but said nothing. Robin shifted closer, one arm under her head and began to stroke her body from shoulders to thighs. Under his hand, her tense body seemed more submissive than willing, not coming to him eagerly as she always did. After a time, Robin left off, up on one elbow over her. Whatever, then, they might as well have it out now and plain. "What is it, Marian?"

"I'm not for it tonight."

"Not your courses this early?" Robin knew the rhythms of his wife's body as any husband came to. Her flux ceased ten days ago, wasn't it?

"No." She shifted again, one arm over her forehead. "I spoke with Father Beorn today. Not confession, though I've had that, too." Marian said it flatly to the darkness above them. "Told him I don't want another child now."

The confession was more easily made to Father Beorn, who was a man with a heart, not just a sermon with a mouth. He told her to refrain, then; that abstinence was the only honest recourse when a woman had lost newborn and her last alive by the mercy of God alone.

"And then I told him it wasn't that. I said I'd not bring a child into this world who might never know its father."

"Listen, love—"

"Love be damned!" she flared. "You listen to me." Marian pushed his arm away. "You mightn't come back. You and I know that, or if you do, who knows when or how? There wasn't a loving in this bed that didn't have all of me in it. Until tonight. I must have loved you fearsome hard and deep, Robin, because I hate you that much now."

Robin took the word like a blow in the face. Stunned for the space of a breath he forgot to draw, then hollow, with a sensation like falling. He got up and struck flint to a taper, put it to the rush light in its iron holder. In the dim light, Marian was sitting up, her unbound hair tumbled about her narrow face—and why was a woman all the more lovely when you couldn't reach her? "*Hate,* girl?"

"For what you've done to us. Taken from us, Edward and Moira as much as me. You've taken all of us and thrown us out like dice for some dream I can't understand. I know nowt of kings and books and that. I was happy, that was enough for me, but not for you. You had to be at them, *at* them year in and out. Ralf told me about the writ, how he and the bishop wanted you to change it before they had to take it back entire, but it's too late now, ent it?"

"Yes,"

"And what's for you now? Hanging? Prison? Run into Sherwood again and expect the men to follow you? You're all past it now."

"No. No more running," Robin said heavily to the sudden stranger beside him. "It wasn't William's doing."

"What matter, him or his rotten little clerk."

He bit off the truth through a growing misery. "Something had to be done."

Marian didn't understand such things. Deeper goads worked in her soul and flesh now. "How many more months or years will I be waiting for you to come back, or Ralf to come one day to tell us you're not coming at all? Nay, don't look at me like a false wife or traitor." All their years together, what was their first unbreakable rule, like the bargain on the oak? Care for the land, but first feed the children. How often in bad years, and last year the worst, did they go hungry that Edward and Moira had enough? "It ent that you didn't tell me what you were doing with all this reading and writing. I wouldn't understand the half anyway. Don't mind—much—that it came even before me. There's much of you I don't know and can't claim. But you put it before our children."

"Never!"

"No? Right then. When you're back from Winchester and chide me for a scold, I'll bow my head and beg my lord's forgiveness."

"Marian, stop this. You don't want me to love you now, well enough, but don't—"

She was unforgiving now. "Don't what?"

"Don't be away from me, not tonight."

"Blow out the rush. No use wasting."

"I said don't! Christ, you don't know all of why I did this."

"No, only that you've been playing God just like that priest in Winchester. Oh, I've seen it in you, Rob, seen it from the day I came to Denby. Will says your da was the same. You set up your judgment on the world—so! Pour the wax, stamp the seal, there's an end."

Marian lay down, turning away from him, the grieved voice half muffled in her pillow. "The morning after our wedding, you put this ring on my finger and said good-bye. For four years, day after day, I waited for someone to tell me you were dead, and one day they did. You never felt death that close or cold, Robin, not ever. Leave me alone. Go to exile, go to hell. I can't go through that again. There's more than you to love now, thank God."

Robin looked beyond the casement to the near fields silvered with moonlight. A good harvest, there was one mercy. Whatever passed, Mauger and Marian would hold the place together, the family and folk would eat. Small comfort in this bleak moment. *Mauger says some men think hell is all flame and agony, but that once he'd met a Benedictine who thought hell was far worse than fire, that it was being apart from God. I can believe that now, close enough to touch the woman and her turned away, far away, putting her heart out of my reach. I should have made her more a part of the purpose, shared more. Feed the children? Christ, Marian, do you think it's just bellies go empty and bodies into the ground?*

"You were right about Da and me," Robin said to her dim back so far across the shadowed bed. "The kings and the earls gave the orders, but we were the ones who brought them to the folk, the link between one and the other. You . . . you get used to seeing things done right, so understand when I say it's my country they took. Not the king's, but *mine,* Marian. Then my father and even my house, and even that wasn't defeat, no part of it. They woke something in me. It's the same as Mum said about loving Da. You see someone die, *see* them go into the ground, and you know they're gone. Mum didn't have that, just cut off like the rest of us, and I keep reaching out for something that used to be there, that should be there, save there's nothing left but the bones of the law for men like me, folk like us. I'm not God-touched or God-gifted, but I know that sure as I've always needed you. I can fight the king, fought him seventeen years. But there's not the heart in me to fight you, girl."

He rose heavily to snuff the rushlight, and heard the rustle of bedclothes as Marian turned toward him. No anger left in her voice, but no yielding either. "Then give him what he wants and come home."

"What?"

Her eyes were huge and black in her face. "Do what you have to. Go on your knees, beg his forgiveness. Crawl if you have to."

Robin couldn't believe Marian would speak so. "I've been on my knees. My children won't be."

"Give him—"

"No."

"Then don't speak of loving or needing."

He spat out bitterly: "You don't understand."

"That's true, thick as I am," Marian said. "I can't read or write, just tend my house and children. Very well, husband. I'll put your food and needfuls for riding tomorrow and have the children there to say good-bye. And for the rest, Robin Aelredson, be gone and be damned."

They stared at each other across the dark with a helpless bitterness born of no real strength but the love it denied.

14

PORTLY and formidable, the king's chief steward William Fitz-Osbern emerged from the audience chamber of Winchester Castle to address the waiting groups of men. "My lords, the king has been occupied with officers of his treasury but will summon you presently. Where is Edward of Denby?"

Robin stepped forward. "Sir."

"Indeed." Fitz-Osbern looked him up and down, clearly unimpressed. He withdrew, closing the heavy door behind him.

Robin stood a little apart from his fellow culprits, Ralf and Osmund, talking in low tones to Will Scatloch. "Stay close to me when we go in, Will. I think I'm for it."

The corridor area near the audience chamber was crowded with the clerks and attendants of Bishop Osmund and Vicomte Ralf. All including Robin had dressed for the occasion except Will Scatloch, a rustic contrast in worn Lincoln trousers and tunic. He carried Robin's wallet, which held a change of clothes for his friend and lord.

A stir and flutter now from the stairwell, a gabble of rapid French. Ranulf appeared with his own entourage of clerks bearing record rolls, and bore down on the waiting men. The keeper of the Chancery seal wore very unclerkly scarlet and gold this day. He paused before Robin, languidly holding up one hand on which four large rings gleamed. His followers hovered dutifully behind him. Ranulf vouchsafed Robin a smile Mauger would have described as reptilian. "How is your health, Denby? You will need it."

"Excellent." Robin returned the chilly rictus in exact measure.

"How's your dear wife?" A foolhardy taunt, but Ranulf made his hackles rise. He could not resist the temptation. "I'm flattered you dressed for me, but . . . you do put one in mind of an overdecorated courtesan."

"And you as one imagines a traitor. You simply do not understand, Denby. Beyond the personal gratification of scourging such as you, there is the necessity. The matter will hardly require much prosecution. You convict yourself. Good forthfaring, Robin Hood."

The ringed hand waved again; Ranulf's entourage entered the audience chamber. Ralf beckoned Robin to him and Osmund. "For God's sake, why do you antagonize him further?"

"Why do dogs chase cats?" Robin couldn't say beyond the bristling of natural enemies. "Subtle little manny. He didn't say 'good-bye,' but 'good forthfaring.' Farewell to someone leaving this life for the next. Well, do we stand together?"

Osmund nodded gravely. "Insofar as possible, Robin. I can claim ecclesiastical immunity up to a point, appeal to Rome if need be, but . . ."

Ralf was more direct. "We signed what we signed. But there is more. There are Judith and my children."

Robin understood. "Yes."

"We urged you to modify the proposal," Osmund worried, glancing about. "You wrote too hastily."

Perhaps. Certainly Robin comprehended their position now. Both were brave beyond the vavasor's blood-witted definition of the word, bred to one way of life, but risking much for the sake of change any conscience would see as necessary in pure self-interest. Of the two, Ralf hazarded most, not having the Church for a shield. Between two fires, as Will would say, between conscience and love, and the trouble of all that clouding his eyes now. Ralf would not renounce Robin or their mutual aims, but neither would he throw his own family into the fire.

And that's what Marian says I've done. Is it true? Is it vanity drives me as much as Ranulf? All I know is how deep the feelings went as I wrote, trying to recall for other men what we had once and from that shape what should be. Do you think, Lord Ralf, that I was not lonely in that and scared as you?

The chamber doors were opened by two soldiers. "My lords, you are summoned into court."

The defendants filed into the audience chamber with their men. William sat on a dais at the far end, Ranulf and his clerks at a table down the left side of the dreary stone chamber lit by shafts of cloudy light from two small casements high in the walls. The men from Sherwood and Nottingham were directed to a table opposite.

Robin discerned as much as he could from the forces aligned against him. He had not seen William personally for years. The king had grown markedly more corpulent. The embroidered skullcap, habitually worn to mask his thinning red hair, now rested on a probably near-barren pate. William looked rumpled and underslept. He hadn't bothered to change clothes, still in the salt-splashed mantle and tunic he'd sailed in. Robin had seen the royal barge crewed and ready in River Itchen by Eastgate. Common word had it that Queen Matilda was not expected to live and William would recross to France at the earliest possible moment.

Flanking the king on the dais were old Fitz-Osbern, a number of grey-gowned officials of the treasury, and a self-possessed young boy of about fifteen in rich, well-cut clothes.

"Prince Henry," Ralf informed him. "Summoned to be with his mother, I expect."

This was Robin's first view of the royal children beyond Princess Adelaide years ago. Henry was unique among the brood, the only one born and raised in England—groomed, patted, and shaped by tutors and servants, many of whom must be English. Said to be literate; that could sort well with English purpose. How much of this boy will be English? Robin wondered as pens scratched, parchments rustled, and chairs scraped, punctuating his own predicament.

Prince Henry shifted slightly in the heavy chair, not with adolescent awkwardness but an economy of movement beyond his years. A watchful face, Robin would say. Would this small-boned boy who resembled his mother more than William come to love this country as Ralf had? *How much of Willy Bastard's in you, boy? Will I be standing before you someday, older and stiff in the joints but the same ancient war between us? Good God, I hope not. A man can grow weary.*

William had been perusing a tax roll. He passed it to a treasury clerk. Fitz-Osbern rapped smartly on the dais with his white staff of office.

"Give ear! The curia of William, by the grace of God King of the English and Duke of Normandy, is now convened to inquire into certain writings published in the shire of Nottingham. Father Ranulf present for the royal Chancery."

Ranulf rose and took several sheets of notes from the table before him. "Let it be recorded that the two items in question are, first, a proposal of three articles in regard to legal procedure. Secondly, a treatise titled 'An Inquiry into the Natural Rights of Subjects.' The first is chiefly subscribed by the bishop and sheriff of Nottingham and one Edward of Denby, admittedly the author of the mischievous work—and other men of the shire. The second is the signed work of Denby alone."

Ranulf riffled through some misplaced pages. In the pause, Bishop Osmund rose. "I hear no charges read. I ask the specific nature of this court, be it trial or merely inquiry as Chancery states."

William glowered at Osmund, who had ridden knee to knee with him through the hell of Hastings and Chester. His voice was testy and thickened with a cold from breasting a rain squall in the Channel crossing. "It is inquiry while our authority deems it so, trial if and when that term applies. Don't waste our time. Bayeux, continue."

"This court is convened to determine if these writings constitute treason and in what degree. By your lordships' leave, I will first put forth the proposal submitted to the crown. The first article charges that the Chancery, without royal warrant, executed a man for speaking treason against the king's person."

"So you did, Bayeux," Robin accused with even contempt. "You hanged Alan to get at me."

Fitz-Osbern rapped with his staff. "Silence!"

Ranulf proceeded. The meat of this pernicious writing, which had spread like blight through Nottinghamshire, was that the arbitrary hanging endangered the rights and safety of all men, that no man should be executed without due trial within the venue where his offense was committed. Third, that the king swear in his coronation oath to uphold this safeguard.

Ranulf addressed the king directly. "A false assumption of right in contradiction to every custom of *jus sanguinis*."

"Objection," Osmund snapped, rising. "If the pope himself denies that right in his *Dictatus*—"

"Your Grace, forbear," William warned with the irritation of an ill-tempered bear. "You are a brave man, but you tamper with the very authority that created you."

Osmund was not unmindful of that, but neither was he abashed. "In my temporal lands, sire, but my pallium was blessed and sent from Rome."

William heaved his great bulk out of the chair. "Osmund, you were always prudent, if you comprehend my meaning. Why is your name first on this upstart writing?''

Osmund hesitated; not from faltered resolution, an intelligent man not native to the ideas to which he had subscribed. ''Because—''

''Your Grace.'' Robin rose. ''I may perhaps better answer that.''

''Please do.'' Osmund sat again, clearly relieved.

''My lord king, it was needed. Chancery usurped your authority in this execution and created a dangerous precedent. For, if this overzealous clerk can assume royal approval, where will he stop? Who is next, high or low?''

Ralf Fitz-Gerald stood up to lay a cautionary hand on his friend's arm, speaking hurriedly in English. ''Let me. I've always had the king's favor.''

''Then be wise, Ralf.'' Robin slid his eyes toward a soldier standing against one wall with a set of manacles draped over his arm. ''I think the verdict is already in, but there's only one set of chains. They could fetch more.''

''It is a matter of honor.''

''Will you stuff that? It's plain common sense. We need you in Sherwood. Please, Ralf.''

''Trust me,'' Ralf persisted. ''I can put it best. I'm his kind, you're not.'' Then raising his voice, ''Sire—you have asked why, against my loyalty and my love for my king, I subscribe to limit crown power.''

Ranulf pounced. ''Then you do admit your desire was so to limit? Let the record show that.''

Ralf ignored him, addressing William. ''Ten years ago we had barely tamed this country. Now I have sons who are half Saxon, who speak and *think* in both languages. There are many like me, daily close to the native people. As we change them, they change us. Looking back, I cannot see how the matter could have been otherwise.''

William paced the dais. He seemed distracted, inattentive, continually glancing toward the door as if momentarily expecting some arrival. ''You have a point, Vicomte?''

''Sire, I do. We are the men who came first with you. This is my country now, and I love it. So perhaps does Prince Henry''—Ralf inclined his head to the silent prince—''whom I greet in my duty. But all the more does Edward of Denby. We are all woven close together here and what blights or blows down one stalk bends others in the same way. If Bayeux acted on your authority, which surely he did not, then all your lords must wonder. And if he did not,'' Ralf threw a scathing glare at Ranulf, ''then anyone can see that an ill-broken hound is better leashed than running free.''

''I do not take offense at the vicomte's sentiments, my lords.'' Ranulf fingered through the parchments, found one indexed with a bit of red ribbon. ''The good servant endures much in loyalty to his lord. Since dangerous precedent is in question, let me refer to one most illuminating. Might I inquire of our learned farmer from Denby when he wrote this matter on the rights of subjects?''

''Over a span of six years,'' Robin said.

''So long?'' Ranulf's brows arched with exaggerated perplexity. ''Then you are hardly reckless, but deliberate. My liege and lords, I will not pursue common gossip about this man, such as that he harbors a witch among his tenants, but will instead invite royal scrutiny to one action recorded in this so-called inquiry that does not *imply* treason, but hurls it like a naked challenge.''

Now it was Robin's turn for strategic objection. ''Please the court, some passages of that work were written when I was not yet well versed in the Frankish tongue.''

''Indeed?'' Ranulf countered. ''If the language is halt, the treachery is yet nimble.''

''For the better understanding of the court, I would ask what passages you intend to read.''

''Of the revolt against Earl Tostig by his sworn vassals.''

Robin confessed that his French had been clumsy in that narrative. ''I will read it in English.''

''Prejudicial,'' Ranulf refused. ''You will not.''

''Then read it yourself, clerk. But honestly.''

Ranulf turned to the king with a sigh of strained reasonableness. ''Alas, my lord, I do not read the Saxon tongue.''

''Father, may I?'' The boy Henry rose. William was about to answer when a messenger slipped in, tiptoed along one wall, urgent but mindful of where he was. He knelt to the suddenly attentive king, offering a sealed dispatch.

''Yes, Henry, read the damned thing.'' As the king broke the seal, Robin caught part of the courier's hurried mumble: '' . . . matter of time, my liege.''

Prince Henry took the pertinent page from Ranulf, glanced through the content, and read aloud in a voice that quavered with adolescence but never lack of confidence or learning. His royal father had slumped into the chair, the written message dangling from one hand. The king read even his own language haltingly; his lips had moved laboriously over the content, word by word—then ceased. He appeared barely aware of Henry reading. No other sound in the stone chamber but the boy's voice and the busy scratching of quills.

Earl Tostig, though beloved of King Edward, was a tyrant. He robbed, imprisoned or murdered men who opposed him, until his thanes knew they must rise against him for the good of Northumbria. Then, consulting in secret with the Witan, they overthrew Tostig, who was away hunting with the king. They seized his treasury and sent to King Edward that he give them another earl. When Edward refused and called up men against them, none came to his aid. The Northumbrian thanes themselves chose Morcar for their earl. This shows the rigid theory of the absolute against the more pliant custom of the practical. The thanes had a right to such action where the king would take none. More, in the eyes of the men they governed, they had a clear duty to divest themselves of the unfit, not in order to throw off honest rule, but better to adjust themselves within it.

"My lord prince, thank you. That will suffice." Ranulf retrieved the page from Henry. "You are an admirable scholar. Does my king hear what this passage means."

"Yes." Slumped in his chair, William held out the written message to his son. "Go fetch your body servants. You sail with me."

Henry read the dispatch quickly, exchanged a swift glance with his father, and hurried from the chamber. The king rose, his red-rimmed eyes impaling Robin though he addressed Ranulf. "I will conclude this matter now."

"But did my lord note—?"

"Be *still*." The powerful command echoed from the stone walls like iron hurled against them as the king planted himself before the three defendants. "Fitz-Osbern, the queen is failing. Ready my barge. You clerks record that I have heard this case and here render judgment. For Bishop Osmund and Vicomte Ralf Fitz-Gerald—"

Both men rose to hear their fate.

"—whom I would have expected to suppress subversion rather than subscribe to it—I will not charge you with treason, though neither of you knows how close you struck at it. Osmund?"

The bishop stared straight ahead. "I have said, my lord."

"Sire, we . . . " Ralf faltered into silence.

The king turned that lethal glance on the erstwhile most trusted of his sheriffs. "Yes?"

"We acted in conscience for the good of your subjects and your realm."

"Did you? You used to be a careful man, Ralf. Now you presume to know the good of my realm better than I?" William's large-veined hand clamped on the younger man's shoulder. "You won Norwich for me."

"Of that day, pray my lord remember that it was Robin of Denby as much as—"

"I forget nothing." The hand tightened cruelly on Ralf's shoulder. "Nothing, Fitz-Gerald. Including presumption. Speaking of which, Father Ranulf, you will not again execute a capital sentence without royal warrant. Clear?"

Ranulf bowed low. "I crave pardon of my lord if I have exceeded my office in my desire to—"

"And *never* presume to know my mind before you hear it. It is our judgment that Osmund, Bishop of Nottingham, henceforth furnish ten additional knights to my annual need or the equivalent in gold or silver. That Ralf, Vicomte of Nottingham, shall render the same. Bayeux, I want that sealed before you leave this chamber."

"Instantly, sire."

"This too. Those hides which these officers denied me in summer will be relinquished without delay, courts and appeals be damned. As for you Denby—" William descended on Robin like a storm out of the North Sea. "Golden Arrow of England. Robin Hood, whose very son was delivered alive by my queen's own hands and her kindness. I pardoned you once, God alone knows why, and by way of gratitude you send to me suggesting that treason and revolt are no more than a vassal's duty to some vague notion of responsible rule. *Pardi!*—guard! Bring the chains."

The soldier approached and manacled Robin's hands. William spoke his sentence over the Englishman. "I should not have had to leave Normandy to deal with such as you. I lend you your life, Denby. You may walk in it, breathe in it, but it belongs to me. You've seen the last of England. You're banished, you hear that?"

William whirled on the clerks. "Set it down, pour the wax, set the seal. Denby is banished from England throughout his natural life. Pack up, Puck-Robin. You're for Normandy."

Book II

When Strong Dies

15

BANISHED," Will reported sadly to Marian and Mauger when they met him at Denby gate. "Taken in chains to the king's ship, the forest courts swept aside and the land to be enclosed. Robin embraced me and sent his love to his lady and children."

Robin's wife received the sentiment with no visible emotion, her mouth a bitter line, which Mauger guessed was not all for Normans. "His love. Yes."

There was more, as Will remembered, something touching Mauger. "He said that when he could write, letters to one would be message to all and that Mauger would know his meaning."

The little steward nodded. "Quite."

Marian glanced at the racing clouds overhead. "I must tell Edward and Maud. Let's go in. There's an east gale coming."

She would be the one to tell them all, and that angered her even more, because he need not have done this to them.

"Banished," Ralf told Judith in the hall of their house at Nottingham. He embraced his wife fiercely. "God help me, you are dear to me. And I might not ever have seen you again to tell you. I could think only of that. Damn me, I deserved to go with him."

"No, no, that is not sensible, my love."

"I tried," Ralf struggled. "We did what we could—no, that's not true. I thought of you and the boys. I was cautious. I feel ashamed."

"Ashamed that you wanted to protect us? Ashamed of what I love you for?"

"Why didn't I *fight* for him? I believe in his cause, our cause."

"You would not endanger us. That is only human, husband, not shameful. Robin will understand."

Ralf was not convinced of that. "I've known his delusions for years. He's *thick,* Judith, a man with a fixed idea. He thinks in generations and passing years. I stood there before William and thought: The king is *now* and so are you and my boys. What I give you all comes from William. Robin is trying to shape himself into a future to throw at now."

Ralf unclasped his mantle and dropped it on the bench, sitting down wearily. "I saw that clearly as my own delusion that I am a man of courage. He's a contradiction to the truth of the world; he can't *exist.* He's going to die, Judith. I'm glad he's gone—and that is why I feel so ashamed. Because I am the king's arm. Whatever king, whoever wears the crown. And pray God it's not my arm that must strike Robin down."

Judith sat beside her husband, one arm through his. "And what of you? Are you accused at all?"

"No, I'm . . . safe." Ralf bathed the word in the self-contempt eating him. "Poorer, but safe. Just a warning that nothing goes forward without that savage old man's word. Don't be surprised if I get drunk tonight."

Judith considered that fitting in the circumstances. "Allow me to join you." They would drink and make love and try not to think how they had been dared by the force of Robin or how frightened they were of him.

"Banished," Ranulf informed his steward in a letter of household instructions from Winchester. "You will recall a knave at the Feast of Saint John in the semblance of a priest and very clever in his own estimation. A troublemaker, a nobody. I convicted him with his own writings and out of his own foolish mouth. He was conveyed to ship in chains and from thence, one assumes, to oblivion."

The information was hardly germane to the steward's needs, more a pointed lesson to Elfled, who appeared altogether too interested when the subject of Denby arose. Suffice to say, Ranulf at twenty-three was more clever than wise. He knew nothing at all about women.

To ship in chains, then to limbo. In the fertile seedbed of Elfled's imagination, her husband succeeded only in lighting a martyr more starkly against the shadows of his unjust fate.

* * *

134

When they sighted the Norman vessels, the Danish pirates prepared without haste to move in. For any but their own sea-hardy kind, this was late in the year for Channel crossings. The raiding *drakkars* discerned from the configurations of the three Norman craft that men of note were aboard: aft sections sheltered with wooden superstructures and as easy to overhaul as crippled children. The *drakkars* hoisted sail in a stiff northerly wind and made ready to move in.

In October weather, the king's ships would normally have coasted east to Dover before standing out for Calais. Neither William nor Fitz-Osbern thought that wise. The count of Flanders was in contact with the Danish king and might not hesitate to hold William and Prince Henry as hostages to be sold to Canute. In all events, the royal party would have a tedious journey to Rouen, expending time Matilda might not have. The king's instructions to Prince William were explicit: rendezvous with fresh horses at Fécamp. He had already lost time fretting overnight in Hamble estuary waiting for the treacherous Solent tides to quiet.

For safety and prudence, the royal party had divided among three ships, William, Henry, and Fitz-Osbern each traveling with officers of the entourage, each keel with a sailing master and crew of thirty-odd experienced mariners.

Oars were shipped this last hour but would presently be put out again. The rowers sat against the beam planks on either side, out of the wind, enjoying the misery of the one poor landsman among them. Wrapped in his old dun traveling cloak, Robin hunched over his manacled wrists waiting for the next wave of nausea—or death, not caring which came first. He had been terrified at first, never away from firm land and that land now vanished from sight, leaving him to this grey, rolling nightmare deep that heaved under him from horizon to horizon. No swimmer at all, Robin recalled dire stories of sea monsters that rose up to bite ships in two and drag the hapless sailors to the dark bottom of the world. As the sea grew rougher, he paled with a worse malady. In spite of the stiff wind, the sweat started out on his cheeks and forehead. His stomach began to rise and sink with the motion of the boat. Never, not even arrow-shot and half dead in Wytha's hut had he felt this miserable.

One amused sailor suggested he swallow some salt pork, but the sailing master, Walfred, a burly Saxon with salt-stiffened white beard and hair was more practical.

"If it's coming up, nowt you can do. Get well over the downwind side if you don't want it all back in your face.''

Robin was doubled over the port rowlocks when one of the rowers, peering to the north, hailed the sailing master. He pointed to three narrow smudges several miles north. "Are they merchants?''

Walfred scrutinized the three keels looming larger. From a bow-on view, he could see little more than the prow and the A-frame outline of their leather tilts.

"Cargo knorrs,'' one man grunted, turning away.

But the sailing master just growled, "No. Too narrow in the beam and they don't ride like knorrs.''

"Jesus defend—look!''

They were sharp-eyed men used to making out detail over distance. Even as they watched, the tilts were collapsed, revealing no lashed cargo but men aplenty. Walfred bellowed: "Man oars! Pirates!''

Around Robin and his misery, the deck came alive. He was shoved off the rowing bench to lie in the scuppers while the men set oars frantically. He staggered erect on the heaving deck as William emerged from the afterhouse with the sailing master.

"Can we outrun them?''

"Not *drakkars,* my lord. Best chance is to fall off and run before the wind, give 'em the smallest target.''

"Give the order.''

They veered sharply south, caught the wind full and leapt forward with new speed. The three Danish ships were still gaining on them. William's mariners unhooked the shields hung outboard along the beams and set them higher for protection while rowing. When the Danes got close enough, it would be axes and hand to hand, but the arrows would fly long before that.

William reappeared on deck in a mail coat, sword belted around his thick waist, carrying a short bow and full quiver. "Signal the other ships to run before us. We'll be the bait.''

One of the king's clerks, wet through and nigh pale as Robin, caught at the king's sleeve. "Sire, do not. You cannot expose yourself this way.''

"Out!'' William roared, shoving the little man away. "My son is my future and my steward knows my will. And by *God,* this has been a week to test my faith!''

The orders were arm-signaled to the other ships, which immediately fell off, running due south ahead of William. The king booted Robin out of his way like a dog and leaned over the side, gauging the speed of their pursuers, an almost pleasurable grin on his face.

Enjoying himself, Robin thought, fighting another surge of nausea. *There's summ'at to kick at last, the Danes and me.*

Something plopped into the water close by, then another. William's predatory grin broadened. "Getting our range. When they're close enough, there'll be fire arrows coming at our sail. Frightened, Denby?"

Robin gasped weakly, "I would be if I weren't so flamin' sick."

"Bring my shield!" William roared. "Give me some cover. First four rowers on either side, ship oars, take up bows and prepare to loose."

Arrows were thudding into the hull now. William's shield bearer was hurrying forward with the long oval shield when the arrow caught him low in his leg. He went down with a howl of surprise and pain. Robin scurried to pick up the shield. Holding it in front of him, he ran back to plant it before the king, seeing the Danish ships no more than three boat lengths behind them now. The swift sea raiders cleaved the water surely, those to port and starboard angling out to overtake the sister ships, but the middle one coming on. Sixteen sets of oars dipped, stroked, and rose in perfect rhythm. Robin's seasickness receded under a deeper terror. *I ent going to drown where no one can find my bones.*

King and anyone else be damned. "I am not going to drown. Unchain me, let me fight."

"Just hold the shield," William said imperturbably, fitting an arrow to the odd-looking saddlebow. The detail of archers hurried aft to take up positions on top of the pitching afterhouse.

Robin winced as an arrow thudded solidly into the shield. Not death he feared but dying here where his corpse at best would be pitched overboard to sink. None to find him, not Christ or *scin-laeca,* the ghost warrior whose task it was to collect the valiant dead from the field and guide them to Valhalla. In this moment of naked terror, Robin gave no thought to his inconsistent theologies. He couldn't run and he wasn't about to drown.

"Ai—"

William had exposed himself to shoot when the Danish shaft hit him, ripping through his left sleeve in a long, shallow wound along the upper arm. The big man reeled against the gunnel. "Denby, cover me . . . "

"Help the king, he's hurt." Robin placed himself and the shield before William—awkwardly, since the chains between his hands were not very long. Valiant or desperate, three of the king's attendants ran forward. They stripped the quiver from William's shoulder, helping him toward the afterhouse. Robin clutched at one of them. "Weeping Jesus, get these chains off me."

The man looked at him as if he were mad. "You are a royal prisoner."

"What are you, bloody stupid? Where in hell am I going to go? Lord king, tell them to unchain me. I'm the best archer on this ship."

"Go on, free him," William winced as they conveyed him to the afterhouse and onto his bed within. Freeing Robin took some time. In the present emergency, no one remembered who had the keys. When the chains were off Robin, William held up his impaled arm. "Be of some use, Denby. You know how to pull an arrow."

With the king's small dagger, Robin cut the tangled blood-soaked sleeve away from the thick-muscled arm. The pile had entered just above the elbow and coursed along the extended upper arm to extrude just short of the armpit. Robin cut the shaft forward of the flights, snapped it off, and carefully cleaned the end of loose splinters. "Hold your arm up, sir."

William gritted his teeth but made no sound. Robin grasped the arrow pile and pulled downward with a steady pressure until the missile came free. The king appeared more inconvenienced than stricken by his wound. He inspected the arrow briefly, then passed it to Robin. "*Merci.* You are deft. That's a Flemish arrow," he remarked to his anxious officers. "I was right to avoid Calais."

"Badly made," Robin judged of the missile. "Fletching's not right, poor balance. Wonder they hit my lord at all."

"Join my archers." William added as an afterthought, "If you die in my service, that spares you exile."

"If I die today, sir, at least I'll feel better," Robin confessed greenly. "Sick as I am, death would be a gift." He lurched to the leather flap that separated William's quarters from the open deck and disappeared through it.

"One might think he didn't take to the sea. This filthy thing's bleeding," William fretted. "Quick, one of you fetch a poultice."

When Robin emerged onto the sharply canting deck, the Danish keel was abeam of their port side, no more than fifty yards distant. Robin took several deep gulps of air against the seasickness and staggered forward to retrieve the king's bow and quiver. A strange weapon, not carved from a single bough, not of wood at all but overlapping strips of animal horn. Robin tested the pull: heavier than a longbow. The quiver was designed to be carried at the waist; as usual, the Normans did everything backward. Doubled over for maximum cover, he ran for the ladder leading to the roof of the afterhouse, where eight archers loosed at the *drakkar*.

Under Walfred's bellowed rhythms, the rowers worked like men possessed, oars rising and dipping like knives eager to be at carving. One of the archers went down, hit, and Robin took his place—"Cover me!"—as he judged distance to the target. William's archers were not shooting effectively, not concentrating their power.

"All of you loose together on my command. Aim there, the bowmen forward. You, shield bearer." Robin grinned at the white-faced young soldier whose archer had fallen. "Stay close, boy. Don't let me feel naked."

The soldier swallowed hard. "No fear, *Anglais*. I'm not going anywhere."

"Where's the king?" one archer challenged Robin. "Who put you in command?"

"Someone better be, boyo." Robin fitted a shaft to his string. "For all the aptitude in you lot, you're going to be a long time dead. All together! Set and press and—loose!"

The concentrated storm of arrows took its toll on the Danes, who were close enough now for Robin to discern individual faces. Bearded men with long braids dangling from beneath their helmets, only a few in mail shirts. "Loose!"

Close enough to hear them roaring challenges across the narrowing distance. Robin's controlled fire kept them ducking, but three snipers were clambering up into the *drakkar's* rigging to shoot down on William's ship.

"Those three up there. All together—loose! More shafts up here."

"Aren't anymore."

"Lovely. Loose!"

Two of the Danish snipers dropped, clawing at air as they fell. One smashed to the deck, the other disappeared beneath churning water. The Danes were no longer veering in toward them; they'd lost too many men from the directed fire for an effective boarding, Robin guessed, but his own men were critically short of arrows. He swept his eyes along the Danish deck like a wolf deciding which sheep to extract from a fold. Found it.

"There. The steersman."

A brave, wounded man, an arrow protruding from his shoulder but yet braced against his tiller. Robin set his feet and pressed the bow. In an almost meditative calm, he measured distance and wind, reached out to become part of the target. Loosed. The man shot away from his tiller with the arrow in his chest. Uncontrolled, the tiller swung loose and the keel yawed, spilling wind from its sail.

"There's our mark! Keep 'em away from the tiller." Robin pushed past his shield bearer, gripping a sail rope, roaring across the water. "You ent about to catch me!"

A single shaft whistled past his ear, but what was that? What of that to a man like him now? They'd taken him from Marian and home, killed him already. To hell with king and country and world to boot, to hell with it all. "Here I am!" he screamed at the Danes. "I'm Robin Hood! Ask of me in Sherwood, by God. Ask who it is that's fought you off. By Dunstan, I'm Robin Hood!"

Dead already but he hardly felt sick at all now.

"Keep them away from that tiller!"

Frustrated, betrayed by age, William wanted to return to the fight, heaved to his feet—then the fight drained out of him. He stared down at his own body with a kind of hurt. He'd willed it to work and been ignored. His attendants urged him back to bed. "You are weak, *mon roi*. Rest, or you will start bleeding again."

"Only a moment," William surrendered in a voice stronger than he felt. "What is the condition out there?"

"Sire, the Danes have broken off."

"*Ow!* Easy on, damn you!" The leather flap pushed inward before a sailor's back. Borne between two of them and obviously incapacitated, Robin blistered the air with the most inventive profanity that ever took God's name in vain. William raised on one elbow. "Denby, what happened?"

Walfred the sailing master barged into the cabin, drenched with spray but jubilant. "Never saw the like, my lord. Never! This one"—pointing at Robin—"he just went for them and *went* for them until they had to sheer off. Lost half their crew."

Walfred broke off with cordial admiration for a countryman. "Didn't know *you* were Robin Hood."

The stricken casualty took Walfred's offered hand. "Of Sherwood. Give you good day, sir."

William broke in. "Denby, are you hurt?"

"Nothing at all," the sailing master laughed. "A landsman, sir, a landsman after all. When he did for the second steersman—aye, and with your own bow, my lord; never saw the like—he goes dashing down the deck, smartly turns his ankle, bashes his knee on a rowing bench and cripples himself more than any Dane could this day. If there'd been any loose line about, curse me if the man wouldn't've bloody hanged himself, he's that clumsy.''

Robin's swollen ankle was bound. William gave orders that their convoy resume an eastward course for Fécamp. He dismissed all but Robin and settled himself on the side of his bed, pouring wine into a silver goblet and passing it to the Englishman sprawled on the deck at his feet.

"You are strong, Denby. No one has ever been able to pull my bow.''

"One doesn't pull a bow, sir. It's pressed.'' Robin drank deeply of the watered wine. The king poured a second cup for himself.

"You did well.''

"I've no love for Danes.''

William found that beyond dispute. "What galls me is that my own ancestors taught them how to build the fastest ships afloat.''

"God knows why,'' Robin wondered. "Worth a man's life to board one.'' The wine flowed over his fatigue like syrup; his shaggy head drooped over the cup.

William studied the man who had been so much of a factor in his life for the last thirteen years—minor but *there,* like a dog always underfoot and needing to be booted out of the way as he had on deck. The boy-thane arguing law even as he knelt in forced fealty, the outlaw eluding capture for years, and then—to speak of inconsistency—turning to fight for William against Waltheof.

"Why always you, Denby?''

"Me? My lord must be patient.'' Gingerly, Robin massaged his ankle. "What with pain at my nether end and a very uncertain stomach, I'm not the keenest wit today.''

"Why did you attack my rule?''

"Attack?'' The mild blue eyes lifted to William. "My lord is the strongest king in Europe. To attack you is to destroy the roof pole of a house and expect it yet to stand. I only questioned the nature and properties of kingship.''

"Which, I assume, God has given you to understand more clearly than myself?'' Clearly the man lacked humility as well as caution. William was reminded of the wolfhounds bred in Wales and Ireland— huge hairy beasts with natures aloof and placid as their jaws were terrible. Selective breeding gave them the long legs to rear up and clamp those Leviathan jaws on the back of a wolf's neck. Was God breeding Saxons so, to rear so far above their natural station and descend on anointed heads?

Such overbred hounds did not live long, nor perhaps such men. Dare he deem that a blessing? William stared at the closed, impassive English face—on first, casual glance, a face that told you everything about the man; then, later, nothing at all. This man and his whole family overshadowed William since Hastings, and why? Why should God thrust this *commoner* between a king and his holy right? The question was like a trick sum that could not be made to come out even, no matter how long one worked at it.

He could throw Denby into prison and forget him. But what the man thought and wrote . . . what he *was* might be better employed elsewhere. Behind Robin, in his description of English law and custom, William could sense a ponderous, mystifying machinery, unique, ancient, and yet far ahead of any other custom of rule in the world. As a king, he wasted men no more readily than money, a miser with both. Perhaps this was part of God's plan for the dynasty he labored desperately to secure before dying. That time could not be far away, and what provision made, what settled or secure even now?

I will keep this Denby close, paid tuppence a day like a common groom. No, that's too much, extravagant. One penny a day, a lackey's wage and let him know it.

That would instill humility, which Robin and his whole breed sadly lacked. William drained his cup and lay back on the bed. The bandaged arm hurt savagely. He prayed silently to be in Rouen before Mora died, not to let her slip away before he held her again and let her know she was not alone. So tiny a woman that Denby's own servant once thought her one of the fey folk, yet tall enough to bestride a kingdom on both sides of the Channel.

How little God makes us before we die. Mora is in pain every day. I could be angry with God for that, hate him as Denby hates Danes, for making her suffer needlessly. Oh, I will humble you, Englishman, as God takes the whip to me.

The planks creaked, the sea sluiced under and by them in its rushing. William closed his eyes, feeling every one of his fifty-five years.

16

▶▶▶▶▶

THROUGH earnest prayer or sheer luck, the Channel wind veered westerly. The royal ships, steering through the night by overcast stars, instinct, and each other's lanterns, sighted the high, white cliffs of Fécamp at dawn, and the beach between them leading back into a narrow valley. As day brightened, Robin heard a church bell, faint but furious in its clanging.

"The monastery of Holy Trinity," King William told him. "We will hear Mass and give thanks for safe deliverance."

Robin's stomach had calmed with the subsiding waters, but gratitude was certainly in order. As the three keels worked inshore, he spied the horsemen at the water's edge. "Friends, my lord?"

"Among the few I trust," said the king. "William my son and his knights."

The shallow-draft vessels knifed in a line to the surf. When the prows nudged gently onto the sand, there was a general rush of men leaping over the side, wading up the beach to hail and embrace friends. Escorted behind the king, Robin saw Prince Henry churn through the shallows, calling out to a blond, powerfully built young man who threw out his arms to the boy.

"Rossel!" Henry boy-squeaked as they collided. "*Mon Dieu, how long has it been?*"

"Too long. By Lucca, you're getting too big to lift. Father!"

Robin's first impression of Prince William, or "Rossel," was a younger image of the king. Not as tall, but the same red-gold hair, ruddy complexion aglow with vitality, a man rarely indoors, with a body that seemed to exult in sheer being. Rossel snatched a half-eaten apple from another vavasor, ravaged two quick bites, and tossed it back before kneeling to the king. "Greetings, Father. I've brought your horses." Rossel bounded up, roaring salutations to those men he knew, pausing on Robin. In his homespun English tunic and trousers, the Englishman was a drab contrast to the bright colors about him. "What is this?"

William shoved Robin forward for inspection. "This? Rare as a unicorn, my son. A farmer who reads and writes treason. An ambitious mite in the royal cheese. My prisoner."

"*Ah, oui*. The one old Lanfranc called Robin Hood. Going to hang him?"

"Oh, I think not," William declined casually. "Not yet, at least. What news from Epte and the Vexin?"

"Nothing, sir." William's husky namesake dismissed the border situation negligently. "Very quiet. We see them across the river. Now and again we cross to drink with them, but no raids. Eudo de Gernon's in command—dear, predictable mule's arse that he is. Ah—and now a word from God."

A welcoming deputation of monks issued from the abbey gates toward the beach in procession behind their abbot, Willelm of Rots. William shifted impatiently, grudging every moment spent away from his ailing queen. Nevertheless, protocols could not be slighted. He must acknowledge the obeisances of the abbot's chief officers from precentor through the almoner, cellarer, and sacristan, even the rheumy old infirmarian. That duty done, William summoned his men to follow to the church. Prince Henry took Robin by the arm.

"Come," he directed in good English. "Surely you will want to pray while you can."

Robin noticed Prince William departing in a different direction. "Your brother will not hear Mass?"

"Rarely does," Henry told him blithely. "The abbot frowns on my brother. Rossel returns the sentiment with interest." Their eldest brother Robert *had* to stay on good terms with the clergy, since he would be both king and duke one day. "But Rossel doesn't care who likes him or not."

Some distance from them, the stocky Rossel gulped from a wineskin with spluttering relish. "Evidently not," Robin said. As for young Henry, Robin could hear the graduated affection the boy held for his

brothers in the way he named them. For Rossel, a younger brother's open hero worship toward a soldier. For Robert, an audible coolness toward a sibling seventeen years older and a virtual stranger.

The king's party filed through the abbey gates toward the low-roofed church, entering by the monks' choir. Standing in the crowded nave, Robin began to feel uncomfortable, constricted. The heavy stone walls and thick columns seemed to be crowding in on him. His prayers were heartfelt but distracted. He experienced a sudden, irrational fear of this clammy, shadowed nave, be it of God or anyone else, and looked about him at the king and Fitz-Osbern, their hands clasped in devotion, the monks chanting in Latin—and knew with an instinct strong as the terror of death that he must be *away,* out from under these arches that would fall on him, smother him to death or worse. Not the house of *his* God, this place. Not knowing or caring why, he must get out *now,* to where he could breathe, let the guards follow as they would.

Never to know precisely why, Robin would always be oppressed by Norman buildings, churches and castles alike. The great early poets of his race were gone, but they and those yet unborn who would forge English and Frankish into a language like a bright sword could have told Robin why he needed to escape from the church as from an airless tomb. Long before Christ came to the north, Robin's dim ancestors had watched the Roman legions from across the Rhine or the misty lowlands of Frisia and Denmark. They bargained with the legions, ambushed them in the Rhine forests, but never submitted. Later, in Britain, they gazed in awe at the massive stoneworks these Romans erected. Impressive but alien. They shunned these edifices as doubtless housing gods and magic against whom their own Woden might not avail. To the end of his days, Robin would never be at ease in a house, church, or any building where he could not feel earth or at least living wood beneath his feet.

Disoriented and miserable now, the chanted Latin from within the church wafted no comfort to him. He threw the folds of his old cloak over his chest against the sea wind, noting a dozen or more folk filing down the high paths to the valley from the east.

"Here they come! Heigh-ho for miracles. Hey, *Anglais.*"

Rossel had hailed him from a picketed line of horses. The prince beckoned him in a flutter of the bright yellow mantle thrown over his mail. Robin's two stony-faced guards followed at a distance, hardly worried he'd escape. There was nowhere to run.

The tanned young prince inspected Robin with indolent curiosity, then looked off at the folk approaching along the cliff paths. "Miracles. They're good business for Fécamp."

"A patron saint, my lord?"

"On my word, the most sanctified."

"Who are those, tradesfolk?"

"Pilgrims." The word rippled with amusement. "Father said you were educated. You do not know the legend of Joseph of Arimathea?"

All Englishmen did. Joseph went to Glastonbury, where he founded the first Christian church in Britain, or so the Welsh said.

"Like the fugitive Jesus, Joseph was apparently everywhere," Rossel observed. "Positively footloose." As the story went, when Joseph and Nicodemus took Christ down from the cross, Nicodemus placed a vial of the holy blood in a tree trunk. Set adrift, the tree floated all the way from Antioch to land conveniently at Fécamp. "Naturally, the tree sprouted and began to dispense miracles on the spot."

Despite his feelings toward Rome and foreign popes, Robin felt the prince's flippancy a shade much. "Our church at Blidworth has a lock of hair from Saint Dunstan."

"Which no doubt heals lepers."

"Men have recovered from mortal sickness or wounds when the reliquary was brought to them."

"Would have recovered anyway," Rossel scoffed. "Or died. Man, there are vials of Christ's blood from here to Hungary. Fellow must have bled buckets." The prince took a brush from the saddlebag on a huge bay and idly groomed the animal's neck and shoulders. "Because I have no consuming devotion to his institution, the good abbot believes I follow Satan and the old religion. *Merde*. I don't follow anything old, I'm interested in now. What I eat, what I ride, what I hold. Bugger the rest."

Abruptly Rossel jammed the brush back into the saddlebag. "So— what's your crime, *Anglais?* Why are you so unique a prisoner that Father keeps you close?"

"That is complicated, my lord."

"Simplify. Despite my mother's despair of me, I've been known to think."

"I suggested improvement in royal law."

Rossel whistled, impressed. "That would do it."

"Aye, sir. It did."

"I've been in your country. Odd sort of people. But Father is fascinated by things he can't understand, like God and England.'' The prince allowed Robin was uncommonly lucky. Most dangerous men usually hung or disappeared, like the usurper Harold's young brother Wulfnoth, who was incarcerated thirty years ago as a hostage and languished yet. ''Growing moss by now, I suppose.''

''Yes.'' Robin let the sharpness bristle in his retort. The fate of innocent Saxons like Wulfnoth was no joke to him. ''God give him ease.''

''Or easeful death,'' Rossel amended. ''But you see what ambition pays a man when he gets in my father's way.''

Robin said nothing. He'd seen that much for years.

Mass was done. The king and his party were coming from the church. Rossel unhitched his bay from the picket line and prepared to mount. ''Ambition, *Anglais?* You must cut it to your size like a garment. My brother Robert was made a count at eleven and screaming every day since to be duke and king. Mother spoiled him, Richard died . . . and me? My ambition fits perfectly. I'd like some money now and again. Sacks of it, in fact. I want to be rich.''

Rossel mounted the bay. He looked down at the Englishman with an amused smile that might hide considerably more than laughter. ''This is Normandy, fellow. Keep your eyes open and your head down, and you might live a while.''

17

>>>>>

THIS William was a king of moods, most of them foul from Robin's harried view. From Fécamp to the Seine Valley, it pleased William and Rossel's raucous vavasors to have the Englishman walk between mounted guards, sometimes trotting him for miles at a stretch. Later, when William fretted over losing time, Robin was thrown over a pack-saddled mule.

When they briefly rested the horses, Robin took a farmer's natural interest in the verdant Norman countryside. The earth was better by far than Denby's, dark and rich, able to grow anything, but the common serfs were a different breed from home. They took pains to avoid the king's party. If summoned, they stood hangdog and mumbling, never daring to look lords in the eye. Once, two of Rossel's knights spurred after stray cows, spearing one of them for pure sport. The license and waste appalled Robin: just killed a man's cow with the poor serf unable to stop them or even protest, and not a word from king or prince about payment.

Knights they might be, but hardly lords in any responsible sense. Crude, foul-mouthed, pig-ignorant and proud of it, lusty young animals with big shoulders and legs bowed from a lifetime in the saddle. Younger sons of minor houses, their only recourse for living was the Church or knighthood, in which latter condition they appeared to Robin little better than mercenaries. If the prince ceased to pay them, they would offer themselves to France or Flanders without hesitation. Robin held aloof from them. *True what we always said of their lot: No proper upbringing.*

The royal party wended east along the snake-winding Seine until the walls of Rouen were in sight. A herald galloped out of the city gate, cloak flying behind him, to salute the king and bring news. The queen still lived through God's mercy. Count Robert had arrived and, in grave haste, the royal daughters, Cecily, Adela, and Constance. All awaited William at the west gate of Rouen, including Simon Rollo of Crepi, who came to do honor to Matilda, his foster mother.

"Simon? That idiot," William snorted. "*Sans doute,* there is joy in heaven when a man renounces a county for God, but it can be damned inconvenient for a king."

The last mile to the city was more hurried than grand. Within the west gate, a dazzling panoply was drawn up for the king, a full hundred or more knights and men at arms, clerics, the royal children and their retainers. William Bon-Ame, Archbishop of Rouen, had turned out in the full canonicals of his office, jeweled crozier glittering in the sun, his chaplains, sacristans, and priests behind him.

To the fore were the king's children, the three young daughters and Robert, Count of Maine, heir to the double crowns of England and Normandy, astride a magnificent dappled grey Flemish whose bridle jingled with silver. Robert would be slightly younger than himself, Robin estimated from sight and hearsay, a blaze of the tailor's art from scarlet cloak to short yellow tunic and close-fitting trousers, boots spurred with gold. He was planted before a cordon of his knights from Maine and greeted his father from the saddle as an equal.

"My respects, Father. And to my brothers, William and Henry."

To Robin's sharp English eye, keen at detecting nuance, there was no love worth mentioning between Robert and his siblings, each of them markedly different from the other two. Like Waltheof, Robert *looked* the magnificent stuff of which popular kings were made. If Rossel glinted like bronze, Robert was the sun at noon, handsomest of Matilda's boys and aware of it, every word or gesture performed for an audience comprised of all Europe. Next to that shimmering crown jewel, Rossel was clay and young Henry virtually disappeared—or almost, as Robin contemplated him. In contrast to dazzling Robert and rough Rossel, there was something hooded and self-contained, less easily labeled in the boy.

Princess Cecily, Abbess of Caen, was no more than twenty, a slight figure in holy black. The younger Adela, Countess of Blois, was resplendent in white and gold, her ladies in waiting as sumptuously turned out. To the plain but astute Robin, these Norman birds knew the display value of their plumage.

The king embraced his abbess daughter. "Cecily, most welcome."

149

"My father and brother in Christ. I wish we met on a happier day."

"And I. Adela! I'm pleased to see you in health. And Constance"—as a stocky child of twelve was assisted from her palfrey and ran to William's embrace—"Come kiss your father."

Adelaide, who had come to Denby with her royal parents in 1070, had died of fever five years later. Affianced to Alfonso of Spain, Adelaide died a virgin and therefore, as Judith remarked at the time, presumably became an ornament in God's house. Judith's private opinion of the girl was more acerbic.

"One should never speak ill of the dead, no matter how pleasurable, but Adelaide was a spoiled brat. Let her annoy the angels hereafter."

Robin remembered the searing judgment as being rather severe upon a dead girl deserving of prayer at least, but Judith spared her none. "When you were forced to kneel to William that day, the little bitch laughed at you. *No* one does that to my blood."

So Judith slammed the doors of eternity on Adelaide, looking just then very much like her aunt Maud.

Greetings concluded, William mounted to ride on, but Bon-Ame whispered in his ear. The intelligence apparently did not please the king. "Well, let him be quick."

A tonsured, black-robed monk came forward and knelt before the king. William acknowledged him curtly. "Oh, get up, Simon. Must I be burdened with you now, you boil on the fundament of chastity?"

An uncharitable address to a lay brother, Robin considered . . . but beyond that, there was something familiar about the monk. The set of the man's head, a certain residual arrogance beneath the humility of his order. He protested to the king now that he came from Saint Claude to pay last respects to his foster mother.

William remained unmollified. "Belated gratitude. If you'd been man enough to bed your bride when you should have, Philip would not be at my back door now. Out of my way, monk."

On the way to the palace, Robin's mule went contrary and had to be led by one of the grooms. They were the last to reach the palace courtyard. The royal party swept like a riptide into the palace, through the corridors and cordons of attendants bowing like a stand of wheat before a wind. Up the stairs through more of them scurrying out of the king's hurried way. Robin's guards conferred briefly as they hustled him forward between them. "What do we do with this one?"

"I don't know. Just bring him along, I guess."

Robin was borne on the tide into the already crowded chamber of the dying queen.

Matilda lay in the big bed, her emaciated body supported on embroidered samite pillows. William threw his mantle to a knight and went down on his knees beside her, pressing his wife's hand to his lips. "Mora . . ."

But for those times when pain vanquished her entirely, Matilda was very much in possession of her faculties. Her time had come and she knew it. She had never feared to live; to fear death would offend both dignity and her sense of proportion. Her mind and sight were clear. Gilly had come in time as she knew he would. Robert stood close but stricken, the younger princes and obedient daughters to one side.

Yet, Matilda fretted privately out of long habit, there was always something to attend to. Constance must be betrothed to Brittany when that county was once again at peace with Gilly.

William half lay across the bed holding his wife, hardly trusting himself to speak. "Back from us, all of you," he warned the solemn company. "Stay back. Give place, I say."

The silent watchers moved back dutifully, retreating into a huddled crescent about the royal bed.

"You know the one thing I have missed all our lives?" Matilda whispered against her husband's cheek. "A little privacy. But—nine live births and a kingdom. We did not do so badly." As if she were merely kissing him good night until morning, Matilda pressed her lips to the stubbled cheek. "Gilly, I am very tired. And I must speak to the children."

As she regretted, privacy had never been among Matilda's royal privileges. The farewells were conducted by precedent, as everything else in this court. First by right, Count Robert knelt by his mother, tears streaming down his face. "Mother, bless me."

"So I do, my son. It was good of you to put aside your differences with your father."

"Forgive me, my mother."

"Poor Robert. You never managed your heart well. A pity. You are all heart and little head. Attend me." Matilda took her son's handsome face in cold hands. "It is my last wish that you make amends with your father. Stand by him, Robert. Philip is false."

"I have sworn oaths," Robert agonized. "I do not know what to do."

Nor would he ever, this beautiful child of hers. Matilda kissed him gravely. "*Je t'aime, mon fils.* Go with my blessing."

The prince backed reluctantly from her presence. In the shuffling of the courtiers about the oppressive, medicine-rank chamber, Robin of Denby and his guards were pushed to the fore between Adela of Blois and the queen's women.

"Prince William," Bon-Ame summoned in a hushed tone, "the queen will see you now."

Robin saw the young man wince as if slapped—then mask whatever emotion he felt. *As if he were granted audience merely out of duty.* Rossel approached the bed, went on his knees and kissed the hand offered—allowed—to him.

"Rossel, my son. My little bird, I have never pretended to approve of your life."

"That life has not one shred of lie in it, *ma mère.*"

"Amend it, Rossel. Do not let my own flesh be an affront to God."

Robin caught the small, subtle rejection. Rossel would have nestled his cheek in Matilda's hand, but it was withdrawn. "I cannot lie before heaven, my son. Certainly not this near to Him. You were a hard child to bring into this world and harder to love thereafter. You may kiss my cheek and call Henry."

"Yes, madame."

The queen's farewells to Henry and her daughters were quite affectionate, though Robin could not help sympathy for Rossel—summoned more like a servant than a son, admonished in bare duty and dismissed with a meager ration of the warmth his mother showed the other children. Rossel stood by his father, staring straight ahead, but as the daughters went one by one to the bed, his head drooped gradually.

They were done now, the children, the archbishop approaching the bed with a young priest at his elbow. Suddenly Matilda seemed to flare up with her old energy. "Here," she ordered a chamberlain, "fix the pillows." She peered straight at Robin. "Denby? It can't be you."

He stepped forward, bowing. "Yes, Majesty."

"Come here," she ordered, imperious as ever. As Robin knelt to her, Matilda surveyed his salt-stiff clothes and untrimmed beard. "What a rumple you are. From the first day I set eyes on you, you always looked as if you'd been plucked from a hayrick and thrown on the mercy of an indifferent tailor. And in trouble again, one hears."

"*Oui, ma reine.* The king does not approve of me."

"Neither do I," she said with her old tartness. "Marian was always more deserving. How is she and the boy I delivered?''

Both did well, Robin assured her, nor did Marian ever forget the queen's kindness.

Matilda's voice had grown faint and reedy again, the last energy burning away. ''You are an impossible people, gross, dull, and blind. Shall I tell you something, Denby? If you English had any sense of reality, you might have been great. As you do not, God gave you us for keepers. For your wife's sake, try to avoid the gallows.''

''Diligently, madame.''

''Leave me now,'' she dismissed him, gazing among the press of people about the bed. ''Gilly, where are you?''

So like his independent wife and queen to spare a moment, precious as they were now, on an English commoner. William gathered the small figure in his heavy arms. For all the others hovering hushed and reverent about them, William was alone with his wife, would be so alone from here out. His life truly began in her arms. Hers would end in his. Mora should go with no fear.

''Wouldn't you know,'' she whispered. ''My feet are cold.''

''I'll rub them.''

''No, don't bother. What a time we've had, Gilly. Do you remember the day I kicked you so efficiently?''

''I deserved it. I kicked you first.''

''I bade Robert make peace with you, to show some sense and come home.''

''Don't trouble over that now.''

''Oh, but you know how I hate loose ends. It is important.'' Matilda sighed against her husband's chest. ''But the truth is, my love, I am just worn out. Send the people away and let me sleep.''

William held her. In a little while, his love did seem to be asleep in his arms.

18

▶▶▶▶▶

La reine est morte.

L When Bon-Ame and Rossel gently took Matilda from his arms, the world had receded from William, discerned only faintly like soft voices under rushing surf. Someone helped him to a chair. From a distance, he heard Robert weeping by the tiny remnant in the great bed. Someone said in a hushed voice, "Let the women prepare." Certain sequels were to be set in motion. Women in waiting hurried away to change into white mourning. Matilda's chamberlain sent to inform the household.

Yes, these things must be done, but give me a moment. Who are you, who speaks to me? Leave me alone. You've been at me all my life and all of Mora's. Leave me alone!

Even as his spirit snarled and warned them back, the king in William responded from habit, lifted his heavy, tired body from the chair, allowed someone—Rossel, yes, good boy—to fix the mantle about his shoulders.

"The men are waiting in the courtyard, Father."

Rossel it was who guided him from the room in a sea whisper of voices, sons and daughters, stewards, chaplains taking their ranked places in his wake, climbing the stone steps toward the open parapet that overlooked the palace courtyard. Others joined the train as it proceeded, lately arrived messengers from England, from diligent Ranulf in his Chancery, and steadfast Lanfranc. Envoys from Maine with dispatches for Robert, nuncios from Flanders conveying meaningless messages to lull and delay while that county aligned with Denmark.

154

Ambassadors from France, dove-drooping in sympathy and condolence while Philip wiped away the tears for his dearest cousin Matilda and strengthened his forces along the border Rossel patrolled like a harried watchdog. All of them would ask, though never aloud: What change hereby in the duchy, the kingdom, the status quo?

None, damn you all. What she and I built will last a thousand years. The flag is torn, the heart of me going in the grave with her, but our house stands. Robert, Philip, all of you. Nothing is changed. Do I not yet move as if I were alive?

He was out in the light and open air now. William dragged it into his lungs, conscious of the fatigue and the awful heaviness of his flesh—nurtured, armed, and forged to the merciless demands of destiny for more than fifty years. He looked down at the lines of men and horses in the courtyard below him. Habit and ritual lifted his arms out to them like ponderous dead weights. "The queen is dead."

The sea of upturned faces lowered, the men knelt. At William's side, Prince Robert added huskily, "Heaven receive her soul."

"My liege men! Your king asks your prayers."

At Bon-Ame's order, couriers had galloped through the streets of Rouen to the new cathedral of St. Vitricius and the abbey of St. Gervais. Even as the king loomed over his men, flanked by royal sons and daughters in their sorrow, the great bells began to toll beating the measure of William's own requiem.

All of this was distant and unreal to him. In a few minutes, a half hour at most, this solemn pause would dissipate and the pulse of empire beat again. Men would go about their business and expect him to do the same. William could not. Damn them, let them wait this little time. Long ago there had been days when he and Matilda found small secret pockets of time to call their own. Not so later for more years than William could gaze back across. If God gave him truly to be king, the crown was so dearly bought. . . .

How have I lived near threescore years with so few to call friend? Only Mora, really, and I must see her to Caen to be buried in the convent she founded.

So many years dodging or in pursuit of necessity, never without fear, never able to show it. Always having to lead men or drive them, because not one of them in a hundred were quick mettle but dull, greedy human dross. Spineless burdens to be pushed and dragged this way or that. I am not a brute, Denby—but brute or angel, I know men. I respect you as I did Fitz-Gerald. If you had Ralf's loyalty, I might have advanced you, but you are out of measure to your times. Fealty to a king, to the symbol of power, is the way of things, the only way men know. Fealty to an abstract ideal is a dream with a bitter waking. Learn that, Denby, learn it well while you follow at my heel.

Don't you see, any of you, that I am a jongleur in the balancing of men? It is my skill, my strength, my fate and Mora's. We made few mistakes. But I am and will be lonely without her, desolate now without one friend to share with, to talk with, or to whom I may show my weakness or my tears.

No man is a god to his wife. Mora knew my faults and fears and folded her life about me to protect them. I fear no man—but trembled since the conquest of England at the judgment of God. Yet I don't know how I could have managed otherwise from the start, except to let my father's enemies kill me as a boy. Oh, they would have loved that, all the great houses that bow to me now. But destiny was mine, the very comet blazing in the sky that Easter was mine, and Edward promised me England. Harold was the usurper, not me.

If I could only rest assured of that. How many devotions, donations, how many churches founded and abbeys endowed to the glory of God? I am not guilty, I had the right. Otherwise, God would have shone on Harold at Hastings and shadowed me.

And is not a king anointed by God's will? To take that place unchosen is mortal sin, and if I am chosen, why are the shadows still there? Zealous Gregory, congealing in his virtue and conveniently failing health, writing me like an overlord, telling me I am no more than a provincial servant of holy empire. Good, true men like Ralf and Osmund asserting their rights against mine as "English" landowners, so please you . . . and the little men like Denby, the stubborn, splay-footed farmers with their own perverse spelling for right and wrong.

Only you were my lover and my friend, Mora. How many nights did I lie in the dark with you so small and comforting in my arms, and tell you of these deep fears? You were the best of me. Without you, I would not have become half the king. One wouldn't think a woman so tiny could be so strong, so enduring. She was against our marriage at first. Even after Val-ès-Dunes, when the barons learned that, young or no, I meant to *be* duke, to Matilda of Flanders I was still an illegitimate nobody. God's holy face, that made me angry. Not consider me? Not even see me? I rode to Bruges in a white rage, forced my way into her very bed chamber and called her to account. So furious I kicked her in the backside.

If that was a wry footnote to *lèse-majesté*, it was also a mistake. One didn't boot a count's daughter in the rump. Mora let out a yelp! and then kicked me hard as a mule in return, and so well aimed, there I was, doubled up on the floor with Mora on her knees over me, cursing and laughing all at once, and when I could think beyond my suffering privates, I knew we'd be wed and so did she.

So we married and changed the maps, the balance of power, the world. So God takes her from me, and from her loss I will reckon my old age. Ambition palled long ago; no more now than a ploughman's daily stint. Our children will ride home to their lives: Cecily to prayer, Adela to Blois, Robert to more rebellion, very like. We spoiled him, Mora. We gave him too soon to expect too much before making sure of the man to come from the boy. Now he is shattered by the loss of you. Weeping. I won't deny his grief, but his tears are tedious, *de trop*. When he wipes them away, Robert will be importuning me as always, demanding his due, his duchy, *his* crown. When I'm ready, scion and son. When you are a Fitz-Gerald with as much steel as fervor in your blood. When I can trust you—oh, enough, boy. Leave weeping. I'll give him something to do, that's best. One of us must see to Mora, and I haven't the heart just now to look on my love gone. Not until the bleeding stops.

"Robert," the king murmured aside to his stricken eldest son. "Listen, I would have you look to the queen's women, see they prepare her."

Robert was red-eyed and incoherent. "Father, I . . ."

No, the young man was not capable just now. For all his dash and repute, Robert never seemed apt to the moment's need. In that moment, blunt Rossel was at his father's elbow, modifying the request with delicate assurance.

"My brother has too much of sorrow like yourself. I will see to the queen."

In a more collected moment, William might have refused. The directive had been issued to the heir, let him carry it out. After her darling Richard, Robert was always Mora's favorite. But William was weary. Easier this once simply to let it go. "Very well, Rossel. See it done."

* * *

A litter had been placed by the queen's bed, but no member of the royal family was present. Where were they to take the queen now? No one clearly knew what to do. A hushed, uncertain wait ensued, Robin standing between his guards as women in waiting glanced expectantly to the queen's chamberlain, who peered continually out into the drafty corridor. With no orders about the English prisoner, Robin's guards held him in a corner of the queen's chamber. All about him, he saw the impatience of ongoing life begin to stir from the shock of death, asserting itself within ceremony. The autumn sun had crept westward, leaving the room in shadow, the usual dinner hour long past. Once more the chamberlain leaned out the door—almost colliding with Rossel as the prince swung into the chamber and went straight to the bed.

"Take her up."

The women were awkward with respect toward the body. Rossel's hovering, vital presence seemed to dare them to be clumsy, and so they were just that. They had to pull the corpse toward the edge of the huge bed to lift it. One woman fumbled over the task and lost her balance. Rossel waved the chamberwomen aside.

"I will do it."

His gruffness vanished as he bent to lift his mother's body. Whatever this cynical young man thought of God in general, Robin saw boundless reverence in his arms bending to their task. As Rossel raised Matilda, her head lolled back. Robin hurried quickly to support the queen's head while Rossel lowered her gently onto the litter.

"Thank you, Denby. Help me with her."

A number of male attendants stepped forward, but Rossel chose two of his own knights to take up the rear of the litter, Robin and himself at the head. They carried the queen carefully in the wake of the chamberlain and priest who led them down to her private chapel, where the women waited to wash and clothe Matilda. One of them stood to one side with the rich white kirtle and jewel-sewn mantle draped over her arms.

The litter was laid on trestles before the altar. Robin gazed down at the dead face gaunt with the sickness that had wasted her, but composed. Remembering Matilda's no-nonsense manner in life, Robin thought: *She looks as if she's made a good working day of it.* "There, that's accounted for. What now?"

Rossel curtly ordered the knights and women out. "All of you go."

The two knights departed quickly without a word, but the women charged to prepare the body hesitated. "I said *go*. Wait outside. I'll call you. Denby?"

About to depart with the women, Robin turned. "Sir?"

"You stay." Rossel waited until the door closed behind the women, still studying his mother's face, perhaps searching for something never seen while she lived. "Does your mother live?"

"Aye, sir. Like the queen, she is small but hard to vanquish."

Matilda's toilet articles stood ready in a small silver chest placed on the altar. Rossel took an ivory comb from the chest and began to work it carefully through his mother's hair. Robin recalled the shade as brownish-red when he knew her thirteen years ago at Denby. Faded to pale brown now and shot through with white.

"Do you love your mother, *Anglais?*"

"Of course."

"In duty or from choice?"

The cold query amazed Robin. *Choice?* Love simply was. Like the hall itself, the bargain oak, and Holy Pool, Maud was part of him and the very soil of Sherwood. "I can't imagine home without her."

"Then you may understand." Rossel put the comb back in the chest. "Those two who carried her with us. And you. My mother had to live with a great many liars. I would at least have her carried by honest men. The change will refresh her spirit."

As Robin listened, he felt the man was not uttering what he would but what he must. Now and perhaps never again. Things he could not risk saying except to a stranger behind his back, anonymous as a priest in confession.

"Been so much weeping today: Father, because he loves her and probably never will love again, God help him; Robert, because he is sad for a moment, and a moment is all he can stand. They say you English are very sparing with your tears."

"We are not raised to show them, my lord. Lanfranc called it our national constriction."

The prince's head, bowed over Matilda, wagged slowly in conviction. "No, it's—tidy. I grew up in camps among soldiers and horses. Strong, because I had to be, but I learned there's more between men than killing one another in the trappings of honor. So Robert calls me a catamite, so does the Church. Whatever priests promise of the next world, this one's a sewer. One should enjoy the few clean bits when they're found. My father tries to care for me. I saved his life in battle once. I would again, gladly. Yes, he does care for me. My mother never troubled. I had to love her without her permission. That tends to keep one dry-eyed.''

Rossel bent over his mother and kissed the pale forehead. ''Get out of here, Denby. I will tell the women when they may enter. Go back to your guards.''

19

H E was not exactly a prisoner, nor much of anything else. Robin was told by an officious chamberlain that he was to receive a penny a day. A balding, bustling little man who had few responsibilities beyond minor accounts like Robin and the servants while creating the illusion of continual crisis and unceasing toil therein. His cubbyhole work cell was a chaos, every flat surface covered with records and pipe rolls. In his absence one day, as the rains of autumn soaked and chilled Rouen, Robin took a diabolical notion to straighten the piles of parchment. As he predicted, the chamberlain was depressed and disoriented for a week, unable to find anything or even function, miserable until time and habit eroded the neat stacks to disorder once more.

The royal family accompanied Matilda's remains to the abbey at Caen to see her interred. Robin was left in a tiny chill closet near the guard room on the ground level of the Rouen palace. There was one small stone casement which served only to waft the stench of the garderobe into the chamber. For warmth, there was a smoky brazier in the middle of the floor.

Rossel returned to Rouen a day in advance of the king, sweeping up Robin in his gusty wake and naming the Englishman's immediate fate. "Father has given you to me for the nonce. You'll need a horse, I suppose. Penny a day. By Lucca, it's good to know someone in his service is poorer than me."

Before departing for their patrol area around Gisors, Rossel lost considerable time collecting his vavasors for a series of conferences. Robin was present for some of them. If the knights weren't drunk they were quarreling, usually to be found on or near their huge Flemish horses, which they matched for rankness. Indeed, to Robin, all of Normandy reeked of horse lather and a peculiar ambitious fervor with Rouen at its heart. Everyone was restless, all wanted something. By comparison, England seemed a tranquil backwater. But here, the ferment was at the top around William and his barons, calculating men no more manageable than half-broken stallions. There was no class here comparable to Robin's own, the minor thanes who had always been buffer, balance, and link between commoners and crown. Normans were a foreign nobility battened on this lush, fertile corner of the continent. Their Frankish serfs hardly seemed to exist, seen but never heard as a voice, given no more consideration than oxen in the field.

Robin had spoken fluent French for years. Now he tuned his ear more precisely to the Norman dialect, unobtrusive at Rossel's conferences, able to read the maps and digest what they told him. Not subtle politics but naked power was the game. There was a veneer of diplomacy between William and the crowned heads he dealt with, but always backed with the sword. Rossel was the keenest blade. If Robert was beribboned *beau chevalier,* Rossel was the working soldier. He might stumble into council smelling of wine and whores, but once there, he tolerated no sluggards. If one of his vavasors dozed after a night of carouse, Rossel might break off in the middle of a thought, lift the stupid sod out of his lethargy, and belt him silly.

War with France was undeclared but inevitable. Southwest: Anjou, nominally allies but unreliable. To the southeast: Maine under Count Robert, difficult to handle under the best conditions. North: Flanders, already sending love notes to Denmark. The most present danger was Philip of France and the small, strategically placed county of Vexin, just southeast of Rouen.

For a hundred and seventy-five years, the accepted boundary between the lands of the Northmen and France had been the River Epte, where Rollo the Viking signed his treaty with Charles the Simple. The Count of Vexin was vassal to the French crown, though early in their astute reign, William and Matilda had managed to secure Simon Rollo of Crepi, heir to the county, to be brought up by them in fosterage at Rouen. The duke and duchess saw this as a brilliant coup. As balance between Normandy and France, a Vexin favorable to Rouen was an obvious advantage to William. Simon grew from an unexceptional boy into a thoroughly conventional young nobleman with a narrow mind unclouded by thought in any depth. As a knight he served William at

Chester in 1070. He caused a flurry of trouble between William and his own father when a despicable Saxon brained an expensive horse out from under him in Sherwood.

"Weeping Jesus!" Robin twisted about in the saddle to face Rossel, as the column of horse plodded toward Gisors and the River Epte. *"That's* where I've seen that manny before. I killed his horse."

"Really?" Rossel responded. "A lovely Flemish worth two of you? Unspeakable."

"The lot of them demanded hospitality at Denby. Simon insulted my cousin, wouldn't even believe I was lord. Cheeky little sod. We ate the horses."

For once Rossel was at a loss for words, flabbergasted. "Name of a saint, you didn't!"

"Not bad for taste. Bit tough."

The column moved on through mud in which their mounts' hooves sank to the hocks. Rossel rode bareheaded, sometimes tilting his head back, mouth agape to savor the soft, flat-tasting rain. He was much more a creature of earth than anyone in his family. *"Bien,* Simon complained through his father to mine. Father found it best to replace the horse. He hates to spend money, but that was nothing beside what Simon did later."

In time, the Count of Vexin died and Simon succeeded to the honor. A marriage was arranged with the daughter of the Count of Auvergne— "Curse me if I can remember the wench's name"—and the union solemnized with highest pomp. Not consummated, however. God alone knew what took Simon on his nuptial night. There was his bride waiting in the flower-scented bed—

"And in wafts Simon in his nightshirt and new halo, and tells the girl he's decided to become a monk at Saint Claude. Then and there on his knees he vowed chastity and urged his bride to swear the same."

"On his wedding night?"

"Without so much as tupping her once."

"But why?" Wet and saddle-sore, Robin was hardly inclined to charity. He judged Simon a mean-spirited fool, at very least an idiot. "I should have brained *him,* not the horse. Could at least have waited until morning. Loved her a little and that. Seems downright . . . indecent."

Rossel agreed on principle. No bed should be passed up summarily. The bride's feelings were not recorded, he said, though one might assume a certain anticlimax. "Off they went, Simon to his monastery, the girl to a convent, and my parents to something like political seizure.''

With Simon chaste, childless, and gone, King Philip snapped up his vassal's vacant honor. Within a week, French troops were grinning across River Epte at William's men, and so they had remained for the last four years. William and Matilda could only grit their teeth and accept the most inconvenient attack of religious fervor since the emperor Constantine's vision at Milvian Bridge.

"And so we must ride this river for the king," Rossel concluded. "Sometimes we drink with the French, sometimes we fight them.''

Robin recalled the knightly fraternal nonsense at Norwich that so frustrated himself and Ralf Fitz-Gerald. "Just so.''

"I'll present you to them if you want. Father says you're a rarity.''

No, thank the prince just the same. If Normans lived by a thoroughly impractical code of honor, Robin saw no sense in drinking with men he might have to dodge or kill.

His mother laid in her crypt at Caen, Robert intended to bid his father a civil farewell. That was not to be; one word led to another, father and son each intent on their own purpose and right, and the flimsy truce of the funeral tore apart.

A day of hunting had been arranged along the banks of the Orne, though neither William nor his son had much taste for it this day. They rode apart from the main party through weather unable to resolve between sun and rain shower. William tried to be paternally patient, but the truth was he lacked Matilda's indulgence toward Robert's demanding arrogance.

"Robert," he advised gravely, keeping the black hunter to an easy walk, "Normandy is no longer a mere duchy, but the heart of a kingdom. *One* kingdom. Remember how Canute held together three countries under one crown. If he'd had sons as wise, that empire might have lasted. He did not. Now his blood is on the outside trying to grab it back from me. Be schooled by that.''

"You are not young, Father," Robert said. "Time is passing. I am not a boy anymore. Again and again I have sent to you with the one question—why, when I've already been named to inherit your crown, will you not at least name me duke now?''

William stared ahead along the river bank, collecting his thoughts. *I can't. You are still a danger.* "Not yet, Robert.''

"I am the eldest," his son insisted. "When she was dying, Mother begged me to compose with you. I have tried, Father—no, don't look away. I have *tried*. You trust me or you do not. I demand—"

"Demand?" William reined the hunter about to face his son. "*You* demand?"

"It is my right."

Denby is a great one for his rights, too. Staring at his son, William found himself comparing the man to Robin. Close to an age, though the Saxon was far more mature.

"You do not trust me," Robert sulked.

"Very well, I do not. Not until I know you are my son in regard to Philip."

"Philip already hails me as duke. He trusts me now. And we are his vassals."

"Vassals." William hissed out the absurdity of the term. "Name of God, wake up, see facts clear. France recognized Normandy as a separate power because Philip's ancestors knew ours would have sacked Paris clean if they didn't, plain as that. Vassals! *Sangre du Christ*. We are enemies, always have been. Every year or so I've sworn fealty to France and for the last four of them, Philip and I have both wondered which of us would cross Epte first. Before I put the crown on your head, you will clearly remember that you have allies and enemies, but no friends, Robert. Not as a king."

His son rejected that out of hand. "Philip has shown himself my friend."

The father's hard smile was tinged with sadness. "When you know that's a lie; when you know it so well it robs your sleep of nights; when you realize that everyone wants something of you and wants you dead most of all—then I'll call you duke, not before."

"There, I told you so. You do *not* trust me."

"Not your judgment, no."

Robert's even features soured to petulance. "Perhaps you will look to Rossel. There's a fitting king for you. The family deviate."

William fought to keep his temper; he had no time for such whining now. "At least Rossel knows how to follow orders."

"Indeed? Then try to make him king," Robert flung back, wheeling his horse away from the confrontation, ending it. "Try, Father. I'll hit England with Philip and Scotland *and* the Danes at my back, by God. I'll hit you so hard you'll think it the Second Coming."

Robert put spurs to his hunter and galloped away.

Sitting his horse, William watched the departure of his hot-tempered, unstable son with the sadness of kings great enough to make great heirs unlikely. Rossel king? He had not seriously considered the possibility until Robert threw it in his face. Even now he prodded the notion gingerly before discarding it. His England had been created out of Normandy as Robert from Mora's body. One flesh not to be sundered.

For Robin, riding River Epte through autumn rain and winter snow, the question of succession was very much with him. Whatever their opinion of Robert, most Norman lords in England believed in the unity of one crown over both sides of the Channel. The middle rank of Englishmen like Robin, former thanes and landholding freemen, saw security only in a king who stayed at home, with the Channel a natural boundary since time out of mind. To Robin, the logic was clear as a fist in the face. If Robert could not be separated from succession to Normandy, then England must be amputated from the duchy. That he was a penny-a-day pawn on a drawn battle line did not trouble Robin, nor the unreliable and squalid natures of the men around him. As in chess, he was thinking many moves ahead though taken one at a time through the ridiculous situation on Epte, half war and half drunken debauch.

In time, when he was given permission to write home, once a month and in French subject to careful scrutiny by suspicious Rouen clerks, the code prearranged with Mauger told Robin's steward the exact situation. The lengthy letters were addressed to Marian: innocuous, rambling between affection for her and the children and comprehensive instructions to Mauger for the harvest or to Will Scatloch on forest matters, nothing at all in them to be censored before dispatch.

"*L'Anglais* has a feeling for our tongue," William's clerks admitted, "but no grammar or spelling."

These errors were systematically extracted by Mauger and converted via the matrix of his cipher into intelligence transmitted to Ralf Fitz-Gerald and Bishop Osmund.

"OUR BEST INTERESTS SUPPORT PRINCE WILLIAM."

Marian hovered over Mauger as, letter by letter, the message emerged from his love for her and the children.

"WAR WITH PH ONLY—"

"Only what?" Marian fretted. "What's *PH*?"

"Philip," the steward muttered over his task. "France."

"—MATTER OF TIME."

"War where? Where Robin is?"

Mauger didn't know for sure and would not venture a guess that would only worry Marian the more. He was more candid with Ralf Fitz-Gerald.

"Just there, I imagine. Where Robin is."

20

〉〉〉〉〉

SIMON of Crepi's attack of religious zeal had caught Normandy unprepared for France aligned a few dozen yards across River Epte. When William finished cursing Simon, he hastily threw up several timber castles along the river. One of them, near Bois de Gisors, was base for Rossel and his men.

"Dirty Geezers," Robin called the castle: a circular keep on a mound, stockade and bailey buildings much like the one at Hough where Maud had been held, and as filthy. Robin shared a barrack in the bailey with the lower ranking men at arms, rough and ignorant sorts grateful to be raised this high. In the manner of common soldiers anywhere, what rumor didn't tell them of the Franks facing them they pieced out from experience. Robin listened carefully. Philip was quietly building up strength along Epte, but where and how many?

"They will probe here and there," Rossel surmised in dispatches to his father, "and possibly raid. Eventually they will come in force."

The situation clearly called for precise reconnaissance, a weak point with Norman knights. They made deplorable scouts, always readier to challenge and fight than to observe and get back with information. In this regard, William was some few steps ahead of Rossel:

Suggest you employ Denby in this capacity. As an outlaw he learned how to move unobserved as if his life depended on it—which it did. Don't get him killed just yet, as I may have other use for him.

Robin welcomed the duties of scout since they kept him away from Rossel's vavasors, as appalling a collection of brutes as ever donned mail. Rossel himself, disdainful as any knight of evasive tactics, thought his offer of a Flemish warhorse to Robin a magnanimous gesture. He was astonished at the Saxon's refusal and rather put out when Robin laughed at the notion.

"Need something much faster, Prince. This flamin' great ox—"

"Ox!" Rossel might joke about anything else under heaven but not a blooded destrier. "You know the blood lines of what you call an ox?"

"Too damned well, sir. They need fifty yards to get up any kind of speed. We butchered 'em by the dozens at Norwich."

Rossel winced at the sacrilege. "You are an authority on horses?"

"I learned from a man who is. I need small, smart, steady, and *fast*." Because, as he explained, his duty was to see and live to report what he saw. In view of this, a gallant death on a slow horse worked against the prince's need, thank his highness all the same.

Bois de Gisors was part of a ducal manor and a large portion of its livings went to the castle maintenance, including two large stables in the bailey. Robin chose a black Welsh cross-breed mare fifteen hands high. Ralf had praised the strain for its intelligence and endurance over hard country.

"For spirit, a Flemish. For brains and stamina, a good cross-breed." So said Ralf, who knew his stud book as Judith her Bible. "Any horse you must depend on, let it know it can trust you in return. Approach upwind at first, so it learns your scent. Curry and feed it yourself, talk to it, spend as much time with the horse as you can. Be gentle, but firm. Never let a horse learn that it's stronger than you."

Robin courted his mare with a carrot as opening gambit. He decided to name her Hratha for luck. "It means hurry," he whispered in her twitching ear. "It means quick." He rode with the lightest saddle, no more than a cinch for stirrups attached to a broad piece of soft leather with a fleece sewn over it.

The summer of 'eighty-four was deceptively quiet along River Epte. Given his duties and left to his own devices, Robin followed Ralf's advice and spent more time with Hratha than any biped in Gisors, feeling the mare better company. He must know the river feature for feature as well as Sherwood, and on both sides. North of Rossel's keep an ancient timber bridge spanned Epte, Norman sentries on one end, Frank on the other. Robin rode by the prince's sentries every day, learning where Epte was narrowest and most fordable from either side.

Once a week manor serfs plodded into the bailey, leading pack mules laden with fresh supplies. Stoic and resigned as the mules, the peasants never looked up when the castle steward addressed them. They answered in monosyllables and got away quickly as possible. The lot of them looked pathetically undernourished and spiritless to Robin. They were Franks, not Normans, and spoke a different dialect altogether. Rossel's knights considered the difference a point of pride. They themselves were Northmen, descended from Vikings, dominant from the time of the first dragon ships and never beaten.

They've no middle ground, no middle folk like Da and me, Robin reflected. *Just those on top taking it all and those on the bottom having to give it to them without a whisper of complaint.*

With summer came the camp followers for whom Rossel's following was notorious. On foot or in wagons, some favorites riding good horses, they trickled in with the sultry weather and set up more or less permanent housekeeping in the bailey. There were as many young men as women, both used indiscriminately by Rossel and his men.

Rossel hunted the *bois* nearly every day. As often as not, the French garrison crossed the river with huntsmen, beaters, kennelmen, and dogs in full cry and high spirits to make a fraternal day of it. Robin observed them with silent disgust. They'd make life hazardous for the local game, catch a good dinner, and then the lot of them would gorge until dark and drink until they rolled under the table or staggered away with a favorite of the moment under one arm, sometimes two.

Robin quartered with the men at arms, not considered worthy of the high tables and personally content with the disposition. Frank or Norman, these roaring, guzzling knights were all enemies. He wanted none of their company. Rossel was tolerable by himself. William's son had a facility for command, the knack of being at once informal and a little apart from the men he led. Even Eudo de Gernon, commander of Philip's garrison on Epte and arrogant with others, reined himself in with the soldier-prince.

Baron Eudo was of Ralf's age, Robin estimated, and harked back in build to the northern giants who first settled Normandy. Enormously tall and with the bulk to go with it, Eudo took great pride in his ability to vault the back of a warhorse in full armor without touching the stirrups. He took wagers on this feat, always won, then swaggered away to a drinking match with Rossel, which he invariably lost along with a portion of his earlier winnings.

There were even class distinctions among the female whores. Those earmarked for the *noblesse* did not mingle with those used by the men at arms. The whole matter was cheerfully cut-and-dried and a lusty camaraderie existed among the men of Robin's barrack and the worn, profane women who always greeted them with screeches of pleasure and usually stole as much money as they earned.

"Ysabeau, *ma belle*! You mother of all beddable women! Come here, I've missed you."

Ysabeau was a camp regular and durable as a mule. She'd gone through the men of Robin's barrack more often than camp lice, squat and square and apparently indestructible. She had worked through a number of groaning but satisfied soldiers when she came out of the barrack door for a breath of air. In the flickering spill of light from the knights' feast tables across the bailey yard, Ysabeau saw Robin sitting against the barrack wall with a skin of wine.

"Eh, *Anglais*, give us a drink?"

Robin offered her the wineskin as Ysabeau slid down beside him. "Getting rich?"

Ysabeau drank and wiped her thick lips. "Might if you helped."

"Not tonight."

"My, aren't we pure!"

Fastidious rather, though Robin would not hurt Ysabeau's feelings. She was as efficient at her trade as Blidworth reapers going at the wheat, and as indiscriminate. "Not in the vein, dear."

"Think you'll ever get home?"

"I have to believe I will. Someday."

They rested together in the dusk, watching the knights from both sides drink themselves into vomiting oblivion. Ysabeau had a pragmatic attitude toward the whole matter. Days like this were good for profit and she wouldn't have to leg it across Epte to work the French camps, even though they were solvent. Their pay had come through two days past.

"At least they *got* paid," Robin noted enviously. "Someone dipped into mine before it left Rouen, I'm bound. Christ, this is a dishonest country." He offered the last of the wine to Ysabeau who drained it, gargling noisily before swallowing. "Who brought their money, then?"

She didn't know for sure. "Great company of knights."

"How many?"

"Did I count them? A good many. Getting to be a proper city east of here." Ysabeau glanced sideways at the Englishman's bearded profile. "What's it to you?"

"I'm a curious sort."

"Here." She captured his hand and pressed it firmly low into her broad lap. "Get curious about this. Best you ever had."

Robin retrieved his hand. "That would take considerable best, girl."

Ysabeau was hardly offended by the rejection. "Just asking in the way of business. You could be dead tomorrow, so could I. Whatever you're waiting for, the world don't get any better than this."

"God's blood, I hope so."

"*Jamais*. Never in your lifetime. Go to Mass, what does the priest tell you? World don't change, amen." Ysabeau gazed off toward the riotous feast where a clumsy wrestling match had begun between two knights too drunk to stand straight. "And you can see it don't change or get better, so get yours while you can. The prince will. You just watch that shrewd bastard."

Robin rested his head against the wall, wanting to sleep. "You're a dark philosopher, Ysabeau. Don't you want anything beyond this?"

"What is there?" she asked blankly. "My village was burned out twice, one side or the other. Always hungry. Look clear through us, them knights do. On the bottom you get used to looking up, so make some money out of it like me. And always get paid first. Beyond this? The dirty knights took everything beyond this. You're a fool, know that?"

Next morning, the bailey yard looked like the aftermath of a battle and smelled worse. Long after sunrise the bodies strewn around the tables, those too drunk to reach any bed, were still inanimate. As Robin threaded his way through them, a vavasor here or there wheezed and sat up, cursing feebly for someone to fetch them water. A few hardier souls were already walking their horses out the bailey gate. Huge in the saddle and apparently little the worse for the night's debauch, Baron Eudo swigged deeply from a wineskin and threw it to a groom before departing.

The two guards at the door to Rossel's bower looked unraveled themselves, blocking his way with pikes but no energy. "Business?"

"I need to speak to Prince William."

Not at this hour, they told him. Come back later.

"Later? The sun's up and the village church rang Prime half an hour gone. He must be up."

"If he is, he's in no mood to be disturbed. Had a drop too much in last night."

Robin had just turned away in impatience when the door cracked open. Rossel hung onto the lintel for support, still in his nightshirt, tousled and pale. "Denby," he rasped out of a dry throat. "What in hell do you want?"

"Urgent, sir."

Rossel groaned, working a dry tongue over a wine-parched palate, clearly uninterested. He muttered something to someone within the bower and yawned. "Well enough, come in."

The prince's bower was not opulently furnished except for the wide, comfortable bed. His mail hung on a rack, clothes from the night before strewn over the floor. Sitting on one side of the bed, a handsome young man was wriggling into his clothes. Rossel sped him with a negligent shove. "Out. Dress outside."

The prince's entertainment gathered up his belongings quickly. As the fellow sidled past him with a nervous smile, Robin noted the remains of rouge on the pouting lips. Rossel collapsed on his pillows. "Sweet boy."

"Not half."

Rossel squinted wryly up at him. "*Ma foi,* but you look so damned English and disapproving. You and my mother. She warned me primly of the path to hell, then washed her hands of the matter. Hell is maybe, this is now. I'm not going to get rich at Father's rates. If my arm is his, my cock's my own. So—what's so important it can't wait until I feel human?"

"We know Philip is reinforcing Epte all along the river."

Rossel groaned. "Of course he is. That's your news? Get out of here, I'm suffering."

But what they didn't know was how many and where, how deployed. Robin recounted what he'd learned from Ysabeau last night. "She said a great company, sir. Worth a look and a counting."

"Impractical," Rossel considered. "My heralds are escorted to de Gernon with no chance to see anything. They try. We all do."

"They wouldn't suspect a Frank peasant who might wander about before finding the baron."

"*You* pass for a Frankish serf?" Rossel chuckled at the image; the effort did not help his throbbing head. *"C'est drôle."*

"Oh? Watch."

Rossel blinked. Last night's wine might have affected his sight as well as his wits. Suddenly Robin appeared inches shorter, vacant eyes downcast. Servile, gelded of manhood and pride, defeated since birth.

"Great lord, my good master who is the Prince William, asks if the baron and his honored knights would come, if it please them, to hunt again. At their lordship's pleasures, my master asks."

"Ve-ry good. But Father says I'm not to get you killed." Still Rossel was clearheaded enough to see the value if Robin could carry it off. "You would have to see much and remember it all. No, I couldn't send a serf. De Gernon would take it for an insult."

"Why send at all, sir? Why not—oh, a minor cleric from Paris?"

"Um. Doing what?"

"Whatever such witless piddlers do for the Church. Errands, liturgical letters from the Metropolitan, saints'-day schedules."

"Even better. Yes, do it." Rossel began to relish the fun of the prospect. "Father said you were devious. Oh, would I love to put this over on de Gernon. Never liked him much. Yes, a priest. Just pray no one asks a Mass."

No fear. Spying contained an element of creativity. Robin could do a very believable Mass if need be and had passed for a priest before. "A very honest face, my lord."

"You have leave to try." Rossel felt better already, sputtering into his wine cup: "Take the word of God to the god-damned French."

21

▶▶▶▶▶

I F war had to come between William and Philip of France, each
naturally would have preferred time and circumstances to their own
best advantage. Philip would consider it a punitive expedition against
a rebellious vassal. William, if he won, would gain that much more
political leverage in future dealings with his nominal lord.

The conflict began without their permission.

When Robin set out to spy on de Gernon, his interest in the baron
was purely military. It became personal when Robin took the measure
of the man, and mortal when de Gernon found he'd been had. Philip
was diplomatically embarrassed, Rossel embroiled in an undeclared war.
The serfs suffered most, but what of that against the flouted honor of
a French baron?

Robin's reconnaissance required careful preparation. He had to pay
out hard cash for a priest's soutane and more for new parchment and
ink before forging a number of liturgical letters from Paris. He shaved
his beard, Rossel's barber tonsured him authentically, and Father Bernard set out north through the *bois* on Hratha, accompanied by a groom.
At Gisors gate, he saluted Rossel in farewell.

"What's the wineskin for?" the prince wondered. Robin's supply
was far more than ample for an abstemious cleric.

"Bless you, sir. Father Bernard is a good man with a certain weakness. God keep all Christian souls, my lord."

Seven miles upriver, Robin parted company with Hratha and the
groom, forded Epte by night, slept until dawn. With the first grey light,
Father Bernard began his journey.

175

The western Vexin was still heavily forested, not as wild as Sherwood, but as beautiful. Robin removed his hand-me-down sandals and walked barefoot to feel the dark, moist forest earth under his feet.

Through the last days of June and early July, he wandered this way and that, always appearing to have come from the east, apparently lost and more than a little bewildered. He saw squat stone castles now and then, but few knights in residence. Like Baron Eudo, most of them were pavilioned through the woods and meadows, enjoying the good weather on a more or less permanent hunting party.

For vigilance, French pickets were a joke. After eluding Ralf Fitz-Gerald for years, Robin glided like a shadow through one guard station after another, seen only when he wanted to be—

"I am Father Bernard, carrying liturgical letters to . . . could you direct me to . . . ? Ah, yes. Blessings on you and thanks."

Bibulous Bernard shared his wine with any man to give him information and directions, an earnest fool trying to sound better educated and soberer than he was.

"Baron de Gernon, you say? Yes, I would see his lordship. Is it safe to cross Epte? Will the Normans give safe conduct to a man of God? South? Pardon, I thought you said west. Blessings. . . . "

When Father Bernard finally reached Baron Eudo's summer quarters, the hem of his robe grimy and unraveling, one sandal strap sundered and flapping about a grimy ankle, the French knights were quite used to the sight of him. Some casual word had already been passed of him to Eudo's camp, which was almost in sight of River Epte. No, he could *not* see the baron just yet, the baron was not awake. The footsore priest would have to wait. No, they could not tell him where the nearest church was. Not much of a priest, they judged. Someone's errand runner from Paris. The Church was full of them nowadays, but the fool knew good wine and shared it liberally.

The bumbling, harmless priest sagged down against a tree to wait and doze in the afternoon heat, only a few yards from Baron Eudo's red-and-yellow-striped pavilion. Behind his closed eyes, Robin concentrated fiercely, laboring memory to fix the numbers and locations of men and war engines noted up until now.

A sound intruded on his calculation, a short, high-pitched cry like a child in pain. Then a deep animal grunt. Robin closed his eyes again. With any luck, he'd be at Gisors by evening. Just to be sure . . . one more time through his numbers and notes. Again he conjured his mental map, dotting it here and there with men, horses, and engines. Tightly focused on his effort, he became aware of a soft but persistent whimpering from the baron's tent. The pathetic sounds died away; a few minutes later, a small figure ejected suddenly from the tent as if roughly propelled from behind.

A little boy, perhaps nine years old, a serf's child from his ragged clothes and the grime on his feet and spindly shins. The boy fumbled dazedly at the ragged drawers under his shapeless smock. He wiped at the tears of numb injury with a dirty hand, yet kept his head down among these superior brutes in iron, sidling away as unobtrusively as possible, fearful that one of them might harm him further.

Robin felt faintly sick. As far a cry as this miserable boy was from his own Edward, the images merged with a stomach-turning swiftness and would not separate.

At least Rossel's playmates are whores by choice, like Ysabeau. This is a—Jesus, give him a chance and he could be Edward. So he goes home, one more loss laid on all the others since he was born, aware of life with his first breath and of defeat with the second. There's that you don't take from a boy and expect him to stand up ever. You, de Gernon. You should be thrown on your knees before Judgment with no mark of honor about you to argue against hell.

The huge man in a soiled nightshirt pushed the tent flap aside and stood stretching and yawning in dappled sunlight. He flexed thick shoulders and slapped his belly like a contented animal with its appetite and thirst slaked for the time. Eudo did not notice the shabby priest awaiting his convenience, which was for the best; he might have caught the gleam of something predatory as himself before it hid behind the shy, deferential priest laboring clumsily to his feet. "Good my lord—"

"Comment?" Eudo stared impatiently at the scarecrow cleric. "Where in God's jakes did you come from?"

"Father Bernard from Paris, *mon seigneur*. I carry schedules for the observance of—"

Poor, stammering Father Bernard got no further. He ceased to exist for Eudo, who lurched away to relieve himself against a convenient bush. "De Cours! See what this fool wants. Damned flies are bad enough, now it's priests."

Between Rossel and his castellan, the vicomte d'Alençon, Robin bent over the detailed map just drawn on new parchment. "Here, thirty-five vavasors with squires. Here, the bulk of their heavy equipment. Five catapults, two siege towers, fifteen knights, perhaps twenty sappers. The rest laborers, and a rare rank lot they are.''

The prince and d'Alençon were impressed by the thoroughness of the report—but siege towers? How was de Gernon going to get them across Epte with any dispatch?

''Impossible,'' the castellan asserted. ''We'll destroy all bridges at the first sign of their advance.''

''Float 'em across. They're not assembled,'' Robin said. ''They'll bring them in sections as King William took castles across the Channel. Now here: A good way back in the *bois* there are two large camps of knights, perhaps two hundred in each. Places stink. Crawling with flies. They'll be down with water sickness, some of them.''

A good many, by virtue of Robin's forethought. Whenever he had found a dead bird or squirrel on his journey, he'd saved it to throw into streams and wells from which the French drew their water. The tactic had devastated whole Norman squadrons at Dover in 'sixty-six.

Robin's finger came down decisively. ''And here, another seventy knights with the *honorable* baron.''

Both Normans heard the contempt. The castellan d'Alençon inquired, ''You have some quarrel with the baron? Some difference?''

''No quarrel, my lord,'' Robin replied, ''but a vast difference.''

Rossel dismissed the castellan, but detained Robin, quizzical humor flickering about his lips. ''What happened with the baron?''

''Nothing really.''

''Oh?'' Rossel remembered de Gernon's proclivities. ''Don't tell me. A young boy.''

Robin rolled up the map, keeping his eyes averted. ''Yes.''

''Very young, no?''

''A child.''

''Eudo likes them so,'' Rossel shrugged, as if that explained and dismissed the subject. ''Shouldn't wonder, his wife's an absolute cow.'' He took the map from Robin. ''Well done, Denby. By the by, it appears that little shit in the Rouen Chancery was indeed stinting your pay. Father has already found another post for him, something modest enough to remove temptation from his path. That's all.''

The prince dismissed Robin as he did all subordinates, pleasantly enough, but definite. He valued men in direct proportion to his need for them. As yet, he neither liked nor disliked the Saxon beyond a growing respect for his eclectic abilities. Interesting man and valuable— but, as the king said, quite unable to accept the nature of the real world.

"Anglais."

Robin paused in the doorway. "Sir?"

"Have you read the Greeks?"

"A little."

"My brother Henry got the lion's share of learning, though I'm not entirely uninformed. The young students of Greek masters were expected to take care of all their tutor's wants—which now and then included shaking the dew off the master's lily. It's all in the point of view."

Robin looked out into the darkening bailey yard. "He's scum."

"Eudo? He'd be wounded to hear you say so." Rossel laughed, a short, explosive bark of healthy mirth. "Name of Lucca, but I love the English expression of moral outrage, that tight-lipped look that usually means another stiff note to God."

"There are some things—"

"Many things. Leave it, Robin." Rossel put a firm period to the matter. "You've nastied their wells, which will give them all the runs for a week. Enough. There are few pure men in the world, but many de Gernons. He takes the world as he finds it, so do I. If you want to survive, *mon vieux,* so will you. When you live on a garbage heap, it's foolish to wear white."

"A demain, seigneur." The door closed. Rossel remained by the table, humming softly. He unrolled the map with its neat markings and numbers. De Gernon outnumbered him three to one; he must have immediate reinforcements for Gisors and the other Epte defenses.

Before the French came in force, there would be more knightly visiting back and forth. Rossel smiled at the thought. Of all William's children, he had the keenest eye for the gap between ideal and actual. Within the purposes of kings, he and Eudo played a ridiculous game of their own. The baron had been a bore of late, overbearing and smug, and why not? He could take Gisors and Rossel himself any time for a considerable profit in ransoms.

Rossel's smile broadened to a grin, then a deep, gut-satisfying chuckle. Denby disapproved of the baron. One had never heard the word *honorable* wrung through so much grime in mere inflection. That would be only prologue to the joke Rossel had in mind. His own jest would rise like cream from milk, thick and rich when he removed the cloth, savored its excellence, then threw it in de Gernon's face. But at the right time, the perfect moment. Beautiful.

Rossel began his tuneless humming again, quite pleased with himself.

22

ROSSEL's reinforcements clattered into Gisors shortly after Lammas in August amid enough uproar to wake the dead. No need for Eudo to spy; he needed only someone to sit on the river bank and count. For his part, Rossel affected a hail-fellow ignorance of Eudo's augmented forces when they parleyed at the near bridge. Beside himself, only Robin and d'Alençon knew of the Frank superiority in any case, which Rossel judged wise for the time being. Sooner or later Eudo would come in force. The king's high-spirited son preferred sooner, while the good weather held, but sober instructions from Rouen counseled otherwise.

William had crossed to England and worn his crown at Winchester during Pentecost, mainly to review available taxes against the Danish threat. Flanders was now openly in league with King Cnut Sweinson, who would almost certainly revive his claim to the English throne. A large force must be raised in defense.

Philip is not our greatest danger just now. Since all is quiet on Epte, I would have you keep matters thus. At the moment, we pull our wagon with a half-broken lead horse. I sent to Robert for a pledge of unity and aid in the event of a Dane-Flemish attack. Your brother sent answer with a price attached. No aid from Maine unless he is crowned duke in Normandy now, and guaranteed England on my death.

Looking all his life to his father and not the crown he wore, Rossel kept the letter and his feelings secret. Beyond the political danger, was Robert so blind that he could not measure their father's pain?

—only a little after his mother's last wish that he hold loyal. You were there, you heard. She begged him.

Begging, yes, but holding her dear Robert like a last delight while I was merely summoned, allowed to kiss her cheek and sent away. You have your pain, Father. I have my own.

The long-smoldering resentment in Rossel was only the other side of natural love from a son who loved instinctively. If he sometimes drank himself to stupor or rutted to exhaustion, let not his mother's frowning shade condemn it for sin. Let not Denby think he was the only one able to feel for a brutalized boy. Rossel remembered subtler cruelties. Children reached out; if one hand was denied them, they grabbed at what was offered.

Meanwhile, Robin rode swift little Hratha through the last of summer along the tranquil Epte, reporting nothing unusual. He would never accustom himself to the Norman-Frank notion of nobility. Vacuously stupid men, most of them, who drank together and occasionally wept over certain sentiments held in common, and just as ready next day to kill or ruin one another in ransoms. Civilized England could no more absorb this madness than Robin would take lepers into Denby hall; yet this crucible of violent absurdities had produced Ralf Fitz-Gerald and the monolithic William.

So much for an outlander's viewpoint. Neither at Norwich nor here had Robin sampled more than the *vin ordinaire* of absurdity. Presently he would taste the very soul of the vine. These men on both sides of Epte were not the disciplined Fitz-Geralds, Osmunds, or de Coutances. Bred of the same system, the bachelor-knights under Rossel and de Gernon were their own mixture of pride and ignorance. Thought was not only unfashionable but foreign to them. They were still no more than a fellowship of rough horsemen. For excitement and profit, the battle meant more to them than its motives; personal honor, more than anything; a noble horse more than a noble cause. Even Rossel in his playful malice could be stung beyond caution in the loss of a lavishly expensive warhorse.

On August 15, the Feast of the Assumption, Baron Eudo rumbled across the Epte bridge with an escort of fifty magnificently mounted knights, squires, and a train of grooms. The feast day would commence with a short Mass (to Rossel's taste, the briefer the better), followed by a grand melee with blunted weapons and token ransoms only large enough to make the contest interesting. The mock combat took place with considerable noise and enthusiasm in a meadow outside the bailey. The French vavasors were less aggressive than usual, recently afflicted with a sudden and widespread attack of water sickness.

Rossel clucked solicitously. *"Quel dommage."*

"It was mischief," Eudo swore darkly. "Our wells were poisoned."

Indeed, he looked a bit wan to sympathetic Rossel. "Clearly mischief. I hope you don't think that I or any of *my* men—but to horse, Baron. One more pass and then to feast."

Sick or not, Eudo unhorsed Rossel in the last engagement of the day. A splendid pass. Both of them had disengaged from the general melee, recognized each other, and spurred forward, blunted lances couched. Rossel was hit cleanly and flew out of the saddle, landing with a bone-rattling crash. Eudo leapt from his horse, exultant. "Yield and ransom, son of William!"

As his squire helped him rise, Rossel felt gingerly for what might actually be broken out of everything that felt that way. "I yield, knight," he wheezed reluctantly. "Ransom is yours."

Ransoms that day were half in jest and wholly in earnest. Most bachelor knights were impecunious younger sons, and ransom was a considerable part of their income. Still in all—Rossel complained through his teeth as linament was rubbed into his bruises—Dancer went beyond the bounds of sporting ransom. He had ridden Dancer that day, a grey Flemish raised, saddle-broken, trained, and pampered at his own hand. Dam and sire, he could cite the stallion's lineage on both sides for four generations back.

"But I love that horse; we are practically related," he pleaded with Eudo. "Any other destrier in my stable. Any two, but not Dancer."

The baron insisted. Dancer it was. Rossel held out, enlarging his offer. Any three blooded mounts. The deadlock swept the feast tables that evening. A mock-serious court of honor ruled Prince William had to pay in good faith, which decision the vanquished accepted with outward grace and inward grudge.

If Rossel knew how to lose, Eudo demonstrated little of how to win. Behind this ostensibly friendly joust, both sides were flexing their might toward more lethal contests. Cup by cup of wine, Baron Eudo crowed his victory and the ransom to death. Their tilt was uproariously recounted, the unseating of the prince couched in terms usually reserved for the deeds of Roland or his ilk. Rossel's good-natured grin grew more forced with each of Eudo's sallies.

The feast wound down from exuberance to the mood of tired but still devilish children. The sun was low in the sky when Eudo leaned over Rossel and said, "Let them bring my ransom from the stable. His blood is as fierce as my own. He will welcome a new seat."

More than half drunk, the burly baron did not notice Rossel's fleeting change of expression, which a more perceptive man would have read: enough is enough. Rossel called to his own grooms, "Bring my Dancer. Baron has won what he has won, and who am I to argue with honor? You, d'Alençon, send one for those trifles in the case on my bower table. And for Denby."

Dancer was being groom-led about the space between the admiring tables of vavasors, when a man at arms laid a cylindrical leather case before Rossel's trencher. The sun was down now and smoky torches lit to discourage the flies buzzing about the tables. Eudo took Dancer's bridle and paraded him before his men, halting finally in front of Rossel. "A beauty, Prince. I quit you of debt."

"That is large of you." Rossel rose, the case resting jauntily on one shoulder. "Now for *my* ransom."

The laughter about the tables faltered and petered out expectantly. Rossel was known for the sting in his jokes; right now he looked more like a man who'd won than lost.

"*Adieu, mon Dancer.* The baron has won fairly and lost what he's lost, unseated himself by the lance of a sharper wit. Regard, Baron: your detailed dispositions on Epte. Where camped, in what number, how armed and with what engines of war. This copy goes with the horse." With a ceremonial flourish, Rossel displayed the map to all before presenting it to Baron Eudo. *"Pour souvenir."*

Low appreciative whistles from Rossel's men, surprised as the French. Not strictly honorable perhaps, but a fine joke that clearly took the wind out of de Gernon's puffed-up sail this night.

Baron Eudo lost no more gracefully than he won. He stared at grinning, impudent Rossel, then around at his own men as the heat of mortification rose and throbbed about his ears. "This is no joke. This was not honorably done."

"Oh, come," Rossel scoffed. "You've counted our noses every time you crossed that bridge. Didn't want you to think we were napping."

Eudo flung the map to the ground and spat on it. "You laugh, any of you?" he challenged all. "Who dares laugh? This was not done in honor."

"Say rather in marvelous common sense," Rossel replied aimiably. "Ah, Denby. There you are."

Robin stepped reluctantly from dusk into torchlight. The prince clapped a proprietary hand on his shoulder. "Fair trade, Eudo. You've made a horse in ransom. My man's made an ass of you. Father Bernard, *à vôtre service.*"

Good God, Rossel, why don't you belt up? Robin cursed savagely. What they'd learned was worth a hundred horses. Why tell the Franks?

Eudo glared at him in murderous recognition, too drunk for caution and much needing to save some dignity. Robin could not erase the memory of the peasant boy. He tried to put aside the cold, vindictive rage for a meeter moment when he could cheerfully kill this animal who prated of honor but had none. He met Eudo's glare eye for eye, unable to mask the contempt.

"Your servant is impertinent," the baron said at length. "A serf bows his head before me."

Robin kept a tight rein on his feelings, but he spoke to be heard by all. "I am not a serf, Baron. I'll bow my head when you take it off my shoulders."

"What? Tell me," Eudo appealed to Rossel. "What is he, simple?"

"No, just English. And much valued by my father," Rossel added to forestall violence.

That was William's care, not Eudo's. He reacted as he would toward any inferior turned insubordinate. He scooped up a clay wine cup and hurled it at Robin's head. The movement was vicious and swift; Robin had bare time to duck before the missile caught him a glancing blow at his hairline. In a flash of exploding color, Robin staggered, shaking his head to clear it. As Eudo bore down on him, Robin's dagger was out and slashing. Eudo stopped with a grunt of surprise, looking down at his middle. He was not wounded, but the blade had parted the linen of his tunic.

Robin crouched, ready to cut again. "Aye, come on. You are without honor, de Gernon. You touch me and I'll gut you like a chicken."

Unbelievable. When men found their voices, the sound turned ominous as the circle of them tightened around Eudo, Rossel, and Robin. Even Rossel's men considered the insult tantamount to *lèse-majesté.* Some mentioned a rope, others flaying.

Eudo mastered himself with some effort. "Prince, neither your royal father nor yourself will object to my flogging some respect into this peasant. Bring me a whip."

Rossel shifted uncomfortably with the aspect of a man whose joke had turned against him. "Well. Now. A moment."

"You *saw*!"

"Eudo, come. We hold a friendly feast. Denby is not so important. You are larger than this."

Eudo threatened in a low voice. "I could make this quarrel larger. I want this serf punished. Will you do it, or shall I?"

Rossel quickly read the faces around him—and Robin devined his conclusion. Punishment would be the cheaper way out. The prince spread his hands in something close to personal apology. "Denby, perhaps—"

"Don't trouble yourself, my lord. I will satisfy the baron. I have the right to meet him in arms."

"Right?" One of the French knights brayed mockingly. *"Right?"*

Others took up the joke on both sides. This was turning out a rare evening. First the Norman prince's horse, then his embarrassing map, now the incredible *Anglais*. Grand sport; there was wine aplenty yet to drink and there might even be a little blood.

"I have the right," Robin repeated patiently. "I will satisfy the baron. He will satisfy me. I was born to a thane's holding—what you call an 'honor' or title. If the baron overbears me in that, it is not by much."

"This country fool is mad," Eudo decided. "Bring a whip, I say."

"Not mad," Rossel verified. "His family holds his land from the vicomte of Nottingham, so I hear."

"You mean, I must trouble to meet this little dog of yours on equal terms?"

"If he speaks truly," Rossel answered neutrally. "Why not forget the whole thing? Denby, get out of here."

"No." Eudo didn't budge.

"Baron, you embarrass me."

"Over a serf? Prince, do you wish this to be a quarrel between us, then?"

"No." This time it was Robin, intractable as Eudo. "I want to meet you."

"Mes seigneurs!" A young Norman wag leaped onto a table, waving a torch snatched from a groom. "Court of honor! We must reconvene. Surely, our Englishman deserves the justice we accord a good horse— or almost."

Among the half-drunken knights, the notion was fire in tinder. They insisted; the cry went through their company. Court of honor! Even

Baron Eudo caught the spirit, holding up one hand.

"Whom am I to stand in the way of honor? If he is worthy, I will kill him; if not, I will have him flogged."

The matter seemed to have been resolved, though Rossel was far from happy. "A moment, friends. This is serious matter. Choose your court."

He led Robin aside from the crowd. In the deepening dusk, he wiped a trickle of blood from Robin's forehead. "Denby—*hélas*, every now and again, I out-clever myself. Eudo might well start his own war now. He has the men and he's stupid enough."

"Let it be arms. He doesn't exceed me by birth."

"The court will decide."

"What's a court of honor? What's it to decide?"

Three knights from either side would scrutinize Robin's claim to be worthy of single combat in arms. "Eudo will urge their diligence. He'd love to kill you. You have some connection of whom they may inquire? Vicomte Fitz-Gerald?"

"Yes. He is married to my maternal cousin. She," Robin emphasized, "has blood tie to the old House of England."

"Truly?" In the gloom, an insect buzzed between them. Rossel batted at it absently. "All right, but if they rule against you, one hopes you can stand a thorough flogging. I have a certain affection for you, Denby. And a respect for your common sense until now. Clearly, it is unreliable."

"Oh? My lord is the one who spread the map like a bloody flag."

"Well, yes—"

Robin did a very creditable imitation of Rossel. " 'He's made an ass out of you.' With all respect, Prince, you've an odd sense of occasion."

"Guilty as charged. But I live in a world that refuses to laugh."

"Eudo owes," Robin maintained stubbornly.

"Owes what, for God's sake?"

"He owes. What my folk call *wergild*. The price of injury to someone. He owes."

"Name of a—" What he did not understand, Rossel decided not to delve. He vented his staccato bark of a laugh. "Speak of asses, I don't know who's the purer—you, me or the *foutredieu* baron."

He lifted his arms and let them slap heavily against his thighs in resignation. "So be it. Court of honor."

23

THE current of Rossel's mind was not deep but swift. In the furor over the challenge, he quickly saw trouble and advantage alike. Trouble, if his father heard of it; advantage, in that while the court of honor was occupied with Robin's claims, conditions on Epte were quiet, giving him the time to further strengthen the defenses on Epte.

D'Alençon headed the Norman half of the court and sent an ill-spelled letter to Vicomte Fitz-Gerald requesting certain information from his lady. Judith was irritated and not a little confused.

"What do they mean—*is* he my cousin, *was* he a thane, and what is a thane?"

Robin in trouble again. Ralf mused ruefully over the letter. What now? "There's been a personal challenge *outrance*. To the death. Matters of lineage are vital in such cases. They need to know your degree of consanguinity with the old royal house."

"Aunt may have to refresh me there. A challenge?"

"Robin and some French baron." Ralf handed her the letter. "I think you should answer this privately."

Judith quite understood. "Yes. No need to trouble Marian with this now."

They kept the concern to themselves. Judith made detailed reply to d'Alençon. Her letter clarified little for Normans or Franks, since there was no Continental equivalent to a thane. A thane might rank equally with a baron, depending on the derivation of his title and how much land he held.

"Roughly a baron—*bien,* more or less," d'Alençon translated for his court.

But of knightly rank? No, that had been something called a *carl* in England—no longer, of course—and a crown thane, which Denby appeared to have been before his outlawry, had precedence over a carl. The court debated as they would over the bloodlines of a well-bred horse, trying to untangle the Gordian knot of ancient English custom. Judith's lineage *seemed* to validate Denby's claim, if one wished to trace back nigh a hundred years to a cousin of Aelfgifu, queen to Ethelred II. This cousin sired the obscure younger-son carl who was Denby's maternal great-grandfather. Well enough, though the court would be remiss if the paternal line were not searched. Denby's grandfather Brihtnoth had been a carl raised to thane by Canute, but his beginnings were quite common, being sired by a "sokeman" farmer.

Denby must clarify: What was a sokeman? His answer, verified by Judith and simple enough, told the court nothing explicable. A sokeman was an untitled landowner who owed specific duties (or perhaps not) to a lord or king, payable in cash or service. *Now* did they understand?

Oh, enough, enough! Baron Eudo was growing impatient with this absurdity. The court threw up its collective hands and allowed Denby could be slain in knightly honor.

September chilled and dampened toward the rains of French autumn. A herald crossed the bridge with Eudo's standard bearer and cried entrance to Gisors bailey. Standing with Rossel, Robin heard the challenge. The gauntlet was flung, he retrieved it. The time: the next morning on the west bank of Epte by the bridge. So they be honorable, Eudo negligently deferred choice of weapons to the Englishman.

"Choose shrewdly," Rossel advised. "Eudo is a bull."

"Thought about that." Robin sniffed at the air with a farmer's nose—and returned his choice to the baron: armor and broadswords without shields. There would be rain; rain meant mud. Possibly the bull would not be so sure-footed. Ralf had taught Robin that the balanced foot was all-important to swordplay.

"As important as your arm and blade. It is a dance, Robin, every move balanced and planned."

Robin honed his dagger toward its part, recalling the painful, sweat-drenched lessons under the best swordsman in the Midlands.

"Every stroke implies a counterstroke. Don't think one move, plan three. *Hé la!* So. One-two. One-two-three. *Don't* let your eyes or body tell me what you're going to do. Flow like water, like light over a smooth surface."

Over and over until Robin's shoulders and arms were agony.

"Forget that. The sword is not heavy, it's a feather in your hand. If he attacks high, if he leads you high in parry—see? I caught you low. And always attack. Defense is only preparation for attack. *Go* for the man, but cold. Cold you think, angry you don't. Be ice, Robin."

There would be no anger, no feeling at all. He learned that winning the golden arrow at Grantham. Nothing existed but the true line drawing his shaft to the center of the clout.

Now his dagger bore a razor edge. Robin wiped it clean, sliding it home in the scabbard. The sky was gravid with coming rain; he felt it in the old scar on his belly, the one Ralf gave him long ago. They were enemies then, but Denby still survived. The hall stood, crops and children grew. Somehow in the cosmos men thought unchanging, something moved forward in the long game.

Thoughts of home came flooding back. Did they get the hay in before rain? They'd be sowing rye now, Mauger preparing to collect the Saint Michael's Day quarterly rents, Father Beorn announcing at Mass which barn would be used for tithing to the church. Everyone would meet there, part work, part celebration. Gossip would pass and perhaps a few troths plighted, and Beorn would say out the banns for the new young couples. Marian would be there. . . .

Under dark September overcast, Robin closed his eyes and conjured mellow sunlight and Marian gold in the soft glow. *Moira is two now. God be thanked for sparing her to us. Edward's twelve by my reckon, all legs like me, part of the forest and the bargain oak. God, I want to hold them all in my arms. And leave them what, then? Damn all you foreigners—aye, and you, Rossel.*

He looked on Norman and French knights with indiscriminate hatred. What difference between them? Like mistletoe on the oak, supposed to be magical, touched by heaven, so Angharad said, but only parasite after all and death to the tree it battened on.

Rossel was at some pains to find a knight tall enough for his second-best mail to fit Robin. The knight chosen put the mail coif, shirt, and drawers and the scale armor surcoat in Robin's arms with the air of one bringing funeral gifts to a bier. He departed shaking his head. Rossel loaned Robin a well-balanced sword with a wide hilt, once the pride of a Danish pirate who died raiding at Calais. There were runes etched into the blade. Rossel couldn't read them.

"Some old charm, damned if I know."

"It's a prayer to Odin. Well enough." Robin scraped a thumb along the keen edge. The runes were meeter now than any prayer to Christ. He would appeal to God when the time came, but Woden would judge between him and Eudo de Gernon.

The morning dawned dark with overcast and a mist that resolved to thin drizzle by the time Eudo rode across the bridge with his cordon of knights. Two hundred men on each side faced one another in two ragged crescents as the combatants met between them. The dampness was already seeping through Robin's mail to the padded tunic beneath. His coif and helmet felt awkward. He hadn't counted on the weight factor; with armor and sword, he weighed a good stone and a half more.

They met on a grassy space along Epte bank. Since the proceedings were directed by the court of honor, Rossel acted as Robin's squire, Sire Guy de Cours for Baron Eudo. The Vicomte d'Alençon mediated, barking out the ritual questions.

"For what purpose do you come here?"

"Personal affront not to be borne," Eudo stated.

Robin replied in a flat voice. "The baron has said."

Gradually the crowd of knights tightened about the ring of spears as men shifted this way or that for a better view, turning up the hoods of their cloaks against the rain.

Leaning on his sword, d'Alençon addressed the mortal enemies. "I am constrained to ask if any honorable conciliation is possible."

Eudo grinned coldly at the Englishman, who gazed sleepily back at him. "None."

A silence. D'Alençon prompted Robin. "Denby?"

"None."

"Then may God defend the right."

The combatants drew apart with their squires. Robin took the sword from Rossel, knelt, and kissed the hilt. "Christ be my arm today."

"Oh . . . amen," Rossel remembered himself, down on one knee beside him. "I rubbed dirt and honey on the grip. Won't turn in your hand."

Robin plucked up a handful of grass, put it to his lips, and let it fall. "From dust I come and to this dust I return until Your trumpet."

"Robin, listen. We've not much time."

"I'm yet at prayer." An older prayer this time. *Woden, I call on you as well. By my father's place among the honored companions in your hall, find me worthy and guide my sword.*

190

"This is no time to let your mind wander," Rossel worried. The Englishman seemed unaccountably absent. His eyes lifted drowsily to his waiting opponent; he did not break that gaze again.

"The archer's way, Rossel. The target is part of my weapon, part of me."

"Glad to hear it. I thought you were dozing off." Rossel threw an apprehensive glance at Baron Eudo, stanced and flexing the sword in both hands. "He's got the weight and reach. Use distance, don't close."

"Let be. Just keep the Franks off me when he's dead." Robin rose and stalked away toward de Gernon.

Rossel stared after him. "When *he's* dead?"

Crouched, circling at guard, Eudo had no fear of his adversary, but frustration rapidly darkening to fury. Each time he moved in, Denby gave ground, moving with precise dancer's steps. Overhand, left side, right side; if Eudo tried a triple pass, the other sword flicked out like a snake's tongue in a fourth counterstroke. Panting, Eudo roared his contempt. "*Lâche, tu es un lâche!* Coward, why do you run from me?"— as Denby's blade flicked out.

Caught off guard, Eudo gave ground. Only a lifetime of experience saved him as Denby's sword whirled like a scythe in the hands of a demented reaper. Eudo parried blow for blow, then opened out in his own attack, slashing low at Denby's thigh, feeling the other's parry meet his blade but an instant too late, the hard denial of iron, but the bite through mail and softer flesh. He'd hit the Saxon, shock and pain leeching color from the man's face. Only a matter of moments now. Eudo had never doubted the outcome.

"Now, *Anglais,*" he panted. "Your dance is done."

Slow—just a mite slow, and now Robin was bleeding like a hog at Martinmas. He'd worn the bigger man down, but there was no more time, his left leg already stiffening under him, his own breath harsh with exertion. Had to be now. Robin knew the deception in the series of overhead attacks that should carry Eudo's blade too high above his huge body. After Ralf's obsession with square parries, Robin could see the lack of precision in de Gernon's slant responses that took an instant to recover leverage. *Attack. One-two-three-four. Five count now, sit in the middle of your balance. Remember how Ralf did it. And now.*

Robin's overhand chop was the merest feint, caroming off Eudo's high parry. He lunged with the last power of his wounded left leg, kicking far out with the right, his whole body swooping low in the lateral swing, as if he were sinking an ax into oak. The blade went home.

Eudo stumbled sideways with a gasp of expelled air, already dying.

Again. Ralf's voice lashed across the last of Robin's will. *Again*— as he sliced through shoulder and collar bone. The bigger man went down on his knees, then fell on his side.

The last thing Eudo de Gernon saw was Robin bending close over him. The man's eyes, expressionless while they fought, were now madness carved from ice.

"Still with us?" the voice spoke to him. "This is for the boy. You remember the boy?"

What Rossel looked on sickly, only a few of his kind had heard rumored, none witnessed. And the sound, a bone-chilling wail that rose as the Saxon thrust out his hairy prize to the grey northern sky.

"Woden! Deny him!"

24

▶▶▶▶▶

THE steady downpours of autumn had not yet set in. On the first
clear day following the combat, the French cavalry, howling for
Eudo's vengeance, thundered across the bridge or forded the shallows, laying waste to much of the royal manor, circling Gisors' walls
with insults and challenges. Savagery was their grievance. For *l'Anglais*
to kill their baron in honorable combat was one thing, to mutilate him
like a berserker quite beyond tolerance. No casualties resulted except
serfs luckless enough to be in the way, and only the incomprehensible
Englishman took note of those.

"These are raids, not a declared war," Rossel reported to his father.
"I have the situation in hand. Truly, Father, it puts spirit into my
vavasors and gives them work to their liking." He reluctantly reported
the cause while swearing to his sire on a clutch of saints that the personal
quarrel had been foisted on Denby, who had no choice.

Unsubtle but diplomatically shrewd, King William salvaged as much
as he could from the affair, dispatching his most experienced nuncios
to Paris, older men who chilled their courtesy and cut it to the measure
of their lord's outrage over violated boundaries.

"Unknightly! Recreant and un-Christian. So says our king and your
most loyal duke in Normandy."

Philip of France, born in the same year as Count Robert, was far
older in craft. Let the nuncios return to William and say that he was
shocked but innocent of any aggression against his vassal toward whom
he nurtured only amicable intentions. That these raids, as Philip understood, were personal matters between men of breeding and spirit. He

193

could not oversee every motive at every moment, though a cautionary proclamation of restraint would reach Epte the next day. The order was drafted in the nuncios' presence and a copy made for William. The copy sent to Epte contained different instructions: fewer raids but let them count. Find where Prince William was weakest.

Political chess moves—while the scout Robin survived because Hratha could gallop faster through sucking mud and pelting rain than lumbering war horses could pursue. Not always; more than once through the first raids, Hratha reached the gates of Gisors bailey mere seconds out of spear range, Robin crying, *Ouvrez!* and praying they could open in time—or fighting at Rossel's side on the parapet as the joyously profane prince, roaring a doxhouse tune, loosed crossbolts at the attackers below, reeling as the answering bolt grazed his shoulder. Robin caught him before he fell. Rossel hunched against the parapet timbers, cursing low and passionately as Robin staunched the flesh wound.

"You couldn't just do for de Gernon," the prince grated through his teeth as more bolts whined over the parapet. "Matter of honor, neat and tidy. No-o, *you* had to have his scalp as well. Ow! Easy there. This is all fun, but it's getting to be a bit much. You're utterly mad."

"This is mad," Robin muttered, working at the wound. Was, is, always will be."

Rossel pushed him away. "Leave off, I'm not that hurt. Lunatic."

Robin snatched up the prince's crossbow and quiver of bolts, winding the weapon and setting a shaft. "Lunatic if you will, and with a mad sight. Look! Look where Woden's war maidens ride through the sky to choose among the brave dead and the bloody stupid! Tell you flat, my lord, you can't cull one from the other."

Robin stood erect, bow jammed into his shoulder, leading his target, loosing. Rossel staggered up, calling for another bow. And this undeclared hell would grind on and on before Philip crossed Epte in a formal war.

25

KING William's eye was now on England rather than France. Against the threatened Danish invasion, vast areas of the eastern coast were burned bare while the country bulged and strained with the thousands of Norman and Breton mercenaries battened on it. To pay for them, a staggering war tax of seventy-two pence per hide of land was levied throughout the country. Norman lord and Saxon churl alike felt the burden of this beside the problem of the lawless foreign troops. Ralf Fitz-Gerald relieved some of Denby's tax and distributed mercenaries in and around Nottingham with strict orders to their officers to maintain discipline. When they ignored the warning, Winchester and William himself grew weary of Fitz-Gerald's pointed reports of justice dealt.

For theft from Papplewick church, the following have been hanged . . . for rape and looting within the honors of Osmund, bishop of Nottingham, these . . .

Ralf kept the mercenaries well away from northern Sherwood. Will Scatloch and Morgan of Powys patrolled constantly with Ralf's own parkers, young Edward often making a third now. Gallows trees at crossroads bore constant fruit. Robin's son paled at his first sight of a hanged man, but Morgan found it edifying. "There's lovely," he purred, leaning on his bowstave and gazing up at the late felon.

"You are a black-minded man," Will Scatloch muttered with his arm about Edward's trembling shoulders. "No, boy-bach, it is not pretty, but your father would do the same and so will you on a day that will come.''

Turning away from the blackened face and swollen, protruding tongue, Edward already knew that for truth. Property was sacred. The law said so, and law was law, no mind who broke or bent it, even unto the king, and Edward's father had damned well written as much.

For all that, William went his grim, heedless way. Through the spring and summer following Robin's banishment, king's men were everywhere in Sherwood, marking out huge tracts to be enclosed for royal hunting, and nowt Uncle Ralf could do about that. Through prayer to Saint Dunstan and Ralf's industry, Blidworth was spared, but many small villages and forest dens were emptied of folk and razed to let the wildwood grow over them, while the displaced folk wandered the roads.

Crops and livestock were good that year, Denby secure from the knife-edged famine of two years before when hall and village alike lived on thin soup and barley gruel, and hungry wolves prowled close to doorways. This year at Michaelmas tithing in Denby's barn, when so much was laid aside for old Father Beorn and his church, Marian and Mauger sadly watched the homeless trail in, their faces heavy with last hopes. None of them had ever farmed as much as a hide. Most worked strips in the open fields, some bordars had eked out their living on the holdings of others. But all showed the mute, baffled rage of folk torn from the only place and life they knew—heads shawled, soles flapping loose on wornout shoes or no shoes at all, children barefoot and grime-black to the scabby knees.

"It is for Lady Marian to say how many of you may stay, but the rest must go," Mauger told them. "You that depart, we will spare you what we can, but you will steal naught on pain of death.''

Then Marian, grave beneath her mended best linen veil told them, "We can take five families of those with small children. God knowing our own need, the rest must seek elsewhere.''

In the end, she let seven families stay, including two elderly couples she hadn't the heart to refuse. Edward stood with his mother and Father Beorn at the door of Blidworth church, distributing more alms than Denby could afford.

"It must be done," Marian told her son. "Foreign lords are one thing, but the folk are our own blood.'' She would be deeply shamed if Robin somehow came home to hear she'd turned away one more soul than needed.

Edward's gran Maud said the same thing from older and iron-bound reasons. Gran was strange these days, missing meals and wandering about in the wood, but when her mind turned on Denby, she was sharp as Will's arrowheads.

"These things must be done because..." Maud gathered the thoughts over her trencher at table, balling the long-skeined past like wool to be stored and woven to use. "Because we endure, Edward. Because we always have and must. Kings and earls come and go, but thanes like your father and grandfather are the bone in England's flesh, the timbers of her house supporting the king, sheltering the folk. From *my* blood," Maud made audible distinction, "your sires in Mercia were trusted knights when those of William Bastard were no more than pirates." Maud signaled Angharad to refill her ale cup, succinctly ending Edward's lesson in the Way of Things. "We do not change our cut to the convenience of foreign trash. Drink your milk, boy."

"Don't want my milk."

"Edward," Marian commanded crisply from her place to the left of Robin's empty chair. "Milk and butter ent so easy coom by that you'll waste when they're on the board. Drink."

"But I don't—"

Ultimate Law, sharper than Maud's and without appeal: "Milk!"

"Aye, Mum." Edward drank and wished it the ale he loved.

After May Day in the spring of 'eighty-five, two letters from Winchester reached Ralf at Nottingham. The first bore the small seal of the Chancery: King William would hold solemn high court at Gloucester over Christmas to counsel with the chief men of the realm on new matters of import. Fitz-Gerald would attend the king there. The second letter, written on worn and wine-stained parchment, was stamped with a seal Ralf didn't recognize, a warrior mailed and mounted. He broke the seal and read the signature. "From Prince William at Gisors."

"Then he'll have news of—" Judith smothered the name with a chill of premonition. If bad news, she or Ralf must bear it to Denby, and why else would young William, a total stranger, trouble to address Ralf?

No more literate than his father, Prince William's letter was likely dictated to the handiest scribe, a village priest not too comfortable with letters himself. The sentiments were set forth in stiff, formal phrases utterly unlike the earthy Rossel.

...respect and love borne in kinship between yourself and Edward of Denby, that you receive the first news...

Judith listened as her husband read, mind and heart racing ahead of the courteous sentiments. "Is he dead, Ralf?"

"They don't seem to know for a certainty."

. . . being charged with a reconnaissance across River Epte from which he never returned. It is unlikely that he has been held for ransom, for I would have heard before this. Therefore, he must be presumed dead. Your lordship being his kin will transmit this to his wife with my deepest regret. I knew little of his mind save that among knights he was modest, among the boastful, silent. Among lords jealous of honor, Robin carried his own like a private vow. My lord vicomte will understand this better than I do, for I have no art to divine the English.

Ralf and Judith sat without speaking at first, the letter on the table between them. Neither wanted to tell Marian, but knew she would rather one of them than a stranger. This was family, not to be shared. Ralf picked up the letter and inspected the seal. "Someone already has. It's been opened and resealed. Ranulf."

"That weasel! Is there no honor left?"

"Not in Winchester. The weasel scans anything of importance passing through." Ralf resigned himself. "I'll ride to Denby in the morning."

"My love to all. Tell Marian I will come when I can."

In a secret selfishness, Ralf was relieved. If Robin had to die, let it be by the hand of a stranger, any but his own. Leave him that much. Let him be that clean. He despised Ranulf and could feel no more than bare duty toward his king. Some men needed to destroy what they could not understand. Robin's ultimate visions were dim to Ralf, but he saw clearly enough the end of the man as the world went. They would cry for Barabbas and throw the prophet to the wolves.

Late spring 1085 brought its own tasks to Denby that must be timely seen to. More often this year, Edward rose at first cockcrow, breakfasted quickly, and rode with Mauger. More and more his mother relied on him to do his share, but Marian, like Maud before her, was the fuel to every Denby hearth, and the folk knew it.

"She hasn't the high airs of the old gran, and that's blessing, but Lady Marian keeps a proper house with a good heart."

The peasant women of Sherwood and Blidworth saw no more than they expected to see. Marian, at thirty-one, tended to house and children and kept her heart hidden away. Robin throbbed and hurt in her; meanwhile, she did what she must. Wounds were not to be shown, and dying was a private thing.

When Ralf came with the letter and read it to the family about the high table, he expected no great show of emotion from these English. Edward only went silent, head lowered over his soup. He put down his spoon and sat a little straighter.

"These reports are so often confused or premature," Ralf reminded them, wanting to offer any possible hope. "Many men have come home even as their requiems were sung."

"He is not dead," Will Scatloch asserted from the low table. "There are those in Denby who would know." Angharad agreed with her husband, young Edward nodded as if the point were self-evident.

"Dead or live," Marian told Ralf as they walked arm in arm to the groom waiting with his horse at the gate, "I only know he is gone from me."

The girl had gone out of Marian as it faded from all country women through work and childbearing. But not plain, Ralf thought. The candid brown eyes were still luminous when she laughed, the face stronger and more firmly defined. One could read sadness there, but no despair. She put her hand over his. "You're not the common lot of foreigner, Ralf."

"Foreign? I've been as long as you in Sherwood."

"*Ach,* then, you know what I mean. You asked for me once. Not many men would still be the friend you have, my dear."

The love was still there, Ralf knew, but the wanting had washed away as a river ran itself clean. "Oh, I am a little wiser now. And I've learned this much about Robin: I'll never believe him dead until I see the body cold, and even then, he might get up and walk away. More luck and lives than the old Puck-Robin Maud named him for. It must be . . . " Ralf throttled the thought that wouldn't help Marian at all. But she caught him up.

"Must be what?"

Must be a pain to have a destiny that never let the man rest content in a world he could never change. "I must be riding home."

"Let Judith come soon and bring the children," Marian said. "I'm that lonely sometimes. There's never enough work to tire that out of me."

One hand on Denby gate, she watched her friend ride out of sight. From Blidworth church, the sound of Vespers bell rang clear over the dale. Two swifts darted low over the gate. Quick, restless birds who fed and even mated on the wind. Maud might as well have named Robin for one of them. . . .

I've heard they live most of their lives on the wing, coming to earth only to lay their eggs. Their legs are too spindly weak to hold them up; they even sleep on the wing and the wind. That's you, swift-Robin. You left me to hide from the law and then for the law, for summ'at I can't understand and a place where I can't follow, so don't expect me to simper, "Aye, love, I do understand," because I bloody well can't. That's the sin I confessed to Father Beorn. Disobedience. The rest is too hard and hot and would take a mickle long time in telling. Nineteen months gone, husband. I've counted every one and the hundreds of days gone into their reckoning. Do you know what you've missed, what I've looked on miserable without you to share? Edward's grown from child to the verge of manhood. Thirteen this Candlemas past, all of a sudden too big for his clothes and shoes. Sometimes in a certain light he'll turn to me and I hear you in his voice, see you in the shape of his head, and my heart breaks because you're not there to share the wonder I feel at what we made together.

You weren't there the day Moira left off her swaddling clouts or to see the first little kirtle Maud and I made for her. Or when I called her and she got up and stumbled clear across the bower to clasp my knee. Not here when Moira spoke her first clear word or after her second year when she discovered *no*—and that was all we heard month in and out—or the day Angharad and I first parted that fine hair with a comb, gathering it into two long wings soft as down and tying it artful with gay ribbons. Not here to see her go from feeble babe— only God's mercy she lived at all—to a sturdy child who'd thrive, who called me *Mum* clear as Blidworth bell and spoke with a smile that knew *me* . . . but how much of you, Robin? Moira is three now; if she remembers you at all, it's dim, and I'll have to be telling her soon enough. Damn you, you knew they'd come for you soon or late. You chose it. . . .

Moira will hear the songs folk sang of you. I could make one of my own for the children lost. Sometimes I try to imagine them on the hearth and alive with Edward and Moira, wasteful and wounding as the pictures are. *Now he would be six and she seven.* They're a loss in me, Robin, gone as you are. You should be in the hall of nights and in our bed that's too big and cold now. Dead or alive,

you're gone from me when you need not have been. Your doing—
and by Jesus, I must love you fierce to clutch at you yet and hit at
your memory for what you've denied me. And nowt but to wait until
the sky itself betrays your wing and you go down like the poor swift
to foreign earth.

26

R ANULF was not uniquely despicable in reading private corre-
spondence. During their regency, Matilda and Lanfranc intercepted letters as a matter of state policy and, as a result, were
somewhat prepared for Waltheof's rebellion when it came. Through the
Chancery now flowed a river of information, including most royal chart-
ers and writs. No one knew better than Ranulf what William granted
or withheld; this knowledge created a continuing need to know. Con-
cerning his king and the realm, Ranulf was a master observer.

As for William, he condoned Ranulf's zeal and tactics insofar as they
kept power in his own royal fist. Fifty-seven now, the widower king
yet drove himself too hard as always, constantly on the move between
Rouen, Winchester, and the far marches of his kingdom. Without Matilda to apply common sense, he drank and ate too much. His breathing
labored nowadays, his color worried his physicians, who urged rest and
a more abstemious diet. The old bull only snorted, called for horse, and
galloped away to the next meeting with prelates, sheriffs, or barons.
William never feared power in Ranulf's hands, since he knew to the jot
how much he delegated. The Chancery priest certainly rendered a precise
report when needed—

**I will personally inspect the Sherwood enclosures and sue for Fitz-Gerald's
cooperation in this. In the matter of the king's heir, Count Robert, the
chief men of the Midlands, notably Osmund, favor his succession both in
England and Normandy. For the Vicomte Fitz-Gerald, one cannot say, as
he evades commitment on the question. He lacks no competence in office,**

yet I must bring it to my lord's attention that his was the second name subscribed to the treasonous writings for which Edward of Denby was banished.

While William had a frugal affection for men of his old guard like Ralf Fitz-Gerald, a Ranulf he merely employed, quite aware of the young man's ambition. Since that attribute combined with diligence, Ranulf enjoyed considerable latitude. That diligence already knew that the king would present a staggering command to his clergy and nobles at Christmas in Gloucester. A vast, comprehensive survey to count every man, woman, pig, chicken, cow, and horse in England, who held what land and how much, and its precise tax value. Few men of his time would perceive the effects of this study so clearly as the keen young man from Bayeux. To Ranulf, "the king enrounded by his chief men" was a quaint obsolescence. True power must be central, else the king was merely an aging man in an ornate chair. Real power was a complex mechanism working efficiently to the purpose of rule.

Ranulf did his master's bidding and kept his ear to the ground. Like most clever and capable young men, he considered his genius polished while it was still forming. The mind able to detect the subtlest nuance of royal intent did not know much about its female counterpart, including his wife's. Elfled had a second daughter to occupy her now, still attractive to Ranulf, who liked the light-colored Saxon look in a woman. They got on well enough when he was home. For all that, his indulgent smile at her fascination with the chimera of Robin Hood was beginning to curdle about the edges. He wondered how much of the fondness involved the reality of Denby himself. While Ranulf was no longer enamored of her, Elfled was *his*. More, he was still young enough to rankle at the personal insults of Denby. Privately he was more stung than amused that Elfled could be so glamorized by a disenfranchised country lord now very likely fertilizing a French meadow. He broke the news to his wife in a carefully offhanded manner.

"So the prince's letter said, my dear: 'missing and presumed dead.' "

Elfled's reaction puzzled Ranulf. She observed only, "That will be less trouble for you in Sherwood, I should think."

Searching for any telltale anxiety, Ranulf found none. Elfled brushed out her hair meticulously as usual before bed, said her prayers perfunctorily, bade her husband good night, turned on her side and went to sleep.

Ranulf lay awake beside her, hands behind his head, while his wife snored softly. He already planned a visit to Nottingham in regard to the forest enclosures; why not stop at Denby? Could he be blamed for a little gloating? He felt quite satisfied in his personal and complete victory over Robin. He had become formidable. Higher-born men trod warily about him. Denby did not, Denby was gone. More than vengeance, there was justice in that.

Elfled's second child had been a difficult birth. Not that Ranulf appreciated the fact, being in Winchester at the time. Elfled understood intimately what drove him so unmercifully, the years of bending his back before less capable but better-placed men, the fawning obsequiousness needed for so much as a nod from one of them toward his next possible advancement. Rise he did and would, though Elfled realized with a woman's and a mother's practicality that Ranulf's star would draw him away from her and the children. To be honest, her marriage had already settled into a condition like a clouded day, not dark but hardly bright. She wasted no mourning on this. The daughter of a hardheaded merchant accepted conditions, assessed her still-fetching appearance and youth, and looked toward a more lucrative and infinitely more fascinating market.

Naturally, she betrayed none of this to Ranulf, certainly not the almost physical sickness over Robin's presumed death. Prince William must be wrong. Robin *couldn't* be dead; not that fine, tender man with the speaking eyes. A piece at a time over the months, Elfled had collected and arranged the details of his life like furniture in a private sanctum of imagination. The lands at Denby, the wife Marian and the children, the very substance of his experience—Elfled needed to see them now. The time had come when she couldn't *not* look on them.

"I would ride with you to Nottingham," she declared to Ranulf one evening when he spoke of his affairs there. "Vicomtess Judith lays a fine table, they say, and I ride too seldom since the baby came."

"You would not be embarrassed?"

To her husband's sardonic question, Elfled matched a neutral tone and expression. "By what, pray?"

"They will be courteous, but not well disposed. We will be received, but not welcomed warmly. The sheriff is no friend to me."

How many were who came to Ranulf's board? Elfled favored her husband with her all-purpose wifely smile and got on with her dreams. If Robin were only a harmless fantasy, the reality of his wife and children would be the last thing she would wish to look on. For all her reasons, he was so much more, a road that led as always to what Elfled perceived as need. Lady Judith was kin to Robin; one could learn much by being innocently attentive in her presence. Elfled would meet the wife cordially while making a steely feminine estimate of the competition and her chances—*he's not dead, can't be*—would smile and find a warm, lighted place for the stepchildren in her generous heart. . . .

Elfled was glad Lady Judith did not accompany them through Sherwood with the sheriff's armed escort. She frankly preferred to be the only attractive woman in any group of men, and the vicomtess was a striking woman, if far beyond her prime. Courteous but cool, tasteful in dress though quite out of fashion. With these qualifications, Elfled neatly tucked Judith away to her satisfaction and took horse with Ranulf, Vicomte Ralf, and their escort through Sherwood on a clear May morning. They would arrive at Denby by midday, ask hospitality, and be away to lodge the night at Mansfield.

The sheriff's reluctance in this visit to Denby was obvious. "They are old-fashioned people, Father Ranulf, and well aware of who you are. Under the circumstances—"

"Vicomte, I am on more business than I may divulge," Ranulf overrode objections with unwavering authority. "You may leave discretion to the Chancery."

Elfled refused a traveling chair and rode a grey palfrey, saddle soreness eased by padded trousers beneath her rich yellow kirtle. The party set off after a quick breakfast and brief Mass at the hour of Prime. The sheriff had introduced Elfled to her personal escort, a charming bachelor knight, Sire Henri Chailliard, who talked easily of this place he now called home.

North of Nottingham, before the broad open heath gave way to forest, Elfled saw three gallows trees, one or two bodies dangling from each. Mercenaries, Henri told her.

"Foreign thieves, Lady."

"But you are foreign yourself, are you not?"

"From Normandy, yes, but this is a special place. An enchanted place. Worth protecting from such crows."

When their route forked away from Papplewick, Henri offered Elfled a bit of local legend. "Just west of here, Robin Hood once waylayed Bishop Osmund and relieved him of a considerable purse. There's a song they still sing in the taverns."

Robin. Elfled brightened. "Did you know him?"

"I was with him and the vicomte at Norwich. I was only sixteen, the vicomte's squire." Henri chuckled at the youthful memory. "Before God, I didn't look to see the morrow when we took our mad stand before the castle. Robin's archers were—*bien,* doubtless you have heard that tale." Henri crossed himself. "Rest him with angels. If he *is* dead."

"One hears they are not sure."

"You never could be with Robin." Henri grinned ruefully. "You need only ask my lord sheriff."

"Robin Hood." Carefully casual, as if merely whiling the time, Elfled inquired, "What was he like?"

Henri glanced across at her from his saddle. "But you have met him yourself, haven't you?"

The knight was not as naive as he appeared. Elfled wondered how much Robin had told him. "At Lincoln, but we spoke only briefly." *So little time. Those few moments I can never forget.*

Henri considered. "There are men one knows too well in ten minutes, others not in ten years. Like most Saxons, a possessive man. Steady sometimes, a little mad at others. I would say a passionate man, Lady. Yes, passionate and stubborn. At Norwich with the priest giving last rites to Little John, Robin hung over his friend, willing the man to fight it and live."

Elfled echoed in her own key: *Passionate . . .*

"That will kill him someday," Henri reflected.

Elfled came out of her own thoughts. "Eh?"

"Nothing, madame."

Their procession wended slowly north. Elfled noted a few newly bare patches here and there, the remains of razed hamlets. This had been Ranulf's office, to clear so many hides for royal hunting preserve. Fitz-Gerald had cooperated, knowing what was good for him. Power like Ranulf's was greater than rank or birth. After that came money; not even a king held sway without it. Thus, riding through the sun-dappled arcades of northern Sherwood, Elfled did her own tidy sums. Now thick-brambled undergrowth pressed close about the ancient cart track. Sire Henri informed her they were on Denby holding.

Beautiful. Tranquil. His place. Robin grew up here, walked this path. "As you said: enchanted."

"Perhaps," the knight said, tilting his head up at the beeches flanking them like rows of ancient, welcoming counselors. "The peasants say a spirit watches over Denby in the form of a red doe. Hallo? What's this, now?"

Just ahead of them, one of the men at arms twisted about to the knight. *"Rien, vavasor,* just Denby's Welshmen."

She was coming close, then. In a flutter of inner excitement, Elfled urged the palfrey forward. "Make way there."

The two Welshmen were passing some news to Vicomte Ralf. Small middle-aged men with the grey standing out like new steel in their ebony hair. Evidently there had been some trouble.

Ralf queried the more civilized-looking of the two. "When, Will?"

"Two days past."

"My doing," the other forester stated dourly. "Nothing else to do, my lord."

Ranulf broke in impatiently. "Am I to understand these men killed two of the king's soldiers?"

"Mercenaries," Ralf said. "They were apparently trespassing."

"All of that and very ill-mannered," Morgan attested. "On a Sabbath, too. There's heavy it is, but true."

"I told you they were old-fashioned on Denby," Ralf remarked to Ranulf. "Foreign or native, a man gets a welcome or one warning."

"They were warned," Will Scatloch warranted. "By Morgan himself at the very gate and young Edward by him, and those two louts climbing over the bars."

"Reprisals?" Ralf asked. "Any others come?"

"No, my lord, and there's the heart of the matter." To Elfled's ear, the one called Will waxed suddenly circumspect. "That you be prepared, and these visitors, is it, we've proclaimed the example plain to the dullest eye. Morgan, nip along and tell Lady Marian the good sheriff's come. And royal servants from Winchester."

Morgan trotted away into thicket with little more noise himself than a deer would make. Will Scatloch walking at Ralf's stirrup, the party moved on through a neatly tended stand of young birch, and then Denby's gate loomed before Elfled. The heart of his holding. She couldn't help a certain disappointment. Squat and squalid by town standards, Denby was no grander than the outlying farms about little Wigford outside Lincoln. A sprawl of bowers, barn and stable, cookhouse, and the low outline of the hall with its weathered thatching.

The view was not entirely bucolic. Two severed heads, covered with flies, stared at the forest from poles, eyeless where the birds had been at them. Elfled averted her sight.

They were awaited, nevertheless. Behind the barred gate there was the forester Morgan, next to him a younger man bearing the white staff of a steward. A gangling boy, bow in hand and quiver slung: Robin's son. Elfled saw the father's lines in the long body and beautiful head, but she gave her closest attention to the tall woman with the shy girl-child peering at the strangers from behind her mother's skirts.

The woman did not move to open the gate, only indicated the impaled heads, drawling a greeting to the sheriff. "Give you good day, Lord Ralf. Will told you of our troubles, then?"

Fitz-Gerald appeared in no hurry to enter. "He did, Lady Marian. What happened?"

"Morgan and me, Uncle Ralf," the young boy spoke up. "We did 'em as Da would have."

As Elfled scrutinized Robin's wife, at pains not too appear too direct, Lady Marian remained planted like a tree. "Breton bastards were drunk. Edward warned them."

"They'd already caused some grief in Blidworth," the boy said. "Threatened us, said it would go hard if we didn't let them in. That one on your right didn't believe Morgan would put a shaft in him." Edward pointed to the other remnant. "That one didn't believe I would. That's the truth, Uncle. You know hearth-right."

Ranulf complained to Ralf in rapid French, not understanding English well and the shire dialect not at all. "Do we have to sit here all day in the hot sun?"

Ralf turned to him, unperturbed. "Patience, Father Ranulf. We enter when the gate opens. I told that scum to mind their ways in Sherwood. You can see why."

Now, for the first time, Robin's country cow acknowledged Ranulf's presence. "You'd be that Chancery clerk."

"Lady" or not, Elfled felt immensely better about the woman. Her patched linen kirtle was caught up in a worn apron passed peasant-fashion between her legs and tucked up in back, revealing lanky shins and bare, callused feet. Dull, Elfled judged. For competition, not worth a thought. *Looks to her children and house, goes to Mass every day, and bores Robin to death.*

From their one meeting, Elfled remembered how he'd spoken of a girl, almost sang of the wench, how she'd shimmered in the light. Elfled wondered if, dissembling as he obviously was as Father Brand, he described Marian. No, not this barefoot bitch.

Now Robin's woman let her disinterested glance rest on Elfled in return. Under the most cordial circumstances, this one would have little

208

to say to a city woman. "Lord Ralf, you are welcome, one of you open the gate."

So Elfled rode into Denby, into *his* place sagging with age and drab as the wife who claimed him—who, Elfled noted with relief, was much older than herself, thirty if a day, with the flat northern sound and manner Elfled had encountered and hated whenever she rode beyond city precincts. Their faces told one without words: They and God knew the right of things. All other judgments were suspect.

Elfled caught sight of a sow wallowing contentedly in the sty hard by the barn, four farrow squirming at her dugs. These people were used to smells and dirt, but Elfled vowed to do much, given time, with a repaired, scrubbed, and new-painted Denby. *We will winter in Lincoln and perhaps spend occasional summers here.* She smiled at the gawky boy and the tiny, shy girl, stepchildren-to-be.

Whatever her image of Robin, Elfled had one trait alone in common with him: Both were tragic dreamers, if seduced in different sleep. In his more perceptive moments, Ranulf might have told her this.

27

▶▶▶▶▶

SEPTEMBER brought soft rains to Sherwood and a brief chill, autumn intruding too soon on the last of summer. The sun came again with a gentle coolness that tinged the oak leaves yellow and gold. There was a tang in the air of woodsmoke and fallen leaves that beguiled memory and drew Maud to the forest this day. She thought at first to take a horse from the stable, but the day was clear as her mind at the moment; she would enjoy a walk.

Basket on her arm, she strolled toward the steading gate. By Marian's order, the Breton heads still blackened on their poles. Maud approved: fitting and good. They could remain there until the skin peeled dry from the bone and the skulls bleached white to teach foreign trash the perils of trespassing on Denby.

"G'day, Gran!" Edward hailed her from the open stable door. He was dressed for riding, and in a sweet rush of memory, Maud saw his father at that age.

Robin was all legs and hands too big, brown as a nut from trailing after Will in the forest. That would have been about 'sixty-three. Aelred and I were fifteen years wed, in and out of love, further out and deeper in each time, and now my bones are hollowed with wanting and lone-liness blowing through them. William made so many widows, so many bone-flutes. Does our music haunt his sleep as it does mine?

Edward called again. "Where do you go?"

"After eldrum berries, sweeting. Minna's cough is on her again."

On this crisp morning, Maud felt better despite the happenings of a tense, miserable summer. Once more Fitz-Gerald had come, bringing others of his kind like dirt tracked into a clean hall. Maud would not sit at table with the Chancery priest. As for his wife, that awkward little tradesman's daughter, with her prim mouth and eyes everywhere, pricing everything. Right fishwife, that one, resentful of her betters, biting every coin at her market stall.

Fitz-Gerald managed to look regretful bringing the news of Robin. No matter, none of us believed it, yet if Robin's dead, Ralf is guilty as the rest. He is yet one of them.

Maud moved at ease along the cart track. She caught sight of Will and Morgan and called a greeting. No, no need to break off their business on her account, she was only searching out eldrum, since the berries came early this year. The two foresters disappeared soundlessly into the thickets. Maud left the track, veering toward the eldrum patch she desired. There was a bush hard by the hall door, but that was Marian's and the lass had strong views on the matter. Maud scoffed tenderly: For Marian, an eldrum bush by the door prevented unwanted visitors, though this past summer might have shaken her faith in its powers. She firmly believed that a spirit lived within the bush. Once when Robin cut a summer sprig of the small white blossoms and put them in Marian's hair for a lark, she removed them quickly, muttering a preventive charm over the eldrum—"Give me of your flowers, old girl, and I'll give you of mine when the tree grows."

Only then would she wear the blossoms.

At the berry patch, Maud filled her basket with enough of the dark fruit to boil syrup for Minna's cough. Poor Minna was her own age if a day and never slacked duty between Denby's kitchen or her husband Wystan, blinded all those years gone by Fitz-Gerald himself. Maud had a special dungeon in her mind for the sheriff; for now it was yet time to smile on the wretch, but a day would come when she need not. . . .

Maud blinked in the sunlight dappling the forest floor as her train of thought raveled and went vague.

Need not smile anymore, and . . . and time stopped for her, the sand hovered, still, in her glass. In the full light of day, darkness swept over her like the shadow of a vast wing; her nostrils remembered the fetid air of Hough dungeon. The basket dangled in her hand.

Pipe tree, that is what Aelred calls the eldrum. Just last week we stopped by a bush like this, and Aelred fingered the wood the way a carpenter does, feeling for the possible uses and shapes within. "I'll be cutting a pipe for Puck-Robin from a piece of this." So he did, and Robin tootled up and down the hall until Angharad took her broom to him. . . .

Maud shook her head against the lovely, luring shadows. *No, leave me.* She was a fool again, hoodwinked once more by the Soft Demon. He could come so easily now between one thought and the next.

Maud crushed a few berries and let the stain run over her fingers. So many uses for this tiny button of a fruit: dyes, wine, nostrums for fever or rawed throat. Would it could set time right, bring her clearly into Now, or ease her once and for all from the remembered dark of the dungeon into the gentle magic of Then.

Take me to Aelred, then, if that is your bent, and do not mock me if I see but one flower where all else about me is weed.

Unaware at first where her footsteps led, then surer, Maud dreamed her way through the cool, shadowed forest toward their tree where Aelred was waiting.

Edward grained and watered his Welsh pony in the stable, currying the gelding meticulously. The brush moved slowly to the rhythms of his heavy concerns. Mum didn't mention his father much after the news came. As such things were understood in their family, he shouldn't either. But Edward would know today for sure, by one means or other, whether his da was dead or not. He would go to old Wytha, who would scry out the truth of the matter.

Edward ceased brushing and leaned his face against the pony's warm flank. Did his father ever pause so at thirteen and think what a perilous age it was to be? Aye, Da was to York and that, and through sore troubles after, but . . . how did he feel when he was just this old, bones pained from growing too fast, voice unsteady between one word and the next, squeaking and deep in the same breath? Did he ever have a boy-summer terrible as this, veering wildly between excitement and horror and gloom? Da was a strong man, stopped a wicked great earl in his tracks and a slew of foreigners at Norwich. Robin didn't speak much of that, but Will Scatloch did, ever spinning a grand tale and all the better if he'd a drop in.

Aye, Will tells and the folk sing of Robin Hood, but who am I?

How did Da feel putting an arrow into a man for the first time? The thing had to be done. The two dirty Bretons at the gate: slovenly men in rusty mail, but armed. Deserters, Morgan had guessed. Just some water, they asked, and perhaps something to eat. Morgan warned them off—softly at first, then more sharply as they began to climb over the gate, and Edward knew the thing would happen, had to happen, no way out.

Both soldiers straddling the fence, then, insolent, neither believing a wee Brit and a scared boy would dare hinder them. Then Morgan's hand streaked to his quiver, and Edward, sick with fear, felt his own arm lift. He seemed to live years in the one breath. They were doing the Forbidden, coming unwelcomed into Denby, and JesusandMary, there was one dead from Morgan's shaft. Edward's arms moved of themselves—every eye in Sherwood would be on him now. He couldn't stand like a *niddering* whelp letting Morgan take it all on himself— pressed and loosed.

Mum and Gran Maud thought the matter distasteful but necessary, like slaughtering hogs at Martinmas, but Edward was sick after the killing, unable to look when Morgan set the heads on stakes with no more ado than spearing a piece of turnip at table. Morgan was not as feeling a man as Will. To Will it was that Edward showed his sick horror, what a terrible thing to loose on a man and see him fall dead. Will held him close and let him shake his bones loose, then poured him a drink of whiskey on the sly. Edward had never swallowed such. Pure liquid fire, but the second gulp steadied him a bit.

"Drink it down," Will admonished. "A man's dram for a man's work. I'll not be calling you boy-bach anymore."

Edward's emotions jittered the words and the whiskey made him hiccup. "Why do they come, the dirty foreigners? Why won't they leave us alone?"

Will Scatloch, with all possible, joyous, and terrible worlds in his eyes, just asked, "How is it with you, mun?"

"When you and Da were outlawed, how did it feel wh-when you had to—"

"Kill?" No quick or easy answer to that ever. Will stared back at years gone grey as his hair. "If you will take my word, one man to another, I never felt better about it than you do now."

Edward kept the deed and the whiskey down, but there were more difficult questions. For years he'd known his father and the forest and hall. Now that Da might never return, there was so much of him Edward felt robbed of, never to learn. If he had to follow in such a man's shoes and fill his place, what was he like among other men? Edward remembered Robin as a small boy would, the safe feel and smell of a father holding him close, even the rough scratch and tickle of Da's beard, part of well-being when he got hugged goodnight. But what of the grownup things, a man's knowledge of another man?

Part of the answers had come earlier from Father Beorn and his sexton Seaxwulf. The old priest walked Edward thoughtfully through Blidworth churchyard to the three small graves the boy knew well enough.

"Your brothers, who never lived to grow as you did," said Beorn. "Your father did not grieve overmuch for them; it was the will of God and couldn't be changed. But against wrongs that could—you follow, Edward?—he spoke and fought. Robin had a sense of justice like a thorn in his heel."

As for stolid Seaxwulf, Edward understood him better. "Your father? Well, then." The sexton paused in polishing the silver altar cups to rub the dust from a memory. "I first met him the day he robbed Bishop Osmund and my own priest—in a good cause, mind. Loovely man, Lord Robin. No friend to Normans, but a saint to his own. Be like him and you'll do well enough."

Like him indeed: There was a task for a boy not sure who he was himself.

Edward saddled the pony and rode out of Denby steading. At a walk he turned north toward Wytha's forest hut near Holy Pool. She once healed Robin of a wound like to kill any other man. The *wicca* woman would know if he were truly dead.

North of Minna and Wystan's croft lay virgin oak forest several miles wide, where Denby had never allowed any clearing for plow land. The pony's hooves fell softly on the thick loam along the narrow path among the oaks growing before Hengist and Horsa first beached their longboats on the island shores. All her life, so Robin said, Wytha preferred the forest to any village, and always chose a site well back from any traveled way. Edward turned off the footpath through the hoary trees into the hidden clearing, loose-tethered the pony to let it graze, and knocked politely at the door of the small hut.

The dry voice came from within, calm and steady. "Who's there?"

"Edward of Denby, wise woman. May I enter?"

He heard a muted chuckle. "A boy with questions. Come in."

The interior of Wytha's home was dark and cool, pungent with herbs hung thick about the rafters and tucked into corners. The old woman lay on her pallet in one corner, raised on one elbow to see him. In her old smock, shapeless and colorless with age as the wearer, the thin bone-white hair falling over her shoulders, Wytha might have been part of this forest since time began.

214

"There's porridge," she said, nodding to the cooking pot on its iron tripod.

"*Ta,* but no." Edward bobbed his head to her, raised to show good manners toward tenants, and no one spoke disrespectfully to Wytha. "Are you ailing, then?"

"I'm too old for ailing," Wytha declared, lying back on her pallet. "But it is time to go."

"Go where?" Edward blurted before realizing with a thud what she meant. "I mean, shall I fetch Father Beorn?"

The wise woman laughed softly at some small private joke. "I wouldn't embarrass the man. But you've come to ask about Robin."

Edward marveled silently: *How did she—?*

"The wind brings me news, and the silly rooks from time to time, or a char-burner passing through. Damned charrys will natter you to death. I married one. That cured me."

"Of char-burners?"

"And marriage. Your great-gran, now . . . well, never mind." Wytha sat up with an energetic grunt that belied any thought of illness. "You've come for a scrying, haven't you?"

"If you would be so good," Edward asked with careful deference. "I'd know if my da's truly dead or yet quick. I don't have any money, but—"

"No need," Wytha brushed the notion aside. "I heard of the two foreigners you stopped in their tracks."

Edward dropped his eyes, not wanting to talk of that.

"I have much affection for your father, boy."

"Is it as the Norman prince said?"

The old woman's head wagged side to side decisively. "There was no death in the runes."

Edward waited in silence while Wytha seemed to look through him to his marrow and beyond. She was the oldest person he'd ever known, but in the sagging flesh of her face and the maze of wrinkles, her eyes were sharp and young as his mother's.

"He's far away, the runes said. Far even from himself."

"I don't understand."

"Neither do I," Wytha admitted with off-handed candor, abruptly taking a new tack. "Well, then. I hear you read Latin like a scholar now."

"A little. Aunt Judith teaches me. She knows the lot."

"No one knows the lot, Edward." Wytha's dry-leaf voice rang suddenly clear as if it were running past winter like a young girl toward the spring of her soul. "No one. The runes, no different. There's truth in them, but how much do I read aright? Your father's far away and troubled. You have to be very live for that, don't you? Have some porridge. It's uncommon good since the basil and hare got in." Wytha lay back again, this time like someone resigned not to rise again. "Or be off with you. It's time for me to go."

Edward felt uncomfortable. Such a woman would surely sense her time to die and ought to have a priest. "I can ride to the church."

"I didn't say die," Wytha corrected peevishly. "I said *go*. Leave. All my life I've had to know the right time for things to begin and end. Beorn and I have different names for the leaving and where we go. I wouldn't strain the dear, difficult man."

Wytha lapsed into silence. A starling lighted in the doorway, found nothing of interest, and darted away. The old woman's eyes were closed, sunken back into their sockets. Edward shifted from one foot to the other, not certain whether he was dismissed or not. "I'll be off then." He cleared his throat.

"Boy?"

He turned quickly, grateful for any further word.

"Nothing dies, Edward. Men knew that before the White Christ came, but that's the rub between Beorn and me. What he calls death is only change. Have you ever seen the old doe they say drinks from Holy Pool?"

"Only heard tales of her."

"And of your great-gran Guntrada? Some say they're one and the same."

So he'd heard, though Edward was not up to sounding such mysteries today. "Is it true?"

"True or not, it does make you ponder on real and not real, I'd think."

"Thank you for good counsel, Wytha."

"May it well become you," she murmured drowsily, the sound of the words like the rustle of fallen leaves. Then: "Your father, there's a man who thinks too much if one were to ask me, but go you and think on changes. Nip along; I've got to be about changing myself."

And that was his word from Wytha. Edward left quietly, shutting the door softly behind him. He was mounting his pony, one foot in the stirrup, when her voice came again from within the hut. "Do you know your gran's gone off to the bargain oak?"

216

"Thought she might."

"A good lad might ride that way," Wytha ventured. "Sometimes she forgets the way home."

Wytha was never seen again by any folk of Denby or Blidworth, though nobody but Father Beorn assumed her dead.

28

HERE in this blessed clearing set aside by God or Freya, where the yellowed grass was daubed purple with heather around the bargain oak, there was always a hush in which Maud could hear herself live. Here was the hut where she and Aelred spent their wedding night before giving their blood to the tree, and so many nights thereafter down the years. She'd borne three children, though only Puck-Robin lived. Why think on that, with one healthy son growing straight and fine? One sweet robin who might well have been conceived here on this simple pallet when the old brown sheepskins were new white fleece.

What time is it?

Maud stepped out of the hut to read the hour by skylight. About three, she guessed. Aelred and Robin were not far off, overseeing folk working to clear and claim bookland, careful that they not cut too close to this virgin plot about Holy Pool and the bargain tree. Since the lady of a steading had little time to herself, Maud prized the rare privacy of this quiet clearing, even loved her husband and son the more when she could be alone to turn the image of them in her mind and heart. . . .

I am twenty-eight, my husband loves me, and I still have my figure after three birthings. Robin is a strapping boy, lusty enough to make up for the two that died. No, the coldest year always returns to summer, nor does our happiness change. It is a blessing how time passes over us, alters nothing, steals nothing from me. Change is foreign, foreign is my enemy. More Normans at court this year than last and too openly favored by King Edward. He is turning our folk against him.

No, too fine a day to dwell on such thoughts. . . .

For our wedding night, Aelred's men laid a peat fire in the hut to give us a soft glow and steady warmth. As if warmth were needed between us. I was frightened, much as I wanted him. Lord knows why, for it was that simple and lovely. In the morning when Prime rang from the church, Aelred brought me his morning-gift, the gold ring that has not left my finger and will not until I—

Where is it? Who took my ring? Who stole it from my hand. Damn you all, who took my morning-gift from Aelred?

No . . . no, I put it aside for Robin to give to Mar—

God help me. What time is it? Please, someone tell me *when* it is. . . .

The old woman with the strong, ravaged face huddled by her tree, one hand against the trunk, steadying herself in time and place. That happened all too often now, never sure where she was, even less of when. But Aelred and Robin had just gone off—yes! Here they came again, all was well and Maud sure of her time. Her heart swelled with a rush of joy at the sight of them. Not lost at all, never lost.

"Aelred! Robin! Come kiss me." Maud sang in herself as father and son leapt the rill and hurried to her. Maud shook her head, blinked. Something was wrong with the two figures. Father and son blurred, lover and the fruit of love melting into a single image. No, Robin alone now, grown impossibly in a few short hours, already taller than herself, smiling down at her, loving but puzzled.

"Where is your father, Robin?"

"It's me, Gran. Edward."

He said more leading her to the pony, but Maud did not hear him. Edward could hardly know how cruel it was to be awakened when the dark and sleep were so much kinder. Maud kept her face averted from her grandson to hide the loss glistening in her eyes.

Judith came to visit before autumn winds sharpened and rain turned the forest paths to mud. It was one of the last warm days before Nottingham goose fair, when Sherwood rustled with fallen leaves and swine rooted for beech mast with their herders looking to them more closely than usual. The foreign mercenaries were still quartered about Nottingham; a significant number of pigs went missing.

Marian had the firepit crackling. The hall was cheery enough. She and Judith settled down to hot spiced tea as the day shadowed toward evening. The hour of Sext had just rung across the dale from Blidworth church when Will's sons, Eddain and Gwaun, trudged back to Denby gate after seeing to the steading pigs in nearby woods. The two young men had just barred the gate after them when a single rider burst out of the forest, pelting toward them.

"*Dyw,* that's a fast mount," Gwaun admired. "One of the sheriff's new breed. Arabs they call them."

"And Sire Henri upon him. Best of the day, sir!" Eddain hallooed. "What news?"

"The best." Henri Chailliard clattered up to them. "Open lads, for it can't wait."

Henri would give his news to all Denby. He seized the ancient horn that hung over the gate and blew lustily. Doors cracked, heads poked out. The knight grinned down at the Welsh brothers. "A letter sent just days ago. Not from Winchester but Canterbury." He urged the stallion through the opened gate.

"What has happened?" Angharad called to her sons from her bower.

"Lord Robin alive! Sent a letter by the good knight," Eddain cried back as he sprinted for the hall. "*Jesu,* Mother, it is glorious!"

Before the knight had his horse to the stable, the news had flashed through Denby steading like purgative herbs through a sick child. Cozy and smug behind the kitchen house bake oven, blind Wystan allowed to Minna, "Tell you flat, I never feared else."

"And I will tell you I did," Minna grumbled over the bread dough she was kneading. "And if Lady Marian says she did not, she'll be a week in confession, brave as the lie was."

Within minutes, led by Mauger, all the folk of the steading congregated in the hall about Judith, Marian, and Sire Henri. Considering the occasion, Marian did not mind little Moira climbing on the forbidden thane's chair to hear and see everything as Judith read the two letters aloud, one from Lanfranc, the other enclosed from Robin. Not a sound in the hall but the logs snapping on the fire and Judith's soft, precise voice.

Lanfranc thanked Judith for her inquiries as to his health, which could be better, please God, and reminded the sheriff of the Christmas court at Gloucester.

"Etcetera and etcetera. 'The enclosed came within this hour from Normandy.' " Judith laid aside the archbishop's letter, turning to the three smudged sheets of vellum which must have been used and erased many times. She glanced with a smile at Edward waiting and eager in his place at table. "This is from your father."

To my dearest wife Marian at Denby, my steward Mauger, my children, and all my folk. Before all else, I send my heart, Marian. Let it fly straight into yours.

At the high table, Marian sat with fingers pressed to tight lips. Lady Maud stood erect by the firepit, her silence barely containing relief and fierce, vindictive joy.

The letter went on to verify Prince William's surmise: captured by Franks, eventually released in a general exchange of prisoners. It seemed to all but Mauger that the missive carried an excess of unnecessary detail hardly of interest to Robin's family.

"Enough of Franks!" Edward burst out. "Where's Da now? How is it with him *now*. Will the king let him come home?"

"Peace," Mauger soothed, reading over Judith's shoulder more matter in the missive than any of them guessed. "Trust our lord to know what he's about."

I presently wait upon the king at Fécamp, where my liege has graciously allowed me to write this before returning to Gisors. Farewell with my love, Marian, and as much to Edward and Moira. How does little Moira? Does she thrive and eat well at meals? Does Edward give the proper time to his lessons? He must be big now, inclining to fourteen, and Moira growing herself. To see you all even for a moment—sweet love, I wish my arms were that long, that I could reach home and press you all so close. A million kisses, Marian. Give this letter to Mauger when read. ROBIN.

When Judith handed her the letter, Marian showed it to Moira with a hug. "From your da, love." Marian stood up in her place at the high table. She made a neat roll of the vellum sheets before passing them to her steward. "I will want this returned."

In the firepit, a log collapsed in a shower of sparks. Henri Chailliard said softly, "I have heard that God is merciful. Today I believe as much."

"No kinder than you for hasting it here, Henri. You are a friend to my house. But hear me." When Henri met Marian's eyes, he learned how black the warm brown of them could turn. "I thank you for coming. We thank you, all of us—but damn your king and your kind that keeps my husband from his hall, and if that's treason, let Willy Bastard banish me, too. *Damn* him, I say—"

"Marian, enough," Lady Maud spoke to check the outburst. "This is not meet."

"Aye, damn you as well!" The curse tore out of Marian like steam from a kettle. The blackened rafters rang with the force of it. Marian faced her mother-in-law like a sword unsheathed and ready. "Not a word, Mother. Not now. Let be."

She caught herself. Custom and nature prevailed. Such display was unseemly. Marian stepped down from the dais with a parting word to all. "I thank God Robin's alive. Mother, you will please head the table tonight. I will be in my bower and . . . and wish to be alone."

Quivering, she was aware of them all looking at her. She clamped her will tight about something that would break free. "Forgive me, Henri. My anger was not for you."

"Lady, I know." The knight bowed to her.

"Mauger, light the hall tonight with the old candle ends. We've none of the new to spare. Angharad, I'll want you. Give you all goodnight."

And that, for Denby and the world to see, was how Marian took the news of Robin's deliverance. She marched straight-backed across the courtyard to her bower, Angharad following after, and bolted the door behind her.

Forgotten, Angharad listened, then knocked uncertainly. "Lady?"

Let her knock, let them all go away for now. Marian would open in time. Alone in shadow, the tension in her wound tight one last time like a bow. Her mouth opened in the shape of an agony and the first strangled sob tore out of her.

She was not a drinker. Ale or beer to Marian were only to wash down supper, of late to help her sleep. The Welsh whiskey she never liked, though now she felt its balm.

"Uisge?" Angharad told her more than once, tasting her words like the drink itself. "Whiskey is to make the moment magic, whatever it is. If there are tears, to let them flow. If joy, music to make it sing. Anger, rage? They'll come sharp and hurtful and go as quick, love will come with no stint or sting. Like the very name of it, whiskey is the water of life, for the pouring over our own to remind us that life's not always brief or hard, that now and again it *is* a bit of magic. There's lovely, whiskey is."

This night, Angharad, who wore the colors of her own life unmixed and unmuted, set the whiskey by Marian's side and left her. Marian lay in the dark, shuddering violently in a riot of joy, gratitude, and guilt.

So Judith found her. When the door opened, Marian sat up, squinting in the sudden light. Judith set the lamp in a far corner and drew a chair close to the bed. "How is it, love?"

She heard a distinct hiccup. "Marian, are you drunk?"

Marian choked into a sodden handkerchief: "Well, if I ent yet, let me get there soon."

There was a last, exhausted tremor in her voice, rawed with weeping, that must have sobbed itself out for hours. "I sent him away, Judith. The rotten king commanded him, but *I* sent him away without letting him touch me. God's my witness we both needed it then, but I was angry and afraid and didn't have the simple *guts* to let him hold me then. I was already seeing my man dead and c-couldn't face that, and I sent him away without letting him touch me."

In the gloom that did not obscure from Judith the exhaustion in every line of her body, Marian drained her cup and poured more, and a generous dram for Judith as well. "Sweet Jesus, much as I loved him, I hated him then. Damn me for a worthless wife, but I did."

"Why, Marian?" Judith reached out to the suffering woman. "You don't hate Robin, you know you don't."

"Hell, I didn't. Then. For all the writing and—and things that put him beyond me, for making the king come after him. And . . . and he wanted to love me that last night, but I couldn't. Thinking it's midway 'tween my flow, just the time I always got pregnant, I can always feel when I'm ready. And then what, Judith? What? Another baby with Robin gone and like not to come back, and the place to be seen to? Another babe to go into the ground because the Normans take everything and there's not enough to keep a babe alive? You're lucky, never lost one. You don't know what that takes from you."

Marian drank again, choked, and sputtered, "How much of this stuff must I swill down before it stops hurting?"

After all these years, Judith thought with a pang of insight, *she's still a Tadcaster girl while part of Robin has gone where she can't follow. Ralf loved her once. We never spoke of it so, but I know he did and don't grudge him that. Whatever the fates spin out for us all, our bonding is a part of it.*

Judith lay down beside Marian, one arm over her, feeling the tears and the moist heat from that suffering flesh. "There, girl. There now. Hush, sweeting."

"You were good to come."

"I wanted to."

"I was so scared of you when I first came to Denby."

"No! Of me?"

"So grand and book-learned. Never seen a real lady before."

Judith owned with a hardwon humility, "I was much older then." They laughed a little over the truth of that. "Oh yes, and terribly serious. A bit much all around."

"Not half."

"Hush, Marian. Lie still."

Marian's breath shuddered with the last of released tension. "There was so much—"

"I know. Here, let me hold you."

"Please . . ."

They lay together in the near-darkness until Marian breathed more easily. The emotion out of her, she sounded merely drowsy now. "He's beautiful, my Robin. Sometimes when I saw him standing in the fields in the sun, it was like the earth was made of clear water or air, and I could see the roots of him going down into the ground. He and I, we feel that way about our hides."

"Just so." Judith held her close and murmured the dear, needed lies about the future. "The king will relent. Robin will come home." She turned on her back with a sigh. "And I don't think it would be amiss to have some more whiskey, and perhaps get a bit tiddly myself."

Marian poured it out for her friend. "Ent it lovely for a change?"

By the glow of two rush lights, Mauger scanned Robin's letter line by line, calling out letters which Henri Chailliard traced on a scrap of parchment. Mauger preened a little over his task.

"Clever cipher, if I did devise it myself. Robin spells perfectly—he ought to, for I taught him—while most men do not, no matter how literate. When the Normans censor his letters, the mistakes or transposed letters are taken for English ignorance of civilized French."

The "mistakes" were then extracted from the text and arranged against a substitute alphabet based on a keyword known only to Robin and Mauger. The message took shape: NO WAR DANES.

"Good, good," Henri muttered, impatient. "Hurry."

"Patience, sir."

CNUT DEAD.

Henri gaped. "The Danish king? How, what? Who killed him?"

"Will you question blessings or count them, knight? No war means the king must dismiss the foreign soldiers he's battened on us."

224

MORE DANGER KING AT GLOU.

Mauger handed the completed text to Henri, who secreted it in his boot. ''Let Lord Ralf read this and then burn it.''

''I hope he knows what it means, for I don't. Where was Robin when he wrote this? I forget.''

''On the Normandy coast at Fécamp,'' said Mauger. ''Waiting for the king.''

29

ROSSEL's report to Ralf Fitz-Gerald was honest; he was quite ignorant of his father's intent, which was conveyed privately to Robin that summer along with dispatches to the prince. Robin was to disappear during a routine reconnaissance, make his way to Rouen, and receive further orders from certain men there—hard-eyed, unsmiling men who spoke no more than they must and whose duties entailed the scullery work of empire. Robin was handed a list of names and specific instructions.

"Read this." The parchment was thrust across the table at the travel-stained Englishman. Considering the extraordinary sensitivity of the content, the orders carried no seal or signature. These men would furnish his travel funds. He would take ship down Seine and north to Jutland, passing himself off, with letters and raiment to that effect, as a lay brother of Canterbury returning home from pilgrimage and seeking a ship for Kent. Under this ruse he would make his way to Odense, where King Cnut was marshaling forces to invade England.

"You will meet the named men at the place set forth. They head a certain faction vital to our interests. You will assure them that Rouen fully subscribes to their aims in Denmark and agrees in all particulars."

The hard eyes searched Robin for full comprehension, as if they expected him to understand without question. "*Agrees:* That is important."

Meaning the price, as Robin took it.

"The first four of these men will then put certain forces in motion. When that is concluded, you will inform the last man named."

Specifically, a group of Danish nobles skilled at detecting the best quarter of the political wind, clear-minded as these issuing Robin's orders, who knew Cnut Sweinson's bid for England would be no less disastrous than his father's a decade past. The last man on the list would pay out the price of progress in Denmark.

"Return to Fécamp when the bells toll for Cnut, not before. Wait the king there and remember, you are in every respect still his prisoner. For all else, you never met us or saw this order. Go now."

Abbot Willelm glided down the cloister walk toward the gaunt man seated on the low wall, meditating on a nondescript bundle of rag in his hand. As the abbot drew near, he saw the object was a crude doll, grimy enough to have been salvaged from a midden heap.

Two years had passed since Willelm first set eyes on the Saxon: more grey in the hair, more weariness in the shoulders, but somehow valuable to the king to be ordered to wait on him here. Willelm wondered at the purpose only briefly; like all the men from the incessant border wars, knights or commons, this one looked battered as his boots.

"The king will be here tonight. Aelredson, do you hear?"

Robin barely nodded. *"Merci, bon père."*

"My chaplain tells me you have not heard Mass this week."

"No."

"Nor confessed," Willelm added. "That shows a slack spiritual condition, my son."

Robin swung his long legs down from the stone ledge. "Among my servants' people, their druids always worshiped in the open, and my own priest as well on fine days. Your church is cold and dark, Father Abbot. I smother in it. I can't find God."

The abbot accepted that without comment; his church was a bit gloomy, but God was even at a man's elbow, and confession was a different matter. "Why have you not taken the sacrament Holy Church offers you?"

The shabby Englishman stared at his rag doll. He appeared to think the question over with his poppet. Willelm remembered the man's eyes at first meeting, bright blue. Now they were faded to the color of winter sleet.

"Confess what, Father? That I am lonely? Absolve me of that; of being kept years from every love that spells out life to me. Dip in your font and cleanse me of the insane waste I've looked on. Do that, good abbot—then tell me God's purpose is a mystery, when I can't even find

227

my own these days. By your leave, I'll settle for a cup of wine in the refectory and a little sleep.''

Abbot Willelm understood now, or thought he did. Many knights had spoken of this peculiar spiritual exhaustion when they had looked too long on death, but none used a child's doll to focus their thoughts.

Robin held it up. ''This is for our puissant king. A messenger from Gisors. My daughter had such a doll when I left. My lady made it out of good linen, bit of red samite for the kirtle. We considered long what face to paint on it. One Moira could talk to and trust with her secrets. This belonged to a peasant child at Gisors. The last Frank raid caught the manor serfs between them and us. Ruined the royal hay.'' Robin lifted the doll in salute. ''Give you good day, Father.''

King William arrived at Fécamp late that evening, soaked thoroughly from the first autumn rain. He summoned Robin to audience in Abbot Willelm's own quarters, as dark and cheerless as the abbey church. The fleshy, hulking old king sat warming his bones before a built-up log fire. When Robin appeared, William waved him without ceremony to a chair facing the fire. A small table stood between the chairs with wine and wooden goblets. Robin would have gone down on one knee; the king prevented him gruffly.

''No, enough of that. Rossel told me of your leg.''

''Thanks to my liege. The wet gets into it.''

''Or perhaps you are not as nimble as before,'' said William with a trace of cordial spite. He indicated the wine. Robin poured a cup. Far better than the swill at Gisors. This wine did not shoot its acid up into his nose, but lay warm on the tongue. ''A friendly vintage, sir.''

''Um. And what of my brother king in Denmark? What of Cnut?''

''At Odin's board, *mon roi*. Or with Jesus, if one will.''

''There was difficulty?''

''Very little.'' Robin grimaced into his wine. ''The Danish earls were so bent that way already, they'd have done him for a shilling.''

''Rest his soul,'' William observed piously, ''and that of the bishop of Rome.''

Robin looked up, surprised. ''The pope is dead?''

''You've not heard? No, I suppose not, traveling as you were.'' The king crossed himself carefully. ''Stainless Gregory. One less paragon in my bosom. The man was mad as you, Denby, though not nearly as useful. When I thought of Cnut, I remembered that no man would want Danes in England less than you.''

228

William bent with a grunt of exertion to pick up a manuscript lying by his chair. "Would you were so malleable in all things. You remember this? Your description of Saxon government from top to bottom."

Or rather from bottom to top. From local hallmoot through the Hundred and forest courts to shire assemblies and to the Witan where the peers of England had argued law with reason rather than swords whenever they could. Two years ago, in levying his war tax, William had been astonished at the dispatch with which money could be collected and reported through this miracle of machinery. He was already formulating more far-reaching uses of the mechanism. He raised his cup to Robin. "I do not read well, but I have troubled to study you, Denby. Several times over."

"My lord flatters me."

"Your lord prudently keeps you under his thumb, and quite right. Your notions are insane."

"Forgive me, sir. I am not insane, nor is what I wrote."

"Unworkable then. A man might paint an angel's wing, but I'd like to see him try to fly with it. Your ideas of government are impossible as a child's dream. Credit me for thinking as well as you write. I am a juggler on a high rope, Denby. Everyone is waiting for me to fall, except God, who says I may not just yet. To complete my sense of well-being, there are too damned many English like you who feel— don't deny it, you've written so on every page—that there is a kind of universal truth laymen may apply to the lords given to rule over them."

Robin's eyes were half closed. In firelit profile he seemed to the king to be terminally weary. "Ideals, my lord. Not always what was, but what should be."

And who was he to say what should be? Speak of presumption. "Why do you think you were banished? No more than a boy when you first troubled me, argued with me, and you're still what your own people call thick. You waste your life in this. God rules, Christ will come again. The order of the world is fixed."

Robin turned to him, respectful but sure. "No, my lord king."

"Indeed? Then grant that I have been given to keep order while I breathe. That is reality. I have just sent you to buy the death of a king with hard money. *There* is reality. You might have accepted the world like other men."

"Like Ranulf, my lord?"

William detected the subtle sting but chose to ignore it. "Ranulf knows his place. He does as he is bidden. If he pinches off a bit for himself, it's not enough to matter. Most capable officers do. I'd not expect else.''

Robin pulled his chair closer to the fire, unclasping the torn cloak. In tossing it over the back of the chair, the doll tumbled from an inner pocket. Robin settled again, holding the grimy toy. "I cannot believe that the world is fixed, sir. It moves.''

Utter rot to William. The man could be burned for such sentiments in certain zealous quarters of Normandy or even England. "I might expect such cant from you.''

"Not fixed," Robin repeated. "Not miracle, but mundane method." Robin could give proof. Did the king remember the end of the world expected in the year 1000? "Not twoscore years before my king was born. My grandfather was a boy when the millenium neared. Many men thought the world was going to end with it. A tidy round number to end the lot.''

But oh, the signs and portents in that thousandth year from Christ's birth. The great comet had come not ten years before, and men thought *that* might have signaled the coming end. The fear in men, the *change* in them. The churches began to fill at every Mass. Men gave away all they owned, lavished kindness on their enemies, even stopped beating their wives. As midnight grew near on the last day, they gathered in churches to wait the inevitable, shivering, but pure as possible.

The first stroke of the hour. Men closed their eyes, held their breath. Clutched crucifixes and relics or those closest about them, listening in terror as the bell tolled away their last moments, hoping their desperate atonement would suffice heaven. One more stroke and the heavens would tear asunder and Christ come striding in fearful majesty. The bell struck twelve and echoed away to silence.

Robin paused. William found he was leaning forward to the storyteller. "What happened?''

"Obviously nothing, sir. Crowded in the church, waiting for time to run out and when it did . . . nothing.''

Silent, rigid, men looked about, hardly daring to breathe. The minutes crept by, became hours melting down the candles. Men began to feel foolish, then resentful. Lifetime habits reasserted themselves. They grew hungry, children squalled to be fed or needed the latrine. Life to be gotten on with. The day came and others afterward. Gradually, men put virtue away for future emergencies and went about restoring the ravages of generosity. Shops reopened for sharp trading, and the world went on.

"Goes on yet," Robin concluded. "Desperately in need of a good clerk. Christ is coming for a surety, but not today, not for a while. We don't get off that neatly. There's our own linen to wash first."

While Robin stared at the foolish rag doll, William savored his wine and considered the tale the Englishman painted in weary, cynical phrases. For a ruler with large spiritual debts, the story offered a certain comfort. William understood ambition in any form; Robin's he could never put name or reason to, and that bothered him. A dangerous man and banished for that, but somehow not self-seeking like Odo or even Ranulf, perhaps not even an idealist any longer.

"Do I detect despair in you?" William found himself hoping he did. Despair gave in where defiance struck back.

"Sometimes, my lord."

"Denby, what is that ridiculous doll for? Have you gone weak-minded?"

"After a battle, a priest said I should say my rosary. Didn't have one, so I used this."

"Devotions to a doll? Rossel agrees that you are difficult to comprehend, but never doubted your sanity."

"This is a sort of delegate to my king. On one of the French raids, our castle held, but the near manor village caught the worst of it. Prince William caught the Frank knights and cut them off from retreat in one of your own fields. At haying time it was. Field was full of serfs."

Robin held up the limp doll. "And their children. Both sides charged together. There wasn't that much time to get clear. Not a difficult calculation: You take the speed of a Flemish horse at full tilt and double that, and that's how fast both sides are coming at the middle, and a wee girl ent that quick."

The voice troubled William's ear like a tired ghost. "Won't see much hay out of that field this year, in case your stewards note the shortage. We beat them back, of course. Nothing changed, though. Prince William had his tent put up just there in the field, his knights took what food was left in the village, and they supped where they'd fought."

Captors and captives were feasting together, discussing ransoms over meat when a sorry, cringing deputation of villagers was prodded into the tent. So please the son of their liege lord, could they have permission to go about the field with their lanterns to find their own dead?

"Ralf Fitz-Gerald told me our women did the same at Hastings," Robin recalled.

"Yes, they did." Some days no man forgot, especially a conqueror.

When William won England in that terrible October day at Hastings, never sure, even now, whether God approved, the Saxon women came crying over the field at night, searching for their men. Some said Harold's handfast wife Edith was among them. Right or not, some hours and the cost of them, their sights and sounds, stayed with a man all his life.

That was what Robin remembered clearest about the field at Gisors. When the knights weren't roaring at one another, he could hear the women searching and calling. Finding. While, inside the tent, those not yet snoring on the table or under it talked of ransoms and honor.

"The peasants were gone in the morning. I found this doll near the remains of a haystack, and later I asked questions of it. What, I asked, can one man, even a gossamer-pure Christ, do in such a world? Despair, my lord? Aye, there's that, but I'd take it kindly if the king would not call me insane."

Robin rose gingerly, favoring his bad leg, and threw the cloak over his shoulders. "My lord has studied my writings to understand England. The serfs at Gisors, they're not all that different. The ideal of a balanced, God-ordained world? Those dead in the field knew what balance means in a famine. It means enough food for another day, another week, so children may survive and not go into the ground when they're barely baptized. Ask them about God's reasons, my lord. Listen to them when you speak of faith or despair. That night in Gisors, I asked of this doll—whose counsel was sound as any present—what it thought of faith and God's purposes. And it replied: God is a clumsy child playing with ill-made toys and breaking them all in time. May I have the king's leave to go to bed? I must return to Gisors tomorrow."

"Yes, certainly," William said quickly. "By the by, well done at Odense. You were the right agent for the task. I will remember your good service."

"Thanks to my liege." Robin put the doll on the table by the king's chair. "But if Christ ent coming this week, we still have to go on as if he were, setting our table for an expected guest."

As Robin limped toward the door, William stopped him, curious. "Tell me something. Truthfully, if you will."

"Sir?"

"All those years ago, if I'd made you a baron as Waltheof promised to do, would you still have been trouble to me?"

"I don't know, sir. Perhaps. Even without purpose, there's the habit."

William held out the doll. "You forgot your rosary."

"That belongs to the king. Royal property like the forests. Bayeux would take it under crown stewardship, I'm sure. Perhaps he'll find a way to tax it. Good rest to my lord."

Unchanged, William thought. *Respectful but quite mad.* No king could free such a man while he lived, perhaps while kingship itself lived.

William drained his cup and reached for more, wheezing at the strain on his now formidable paunch. His heartbeat felt irregular as Denby's limping footsteps fading away.

William looked into the doll's painted eyes and sour-twisted grin.

"Lunatic."

30

WILLIAM's mind, hardening in loneliness and vexed with problems, nevertheless churned as efficiently as the English legal system he admired. At Christmas in Gloucester, he unveiled his master plan for the comprehensive survey of all holdings within England. The inquiry was divided by areas among seven separate commissions. Each section compiled, a second commission verified the findings of the first seven. This *descriptio* was so thorough and thoroughly detested that men high and low began to call it Domesday Book.

Men resisted the survey, since William was obviously using it to tighten his stranglehold on the national purse strings. As if in fury at this added burden, English weather reared up and screamed, breaking loose like a maddened stallion. Nurturing summer darkened like God's own anger and flailed at the land with lightning and thunderstorms, lashing at Denby even as the king's commissioners tabulated the worth of the holding.

A fearsome bolt struck and scorched a wagon outside the barn with an end-of-the-world *crack!* that made all duck instinctively. Before the Normans could even cross themselves, Edward darted across the courtyard toward his sister. "Moira, stay where you are!"—scooped up the squalling child in his arms and dove into the barn.

"*Ma foi,*" gasped one Norman officer, shaking the pelting rain from his cloak. "One would think God himself is out of temper."

"That ent half," Marian grated flatly through Mauger as interpreter. "Our grain's beaten down on the stalk, the other crops nigh ruined. You want to note that in your book?"

With acid courtesy, she went on to suggest what the king could do with his tally once completed.

Totally involved with his survey, William and his appanage plodded into Winchester at Easter for Ranulf's report on progress to date. "My lord, it proceeds but not without hindrance. There have been disturbances in the Midlands and west."

In Sherwood, men resisted the commissioners with curses and hurled stones. Graver news reached William of widespread cattle blight. His officers were duty-bound to predict ruinously poor crops with famine sure to follow.

After Lammas in August, when the pathetic yield was gathered in, the king's survey parties trudged on their rounds while his sheriffs dashed about their territories to control men sharp with hunger, then openly defiant and plundering to feed their own. When the second commission arrived at Denby after Martinmas in November, they were given small welcome and flat facts by Mauger.

"Of thirty swine, we've eaten three and salted six. Three sows we'll keep over the winter; the rest we gave out to Blidworth. The king can have his choice of dead pigs or starved people."

What Marian's steward prudently elided was that Will Scatloch and Morgan had been directed by the lady herself to hinder no man in the taking of red deer. Denby was a living thing, a whole wherein one part aided and restored another at need. So a man stayed within reason providing for his family—well, what he took of the king's venison might not be justice to William, though surely so to God and the English saints.

"Therefore, what such men confess to you," Maud advised Father Beorn in his church, "is between them and God, is it not? We will manage, I think."

"If the salt meat and winter vegetables last," Beorn worried. "If the royal warders don't notice there are bits of everything that goes on four legs hanging from every eave in Denby."

If worst came to worst, there were the horses. Maud gave her priest a smile thin as their resources. "We've eaten horse before."

"Oh-ho, we have that." Beorn looked closely at Maud. "Just there's nary soul at Mass whose garments aren't hanging loose. As yours, dear Maud."

"And yours, you ancient war-horse."

"We'll make do, I suppose," Beorn allowed. "God knows how.

Perhaps we can ask Him. Come pray with me.'' The priest fell back on a long memory of catastrophes weathered on Denby holding. ''It is the young who must be told the sun always comes out again. But aye, we'll manage.''

''More than manage.'' Maud's small hand came down with a smack on the altar rail. When she turned to Beorn, she had the look he had seen many times among carls forming a last shield wall around their lord. In his youth, Beorn had been many times a link in such walls, and Maud was bred from them. ''Mark you, we will endure. As for loose garments, consider the positive uses of vanity, old friend. A little hunger does wonders for my figure.''

A proud joke. England endured but writhed in agony. Some men rose up against their sworn lords. Something ancient, passing through fire, became a new thing.

''This way! Follow me, bring him in. Gently there, he's lost too much blood already.''

Henri Chailliard led the soldiers carrying Ralf, ignoring the clustered servants, pausing only to give white-faced Judith a reassuring nod. ''Sword in his side. Don't worry, he's hardy enough.''

They laid Ralf on a table in the hall and unbuckled his torn mail while Judith sent for poultice and bandage.

''Near Linby Dale. Alan's old freemen,'' Ralf gritted through his pain. ''Swarmed out of the forest with axes, bill hooks, anything. I don't blame them. Christ . . . ''

''Easy, my love,'' Judith soothed as she cleaned the wound. The filthy thing was deeper than she thought. A little more force would have sliced into her husband's vitals. She tried not to let Ralf feel her hands trembling on his flesh.

''I'm glad. . . . '' He tried to raise his head, but the wound screamed against the effort. He lay back. Henri folded a cloak under his head. ''I've been lucky too long, Judith. How deep is it?''

''Deep enough to keep you off a horse for a while. Lie still.''

Ralf groaned. ''I am getting too old for this.''

''Still, I said! Almost done.'' Hating the sight and smell of blood, Judith swallowed back her nausea and fear. The wound had bled freely but would, thank God, leave no more than one more scar on the flesh so much a part of herself. ''Lie quiet.''

''Damn it, I don't feel quiet!''

236

Henri restrained the man firmly. "Will you lie down? Do you want to be weak as a kitten for a fortnight?"

"Using my sword on people who are only hungry and in the right. Thank God Robin is not here."

In that famine-ridden year, less compassionate lords than Ralf or foresters like Will Scatloch caught their gaunt peasants with a fresh-killed buck on royal preserve, and the hangman's ropes stretched and creaked in the wind.

On Steep Hill in Lincoln, famine was a more distant fact. Because he had known poverty in childhood, Ranulf would have nothing but the best now, and Elfled knew the best. Bread was scarcer, the beggars thinner and more numerous at the scullery door. Totally absorbed in the king's survey, Ranulf was seldom home. Elfled busied herself with the children, ordered new material for clothes, and found in her mirror a limpid, fascinating destiny unfolding like an illuminated scroll. No signs of age yet—and her Robin was alive!

The news of his deliverance had traveled with common folk from Blidworth to Grantham honey fair, thence through Ancaster along Ermine Street to Lincoln. At about the same time, a sardonically courteous letter arrived for Ranulf from the vicomte of Nottingham, though penned in a curiously feminine hand.

Since the keeper of the Chancery seal was so prompt in forwarding the news of Edward Aelredson's death, we happily assure him the report has proven erroneous, knowing how much this fortunate sequel will mean to him.

Not only alive, but the subject of a new ballad Elfled heard sung in Wigford market: Robin crossing the Channel to Normandy, attacked by pirates. In one version, his boat was a fishing vessel; in another, he journeyed with the king, sweeping the pirate decks clear with his bow. Elfled heard the songs in a tremulous mood, convinced that fate moved apace, both for her and Robin. Her astrologer had forecast most significantly for her. Elfled's seer was a toothless Scot with a certain seedy panache and a tendency to wax lyrical over his third cup, while never forgetting to exact payment for his services.

"Portents have nae ever been so clear for my lady's sign in this month and house. Great changes are shown. Aye, gr-reat changes. Your life will turn a corner soon. As if on a sea journey, my lady will embark on a venture of the spirit.''

As on a sea journey . . . and the man yet alive. Piece by piece, the imperative came clearer to Elfled. What could it mean, this new direction to her life, but that she would meet Robin in a foreign land, and where but Normandy?

Winter thawed to spring and warmed to summer. Ranulf, with the great survey near completion, could hardly wait to present William personally with the first overall estimate of a country whose potential wealth and the efficient means to tap it would be the envy of every cash-poor king in Europe. William was presently at Rouen. Ranulf would voyage thither and enlighten him. Furthermore, Elfled might accompany him to be presented at court. She had not traveled much, and the time had come for her to gravitate to higher circles. She could have new clothes cut by fine Continental tailors. Yes, Ranulf was pleased with his idea and the generosity it reflected. Elfled would see without having to be told how important and central her husband was to the greatest king in Europe. *Sans doute,* this would be the high point of her life.

Ranulf would never know how high. For Elfled, when he suggested the voyage (after her subtle but persistent hinting), the last hinge of destiny fell into place, the last star aligned in her cosmos. She packed her best clothes, stepped onto the boat, and then from the deck to shore with a high heart, not even plagued by seasickness. ''Life and love have called me to France,'' she trilled. So far from blushing at her overripe conception, Elfled virtually set it to music in what would be—oh, surely!—the most enduring ballad of Robin Hood, his love for the virtuous but ripe and available Lady of Lincoln.

In her complacency at least, Elfled was impregnable. She might have asked the king's view of astrologers, since his own drowned during the invasion of England with no advance word of his own abbreviation. Seers in Rouen were as myopic this year. They read in circle or rune no hint of the French cavalry marshaling west of Mantes, heard no rumbling of the heavy wheels of siege engines as they ground through July dust and heat toward the bridges on River Epte. The strongest salient was personally commanded by young King Philip. William was old, William was ill. No better time to reduce the troublesome vassal to impotence. After three years, the savage, blood-soaked war-in-fact was now war-in-name.

Not much difference to the defenders of Gisors, simply more men and arrows coming at them. Philip would cross the river; Rossel couldn't stop that, but severed bridges would slow him down. That July, while Rossel and his men hacked and tore at the Gisors bridge, his scouts across Epte hunted French columns, Robin among them.

He crouched low over Hratha's neck, the warm reek of her coat mixed in his nostrils with the smell of his own fear as he dashed through the last thinning stand of trees toward the river and Gisors bridge. Pray it still stood.

Too close behind him, the four fast-mounted French knights were laughing as they closed in. Sweat stung Robin's eyes as he slid off to one side of Hratha's straining shoulder for cover, and crossbolts whined bare inches over him.

"Go, girl," he prayed. *"Va, va, go."*

The tough little mare lifted over a fallen tree in an explosion of energy, flattened the line between her head and neck, and broke out onto the river bank, Philip's men close behind. A furlong to the bridge, no more than that. Another bolt grazed Robin's sleeve—

HailMaryfull'vegraceLordiswiththeeblessed—lucky it's crossbows. Can't hit a broad tree most times, but when they do it's all over. Jesus, Mary, and rutting Joseph, get me to that bridge.

He'd made the one mistake scouts couldn't afford, not and live: counting Philip's forces as they got nearer, heat turning the dusty road into mirage where men and horses floated and shimmered in the eye. Nearer then, Philip himself at the column point. Robin found himself fitting a bolt to the ready-wound crossbow.

Foolish; the weapon was useless at more than fifty yards, usually less. But if he could . . . just one bolt, like the shot that won him the golden arrow at Grantham years gone. The sun dazzled on Philip's resplendent mail. A good seventy yards still, but Robin had to try, had to do for that glittering Frank son of a—

Wait, let him come closer . . . closer. So he indulged, forfeited wariness for concentration, forgot that Philip would have scouts as well. They burst charging out of the wood behind him and almost cut him off. Damned fool.

Almost to the bridge. Robin's pounding heart redoubled to the hammering of a demon blacksmith. Rossel's men were in the water, hacking furiously at the bridge pilings; the whole middle span leaned aslant. Toward the eastern end, as Robin galloped nearer, a detachment of crossbow archers crouched behind shield bearers to discourage anyone who made it to the bridge in Robin's wake. They looked nervous, trying

239

to keep their footing as the bridge wobbled and shook beneath them. Hratha swerved onto the bridge planks, hoofs drumming hollowly.

"Get out of the way!" Robin bawled. "Give'm a flight. Cover me, you sods!"

The archers loosed at the Frank scouts, then leaped out of Hratha's plunging way, clutching at the bridge railings. Robin hurtled along the canting bridge, gut-sick for one horrible instant when Hratha stumbled and recovered. Then lighter drumming as she cleared the bridge and brought up short amid anxious, sweating, frightened men who didn't want to die today but knew they might. Robin leapt down and grabbed one by his mail hauberk, panting at the man.

"*Ou est Rossel? Foutredieu cochon,* where's the prince?"

The man's arm jerked toward the churned water and the ax-wielding men. "Down there."

Robin lurched down the bank into the warm shallows where, naked to the waist, Rossel was attacking a timber piling with an ax and a joyous rage. The man's bull body flowed like the river about him. The ax bit and tore loose, swung high, and sank again. Like Little John at Norwich, Robin recalled. The thing had begun, was here to do, and Rossel had never looked so cholerically content.

"Prince!"

"Robin! I see you found the buggers."

"They found me." Robin pointed to the far bank and the tree line that now bled Frenchmen as from a dozen wounds. "One thing about getting shot at: takes your mind off your other griefs."

Rossel wiped at his sweaty face. "How many?"

"At least a thousand. Six hundred knights, close to a hundred sappers and pioneers. Siege towers and catapults on wagons. Not assembled, but plenty of them."

"And Philip?"

"Can't miss him," Robin spluttered, splashing water over his sweaty face and neck. "Gilded mail, riding a dappled grey. Bloody fool's begging to be had. Look! There he is."

The glittering rider pranced his big grey insolently along the bank just out of crossbolt range. Rossel sank his ax in the near-severed piling and surged toward shore with Robin close behind. He gained the shallows and ran like a clumsy bear toward the bridge, thumped along the span swaying and creaking under him, roaring at his archers. "Shoot faster! Keep them at a distance!"

"They'll stay out of range for now," Robin guessed. He yearned physically toward the French king. "One longbow and one arrow, Rossel. One: I could change your father's map right here."

No matter, Rossel was enjoying himself. Hands on broad, muscled hips, he grinned lethally at the distant French king, then bounded away, jumping high for pure good spirits like Robin's Edward let loose from lessons, to barge through his archers and bellow at France—"*Hé, Philip! Tu te fais pomper le moeud par ta petite soeur?* You still doing your little sister in the mouth? You come to Gisors, I'll have your pretty-barbered head on a plate."

To punctuate the sentiment, Rossel chopped left hand into right elbow in defiance of all Franks and trotted back toward Robin, bellowing commands to his archers. "When the bridge goes, jump and swim. You can't swim, jump and pray. Robin—" The prince confronted his scout with new orders. "Walk that silly toy horse of yours until she's rested, then ride for Rouen. Get a remount at Les Andelys or Pont-de-l'Arche. The roads are dry, you can reach Father at Rouen tonight." Rossel tugged his seal ring from one finger and thrust it at Robin. "And I mean *ride*. Kill the horse if you have to."

"Eaten 'em when I had to. Nothing personal."

"Tell Father . . . " The furious forward motion in Rossel paused, suspended. A shade of worry shadowed his tanned face as he glanced back at the French pouring out of the wood and spreading along the eastern bank of the river. East of the wood, the rumble of heavy wheels grew louder. "Tell him the situation and Philip's strength. He'll leave some men here to pin us down, but he'll come on himself. And tell him . . . "

Robin saw all of the man shut down tight around something that Robin sensed without words. He said it for Rossel. "I know. I'll tell him."

"So you will." Rossel gathered Robin in a crushing embrace. "By God, you will. I wish I could trust these here so well as you there. Take care, *Anglais*. Take good care. Sorry you'll miss the fun."

Rossel ran down the bank, leaping into the water. Robin saw him churn toward his ax left buried in the piling. Rossel tore it loose, slung it away, and hurled his whole body against the wood with a roar of released energy.

"Eeeeeaah!"

The timber screamed and splintered, gave way. The whole span collapsed into River Epte. If Philip wanted Gisors now, he'd have to swim and sweat for it.

31

S UPPER was held late, the king closeted long with Ranulf and the business of the English survey. Compline bells had rung a half hour past; servants scurried between the lower tables, bearing away broken meats and other leftovers. The air in the palace hall was humid; scented torches helped a little against the city stink from beyond the uncurtained casements, and now the lively airs of pipe and tabor gave way to a limpid harp that filigreed the murmur from the tables.

Elfled was glad she hadn't worn red, which made her look thicker in the new, fitted styles. Before dressing for supper, she'd inclined to that or the green—the latter worn the day she met Robin for the first time—but finally chose the gold-piped blue with a yellow veil to set off her own fair coloring. The somber old king himself ventured a compliment or two.

The evening meal was informal that night, only five of them at the high table: William flanked on his right by Ranulf and old Fitz-Osbern, on the left by Elfled and William Bon-Ame, Archbishop of Rouen. Elfled and the king ate from common dishes before them. The king must be near sixty, she judged, his once-reddish hair faded to the color of sand around the skull cap that concealed advancing baldness. A strong countenance etched deep with frowning lines. From choleric complexion to his great belly and wheezing breath, the man sagged with flesh and years. He ate and drank a great deal with a plodding indulgence that seemed to take no pleasure in what he stuffed and swilled.

William sat back with a phlegmy sigh of repletion, cleaning his fingers in a bowl of rose water. He smiled at Elfled. "You remind me of the queen somewhat. When she was young."

"God rest her royal spirit," Elfled responded, not knowing what else she could say.

William turned away. A sad gallantry at best. Elfled could hardly expect to plumb its true depths. In truth, she reminded him less of Mora than of his love for her at that age. Observing Elfled, William recalled in a poignant flash a ghost whose clear eyes once told him her every mood before the habit of rule masked them with reserve. William had remembrance in cruel excess now, betrayed all too often by small, dear things lurking where his heart would catch on them. A bag of dried lavender in an old chest, a glove or favorite kerchief still faintly scented. Looking at Ranulf's merely pretty wife in a wine-warmed moment, the old man reached for a shadow. *With twenty more beautiful women in a room, my eye always went to Mora. She was ever the only one.*

William drank the wine that dulled the ache, as the chamberlain hurried down the crowded hall toward the high table.

"My lord! A messenger from Prince William."

Elfled's fingers clenched tight about the wine goblet as the gaunt, limping figure approached the dais. Her stars were unerring, her seer spoke true. But his left leg dragged, and there was more grey streaking the overgrown hair and beard. The shabby stained cloak tossed over one shoulder might have been used often to swab a horse or a hurt. But it was him. Suddenly, the great space of the hall held only the two of them. She saw his eyes flick coldly to Ranulf before the splendid, shaggy head bowed to the king.

"Give you good evening, Denby," William rumbled. "What from the prince?"

"Sir, Philip crossed Epte in force this morning. By now Gisors is besieged and the other marcher forts as well. My lord is at war with France."

"Stay, I will come down." William pushed himself up, signaling the tables at large to remain seated. The hall buzzed with the news of war. The man who brought it stood waiting and far too thin to Elfled, a blade honed and worn long past keenness. *Here I am. I came for you. Look at me.*

He did. Elfled thought she read recognition in his eyes—then he wiped at them to clear the grit of travel and fatigue and followed after the king. That was all. Barely glanced at her. With an effort, Elfled beamed dutifully at her husband and the archbishop, then drained her wine and set the cup down with too much force. When a servant refilled it, she declined the diluting water.

The king stood on no ceremony, but led Robin to the baths in the cellar where water was always kept boiling, ordered the menials out and Robin in, leaning over the lip of the tub while the Englishman soaked, scrubbed, and swallowed nourishing onion soup.

"Don't nod off, Denby. Tell me everything."

So he did, every detail of Philip's strength and equipment. The French king was likely deeper into Normandy now. William should assume that all border forts were pinned down and that Philip might well drive on Rouen.

"Take me?" The notion brought a grim smirk to William's seamed face. "That will be the luckiest day that overweening pup ever lived. How long can the prince hold Gisors?"

"As long as there's breath in his body. He defied Philip. By Dunstan, he did that right enough. The last I saw of the prince, he was tearing Gisors bridge apart with his bare hands."

Robin hauled himself out of the tub and sank down, naked and dripping on a bench. "I know Rossel, my lord. Pardon the presumption, but he'd cut off his arm if you commanded."

William's hard eyes softened for a moment. "I wouldn't know you without the presumption—but you remind me of truth. I know my son's loyalty." He threw a towel at Robin. "Here, get you to bed, I've work to do."

Messengers were already toiling through the Normandy night to summon William's chief nobles. Accommodations within the palace would be alloted by rank. Robin was given a tiny cell below, not far from the one he'd occupied before, and no better appointed. The heat of the day lingered in the stone walls and the rank smell of the garderobe mixed with the pungent effluvium of Rouen at large. A single horn lamp flickered in one corner. In Robin's exhaustion, darkness was light enough. He sprawled on the bare straw mattress, naked to the waist, sweating lightly while he savored raw apple liquor fermented as his thoughts, but a merciful wall between himself and the world.

Ralf would understand. Wish I could talk to him now. My good friend, my old enemy. He's been where I've been, where hell is reality and heaven just a word. Slaughter in the morning, plunder by noon, and Mass at night—all off their dumb-brute backs like water off a duck. Drink more, man, drink faster. If there's no place like home, the next best is numb. Oh, Ysabeau, wise whore, you were right.

When he closed his eyes, he was riding still, Hratha pounding under him toward the bridge over Epte, toward Rouen, the miles and the miles. Sudden tears spilled down his cheeks—despair, exhaustion, drunken self-pity or requiem, Robin couldn't tell, only let them fall while the harsh brandy carried him to numb and beyond.

The faint tap on his door was so tentative, Robin thought he imagined it until it sounded again.

"Aye, what? 'S' not barred."

The heavy door squeaked open, then quickly shut behind the woman. Robin blinked at her. She was a dim presence in low light, a shadow speaking to him softly and urgently. Under the blood rushing in his ears, he heard her from a great distance. Now she came closer. Sat down on the one stool by his bed—shy, murmuring of something he couldn't follow and didn't understand at all.

He remembered her now. Ranulf's wife from Lincoln. But what she spoke or why she perched there, stiff, knees drawn together, was absurd, no more to do with him than the far side of the moon. It hardly seemed to matter to her that he said nothing. The woman went on and on, building in intensity, something in her face, when she lifted her adoring gaze to him, like the ecstasy of a nun at devotions. His silence apparently gave her confidence. She bent forward in the feeble light, whispering, reaching to touch him, talking of dreams and destiny and longing, as if these things concerned him. Yet his own starved body stirred at the nearness of her, basic as the smell of cooked food, no more than that. Not so much a woman but a respite, a staunching, a place to thrust and bury himself inside. He reached for her and through her to all the lost things. Pulled her down onto the bed, felt his mouth ravaged out of hunger fierce as his own. Far away, his hands unlaced her bodice. Less clumsy, she hurried the laces herself.

She wrapped her arms and legs and her foolish life around the dream of him, and Robin took her in despair and, somewhere behind the blood roaring in his brain, an irrelevant drunken pity. It was brief. Quickly done, he fell away from the woman into stupor and darkness—until something moved, made a sound he couldn't identify, and he started awake on guard against the French scouts.

* * *

Elfled didn't know how long he lay like a corpse beside her. For longer than his blunt, brutal invasion of her body. He took her with no tenderness or sharing, not even preparation. She was willing but hardly ready, and so he hurt her. That was the least of it; she could bear with that.

Shaking and cold despite the humid night air that reeked of his male sweat, Elfled lay still beside Robin's inert body. Numb. Where she expected to be filled, she had been emptied, snatched up, sucked dry, and then forgotten. Lost now, she tried to gather the rags of her dream about her, fit them once more to the oblivious stranger who took her body without touching *her* at all, and *why?* when her love for him was so complete and pure?

That was the crossing of their stars, that she would find him in France and he would love her. Still, as she had shyly told him before he took her and the brief warmth of being with him went cold, she had drunk more wine than usual to give her courage, and bribed a minor chamberwoman, who appeared quite used to this sort of thing, to guide her to this drab, dirty cell. So often and for so long, she had pictured this meeting. Then—done, slammed through that rudely, the hard, drunken body flailing viciously at her. He made her feel she was not even part of the act.

In stuporous sleep now, his breathing was shallow. Then, suddenly, as Elfled watched, he started awake like an animal too used to fear and being hunted—saw her and remembered. The snarl that came out of sleep with him relaxed, and his eyes dimmed to a kind of blankness. Elfled hoped he would speak now, say something to her to help her feel close. Robin only rolled off the bed and stumbled to a bucket in one corner, scooping up water to splash over his weather-burned face. He gathered up her clothes and set them beside her.

"Better go, then."

That was all? The hurt and no more than that? "Why, Robin? What—"

"It's nothing. But you must go."

"Look at me, Robin. Please."

He wouldn't. "I don't know why you came."

"I told you why I came. Why did you make it so . . . " Elfled tried to frame what she felt. Rejection and this kind of loneliness were new and alien to her. "As if you don't care about me, when I know you do."

"What are you talking about?"

"You must."

He only looked puzzled and weary. "Woman—"

"My name is Elfled. You have not forgotten."

Robin rubbed the sleep and liquor fog from red-rimmed eyes. Even in feeble light, Elfled could see how mauled the long body was, ribs showing clearly in the thin torso, the dark line of the leg wound that would leave him halt for years, and the paler indentation like a puckered mouth over his left hip. The folk said Robin had nine lives: This was what they cost him. "I was drunk. I'm still drunk, come to that. Don't make it more than it was."

"No more?" Her own voice squeaked with tension. "I came to give to you, to . . . answer you. I don't want to believe you raped me."

"Rape? Jesus, woman, you'd make the Devil blush."

Little better than that. For one savage instant, Elfled wanted to hurt him back with interest, capable of anything, of screaming for guards or anyone else that he raped her—and didn't he just? No, she was the practical daughter of a merchant. Charge rape against a man as important in his way to the king as her husband? The bribed chamberwoman might have an attack of conscience under oath, and inquiry would reveal questionable circumstances. How in hell did he drag her the length of the palace and down a flight of stairs, she presumably struggling all the while to preserve her chastity, without someone hearing? Unlikely— but it would serve him right.

"You tore my clothes off—"

"You couldn't get out of 'em fast enough."

"You threw me over this bed like a sack of grain."

"*Look* at me!"

In the last warmth of her own dream, Elfled did, wanting to be closer, to touch what she loved in him; to tell him that his eyes were what she loved first, so gentle and sad. That she had desired to feast on his mouth. That if he'd been only an afternoon's fancy to a neglected wife, she would never have gone to see her rival. No, the dream would have been more than enough then while she touched her own body and thought of him.

Now, in the cold span of several heartbeats, Elfled actually *saw* him. Saw something no part of any dream, but old, age gathering behind the last of his youth, not kind or gentle, only gnarled tight.

"Look at me, you foolish girl. It could have been anyone who came,

247

do you hear? An old crone, I'd cry on her breast. A priest, I'd babble and care not whether God heard or not. A scullery girl the same. Someone to bury myself in. Anyone.''

"No," Elfled denied. "Not you. You are not so unfeeling. I know when a man wants me."

"Do you? There's wisdom." Robin began to draw on his tattered trousers. "You've a Norman husband, you know lying and smiling's the only way we've survived under them. I can play anything, be anything, easy as a whore smiles, because I've had to. And I do priests very well.''

No, not so. Elfled wouldn't have it. Her life and stars did not sort that way. "I don't believe you."

"No? Ranulf was a danger to us. I had to know who he was. What he was.''

"And tonight?"

Robin turned to her. Elfled felt something in him was trying to be gentle or at least no crueler than needed. "You came here for someone who never was. I was thinking of home and feeling empty. Hold out food to a starving man, you're surprised when he takes it?"

Elfled felt even colder now, miserable. "You took right enough."

"Woman—"

"Elfled! You know my name. Say it."

"Right then," he nodded wearily. "Elfled. See what you look at. Just once, see. I told you why I went to Lincoln. Because of that busy little man you married I've been four years in hell and more to come. Rape is it? There's the word for what he did."

"And you!"

"That's the weather in hell. Don't blame me." Robin held out the kirtle to her. "You must go now."

Elfled took the garment and her shift, holding them to cover herself with a kind of belated, ridiculous modesty. She was still trembling. "You didn't even wait . . . there are some niceties. At least Ranulf would take a little time before . . . not just bulls and cows." *I wanted to give you so much,* she grieved to the impassive stranger who'd taken and given nothing in return. *Not you but him I love. He's in you still, he must be.* "My stars told me to come to you, Robin."

His laugh was arid with disbelief. "Stars?"

"They said my life would change because of you."

"There was a squire at Gisors, decent sort. His stars told him he'd wear a coronet on his head one day. When last I saw him, his head was mostly gone. Whatever you spend on stars, it's too much.''

"They *never* lied to me."

"No, Elfled," he said with dry finality. "You lied to you."

He meant it. Elfled's heart and everything else inside her touched hard bottom. She'd been a fool and used, that was the sum of it. "I see."

Quickly, embarrassed now at being bare before him, she turned her back and slipped into her shift and kirtle. "Do up the laces in back. Do that much at least for a lady."

Which she was in fact, Elfled consoled herself with the prim judgment of her class, even as his cow-wife was one in name. That was their kind: Put *hlaefdige* before her name and the bitch was suddenly a world above her real betters. Elfled felt Robin's hands fumbling with the laces. Damned wife had likely never worn anything fitted, probably call them immodest, even shameless.

"There," he said. "All proper. Goodnight, Elfled."

Barren and miserable, nothing but to leave with what remained of pride. One hand on the latch, Elfled willed back her tears with an effort. She'd begged too pathetically as it was, where other and better men had deferred to and sought her. Elfled felt she'd been thrust brutally against something sharp that pierced and hollowed her out. "When I was—"

Robin didn't move. "You'd best go."

"No, you hear me. When I was little, Norman priests said you were half devil while our own folk thought you half a god. And so did I that day you came. I was so needy then. So lonely. I thought surely . . . oh, I did, Robin. That day and the next and the next, dreaming of you. You had no witting of what you began."

"Elfled, you made a mistake." Robin's tone was gentler now, or perhaps just thin with fatigue. He wilted down on the bed. "No great harm done if you go now."

No great harm? She stared at him. Damn him, did he know how hard it was for her to beg for love?

And you do not know what you may have begun in consequence, Robin. You hurt me and I bleed from it. Never ask forgiveness.

Elfled slipped out the door.

Time to be practical. She must slip unobserved up to her own chambers or at least to the hall where she might legitimately be seen without suspicion. The airless, dank corridor was barely lit by a guttering sconce where the stone stairs began. Elfled hurried through the puddle of light, but faltered in the shadows. Out of his sight what she would not show Robin rose now in her throat like a scream. She began to shake violently; when the trembling eased a little, she went on. If moments ago she thought she might sob with the pain in her, that was past. She was beyond tears now and into the unexpected worst agony of her life.

Ranulf ended his return journey at Winchester, sending Elfled north through London with an escort. She took no pleasure in the bustling city on Thames. She was ill, distracted, slept little and ate less. Elfled wondered if she might be pregnant again and what an exquisite cruelty *that* would be now. However, the weeks went by and, if anything, from the looser fit of her kirtles, she'd lost the better part of a stone in weight. She told herself a hundred times a day she had made a fool of herself and more fool now to pine, wrote the bitter lesson in acid on her heart— and went on grieving.

She lay abed whenever possible, glad Ranulf was away, and gave herself to brooding. No man ever hurt or rejected her so before. The few pains of her young life had been minor and brief, but this grew worse, gnawed and hollowed her out. Where an older or more resourceful woman might have fallen back on strengths or at least grown healthily bored with the matter, Elfled burrowed deeper into self-pity and a soft world of bittersweet. The image of Robin obsessed her still, but the light she bathed him in turned from brightness to shadow. Half devil or half god, they said. Wanting turned to anger and darkened toward revenge. For his sake and pure love, Elfled had gladly committed mortal sin. Not all her fault, Robin was as guilty. More so, a thousand times more. She must confess, but being English as the false lover who led her thence, Elfled would have it clearly understood by Heaven where the greater sin lay.

When he began to invade her fitful sleep and dreams, she was only a step from the belief that the man known even to his mother as Puck-Robin, now showed his true demon nature, seducing her as an incubus.

Since he could not get through siege to Rossel, Robin followed William in the king's personal guard, driving Philip back toward Epte and beyond. Relieving Rossel at Gisors finally, they routed a company of Philip's Genoese archers, some of whom had been equipped with passable longbows. While father and son embraced each other, sweaty and weeping, Robin purposefully salvaged bowstaves and strings, beeswax and arrows from the dead. Plain Norman soldiers who never heard of

Robin Hood remembered the shabby, slack-waisted Saxon who selected his targets like a steward choosing a good wine, and rarely missed. The greatest lords wore the most elaborate armor and were easy to spy out on the field. Attrition among Philip's commanders became critical as the arrow of William pushed deeper into the Vexin toward the town of Mantes, only thirty miles from Paris. Philip prudently retired to his capital. In Maine, Rossel's older brother, Count Robert, held aloof from his father's cause, vacillated and wasted his chances for succession in pride and folly.

July sweated and roiled into August. On the walls of Mantes, the garrison soldiers looked out from their posts to see the first elements of William's army plodding toward them, not to be stopped.

32

▶▶▶▶▶

WITHIN the walls of Mantes, the few experienced vavasors
not drained away for Philip's drive at Normandy knew how
sternly William spelled retribution. Surrender would be futile.
No quarter would be given.

"I will burn Mantes to the ground," he raged at the commanders on
the battlements above him. "Seek you God's mercy, not mine."

Better to fight, as the young knights urged, than to live in shame.
The high-tempered younger sons of cadet houses, their ransoms would
not be much in any case but disgrace everlasting. Puppies eager to be
at an old dog, fatally underestimating the sharpness of his teeth, they
burst out of their walls in a sortie with more fury than aim. Outnumbered
and in disorder from the first, the few survivors retreated within their
walls; before the gates could close, William's squadrons thundered
through in pursuit, and after them, the men with oil and torches. William's orders were brutally clear.

"Houses, churches, everything. In years to come, let the French
wonder where Mantes was. No restraint on the men, let them loot as
they will. I don't care who or what. If it stands, it burns. If it moves,
it dies. *Compris? Allez.*"

To Rossel, as the predators streamed past him into the open city, the
opportunities now presented were obvious. "We're thirty miles from
Paris, Father. Who can stop us? Take Paris, take the crown. *Be* France.
You can do it."

"Why, my son?" Serene now amid carnage, William inspected his
saddle cinch, then threw a mailed arm across the stallion's neck as he

surveyed Rossel and Robin standing nearby. "Do we not carry enough already? Philip is a problem, but he was anointed, chosen. France is not mine to take. Mark that, Rossel—and you, Denby, the next time you cavil about England. Fitz-Osbern, ride with me!"

William mounted with an effort, waving away Rossel and the grooms who would have offered a leg up. The king bent and gripped his son's shoulder, shaking him affectionately. "Besides, he's your mother's cousin. Don't worry, Rossel. I'll cost him more than his crown's worth before I'm through. Denby, come."

The king rode off to join his steward and bodyguard before entering what was left of Mantes.

"Money?" Rossel puzzled after him. "He won't squeeze any money out of Philip."

Disputable crown or not, Robin knew the king who wore it. "Much more: leverage, Rossel. A political lien. Henceforth, when your father kneels in homage for his Norman lands, he'll have one hand in Philip's and the other in Philip's purse. He will ask for very expensive considerations."

"But . . . *Paris.*"

"Think on it, my lord."

To his credit, Rossel could and did. Though never the statesman his father learned to be, the prince could perceive subtle advantage in a game. "Very good," he admired. "Yes, I like that. Father is subtle."

Robin agreed before mounting to follow the king. "Quite, sir. No other term suffices."

Mantes was flaming chaos. As he rode behind William with the royal bodyguard, Robin saw few live people of any condition. Those able had fled through the east gates by horse, wagon, or afoot. William's looters fell on the helpless town in a kind of feeding frenzy.

William rode grimly through the fiery streets, waving his guard to follow, determined to show Philip war until he sickened on it. A few hapless survivors, unable to run or hide, had been dragged out and hung from any beam not burning. Horses had to pick their way over and around the seared carcasses of dogs, an occasional cat, or large rat.

In the market square, three drunken soldiers had pulled a fat woman from her hiding place. Two of them were pummeling each other clumsily while the third rogered their prize against a wall. The smoke was acrid in Robin's nostrils. He tried to fix in memory the clean smell of new-mown Denby hay, and the picture of Marian, Edward, and baby Moira.

His eyes could yet sting with something beyond smoke; he was still sane.

Out of the square now, along a narrow street which must have been a row of goldsmiths and jewelers. Looters were risking their lives to plunder houses where flames gushed out of upper casements and merged with the blaze from buildings opposite. Horses snorted and shyed. One concerned guard rode forward to William: They should try some other route. William denied the man with a glare and moved on. The soldier riding at Robin's knee was a comrade archer from Gisors. While trying to manage his frightened horse, he hissed to the Englishman, "Name of a saint! What is the king doing to roast us like this? Look up there. We'll never get through, it's a furnace."

Robin knew clearly what the king was doing, much like his own exacting of de Gernon's scalp. "William needs this. Don't complain, *mon ami;* one would think you weren't getting paid."

"Not so well as they are." The soldier pointed ahead into the inferno of the narrow street. Two men staggered out of a shop ablaze from cellar to roof, carrying large salvers that, even at a distance, looked more brass than gold. One of them roared out his find to the world. Then, with a hiss and sudden roar, the entire fiery facade of the house collapsed and buried them both.

Robin's horse tossed its head, skittering sideways, more and more difficult to manage. The archer was right; this route was folly. And if houses collapsed behind them, they wouldn't be going anywhere. He dug his heels into the gelding's flanks. A strong animal, the sand-colored mount was steady as Hratha, but now close to the limits of control. Robin ranged at the king's side.

"Sir!"

Face forward, William paced the destrier on, reins firm in his fist. The horse's nostrils flared, eyes rolling, ears flattened back in terror. "Well?"

"Sir, I beg you to get out of this street. There's fire ahead and behind and for sure a better way to the east wall."

"You mean safer?"

"So I do, and the rest of your guard with me, sir."

The king looked about to make some answer, but then his arm thrust out, pointing ahead. "Look there. *Allons.*"

Responding to spur, the king's horse bounded forward. At the same instant, Robin's mount screamed and reared as burning cinders singed its neck. Robin fought to keep his seat, crying out to William. Whatever he'd seen, the king had dashed forward alone—then suddenly in mid-stride, the black stallion screamed high and dug its forehoofs into the cobblestones, throwing William violently forward against the saddle's high pommel. The black reared, terrified as a tongue of flame licked too near. The king fell heavily on the stones, clutching at his stomach. His horse pranced about, trying to escape the fire, then bolted past Robin. When Robin reached the king and dismounted, the old man was curled in a ball, his normally ruddy countenance livid with the unmistakeable shock of grave injury.

"Bearers! Surgeon to the king!"

As the rest of the guard relayed the cry to the rear, Robin knelt by William. "How is it, my lord?"

"Saddle horn," William gasped, eyes squeezed shut. "Hit against it . . . tore something."

"Bearers up here!" Robin bawled as the men hurried toward them on foot.

"Robin." The king lay back, clutching his abdomen, legs drawn up to ease the agony. "Can't straighten out. Quickly: bring Rossel."

Six bearers eased the stricken man onto a litter of canvas and spears. Robin had his horse moving before he jumped the saddle, guiding it carefully back through the flaming arcade, then galloping across the square, his mind racing ahead of the gelding's best speed. The king's vitals were ruptured; such wounds could be fatal to more than one man. William's whole government staggered at the wound. The future must be caught like a shattered flagstaff before it fell with the dying king.

With William so gravely injured, the war against France could not continue. Within days, all Normandy knew he would not live, the news already speeding to England's farthest marches. Its head stricken, the body of the kingdom faltered between one step and the next. Stepped back. Waited.

In too much pain for a wagon, William was conveyed down Seine under sail. From Rouen's wharf, the great weight of the suffering king was conveyed to the palace on a litter borne by eight men. Rossel insisted on being one of them, Robin another.

The most skilled physicians available, Maminot of Lisieux and Gontard of Jumièges, could do little against the inevitable. The worst pain seemed to center in William's ribs and chest muscles, his great belly bluish-black with huge bruises. As the hot days passed, William grew feverish and restive, unable to bear the noise of the city; any sharp sound was agony to him. He must be moved. A more easeful place was found at the priory of St. Gervais, serene on a hill high over the western suburbs of Rouen.

Like worker bees gathering to protect a threatened queen, the buzz of the kingdom rose to one of danger and uncertainty. From Canterbury, Lanfranc sent a deputation of his most trusted monks bearing letters and questions. Prince Henry dashed south from Huntingdon to the nearest port. At Winchester, Ranulf speculated carefully on the development and who would wear the crown and where he would dispense power and favors. The royal steward Fitz-Osbern burned late lamps in the St. Gervais scriptorium to dictate the summonses. Great men began to gather from both sides of the Channel. De Tosny and Vernon, Beaumont and Mortain rode swiftly to the king's side. Many decisions were to be made; there would be little rest for the failing ruler from waking to fevered sleep. Policy must be affirmed, Robert the royal heir brought from Maine to take the double crowns of Normandy and England. Propped on pillows in the great bed, William crept doggedly through his last days and duties. On the subject of Robert, he said only that his heir was being summoned, and presently all men would know the royal will.

"Sent for," Rossel grated privately to Robin over wine, scratching vigorously at his yellow hair. "But I'll lay hard money he won't come. Mother spoiled him. He never gave a damn for Father, only what Father could give him."

Robin saw the matter in a different light. "I think he will, Rossel. You saw him at your mother's deathbed. There's a sentimental streak to Robert."

Rossel agreed. "Don't be modest; he's maudlin."

"Old scores are buried or settled at funerals—if you follow."

"He'll outweep us all," Rossel prophesied. "Then he'll wipe the tears from the crown and put it on. By Lucca, I could weep myself."

But Rossel had done enough of that in private. Old scores settled at deaths? True enough. He had ridden ten years for his father out of love, and for little pay; lived longer than that with Matilda's contempt. If William changed his mind at the last minute and the crown came to him, that would be bare recompense—but, by God, he would make up for the drudge years with a vengeance and turn that crown to profit.

The summons to Prince Robert was entrusted to monks who might travel safely under their cloth through Blois to Maine. Brother Wilfrid headed the party, one of those stolid Saxons who would never be thin or particularly stout. A wispy tonsure ringed his pate. A taciturn man, as Robin judged him, one who thought and observed much more than he spoke, and a Northumbrian by his accent, with a hand hard and rough as Robin's own, telltale calluses on the middle three fingers of the right hand. "You've pressed bow, Brother Wilfrid."

"Still do." The monk glanced about the cloister where they stood to note if any of the passing clerics or soldiers were hovering close to listen. "I was on the walls of York when William came to take it."

"So was I." That pride was old and faded in Robin now, but Wilfrid's bleak northern features lightened a little toward cordiality.

"I know," he said.

"God preserve the king, Wilfrid, and God help England, though we'll need more than prayer. We need what's in the pouch you'll bear to Robert. Is it sealed?"

"Not yet." As Lanfranc's deputy, Wilfrid had been given a private cell of his own. The pouch rested there against his departure.

"Brother Wilfrid, may I be plain?" Robin walked the monk slowly along the cloister. "You serve Lanfranc, the best of statesmen. He would know the present situation to be a pivot."

Wilfrid only nodded, as if Robin spoke of matters to which he'd already given considerable thought. "Your point?"

"Robert is William's heir, Prince William only his father's soldier. If the choice were yours as an Englishman, would you crown the soldier or the vain fool?"

"You verge on treason, countryman. That is a dangerous speculation for small men. I am of the Church."

"And of England."

Wilfrid retreated a little, cautiously. "You know how the Church regards Prince William. The man is unspeakable, a catamite."

"I know his faults, but indecision ent one of them. What Rossel must do, he does. What he has, he holds. Think, Wilfrid."

A suggestion of distress flitted across the monk's eyes. "What are you saying?"

Robin's arguments were reasoned and effective, echoing chords already sounded in Brother Wilfrid, who had learned much of statecraft under Lanfranc. Robert on their throne meant chaos. Rossel crowned would see England sundered from Normandy for the time, perhaps forever. Rule not from across a Channel, but from home, as it should be.

"A man might see it thus," Wilfrid allowed.

257

"Say a man could," Robin pressed. "Would such a man have the courage of his vision? To leave his cell door open and be elsewhere for a quarter of an hour? Not to know what particulars the pouch contained when he closed it? Not to make unreasonable haste en route to Count Robert?"

Wilfrid shook off Robin's arm, astonished at the proposal—and perhaps the inner voice whispering *dare!* to himself. "They said you were bold."

"More desperate. Robert on our throne? Weeping Jesus, haven't we lost enough?"

Brother Wilfrid contemplated the open courtyard formed by the cloister walks. There was a central fountain and a sundial near it. "Quarter hour. If I find you in my cell, I must report you."

Robin grinned gratefully at him. "Would you do that?"

No, not really. Not to a man who, like Wilfrid, had watched York fall and burn and an English future with it. "Go," he said gruffly. "Do what you must. I leave in an hour."

Whatever men or reasons argued for Robert, Rossel was at the bedside of his dying father and had been at his side or call for ten years. William already leaned to him in affection, Robin knew, while Robert inclined to nothing but his own folly, all heart and no head, prize knight but disastrous administrator. An anonymous letter on clean new parchment spilled from the opened pouch in front of Count Robert, along with the summons from Fitz-Osbern and a letter from the king. The unsigned missive was written in flowery, passionate sentences, the intent of a man afraid to write his name but not his feelings, passages aimed true at Robert's nature.

But that my name would cost my life in this, I would set it down, though I set honor above all. Remember Simon of Crepi who put God above the love of his bride. So, as my lord steps onto the throne of England, let him recall that the honest vassal stands higher in heaven than the forsworn lord. Need makes me speak plainly. Against your father, in whose shadow you have toiled with more humiliation than advancement, remember your sworn lord and friend, Philip. Reflect that what your father would meanly allow you and only when he must, Philip openly calls you now, Duke of Normandy. Duty and honor are more puissant than kinship. Remember them when you are king, for by all that this heart holds holy, Philip was ever more friend to you than your father is.

Hotheaded, rankling at what he considered his father's ill use of him, Robert hesitated while August waned and September came on. His father's personal message, if meant to convey paternal warmth, failed utterly in that. He was ordered to appear like a servant. The anonymous letter itself did not sway Robert, only put a rowel to his own nature. He *was* slighted; Philip had said so and many others. Normandy would be his by right and with France's full support. Robert complacently assumed the same of his right to England. Philip was important to him, while his father always treated him more as foolish, sulky boy than responsible lord.

He did not ride for Rouen.

33

▸▸▸▸▸

F OR the king's better rest, the bells of St. Gervais were muffled in sackcloth, the monks awakened with murmurs rather than the clangor of the sub-prior's hand bell, lauds sung softly at Matins and Prime. In the frater, the steward Fitz-Osbern was taking a frugal breakfast of beer and bread with the other nobles when Maminot hurried anxiously to his side.

"The king is awake. Come quickly."

The physician's tone urged more haste than he spoke. The king had awakened perhaps for the last time. Princes, counts, barons, and clerics hurried to attend the dying monarch. They filed respectfully into his chamber, arranging themselves by rank, though at a distance from the bed, the princes William and Henry, the archbishop of Rouen, Bon-Ame, and the king's half-brother, Robert of Mortain in the front. Behind them, the lords of de Tosny, Beaumont, and Vernon, with the minor barons and functionaries on the wings of their group, waiting in silence for the last will of the Conqueror.

Far back against one tapestried wall, Robin took his place among the priory servants. Next to him hulked a large, fleshy man who unaccountably reminded Robin of a fat slug. A moon-faced menial in worn trousers and smock bulging with an ample belly. Robin noted and recoiled from something repellent in that face: the close-set piggish eyes and mirthless, slack-jawed grin. The man nudged an elbow into Robin's side.

"You of the palace?"

"King's guard."

The black-toothed grin widened. "That's good pay and better pickings, they tell. I'm Chabot from the scullery below. Do whatever's to hand, rat catcher, keep on the move. Not much profit here, but they dragged up a few of us from the kitchen to show what a good fellow the old shit was."

Robin edged as far as he could from the man, only a few inches possible in the press of people around him. Chabot missed or ignored the subtle distaste, sniffing the sickroom air. "Stinks in here. He'll go today for sure. Won't last out Vespers."

The rat catcher's small, porcine eyes darted about the chamber like thieves loose in a treasury, weighing the gold in this article, the silver or cash value in that. "He lived good. He got his."

That morning, the eighth of September, William opened his eyes as old John of Tours delicately swabbed his forehead with a cool cloth. The burning pain in his abdomen, for weeks a demon with a life of its own, was gone. He felt drowsy and peaceful, distant even from old John bending over him. The tufted whiskers about John's wrinkled face always reminded Mora of a solemn cat. William raised his head, then let it fall back on the pillow. He was tired of fighting the sickness, of his nearly sixty years, of life itself. He was drifting away without pain. Death would deal with him like a gentleman after all. Perhaps with luck Judgment would be as mercifully inclined.

"Help me sit up," he rasped through dry lips. He would rather sleep, though that would come soon enough. As with every grinding day of his life, there was so much yet to do and not near time enough. "Maminot, what is my condition?"

When the physician hesitated, William made it a command. "Come, be straight."

"My liege, the archbishop and your chaplains have come."

And all the others. "I see. Then you think today. . . . "

Maminot bowed his head over the cup prepared for his king. "I fear so."

William drank half of the remedy, a mixture of boiled comfrey root in wine. It strengthened him a little. His undimmed sight swept over the nobles of Normandy, seeking one face. He could not find it.

"Fitz-Osbern, where is my son Robert?"

"My lord, the count has not arrived yet."

Not even now with so little time left him? "But surely his messengers, some word. . . . "

"Royal brother." Robert of Mortain approached the bed. "Perhaps he fears you will neither pardon nor forgive him even now."

"If he were here," William growled with a hint of his old temper, "that would go far toward forgiveness."

Yet Mortain persisted in his suit. Robert must be fully pardoned for any defection, and Odo of Kent released from prison. Respectfully but firmly the other magnates of Normandy pressed their lord: Robert must be formally invested with the duchy and named heir to England. For Earl Odo, whatever his ambitions, the king's half-brother was a worthy man.

"Worthy?" Rossel derided with a hoot. "My uncle tried to steal the pope's chair out from under him. No one has so large an esteem for Odo's worthiness as Odo. Even as pontiff he would've expected to be resurrected, like Christ, within three days. To hell with him."

"My son, let be," William stayed him. "These are good men and they will have it so. We know what Odo is, but let him be released. As for Robert—"

"No, Father." Rossel dropped to his knees by the bed, clasping William's cold hand. "They're false, both of them. Dangerous."

Quite so; among so many dangers William recognized from a lifetime on guard. *Look about, Rossel. Many of the dangers are here to bury me.* "We cannot afford division now. Robert has so much to secure and mend, here and in England."

Clatter and stir beyond the open casement. In the courtyard below, a mounted party by the sound. William roused himself with a flush of hope, struggled to sit up while Rossel arranged the pillows at his back. "There!" he crowed to all of them. "I told you Robert would come. Just delayed, no more. Quick, go down and fetch him."

Two chamberlains hurried out on the errand. Among the men hovering about him, William noted with satisfaction a subtle shift in mood and stance. Robert was here. Some were relieved, a few like Rossel merely silent, returning to his place by Prince Henry. If sheer love, respect, and loyalty were the holy oil to anoint a king, William would put the crown over Rossel's brow as proudly as he once touched sword to the boy's shoulders in conferring his knighthood. That could not be. Robert was the heir. Beyond that, Rossel would not selfishly tear apart his father's empire to get his due, but Robert might.

The king's head turned toward the door eagerly as a shuffle of footsteps sounded on the stone stair. "Give way there. Give place, let them in."

Brother Wilfrid came alone into the chamber, bowing to the bedridden king. William recognized him. "Yes, you are the one we sent. Is he with you?"

Brother Wilfrid spoke hesitantly. "Alas, my king, he will not come."

The chamber was very still. *Not come? Why? How quiet they all are, all looking at me.* "Not come? His reason?"

Eagerly, angrily, reaching out with his very being to the damned Saxon monk who only looked down at his muddy shoes. "Not even a word?"

"Yes, sire. The count sent word. He said . . . " Wilfrid's Northumbrian burr faltered to silence.

"Said *what,* Saxon?"

"That he has borne too many injuries from his father. That it were a sin to feign love where he cannot forgive."

William's hand trembled on the embroidered coverlet. Some part of his life fell then as the last knife went in and twisted. He looked around at his vassal lords. Solemn and hushed, all of them, so quiet they might have heard the Absalom-cry of a father before he sat up further with a groan of effort. So much for heirs and blood. Kings were next to God, larger than mortal life even in their dying. "Injury? I will show him injury. Since he will not come, *pardi,* he will not rule. Mortain, Vernon, all of you witness to my will and disposition. I accede in part to your wishes. Odo is free, Robert is Normandy. But William—come, Rossel, stand here with me—*William* is my heir in England. Prepare the letters and the great seal to go with him."

He felt the last strength ebbing away, but pushed the inevitable back for a while more because he must, summoning young Henry to stand by his brother and acknowledge him liege. The two brothers had always gotten along; their embrace warmed the old king. Five thousand pounds William bequeathed to his youngest son with the admonition to use it wisely.

As king-elect, stunned at how his fortune had turned like a foot in slippery mud, Rossel announced awkwardly, "All of you hear. We will honor the king's wish in regard to my brother and my uncle of Kent."

"Rossel, come close." His father plucked at his sleeve. In his son's ear, William whispered advice from long experience. "Don't wait. Go now and secure the treasury at Winchester."

"Father, no. I'd stay with you."

"It won't be easy. You'll have Robert to fight. And the English, one way or another. They still think I had no right to their crown."

263

Rossel kissed his father for the last time. "I hope you're not minded to give it back."

A feeble snort: "What do you think? I've asked God often enough. I expect He will answer soon. Go, boy. Don't wait on me."

Rossel called out. "Robin, where are you?"

When the Englishman came forward, Rossel told his father, "My lord, here's one islander I will trust."

"Denby." William exhaled with wry resignation. "Will I never be rid of you?"

"My duty to my lord."

"You wish him pardoned, Rossel?"

"If you will not, then I will," Rossel maintained. "Note that, all of you. My first wish, even before I am crowned. Bishop Bon-Ame, see his pardon writ today."

"You were always generous." William came as close as impending death allowed to a hearty laugh. "Denby was barely older than Henry when he began to give me trouble. Watch him, Rossel; watch all the men like him. They talk of *their* England when *I* made it. Their own kings never made it one country, never could."

William blinked through fever spots dancing across his vision at the gaunt Saxon before him. "That wasn't enough for you. You wanted it always in writing when the world can't read. 'Just a few little rights, if you please.' Like a mouse nibbling a trail of crumbs toward the whole cheese. I thought to know your kind by counting men and what they owned. Might as well try to understand God by counting churches. Damned bargainers, lawyers. . . . "

"We always had to be," Robin explained gently. "We were just weak little tribes. Every man with a sword was carving pieces from us. We learned to bargain before Christ left Bethlehem."

Robin knelt now. William remembered the man's bad leg. Awkward in submission as he was seventeen years ago when the legs were whole but the young back was far stiffer with pride. "You have your pardon, Denby."

"I thank my king for his mercy. He was a strong lord."

"Remember that," William advised in a voice going feeble. "All very well to talk of rights, but first you find a strong man. Rossel, I gave you an order. Make for England now. And call Bon-Ame to me. I have a few debts to consider." He caught Robin's eye on him. "And yes, Denby, I may list England among them, but don't count on it. And they called *me* bastard."

The king of England lay back and closed his eyes, wearier than any laborer, ready to sleep. "Are you there, Bon-Ame? Let us get on with it."

In the stable yard, staccato and clamorous with leavetaking, Rossel gave Robin a purse. "No, take it, you'll need this for passage." Once more he removed the seal ring from his hand and gave it to Robin with the purse. "When I send for this, bring it yourself. And stay with my father until the end."

Standing by his saddled horse, Rossel turned inexplicably shy. "I would ask such only of a friend."

"I will, Rossel."

They clasped hands, one astonished by freedom, the other by a crown. Then Rossel punched his friend's shoulder. *"Va t'en.* I've money to collect." He savored the prospect. "Lots of it. Poor Robert. When he recovers, he'll start a war. Never liked me, you know. I poured a pot of water on him once. From a high balcony. Should have just dropped the pot."

The king-elect grasped his pommel and bounded into the saddle without aid of stirrup, saluting Robin with his irreverent grin. "Remember: When I send for you, don't fail me."

Robin called after Rossel as the prince trotted toward the priory gate with the rest of his party. "God save the king!"

—or save as much of you as England may thrive on. Need me, Rossel? Trust me? We need you to split our island from Normandy, to pull that plow while you can, then we'll need someone else, another ox to the orb and crown. Perhaps Henry. He was born among us, at least. We're not much for the sanctity of kings or any tool not apt to its purpose. Kings aren't crowned by God but husbanded like good stock, and like oxen or horses, we'll force-breed through you and all of William's blood as we must to a new strain of our own. Nothing personal, Rossel. Go haul the plow.

But there are miracles after all. My body's not broken nor my heart yet dead, and I'm going home to Marian.

Robin turned away toward the stairs leading to the king's chamber. "Denby? A moment."

Brother Wilfrid's departing group had just clattered out the gates and down the hill, raising dust and scattering pigeons. Robin peered through the dust about the stable yard. "Who's that?"

Archbishop Bon-Ame hurried toward him from the open door of the warming house through which he'd passed from his scriptorium. "Has Wilfrid gone?"

"Yes, Your Grace."

"But there were more letters to go with him." Bon-Ame fidgeted in irritation. "And short of clerks as well. Do you write Latin?"

Robin owned to a passable facility. "But I promised Prince William to stay with the king until he died."

"The king is dead," Bon-Ame told him, his regret overridden by present urgency. "The barons are making for home, and there are more writs to be done, your pardon among them. Come."

While Robin obliged the archbishop, St. Gervais clamored with departures gradually petering out to silence as men with an eye to state or profit hastened to follow the new king's star or secure their share of the leavings. Robin wrote diligently with two other hastily commandeered monks for an hour, rewarded at the end with his own pardon, signed and witnessed by the archbishop himself in lieu of William:

. . . save he commit no further felony or other offense against the crown.

He might take a horse from the stable and overtake Rossel and the others bound for England. Robin remembered his promise to the prince. There was no need now. Robin didn't clearly know why he turned up the stairs anyway to William's chamber, except that the old king was a man worthy of last respects. The door was ajar. Robin pushed it open. One look and he wished he had simply taken his horse and gone.

The body had been abandoned. Not one baron, lord, knight, or even priest watched by the dead king. The great had rushed off to their own ends. The small, the lay menials who served the priory and this chamber, had obviously crept in like rats to an unwatched table to scavenge. The chamber, richly appointed only hours ago, was stripped bare—bed hangings, plate, tapestries from the wall, a gold cross twisted from the *prie-dieu,* the reliquary of silver and bronze gone. From an ornate psalter on its stand by the bed, the jewel-set clasp had been ripped away with part of the binding.

The corpse lay on a bare mattress, rolled half to one side by scavengers hastily snatching up the rich bed clothes. The king's nightshirt hiked far up through their careless mishandling. The great, discolored belly lolled bare.

Near the bed something scraped across the stone floor. A figure rose, clutching a glazed chamber pot. Robin recognized the grinning rat catcher Chabot, who'd fouled the air beside him that morning.

"I should've got in sooner," Chabot reflected with practical regret. "Not much left." He peered into the chamber pot, shambled to a casement and emptied the stale contents without. "If you were looking to get yours, you're too late."

Robin leaned against the wall, watching the unbelievable sight and the obscene peasant, yet somehow was not moved to stop the man. He felt nothing now but disgust.

Chabot tied up his pickings in a bedsheet, apparently not at all abashed at being caught in the act. "First come, first served, like they say."

"May it well become you," Robin said. "And it does."

"You're the lucky one, getting let off like that. He didn't give away much, tight with favors as he was with money. This is my due and little enough."

Chabot jerked a thumb at the body. "All that shit about God's will. Don't say anything about a candlestick or two no one'll miss. Get yours while you can, *Anglais*. He did, that fat bastard. Even your country, right?"

True. Twenty-one years of hard truth. "I know. I watched him sack it up like you have."

If Chabot heard the contempt, it rolled off his fleshy back and callous soul. He bent over William's body. The nightshirt was of good linen but soiled, not worth taking. Chabot hocked deep in his throat and spat a gob at the corpse.

"He had that coming and not a moment too soon, neither." The rat catcher scooped up his treasure, poked his head warily out the door for anyone who might intercept him, then disappeared.

Robin looked down at the profaned body. *What did you expect, Willy Bastard? If you made England, you made the Chabots as well. Was it all worth this?*

A drab, cruel end perhaps, but justice of a kind. Men fought back as they could, in fury or greed or vengeance. The Waltheofs grabbed for power, the Chabots for the leavings. Robin resettled the heavy body on its back, pulling the nightshirt down to cover the hairy legs.

"Good forthfaring, Conqueror."

Book III

Conscience of the King

34

MOIRA exploded into morning like the sun.
She trusted the world like the animals of the steading and forest around her, smelled and tasted each day without need of names for the feast. Moira inhaled *green* as a scent, delicate in spring, strong as ox broth in summer. This morning, the little girl too full of life to die an infant bounded about Denby courtyard blithe as a grasshopper, bidding her world sing to her small ear.

Five. Mum told her she was five, and she could count twice that, coming out even on her fingers. Moira! she announced to the horses and wallowing pigs and unconcerned chickens. I am MOIRA and I am FIVE. To be either, for a start, was to be little in a world of big, growing but clumsy. She couldn't catch the butterfly flaunting past her the other day, but its bright wings colored her dreams; *small* before the word for it snagged on memory and lodged there. Names weren't close things, after all. Say them over and over, they just became silly sounds. Colors were real and smells and feelings, things Moira could touch. Real was the big, safe people she reached to.

Edward was irritating but annoyable in kind when Moira was in the mood. Not quite as safe as Mum or Gran: Edward chased her when she threw the cowpat at him just to watch it sail and land on his foot.

Five—and fascinated in a huge world that day by day shrank pleasantly to fit her, closer and clearer, rushing into her welcoming wonder like the rill pattering down to the dale where Father Beorn blessed it, Angharad told her.

Moira knew the smell and color and feel and safety of the warming

271

women who nestled, bathed, and fed her. Angharad's skin was darker than Mum's, thick hair the color of night with streaks through it like snow blown across the courtyard. Then why was Mum so light, why was she, herself? Where did the hall and barn and world go when Moira dream-wandered each night? When she slept, floating on colors and bright, surprised laughter, catching the butterfly only to have it grow big as her hands and talking with Mum's voice, threatening doom if Moira didn't let it go. Or darker dreams of crying in a place with no name or time, a place with the feel of fever to it that Moira would never know recalled the first bloodied, birth-dragged moment of her life—all this, and where did the world come back from when she woke?

A world of changes and questions, but Moira knew the feeling of *safe* from the beginning. Ever after, for that word, she conjured the sunlit images that filled meaning from the first. Gran Maud, stern but reassuring, telling Moira she was loved as much as could be expected by a saucy girl who stuck out her tongue at her elders. Aunt Judy, who came sometimes, smelling good and bringing her strange and wonderful things to eat. Angharad, scrubbing her before bedtime, telling her stories of old King Coel or a girl named Olwen, the voice like music itself, lilting and lulling Moira to sleep.

Safe was the thick, comforting smell of the hall, of beer and ale, food, candle tallow, the smoky tang of the big firepit which Moira must *never* go close to when the fire blazed up, and so she yearned to do just that. Safe was old Minna in the kitchen house, shooing her away when she stole fresh bannock cakes, though never before Moira got one at least, savoring the taste of oats in her mouth and the sweet aroma of the peat cooking fires in her nose. Safe was Wystan with no eyes, who could hear mice hunting on tiptoe toward Minna's fresh bread, telling unimaginable tales which Minna said were long ago and boring, but true for all of that.

Most of all, safe was Mum. Moira's word for Mum was the first she ever spoke and little different from the sound she first made at that comforting, nourishing breast. She knew it first as taste and warmth, wobbled, stumbled, and ran first to those arms. Now she could clutch Mum's hand and imitate her long stride when they jumped over puddles in the courtyard after rain. Mum had eyes like the weather: clear or clouded when she worried or told Moira of someone called Da-Robin. Which was confusing, since Moira had already fixed the robin in memory and no mistake. Robin was a bird, and very odd it was to have a bird for a da. When she thought of her "father," then, he was always flying off to nest in a tree.

To Moira, men were Edward, big and clumsy and smelling of horse this year. Will and Morgan, walking soft and sure, talking sometimes in the hall with sounds Moira couldn't understand. Mauger, with his quick step and fun-teasing voice when he swung her up into his arms. Men had a loud, deep sound, the smell of wool and sweat and leather brushed with dry leaves. They were the outer skin that held Denby together.

But now the butterfly was back, a streak of color across Moira's vision, another chance to capture the wonder and see it close. The delicate wings flashed in the morning sun, fluttering away toward the eldrum bush by the hall door. Following, intent, Moira didn't hear the gate creak open behind her.

"Moira?"

She froze. Someone had come into Denby without blowing the horn, someone not of home, bigger than Mum or Will or even Uncle Ralf. Moira stared at him, uncertain. He was a stranger, even though her name coming from his lips was soft the way Mum spoke it. Moira peered at him as he came up the courtyard toward her, came far too close. She didn't know him, didn't want to stay rooted here *to* know. Moira backed away; in the next eyeblink she'd be streaking and shrieking for Mum's bower or the hall and safe—

"Moira."

The huge man halted, keeping his distance, as if her very fear put out a hand to stay him. Slowly he sank to one knee, making himself almost her own size, and his hand came out to her, not reaching to hold Moira but simply offered.

"Moira, don't you know me?"

No. She shook her head. He wasn't part of her place, their place, and what was he doing here? She whirled about to run away—

Then she was caught up safe by Mum, her face pressed to that breast, and Moira felt a new sound rise trembling out of that warm place. She was jammed awkward and impossible between Mum and *him* as he took them both in his arms, and Moira could barely breathe, Mum being foolish like she never was before, saying *Da* and *Robin* over and over, and Moira squirmed in protest, squashed between them like a sat-on cat.

All of a sudden, the courtyard was full of the folk running, and all

273

that day, Blidworth bell rang out wild, spinning clear around on its rods, as if the silly old thing were drunk as Will Scatloch on May Night.

Standing in his courtyard, in his hall and bower and forest autumn-blanketed in red and yellow, purple-carpeted with heather, Robin was home but somehow *not* home yet. To come all the way, Robin drank in the colors, light, and air of his world greedily. Loved things familiar all his life were unaccountably alien, inaccessible to him. Robin searched among opaque surfaces to find misplaced meaning beneath. Once, by the bargain oak, Marian saw him throw back his head, arms and mouth open as if he would will his world to pour all its senses through gates rusted shut.

Robin held his wife and children in those embracing arms, frightened in not being able to *grasp* them as before. Surfaces, movement without meaning. At Nottingham goose fair, Edward striding beside him, Moira perched on his shoulders, Robin still felt painfully apart from them all, unable to reach them, still riding Gisors and the terrible Vexin. He groped, miserable and desperate, for a life remembered, hovered over and delighted in Moira, devoured her.

"Spoils her rotten," Marian muttered to Angharad, baffled herself by the distance between herself and her husband. "Bare lets go of the girl to let her sleep."

With Moira, Robin made up for turmoil with tenderness. Where had he come from? she asked with naked curiosity. She accepted Da-Robin now, but he'd just appeared out of the forest and in through the gate like the old wizards Angharad sang of.

"It's true," Robin lifted her up, pointing. "I come from the forest yon, your forest, Sherwood. Just as Mum told you: I'm Puck-Robin, love. Spying on foxes, minding they don't steal your chickens."

Ever after, when Moira thought of her father, she pictured the forest. He had simply gone back to be part of it again.

"There's dear it is to see them together," Angharad doted, "and Lord Robin home at last."

Home? Not yet to Marian or even himself. When Edward chattered at him over the fletching of an arrow; when Marian told some incident of her day, their voices would more often than not blur to mere sound in his ears, and he would smell lathered horse and sweat-rusted iron.

Ralf at least seemed to understand, thank God, offering Robin hot mulled wine before the fire after Judith, the children, and household had gone to bed. Forty-two now, thickening in the waist, with more aches and ills than he confessed to his lady or anyone, Ralf comforted his friend from an abyss of experience.

"No one just comes home, Robin. Not from such places. Some never do. Others only in time and even then you find yourself there again, is it not so?"

Robin stared into his wine. "As if I'm not really anywhere yet."

Ralf had heard grim tales of the Vexin and Mantes. "Was it truly bad as they say?"

Robin stirred in the chair, deflecting the question without seeming to. "Oh, you would know. Too many people, too much noise."

"Yes, it's always that." Ralf tactfully dropped the subject. In his own time he had elided as much of Hastings and other battles. "Be home, Robin. And be content."

Content? Like other words, mere sound to Robin now. For the first time, he could not trust his own mind, only the deep senses beneath. In the act of loving Marian, her hair soft-washed against his cheek, her whole body ready and wanting to join with his, Robin would see Rossel or William. His body moving with hers, trying to remember a closer union, plunged instead on Hratha over a swaying bridge. The winds of winter whined feather-fletched overhead, the storms of the shire spring galloped as French horse through his thrashing sleep. Marian's arm sliding over him protectively in the night fell on that sleep like de Gernon's sword. Robin muttered and moaned.

Deaf, blind as Wystan in his way, Robin moved, prayed, ate, and slept beside a wife he could not reach through a fog of baffled misery to which neither of them could put word or sound.

Then one morning, sudden and miraculous as the conception of life, Robin's eyes opened and his whole being stretched, shook itself, and came awake. He was leaning against the lip of the courtyard well. He saw Marian—*saw* her as a bolt of awareness poured into him in a sweet, vitalizing flood. Marian had come out of the kitchen house, wiping her forehead, hot from overseeing dinner with Minna. She was not bound for the well, but seeing Robin, she changed her direction and quickened her step.

Something, perhaps the long-striding sweep of her body or the ineffably feminine grace in the motion of undoing the kerchief that bound up her hair, struck Robin in a pang of gladness. The freed tresses fell over one side of her face; she brushed them back carelessly with one hand—something in that simple sight and motion upended Robin like a newborn and smacked him into life.

275

I see you and you are lovely and I love you.

"Minna's wanting some water," Marian said.

Not so; Wystan knew the way to the well without sight and always drew the water at Minna's need. She wouldn't ask the *hlaefdige* to go on such an errand. Marian came here because *he* was here, that simple. In a poignant flash of memory, Robin remembered how they stood just here when he asked her to marry him so long ago.

She reached for the bucket rope, but Robin caught her hand, hardly knowing what he meant before the prayer came out. "Help me, Marian."

Yes, she must have felt his fingers trembling on hers; Robin caught the astonished question in her eyes as they lifted to him. "Help me to come home."

She pressed herself to him. "I will. Help *me*."

"Come walk."

"I want to."

Afterward, Robin couldn't clearly remember where they walked or what they said to each other that differed so greatly from what passed between people for years used to finishing each other's thoughts. All that day and evening they were close. Robin could not leave her side. By candlelight in their bower, he tenderly stayed Marian from lifting the kirtle over her head and did it himself. He knelt to remove her shoes, then both silver pins from her hair, shaking it out while his eyes never left hers. She was bright magic defined in shadow, he as new and strange to her, the grey in his hair and beard ghostly in the flickering light. Marian's lips moved heavily over his body, searching with a delicate hunger, feeling the scars where war had walked. "Are you really here?"

"I'm here. I'm finding you."

Finding her with hands he wished were not so callused coming home to the beauty of her, or so jagged where he had picked nervously at the calluses for years in exile. He wanted to go tip-fingered and faerie-light remembering her. Not gentleness enough in the world for what he felt now, no part of her without wonder. They had never waited so long before taking each other. They would wait longer. Joining was not what they needed now, but the silent communication of touching that was the path to it.

"Stay awhile," Marian breathed against his own mouth. "Stay and take me with you. Oh, so slowly, love."

"No, don't. Don't close your eyes." He kissed them. "See me, Marian. Let me see you."

"So long. . . ."

So long that he would not miss one more breath or instant of her, however fleeting. The four years of her stolen from him he found written on her body. The hard, field-working legs, the muscles between her breasts and shoulders that had swung babes and barley sacks alike, that tensed at his touch over her flat stomach. Thighs hard as a man's to clasp him, the lips softening now, parting to let beauty rush back into her. In their lovemaking, truly that at last, the urgency was not in Robin's body, but in needing to be close. When delight and rapture tossed Marian's head from side to side, he captured her mouth with his own again and again, not to be parted from it. As her body began to tremble in a climax he remembered, Robin held himself back, willed it in order to see her own passion, feast on her helpless, tear-streaked joy, and later, he lay with his face buried in Marian's breasts, stunned by no more than being alive.

In his sleep like a blessed exorcism, the ghosts rose and drifted away from him: a tattered doll in a trampled field, a world of strangers, smoke rising from a gutted, ugly place where an old king writhed on fire-strewn cobbles and began to die—through Robin's sleep all the phantoms flowed and fled away. Not all at once they went, but moving on through cleansing sleep and days that followed, and the gift of summer.

Not an easy summer, that of 1088, or the best crop, but the lord was home, and when he rode the fields now, greeting his folk, his lady was with him. The tightness went out of his mouth and shoulders. Laughter poured from Robin now over work and play. Over nonsense with Moira, who bonded with her father and would not be parted even at mealtimes, squirming and squealing in his lap, making a mess of both their dinners. In ranging Sherwood with Edward, teaching him where the trout hid, where the best apples were for cider or munching when they hunted. Hearing the timbre of his son's voice settle more firmly into the deeper, shire-drawling sound so like his own, not even squeaking in excitement when he placed five arrows in a mark no bigger than a man's fist.

Blidworth folk knew their lord was home and closer than ever, warmer and more tolerant, roaring with the blunt village husbands over beer and the gut-crude Saxon jokes whose points were always more of latrine or wench than wit: "So then the old sokeman says to the traveler, 'Aye, y'may stay the night and welcome, but you'll have to bed with my three daughters . . .' "

Or listening to Will and Angharad singing softly with their grown sons joining in, Gwaun the high silver notes, Eddain the deeper, duskier gold and bronze. Robin's soul held out its hands to be warmed at the fire of theirs. Normans need have no fear. He wrote nothing nor wanted to, spoke no discontent, read little, and Marian felt selfishly safer to see his books, quills, and inkpots dusty with disuse. Sometimes when he trailed his hand down her cheek, she would kiss it with a choked, fierce tenderness; trace with her lips the scar on his palm, the mate to her own, cut the morning after their wedding when they gave their blood to the bargain oak and Robin slipped the gold gift-ring onto her finger. Remembering that, Marian hated the ring he wore now, the one the new king laid on him as a reminder of fealty due, a debt to be called.

She prayed in a woman's way and need. *Take it off, Robin, throw it away or send it back. Don't let this thieving son of a thief-king call you back ever. God, give us these years while the children grow. We've lost too much as it is. So little left, and that so dear.*

Magic summer moved into a tranquil harvest, then toward autumn easy as the rill splashed and sparkled from Holy Pool down to Blidworth Dale, drowning out the distant roil of war. New factions formed against Rossel as king. In France, Robert joined with Mortain; in England, Earl Odo leagued with William, Bishop of Durham. Fighting broke out in the south, Hereford, and York. Odo seized royal holdings and castles in Kent. Men mobilized on both sides and marched. Always more at home in mail and saddle, Rossel went to war with a whoop! to hurl himself against his incorrigible uncle. If his father had a talent for kingship, Rossel had at least the gusto and energy.

"Blood feuds are a day's work," he complained to old Lanfranc. "It's the blood kin that wear a man down."

In alliance with Odo but never in concert, Duke Robert sent a sea force to relieve the besieged rebels at Rochester and Pevensey. Manned mostly by English sailors not about to be invaded a second time, Rossel's keels tore through the Norman formations like vengeance itself, sinking or scattering them in flames. The borders of England rattled and shook with the upheavals of 'eighty-eight, but in untouched Sherwood, in the calm eye of an ocean storm, Robin walked hand in hand with Marian, greeted Ralf and Judith heartily when they came to visit. They were astonished and gladdened by the change in him. Years had dropped from Robin. The long lank-waisted body had filled out, sleekened to the contours of happiness so obvious in the man.

"And Marian," Judith said warmly, hugging her husband with sudden, fierce affection. "Thank Heaven, you and I were born under ordinary stars."

"Long may they move in their ordinary course," Ralf prayed. "I'm a little past the heroic life."

"Which is like English beer," his wife observed. "One horn is fine with a good meal, but it does pall over a whole evening."

"I think you are really home now," Ralf ventured to Robin over subtler French wine in the Saxon's hall. "Consider: Most men with lives like ours are dead at thirty, and here God spares us to comfortable middle age. Do you want for anything more? I don't."

"Nor I." Robin sincerely meant it. Life was a gift lost and returned to him by miracle. To discard the other, more dangerous gifts in trade was still life at a bargain price. "No, I tried, Ralf. I did what I could for conscience. I'm just a man, just one man who doesn't need to fight giants anymore."

"Not even at chess? I would not have you *too* reformed." Ralf drew the chessboard toward them. "Tonight, I'll checkmate you in twenty moves."

"Will you indeed? A shilling says no, boyo. Come on."

Sometimes when they played, as September lazed into cooler nights, Marian would come from the bower in her nightrobe, needing Robin more than rest, to watch them both absorbed and at peace. Her cheek against Robin's, she would smile across at Ralf, and the aging sheriff would think with a prayer and a pang: *Stay home, Puck-Robin, stay and be content. This king is death, there's death at the windows, all around us.*

Then in October, the horn braying at Denby gate, the weary court messenger at the door of the hall bearing a summons: King William was at Grantham; Robin would join him there with all speed.

35

▶▶▶▶▶

SIRE Geoffrey de Coutance, steward of the royal manor at Grantham, his left sleeve half empty since the battle of Chester, was not a man Robin knew well; however, as the aging knight escorted him into the manor hall, he detected an air of suppressed but enduring disgust in Ralf's old companion. While steward to Matilda, Sire Geoffrey oversaw an efficient household. From what Robin heard lately, that was impossible with the new king's retinue in residence. Wherever they battened, the nearby holdings were ravaged and brawled. Any hall where they put up would be a shambles by noon, unspeakable by evening.

Much like Gisors, Robin thought. Vespers bell had just rung from St. Wulfram's. Servants were attempting to prepare the hall for the evening meal, working patiently around a few camp followers of both genders who'd drunk themselves stuporous at dinner, snoring gape-mouthed on the trestle tables or in the middle of sodden bread trenchers. As Robin passed through this slovenly, rank-smelling hall, its sight and smell struck him as the true seal of Rossel, whose reign so far was a disastrous mixture of expensive war and personal orgy. Against Robert and the chronically perfidious Odo, from the moment the crown settled on his ruddy brow, he needed money, men, and support. For these Rossel had made extravagant promises with no seeming thought that they must inevitably fall due.

Robin was shown to a small audience chamber off the hall, a room much used by Matilda for private conference with Lanfranc. Robed in scarlet and saffron-cloaked, a heavy gold pendant dangling over his broad chest, the king was listening to a letter read by a lay monk.

"My liege," Coutance announced. "As you commanded, Edward of—"

"Robin!" Rossel catapulted out of his chair to hug him fiercely. "Thanks, Coutance. You, monk! Out, we'll finish later. Robin! By the face of Lucca, I've *missed* you."

Robin would have knelt, but Rossel stayed him physically. "None of that. Come, sit down. I'm having a good day, didn't drink too much last night. Actually remember whom I took to bed. Wish I didn't." Rossel's bark of rueful mirth shivered about the small chamber. "Touching on that, I do believe your sins have found you out. Some cow you diddled in Rouen. Her husband's here. Wine?"

"No, my lord."

"Lord?" The young king looked up quickly from the goblet he was refilling. "I am lord and liege to my stewards. To all others I am William, by the grace of God and my shit-witted brother King of the English." He threw himself into the great chair so energetically that his wine slopped and the chair shrieked in protest. "But to you who came as an exile and served as a friend, may I always be Rossel."

Robin settled in the chair he was invited to. "I came as soon as I could. Here is the ring."

"Keep it, keep it. You'll be needing a seal in my service. There is a post that you will fill for me." Rossel winked at his friend over the rim of his cup. "The making of you, Robin. I promise. Where was I? Oh, yes." He chortled with conspiratorial pleasure. "Heard a spicy gobbet about you. Her husband's here. The Chancery priest."

Deep in Robin's mind a clammy recollection of a distant, blurred night plucked a note of warning. "Bayeux?"

"That's the man. Something 'delicate' about you and his wife, I gather. Not from him personally, but these things go around a court quicker than camp lice."

As Rossel heard, Ranulf's wife had been anything but secret about the incident, moaning the tale first in confession, then to her husband. "She says you bewitched her." Rossel reached for an apple, bit, and chewed juicily. "Did you tup the silly bitch?"

He'd barely thought of that raw, drunken night since. Elfled seemed unreal. Yet the voice in the back of his mind warned: *Take care.*

Rossel spat out a seed. "Well? Let's hope you have *some* vices to keep you interesting."

"I suppose, yes."

Rossel's brows shot up. "Well, I have heard of Saxon *sang-froid.* Just suppose?"

"I don't remember much of it. That was the day you sent me to Rouen. I was drunk."

Rossel's laugh erupted again, high and abrupt. "That's usually a blessing. Well, it's nothing to me. Bayeux's here on other business. Clever fellow." He cocked an eye at his friend as he swept up parchment sheets lying on a table. "I would say a genius."

"I know his qualities."

"I always need money," Rossel fretted. "First I wanted to be stinking rich, now I have to be, and that little clerk knows how to make it happen. Now, my friend—my true friend, what do you want?"

Robin hedged from habit. Wanting had been dangerous for his kind since 1066. "Want?"

"I'm serious." Rossel stood up. Robin rose with him, sensing a new eagerness in the man, masked with jocularity. "You've always been a bargain, and this month I'm selling. What do you want, Robin? For yourself, for your life. Truly."

Robin shrugged while his lawyer's mind juggled quickly. Rossel made promises easily, but today might not be the time to present that bill. "A good crop at harvest and better next year."

"Oh, come."

"My son to inherit Denby in his own right. A good marriage for my daughter when the time comes."

Rossel made an incredulous face at him. "That can't be all."

To be left alone that I and Marian and our children can stand straight. "Edward to finish his education."

"Gah! To be a common little scribbler like Bayeux? Too modest, man. I'm speaking of honors, Robin. Follow me and you will have them, I promise."

So easily he does that. To Englishmen, Rossel's promises were no more enduring bond that a whore's kiss. For all that, Robin remembered a lonely but loving young man hovering over the body of a mother who had despised him, mourning her. The voice was as tender now and as vulnerable. "Robin, there are many companions, but hardly one man I—come with me, man. I need you."

And to answer that, I should sing the song he needs to hear, save it's not in me, Rossel. Robin affected the smile he reserved for all Normans except perhaps Ralf. "My lord is very generous."

"Ah, *merde*." Rossel threw the remains of his apple into the fireplace. "Come, let's hunt."

Ranulf was occupied most of that year in financing the new king against rebels who tried to shake him loose from his throne. Rossel's troubles were the agile priest's opportunities. One of those risen against the crown, William, Bishop of Durham, lighted a path of inspiration across the fertile mind from Bayeux. He now had a clear impression of the Conqueror's less than kingly son. This bluff, free-spending young man, of his own age but a child for wits, needed him as a fool needed a keeper. Confident and competent, Ranulf was growing into a superb guardian for such men. Control came easily to him, though he would have scoffed at any hint of vanity in the pursuit. That would indicate a flaw in his symmetry, a chink in his armor. Ranulf made a policy of thinking several moves and motives ahead at all times. He did not like to be surprised.

That spring, while Robin plowed his hides and reclaimed his life, Ranulf returned to Lincoln. The leave was not inconvenient; Durham was pocketed by royal forces in the north while Rossel, with roaring gusto, besieged Odo in Kent. Ranulf could spare a week for Elfled. She had been listless and melancholic ever since their return from Rouen. Her husband gave directions for the finest physicians to be engaged. They examined Elfled but found no physical defect at first, gravely diagnosing a "wasting humor of the spirit," and prescribed purgatives, cupping, and judicious bleeding, all to no avail.

In early April, Elfled caught a chill deep in her chest but was too apathetic to throw it off. Weak and feverish, she was as much a slave of death-fear as of her fantasies. She sent up Steep Hill for a priest from the new cathedral to give her extreme unction, confessing her demon-induced passion and its unholy consummation by Robin of Denby.

Unction was a wise but happily unnecessary precaution; Elfled recovered. Even as Ranulf was met at the junction of Ermine Street and The Straight with the good news, his croaking, snuffling wife was propped up on her pillows, drinking hearty broth and tolerating the advice of her personal maid-servant, a Lincolnshire peasant woman who guessed more of her mistress's condition than she spoke.

"Ox broth now, full meals tomorrow. You'll be right as bread again, you'll see. The master will be up presently."

"Bring me my mirror," Elfled husked.

Her own reflection always pleased Elfled; now it impressed her. The red-eyed ravages of the cold could not be helped, but the rest was interestingly wasted. Thinner and drawn, cheekbones more pronounced, the eyes huge and—Ranulf's tongue put it exquisitely—*pathétique*. While believing to her core that Robin had seduced her through witchcraft over a period of years, Elfled was sufficiently self-aware to appreciate the visible side effects. Her mirror showed a woman whose only crime was love, passed through and scarred by the fire of her ordeal. Pathos was the condition she detected, preserved, and gave in greeting to Ranulf with a dramatic upsweeping of wounded eyes to his face. Pathos in the repentance, in the tearful—and carefully laundered—confession she made to her husband.

Ranulf sat close by his wife while she told him brokenly and wept into her handkerchief. Neither his cynical awareness nor any suspicions had prepared him for this. He felt suddenly helpless, pain sinking sharp teeth into his vitals and eating him hollow. Hurt pride, bruised possessiveness, and more than that, astonished to care so much that *she* hurt. For the first time in his thoroughly calculated young life, Ranulf was thrown off balance. He covered it, needing to control the moment as always. Easy enough: He had smiled at men often while wanting to spit in their faces, and could do so now.

"One might have predicted this," he lied, steadying his voice with an effort. "Whatever you insult, wife, spare my intelligence. When Denby limped into the hall at Rouen, wind-blown from distant wars, you all but fell over the high table."

"Not true!"

"I am not blind."

"He bewitched me from the start, cast a glamor to trap me. I am your wife, I have borne your children. That—that night, it was not as you think. I went down from our chamber to fetch some chamomile." Elfled searched for credence in Ranulf. She found only the mask. "To help me sleep, I swear to you. He was in the corridor."

Lurking, waiting. He came close. The light from the few sconces blazed hell-red in his eyes, and Elfled knew what he was then and where his power came from. "He pushed me against the wall. I was powerless. He raped me." All of that, she protested. Bewitchment and rape, and what kind of husband, what real *man* would pause to question such shame to his wife?

Through all this Ranulf struggled not to reveal his feelings, a necessity his life had forged into a virtue. But his hands shook. He pressed them against his knees. "Nicely put, *ma chère*. And has the glamor faded?"

"No," Elfled choked with a feeble shaking of her head. "He comes even now in my sleep to take me still. Surely you know such creatures exist and that they have power over a woman's rest."

"And waking, apparently."

"Surely . . . surely you do not doubt me?"

She did not doubt herself, Ranulf was convinced of that much. Her imploring helplessness was perfection. His reply deftly sidestepped. "My country is more mature than yours in such matters. We also distinguish between the locked gate and the latch left out." Ranulf spoke with a light brittleness, physically suppressing in his throat the truth that threatened to quaver his voice. "It was always a delight to hear you whisper my name when we made love. Somewhat less, in the midst of my amorous labors, when you were swept away and breathed his."

"My God, how can you—? You don't believe me." Through a fresh spate of tears, Elfled groped for her kerchief, sneezed, composed herself again, croaking: "Before God, that was what I most feared, that you would not trust me. I have lived with this torment, too full of shame to go to a priest. Only when I thought my time had come. . . . "

Ordained himself, Ranulf would not put too fine a point on that. As a realist used to deception as a tool, he recognized the glimmer of sincerity within artifice. "So you love him still?"

"Love? Love that *animal*? You know the tales of him and that witch forest he came from." Elfled clutched her husband's hand, pleading, all feminine weapons in play, since she believed every word herself. "My dear and only love, I know you believe me. Your hand is trembling, I can feel that. Trust me."

Ranulf kissed her damp cheek, easing her back onto the pillows. "Of course I do." Of course he did not for a minute. "And he will pay the price."

For both of them.

I am astonished only to find you can hurt me so much, English girl. That you are vain, selfish, and even faintly absurd has never surprised me in the least.

Not sure how he would proceed. But shaking. Hollowed out. Empty.

36

TEN *days,* Marian fumed. Ten days the foreign king had kept Robin from home, worse in a way than the four years imposed by old Willy Bastard, who was no doubt paying for that cruelty now. They were happy, Robin joyfully spending every moment possible with her and the children. They weren't so young anymore that ten such days weren't precious.

"What's the flaming king *doing* with him?" she raged to Maud and Mauger late one night in the hall over warm ale. "I never saw Rob so happy as this last month. No growling about the Chancery or mucking about in the law books. Just content."

"Content?" Maud's tone rang with iron. "Content to let thieves like William and Fitz-Gerald take all from us and then kneel in thanks for the little they leave? Never."

"Not Lord Ralf," Mauger went to the sheriff's defense. "He's kept us from more grief than ever he brought, *Hlaefdige.* And you did give him the kiss of peace."

"Aye, for Judith's sake, and swilled my mouth out afterward." The old woman's glare told their easygoing steward he'd spoken out of turn. "But he is one of them. You were both too young to know England before they came. The earls ruled for the king and the Witan was truly wise."

As always, when she was clearheaded in these late years, Maud never conversed but judged, pronounced, exhuming an England that never was. A silence fell over the high table; the shadows crept closer

286

around them. At length, Marian bade them both goodnight.

"I don't care a damn for what was, Mum. I only want him home."

Two weeks at Grantham and Robin still did not know precisely why he'd been summoned beyond vague mention of some post. Rossel was bursting with generosity, giving Robin the comfortable quarters used by Lanfranc himself when the regent took up residence in former years. For the rest, the king personally rousted Robin from sleep early every morning to hunt or merely to ride for sport as far as Hough Castle—grooms, guests, and hounds trailing behind. The old timber castle at Hough had been in continual use for almost twenty years and sagged with every season of it.

"Damned place stinks like a jakes," Rossel mumbled through a mouthful of baked chicken, clutching the carcass in one greasy fist. He tore off another bite, tossed the remnant among his hounds, and tapped old Sire Stephen Baudreux on the shoulder. "How long have you been castellan here?"

"Since the beginning, my liege. Twenty years." Not young when he came to command Hough, the squat Baudreux now required a cane for the infirmities of his battered sixty-five years, all of them served as a plain knight. Rossel could empathize with the old man in that much.

"Pull it down, we don't need it anymore. I will send orders for you and the garrison." Rossel wiped his hands on the flanks of his hunter, signaling the train to follow him out of the stockade.

Robin had always hated the existence of the castle. "They prisoned my mother in the dungeon here," he told Rossel as they rode toward Grantham.

"Oh?" Rossel tossed off. "Bad luck."

"The place was a sty even then. The dungeon's no more than a pit."

"Wonder she didn't die."

She did, Norman. "My mother wouldn't allow that."

"Baudreux is a good old man. *Hé la*, Robin, will I ever live to be that old? I think not. But I want it razed. Castles are like friends. If they can't help, they can still turn against you. Come on!" Rossel bent forward, putting spurs to the hunter's flanks. "Race you a furlong."

The days passed. Robin was always demanded at Rossel's side. Twice a day the whole retinue feasted in the manor hall, reminding Robin of pigs at a wallow, but Rossel thrived on the chaos.

"Don't talk business at me now," he would protest, offering Robin wine or some new delicacy. "If you aren't a buggering bore sometimes."

"There's the slaughtering and salting at home," Robin reckoned. "I should be there."

"And a provincial bore at that. You came at our summons," Rossel reminded him with a hint of royal chill about the fact. "You will have leave when it pleases us. We have salting of our own to be about, you and I." The chill thawed in the sudden summer of Rossel's disarming grin. "Look, I must be in Gloucester soon enough to try the bishop of Durham for treason. *There's* a slippery oyster for you, secular lord when it profits him, a true son of the Church when that's to his interest. It is to weep. Meanwhile, *if* my sober horse's arse from Denby will approve, I'd like a little fun. Want a woman tonight? Some new ones just arrived." Rossel emitted a sonorous belch and patted his thickening belly. "Fresh meat."

Bishop Osmund had been increasingly ill for the last year. A day after Rossel's summons, Robin and Ralf called on him, appalled to see the doughty old vavasor so visibly wasted. Osmund dismissed his condition with graceful disregard.

"I am putting my life in order. The time seems meet. I've asked for Père Jehan as confessor. Drinks too much but doesn't shock easily. Greetings, Denby. You look well. More circumspect, one hopes. I hear the king has sent for you."

Osmund dismissed his physician and servants, turning to more important matters. He produced a vellum palimpsest from under his pillow, one of those scraps he used repeatedly to scratch memoranda to himself. "The king's promises when he needed money and men."

Osmund had paid his share toward that, so had Ralf. Like all fobbed-off creditors, they had grave doubts about the king's intent to pay. Osmund was of the opinion the royal promises were not worth the ink to spell them out. Both appealed to Robin as a legal mind and an intimate of the disaster on their throne.

He perused the notes with a critical eye. "This just says he promises to revoke unjust laws and taxes from his father's time."

"But the promise is clear," Ralf said, more hope than fact.

"Clear? It's a leaky bucket, a sieve. What laws, what taxes, by what measure of justice? Most of all, *when?*"

The notes contained one advantage: The king had been held to the specific on one article, the return to local lords of all forest lands enclosed since 1083. Not a restoration of local power, but a firm step in its direction.

"Yes. If you can hold him to that alone," Ralf urged. "Laws can be argued, forests are real. Men can live in them."

Robin smiled reminiscently at the Sheriff of Nottingham. "So they can, boyo. The rest we'll have to see about."

Osmund's farewell was more a grimace, the visor of a helm concealing pain. "Godspeed, Robin. Pity I can't be with you. This looks to be a formidable contest."

I mark you, Robin Hood.

So Ranulf did and would act on it, pausing only over method. For the moment, his energies focused on his profitable plan for royal stewardship of vacant bishoprics. Durham's was a prime candidate, a ripe plum ready to fall since the incumbent, William of Calais, was under indictment for treason. After that the see of Osmund, who had conveniently gone to God three days ago. The proposal broke with no existing law or practice, merely made more creative use of opportunity. The incomes from vacated sees were the responsibility of the king, whose duty it was to manage them in stewardship while selecting a successor. There being no stipulated time limit for that choice or any effective control on the royal use of those livings, they could now channel directly to a king desperately in need of hard cash. Delay was a prime factor. Candidates to the bishopric could be barred with clerical or papal arguments. They might bless and send the *pallium* to this man, certainly not to that one. Months and years could pass; meanwhile, the money came in.

Ranulf abode in patience attending the king at Grantham. To clergy and laity alike, young William appeared to pass all his time in hunting and unnatural forms of venery. Ranulf knew him somewhat better. At any moment the crude reveler would discard idleness like a soiled garment, turn about and be all business, but still *nouveau riche*, delighting in the novelty of personal extravagance. To counter this, Ranulf chose his own attire for the coming audience as a general would plan battle strategy. He wore his favorite scarlet tunic over black, tight-fitted trousers, tonsure cut close, bangs arranged over his forehead in clerical modesty—a subtle reproof to Rossel's notorious habit of baring his forehead. The king parted his lengthening locks in the middle, combing them down the sides of his face, a fashion shocking to Norman clergy.

If Ranulf's tonsure was carefully orthodox, he festooned himself with enough silver chain to feed a peasant family for two years.

Summoned finally to the small audience chamber at Grantham, the genius of the Chancery experienced some anticlimax. No one to out-dazzle. The king had just returned from hunting the day before and drinking most of the night, still dressed in rough riding clothes.

"Enter, Bayeux. Sweet Jesus!" The blurting, raucous laugh erupted as Rossel took in the wealth of silver shimmering on scarlet. "You look like an expensive Christmas."

Rossel moved to the hearth where three thick logs crackled lustily. Wall fireplaces were new in England, one of the reasons why Rossel preferred the room. His mother had ordered the fireplace installed when she took up residence as regent. Ranulf noted with some excitement that his vacancy plan lay ready on a table. Rossel rubbed his hands over the flames, then presented his broadening rump to the blaze, beaming congenially at his servant.

"I've considered this plan of yours. Well conceived. Good work."

"My liege honors me."

"Within the law, certainly puts our treasury on a firmer footing."

As Ranulf well knew. The king's privy purse would have its generous share of the proceeds, to be sure, and there would be a steady, predictable flow to Ranulf's as well. So went the world.

"And it takes very little from the Church, which is rich enough already. I tell you, Ranulf—" To the expectant clerk, the king seemed brimming with benefices about to be dispensed. Ranulf found himself almost physically inclining toward them. "—you are a treasure in yourself."

Ranulf flushed with more warmth than the fire gave off. He *had* worked unceasingly, not only toward this fruition which complemented his theories of an unassailable machinery of state, but as anodyne to the still-raw wound of Elfled's questionable fidelity. His loyalty to the crown was unimpeachable. He designed the engine; naturally he would operate the gears, officially or otherwise, as administrator. This was his moment; reward about to be offered.

"And I believe I have found the very man to carry it out, one whom I trust as yourself."

Ranulf blinked. "Sire?"

"Edward of Denby. A lawyer like yourself. I believe you've had some dealings with him."

To acute Ranulf, the remark reeked of the disingenuous. For the first time in an agile career, he found speech difficult. "My lord is justified in any choice, of course."

"Of course we are. But no favoritism. No prejudice. No simony."

"God confound any who would think so—but Denby?"

A hint of displeasure in the tilt of the royal head. "The Chancery has some reservation?"

"In all duty, my liege, yes. And so does the very crown of England. I mean—"

"Bayeux," Rossel reminded him loftily, "*we* are England."

"I speak of the crown enduring, founded by your royal father, grant him eternal rest. Your father who banished Denby for rank treason. Does my lord know the pernicious writings that sent the man hence?"

"They are known to me."

"I know I am importunate, Sire, but let me point out a single facet, one adder's fang among all those ready to strike at my king's heel."

"By God, you're passing good with words," Rossel admired frankly. "I will give you that."

"Then let my liege heed them and decide. In his perverse reasoning of the so-called natural rights of subjects—implying those rights spring from God—Denby states that there are no royal prerogatives, however derived, that cannot be questioned, criticized, and even curtailed by the common consent of the realm."

"Mind slippery as an otter," Rossel agreed, as if presenting a favored son. "You ought to hear him drunk, goes on from here to bugger-all. There's my point, you see. He has—now how did that monk put it?— a *sinuous* turn of thought. Just what I need."

Too much for the honest toiler from Bayeux. He must speak for himself. "Have my own efforts been so inept, my liege? So ineffectual in the crown's behalf these many years?"

"But of course not." Rossel strode to the priest, clapping him firmly by the shoulders. "We thank you for your labors and will amply reward them."

Reward? This king's largesse was as reliable as his choice of lovers. The grey taste of defeat lay sour on Ranulf's palate.

"A man who can so direct my Chancery? Where can I replace you?"

Ranulf was spared the need to answer that. Sire Geoffrey stood in the chamber entrance. "Sire, you bade me announce Denby as soon as—"

"Robin's come?" Rossel brightened like a little boy, forgetting the priest.

"He waits the king's pleasure."

"Send him in." Rossel loped back to the table to fill two goblets with wine. Bitter enough at the moment, Ranulf recalled that this crowned ox had never offered him that small courtesy; the gesture would not occur to him. Even his dismissal was an afterthought.

"That is all, Father Ranulf, but stay close. I may need you before supper."

Ranulf bowed and backed toward the door. As he turned to withdraw, Robin entered. In Ranulf's caustic view the man's new robe and cloak were well cut but dyed in the dark Lincoln green of his shire. With more colors to hand and duty at court, Ranulf considered the choice another sullen English defiance.

"You've met, I believe," Rossel called from the table.

Robin barely inclined his head. "Father Ranulf."

"Master Robin. You yet limp, I see."

Rossel's sudden laughter stung Ranulf like a whip. "Not *all* of him, I hear!"

No misreading the cruel joke. Ranulf froze—then, with a lifetime of practice, he bowed his head in parting and withdrew from the royal presence. In the corridor he stopped and took several deep breaths to cool the heat rising between his ears, willing himself to calm. The king laughed at him in front of the very offender. All his dedicated, diligent life Ranulf viewed the world as it was, his fortune directed by no steersman but himself. Now, he might almost believe in fate or blundering stars as Elfled did. Robin crossed him first in the forest, then in court, at last in his bed. Then this coarse, guffawing buffoon of a king swept up months of work like a pastry from a plate and offered the fruit of Ranulf's work to . . . that.

If one could only scream, make a club of sheer rage to shatter all, smash this king who squatted on the throne like a pig at trough. More than perverse, it was mad, Devil's work. God gave Ranulf a superior mind and the steel of will to advance his gifts, the clarity to envision a machinery to move for the good of kings, but operating without the royal hand on every gear. And this muck-minded lout snatched the masterpiece from the maker's hand like a magnificent toy the infant could not wait to be used properly or even finished.

The king was beyond the reach of mortal vengeance and necessary to one's advancement, but his English creature was quite expendable. Certain facts now fitted together naturally like cogs in a turning wheel. As the whoring but sentimental world went, Elfled's confession—no, say rather her imperiled soul—would be invaluable. What charge to bring against a man the king lauded as other men praised new-bedded brides? William wagged his tail like an eager hound at the very mention of Denby.

Rape? Severe penalty, but slippery in the proof. Denby was able in court, familiar with defense and the ambiguous nature of sworn testimony as evidence in such a case, testimony that could be turned against Elfled. As "evidence" her tale was shaky if not outright falsehood in the light of her obsession with that miserable—

No. Care, take care, not in hot blood but cold. Rape would call for secular trial. *Bewitched,* she said, ensorcelled and ravaged in her sleep by the demon incubus. A charge of witchcraft would be tried by a Church that believed implicitly in such mortal dangers. For the very good of Elfled's soul, after all.

Ranulf felt better, once more meshing with the machinery of which he was so integral a part. An honest wife always impressed males, secular or clerkly. With the right preparation—oh, yes—Elfled would tear their hearts out while digging Denby's grave with her tear-sodden handkerchief.

37

> > > > >

"ROBIN! No other man in England I'd rather greet today." With a sweep of his arm, Rossel invited Robin to the wine and hearth, still sputtering with amusement over his own joke on Ranulf. He perched cross-legged in a high-backed audience chair. "Marvelous to see you."

Robin accepted the proffered wine. "We hunted just two days ago."

"Seems longer. You've no idea of the natterers I have to tolerate. Endless! I must say, with the tailors I've set to civilize you at considerable expense, you could manage a little more style. Cut's fine, but the colors are drab as a sermon."

Robin rather liked his new gown and mantle. Cut was one thing, but muted and sober colors were meeter for a man, leave gaiety to women. Considering Rossel's garish ensemble, to remark on the point would be as maladroit as the man's joke at Bayeux's expense. Rossel had grown giddy with new power and wealth indulged to the glittering hilt, a vital young stallion gauded with too many trappings. He winked at his friend.

"Business at last, Robin. Business and profit."

Robin settled in a chair, glad to be down to that. The king must depart soon for Gloucester. He could go home to Marian.

"I have it all now," Rossel said with cheerful, child-innocent pride. "Never hoped for this, but here it is." He leaned forward to his friend, touchingly eager. "The old men in Normandy and here call me frivolous, and you know what the Church says. You of all men know my heart, Robin. We were soldiers together. There's no stronger bond between men than battle, not even between lovers. Battle fuses men together."

"I'm not a warrior, Rossel. I always thought of myself as a farmer."

"Rot. You're more than that, could be much more. I asked you once what you wanted. Tell me now. Don't be modest."

"Well, then, I've said. My own lands well plowed, my family safe, not much more for myself in all events."

Rossel scoffed with friendly impatience. "Oh, come! I can create you anything I please and I damned well intend to. Listen to me." Excitedly, he summarized Ranulf's vacancy plan, which would guarantee a steady flow of hard cash to the treasury. "The man's a genius in his way. Showed my father how to use the English system of administration as an engine to consistent purpose. A quick mouser, that one. He'll have his bowl and a place by my fire."

Be that as it may, Rossel knew the plan would work better under a native justiciar. They would start with Durham, then the recently vacated see of Nottingham.

"Nottingham? The bishop is ill, I know, but—"

"You've not heard? The old fellow departed this world a few days ago."

Robin crossed himself. "Rest his soul." And one less ally. Robin veiled his feelings in some diplomacy. "He was a man of conscience and vision." Once an enemy, Osmund saw the future and how action could shape to good or ill, perceived early on that the interests of the most loyal landowners must inevitably clash with the crown.

"Yes, yes," Rossel conceded. "Never gave Father or me much trouble. Or any great help. My father's old guard. They became more English than you. Give a king only what he can squeeze out of them. England is an engine, Robin, and money is the grease to the wheel."

Robin said nothing. The old war and the long game had come home to Nottingham and Sherwood. With Rossel, Robin had balanced as long as possible between conviction and personal liking for the bluff, open nature of his friend. Here and now in this comfortable chamber, that balance tipped.

He stood up. "You asked me what I want."

"Now we're down to it."

"Only what many are waiting for: the king to redeem his promises."

"What promises?"

"To revoke any unjust laws and taxes from your father's reign."

Rossel hooted. "Taxes!" He sprang out of the chair, hefted another log, and slammed it onto the fire. "Take a whiff of the world, man. You've shared much with me, but not the throne. Barely time to dress of a morning before they're at me, usually about money and always never enough. Do you have any idea what the Kent campaign cost? Or the fleet that stopped Robert? Decrease taxes now? I need every one of them and more.''

"My lord, hear me.''

Rossel was hunched over parchments on the table before him. He squinted up at Robin. "*Lord* again? You're about to be unpleasant, aren't you?''

"Your promise about the forest enclosures. Your specific pledge there.''

"Robin, Robin.'' Rossel subsided in the heavy chair again, fanning himself with the sheaf of parchments. "The first truth I learned after Lanfranc poured that smelly oil over my head was that a king can't be expected to keep *all* of his promises.'' He thrust out the sheets to his friend. "Read this. It's sweet and legal as a Church wedding. I'm the king, the crown has stewardship—I've told you all this. All *you* need is to see these offices stay vacant as long as possible. Quite reasonable.'' Rossel relaxed in the great chair, pleased with the irrefutable symmetry of his argument.

"Or vacate them forcibly?'' Robin translated. "Isn't that what you're doing with Durham?''

"Bishop William is a traitor!'' Rossel snapped. "He underestimated me, threw against me and lost, that's the luck of the dice. My father *said* you were peculiarly dense. Why in hell are you haggling? What do you really want? A title in front of your name? A barony? Name it.''

Rossel rose again, deliberately, hands clasped behind him. "Be my royal justiciar, sworn to me.''

There it was, either/or. Beyond Ralf's worry or the concerns of dying Osmund, there were the stories Marian told him of the dispossessed during his exile, the pitiful few they could help, so many they could not. "And the enclosures? The land returned?''

"Bargaining, Robin?''

"Rossel, you made *promises*.''

"And you have my solemn word—we'll find some holy relics, make it impressive—that I will consider deeply of these pledges. When I have your oath of office, and that I'll have now. Today. Nothing is free, Robin. Whatever your price, I have mine.''

"My lord—''

"A considered answer.'' Rossel held up a hand to forestall debate.

"There's so much room and no more that I can make even for you."

No room at all. "So."

"Why so sad? A made fortune, not a sentence of death."

"Yes." For one painfully human moment, Robin teetered between right and self-interest, trying to find a middle way, knowing there was none. Refuse, and he would be at one end of an arena, Rossel at the other. For any of them to accede without resistance in this matter of the bishoprics was to give Rossel a lethal precedent he would exploit until no treasury or private purse was out of the reach of his avarice. Accept the post and from that vantage perhaps delay the engine, turn aside its voracity, blunt its teeth . . . and in that compromise become everything he stood against, make a waste of the slow-bleeding years parted from Marian and the children, his life gilded and gelded, an expedient lie. *Aye, and tired of it all as I am, I could do that. Marian would understand, she'd be glad, but always there'd be the taste of shame.*

Traitor to a king was banished or hanged. Traitor to self? What exile where Self wouldn't hunt him down every day?

"I can't, Rossel."

The headstrong king was still smiling. "But you can and will."

Christ, the man left him nowhere to turn. "I cannot."

"Why?" To Rossel the thing was fair and logical, a virtual *fait accompli*. Mad hermits might preach and rail against a king in public, but sensible men did not put their personal leanings before service to a crown. "I say you will, and the damned thing's done."

Robin shook his head, miserable but unable to do anything else.

No, wait: He did not understand, Rossel was sure of that. "You're not used to seeing from the heights, still thinking like a forester. You have seven hides, I'm offering ten times that much and more. Houses, households. To educate your son, send him to Oxford or Paris. Send him to Ireland, if you will. They'll stuff him full of God and lyrics. Or foster him with the best house I can find, page and squire, knighthood when he's of age. Your lady—what's her name?—she'll have town houses and women just to manage her wardrobe."

"She wouldn't know what to do with all that," Robin said.

"Your daughter, then. The best husband I can find among my nobles, and a dowry to sweeten it all."

Robin was surprised at the stiffness in his own reaction. "My daughter will marry whom I choose. A man of her own blood."

"*Pardi* but you're touchy," Rossel whistled. "I always heard you were a clannish race. Your cousin didn't mind when Father put her in Fitz-Gerald's bed."

"That was different. Judith loved him. And Ralf—" Robin checked himself, too close to the heart of it.

Rossel pressed him. "Ralf what? No, don't go slippery on me, but speak. I get enough of that from men like Bayeux. We're friends. Spit it out."

Are we? "Ralf put himself in England. He didn't come to put England in his own purse."

Something heard or induced stopped the goblet before Rossel's lips. "I don't think I like what you mean by that. As you meant it under my father and against him. Don't dare that with me, Robin, *not with me.* Take a friend's advice. I may never be the king he was, but I rule in his example. Forget what you wrote, forget your *foutredieu* Witan. Useless old men haggling and hampering every decision a king has to make. That won't work, Robin. Rein in and learn the horse you ride."

"With respect, sire. Learn the country you rule."

"That's enough." Quiet, but meant. "Step back, Robin." Still friendly but with more warning in the advice. "I am your king and ask where I could command. Must I do that? Let me ask of someone I love."

"Please don't," Robin appealed.

"Man, I trust you with my guts." Rossel came to Robin, embracing him, the trust and so much more, the need naked in his eyes. A man with lifelong rejection still a wound, come to power and able to use that force without restraint. The arms that held Robin now could raise him up or hurl him onto the midden heap.

"I don't know why," Rossel murmured, "but from the first I trusted you, singled you out. Envy perhaps. A prisoner in exile, you seemed to have about you the strength and peace of all you'd lost. Of loving and being loved. So simple. So rare. When my mother died . . . you seemed to understand what I felt."

"That was not hard to see, my friend."

"But you are." The king turned away, as if he'd asked too much of one more bootless hope that would cast him down. "Years we shared. Every day, every battle. You dressed my wound at Gisors, then took up my bow yourself. I will confess to you, I was scared that day; didn't know if any of us would see the sun go down. And I chided you for a mad fool, but thought to myself there on the parapet: Here's more of a brother than ever I had before. That is what I've been to you, not so? When Father was dying and toads like Mortain wheedled and begged pardon for Odo and Robert, whose pardon did I ask and then decree? *I* stood by you, no one else." Rossel released Robin and turned away, and Robin felt a new distance widen between them. "Was my father right? Must I be ware of the mouse going for the whole cheese?"

"Not anymore."

"Then what? For God's sake, what? *Tell* me."

Robin winced with the unkind winter damp in his scarred leg and perhaps more than that. "Rossel, you have my word. Whatever I wrote or spoke, treason or common sense or plain survival, I'm done with that. I'm not God or King Alfred, not the English Furies flying after justice. Not that angry anymore, not that young. What I have, I love all the more for almost losing it. But—"

Rossel caught him up. "I thought there was a large *but* coming."

Robin spoke his truth gently as possible. "It's Ranulf who has a rat's scent for the whole cheese. I won't help him steal England blind."

Rossel stared at him, unmoving. "I say serve, you say steal. Clear enough. Not even for me, is that it?"

Robin slipped the seal ring from his finger and placed it on the table. "With my lord's permission, I will return to Sherwood."

Rossel settled himself once more in the ornate chair. To Robin, there was a subtle difference in the attitude of his body. More formal, closed, about to conclude and dismiss. "That's the sum of five years? Just bow out with regrets, turn away as my mother did in polite disgust?"

"I can't do what you ask."

"Then go. Yes, go home, but reflect on this. Whatever I cut off the fat Church or anyone, call it pay in arrears. God damn you, you know what they owed me."

I've hurt you, Robin thought sadly. *Whatever I refused the king of England, and I helped you to that place, I never wanted to hurt Rossel. You never had a damned thing but courage and loyalty, offering them up to me like a girl trying to please a lover any way she can. Dear Rossel, you never knew whom to love.* Robin bowed his head and took a step backward toward the door. "By your leave, sire."

"Yes, just go." Rossel's mouth was set in a tight line, shut down around something he would crush out. "I will find my justiciar, but let you remember what my father said. Chosen by God, bishops or bugger-all, first you find a strong man."

Which he never was, no more than Robert, merely apt to the moment.

"And then you accept that reality is power, power is the crown, and the crown is me. Be quiet in your forest, Denby. In *my* forest," Rossel corrected precisely through his teeth. "Be very still. Remember that whatever I was not, I am my father's son. Teach your son to write no more than his prayers. Don't allow me to suspect for one moment that you might be so much as that moment's danger to me. Because if I do, you're not banished, you're dead. Get out."

Rossel sat rigid in the gilt chair.

Five years. For all that time Robin had been a friend, a bandage and salve to old hurts, just that much older and steadier to ease the neglect of a father who worked him like any ox in a field and a mother who treated him like a disreputable servant. Let Rossel go, he needs the seasoning. Rossel can do it, he has the experience. Robert we will keep with us, give him Maine, give him our trust, give him the world. . . .

Yes, Conqueror. On the field at Gerberoi when you might have died under sweet Robert's own sword, who took the blow and did the bleeding for you? Yes, you thanked me and stroked me absently as you might a dog, then sent me away, pushed me off again to wherever your power needed patching. If I'm not much for prayer, God's not been much for me. One by one, turned against me or never there when I reached out. Now you, Robin.

One could find a certain relief in complete betrayal. No one left to trust, none to betray. Every righteous soul of them, one way or another, had buggered him from the day he was born.

"But fair enough," Rossel grated to the stone walls hard and bleak as he felt. There were more and readier men to hand than Robin of Denby. "Fair enough."

He lunged at the door like an enemy, threw it open. "Coutance! Find Bayeux, get him back here. Now!"

38

▶▶▶▶▶

THROUGH a wet winter and into the cold spring of 'eighty-nine, Robin stayed at home, tended his folk and stock, hovered tenderly over Marian, Edward, and Moira. Yule came, then Candlemas and Edward's fifteenth birthday. Denby made a feast of the occasion, the hall crowded with Blidworth folk. His mother presented him ceremonially with the second cup of ale and recounted for all how he was brought into the world by Queen Matilda herself. Will Scatloch gave him a new longbow of four-seasoned yew; Morgan, three fine arrows of his own crafting; Robin, a silver-mounted horn for beeswax to keep his staves and strings supple.

Edward's health was toasted, but Robin had the uneasy double sense of joy with his head on the block. Rossel rioted up and down the land, no promises kept, nothing changed. The last wise rein on him, Lanfranc, lay on his deathbed in Canterbury. The Forest Assize met seldom and in a gloom of futility. The enclosures were not revoked; Rossel's licentious favorites battened like locusts on the lion's-share stretches of Sherwood claimed by the king.

Ralf Fitz-Gerald endured that with resignation. Sherwood teemed with game most years, but the shire's greatest treasures belonged to the episcopal see of the late Osmund, whose house was posted and guarded now by soldiers of the crown. While yet making no move to confiscate, Rossel plainly announced his intention.

"Theft's a better term," Robin averred as he and Ralf rode the forest track toward Papplewick, cloak hoods drawn tight against freezing rain that drizzled down through bare beeches and oaks. "No bishop, no holy

301

offices. Want to marry a love or bury a child, a man needs to go searching for any kind of priest he can find. It's impossible.''

"The king doesn't care," Ralf said gloomily. He'd been once to London and again to plead with Rossel on the road from Gloucester, did all but sing the truth of their need at him. "He just doesn't heed.''

On windswept Akeman Street leading from Gloucester to London, Ralf had intercepted Rossel and sued to him for a new bishop; pleaded with a king warming his ride with wine and too drunk to listen. Argued sharply with fur-cloaked Ranulf who rode with the royal appanage, to no avail.

"We have no choice in the matter.''

Robin disagreed; there was always a choice, though he feared it. "What then, Ralf? How when he prances in to snatch up the copes and crosses and all that's not nailed down?''

"You think I have not lived with that?" Ralf reined short, wheeling the mare about to the other man. Grave now, a man who had wandered this maze longer than his friend. "Nothing short of armed disobedience can prevent him. That road is not open to me. Or you.''

The sheriff of Nottingham lifted his head to the winter-bare treetops. A handsome head, grizzling to middle age, the skin under his eyes webbed with tiny wrinkles. "I love this place and what life has given me. I will be your friend as long as you allow me.''

They faced each other through the falling rain and the steam from the nostrils of the snorting horses. "You understand?''

"Yes.''

"Forget Robin Hood. I would have to stop you." Perhaps the mere thought made Ralf grin suddenly to lighten a hard truth. "Hunt you through this damned forest again? With my aches and your bad leg? You've done as much as you can and more, now leave it. Let's age in comfort.''

Ralf turned the mare and walked her on, Robin following after. The thing was said. If any question remained, neither spoke it.

The time was Rossel's, one victory after another. At Gloucester, glittering and incisive as a new blade, Ranulf swept Bishop William into exile, gracefully ushered his king to feast on the spoils of Durham see. He wanted to move on Nottingham speedily, but Rossel vacillated over any direct action toward the town or Sherwood. Denby, of course: one ambivalent, sentimental splinter in the surface of a king whom Ranulf found easy to manipulate except in this.

"Must I remind my liege that Denby is indicted for witchcraft by Remigius of Lincoln?"

"I know."

Ranulf scanned his master's face for any trace of emotional leaning. The royal countenance told him nothing now. "Or who brought the charge?"

He was answered with a noncommittal grunt. Ranulf folded heavily ringed hands before him, bowed, and withdrew. The very inconsistency of this king made him at once malleable and infuriating. Ranulf composed himself and requested leave to attend the trial in Lincoln in support of his anguished wife.

Rossel sent him off with an absent nod of assent. He still bled from Robin's desertion—no, it was no less than that. His hackles rose at any mention of the man, yet to discuss him with Ranulf felt like disloyalty on his own part. Rossel took Elfled's allegations of night-ravaging incubi for absolute rubbish, but Robin was still close, confused and raw in his mind. A more reflective man would deem his own indecision ridiculous. To allow Bayeux to issue a summons to Denby, commanding his appearance in Lincoln, then himself deliberately mislaying the notice in a pile of scrap parchment. To know what the Chancery priest intended, despise him for that and *still* hand the poisonous man direct and damning evidence against Robin.

"No, *he* was the one who played me false," Rossel reasoned, grieving to the walls and his wine. "My conscience is clear. Who will argue the king's reasons?"—and went on grieving and hating and listening to the tread of days like a gallows march. The ecclesiastical court of Bishop Remigius convened, Robin's name thrice called out. Failing to appear, he was tried in absentia. Not even Ranulf suspected how Rossel tried himself over that.

Was it dishonest not to send the summons? I wanted to hurt you as you wounded me, but not mortally. Damn you, be wise in your forest, go to ground. My fist is clenched, I can't help it, but not yet raised against you.

For nearly two decades, Lincoln had grown accustomed to the stone-laden carts grinding up Steep Hill from the quarry at Greetwell. Bishop Remigius, his priests, and deacons were long resigned to limestone dust thick on the altar and railings, the tedious creak of treadmills and pulleys, the irritable shouts of workmen on the high scaffolds, red-eyed with stone grit as they labored to accomplish the bishop's vision. For the trial, therefore, Remigius chose the small Saxon church of St. Mary, down Ermine Street at little Wigford. On a clear evening in April, between Vespers and Compline, the case against Edward of Denby was heard by the bishop and a court of five priests in the small chapel to one side of the ancient altar.

A veteran *causidicus,* Ranulf left no detail to chance. He entered St. Mary's the day before the trial, engaged the sexton in pleasantries, walking about to admire the font and the time-worn designs at the base of the stone walls, the side chapel itself—and gauged precisely the pitch of voice best suited to reach every ear. He could speak with ease. Elfled would have no trouble if her voice was kept at a certain level.

"You must take care that they hear you, my dear."

On the other hand, not *too* composed, burdened as she was with mortal fear. She must look at the court at all times, catch their eyes, and hold them. Her honesty aside, men tended more to believe a direct gaze. She was to wear white, nothing laced, but chosen instead from the most traditional English garb in her wardrobe. No pumice to smooth her complexion nor any other aid to feminine charm. She would conceal her hair modestly with a simple Saxon veil.

Elfled glumly agreed. "I'll look an absolute frump."

Ranulf knew better. "You will be what you are: a beleaguered wife to be pitied and, above all, believed."

He himself would appear in sober black, a plain silver cross on his breast the single stark contrast. Nothing, no smallest advantage or impression left to fend for itself. Beyond those candles set for the court and scribe, every other taper was adjusted by Ranulf to cast the most unflattering play of light and shadow over Elfled, who must be the very image of her plight with no contradiction. She was to enter the church on his arm, bless herself at the font, genuflect lingeringly at the main altar, and give the sexton a purse for the parish poor.

Remigius's five priests included only one Englishman, Father Alric, whose stolid, thick-jowled countenance exuded the skepticism innate to his race. He might be trouble. Ranulf tried to anticipate the man's questions, if any, rehearsing rebuttals to each. He led Elfled to the chair placed for her and surveyed the sum of his preparations. The high, narrow windows of St. Mary's admitted little light this late in the day. Candles flickered in vagrant drafts, trembling the shadows about the chapel, playing on his wife's face. Perfect.

"In the name of Jesus Christ," Remigius opened the court. "Bless and protect us from the wiles of Satan and his minions who roam this world seeking the downfall of men. Amen.''

Elfled made a convincing witness, heightened by her husband's experience in those colors already deep-dyed in her own fancy. Seated before the bishop and his court, handkerchief crumpled and twisting in nervous fingers, she choked and wept her tale to credent ears.

"He first came to my husband's house six years ago on the Feast of Saint John.''

The wizened little scribe prompted her. "Goodwife, you must name him for the court.''

"Edward of Denby.'' Elfled swallowed, one hand to her brow. "He came tonsured and robed as a priest with a pleasing countenance.''

Alric grunted. "They never come ugly, do they?''

Bishop Remigius frowned at the fat priest, wondering if the man was completely sober. Alric was known for the weakness. "You have inquiries?''

"Your Grace's permission, yes. Are we not speaking of the man once known as Robin Hood?''

"We are,'' Ranulf said. "Let the scribe note there will be further evidence on that very point.''

"By all means,'' Alric assented. "And further note the man behind that name. Speak the name of Robin in any house in the Midlands—''

"A known thief!''

"Whom did he rob, Father Ranulf, and to whom did he give?''

"Thief and no stranger to excommunication before this.''

"As other good men have known it, who should never have to. You do not know the heart of this country.''

"Both of you desist. This is far from our inquiry,'' Remigius reminded them. "Does Father Alric have any questions more relevant?''

He did not at the moment. By all means let the woman proceed— but Alric was far from drunk, weighing her every word like a surgeon feeling for a break in bone.

"Soon after he came, my thoughts began to . . . to be filled with the image of him. He came to me at night when I tried to rest, sometimes in the very act of praying before bed.''

Remigius posed a crucial question. Why did she not seek God's help from the first? Why did she wait so long to speak?

"God in heaven, how could I?'' Elfled implored. "I was so frightened . . . so deep in shame. In my dreams, he touched me in ways and in places I cannot speak of. He gave me no rest. His caresses had a heat to them more than a natural man's—oh, God have mercy on me.''

Believing every word she spoke, the floodgates opened. Elfled's torment, far more complex than any court would have guessed, poured forth on an avalanche of tears. As in her agonized dreams, so to the depths of her ordeal in Rouen. The ill-chosen moment to leave her chamber, the unspeakable man waiting to take her in unholy lust, showing his true horrible shape as Elfled writhed helpless beneath him.

"There was flame licking about his body, and the smell of sulfur. I felt myself burning but not consumed, as the Church tells of the fires of the Pit.''

She struggled on, no surcease from that day to this but tainted, tortured, beseeching God, only to suffer and waste the more until Christ her Savior gave her strength enough to make confession. One faltering step toward the redemption she sought. Elfled broke down again; the court barely heard her last smothered plea. "Pray you ease my soul.''

Now the sympathy of the court was a palpable presence to Ranulf. He laid a gentle hand on his wife's bowed head. "Will Your Grace put any questions?''

The bishop would not at this time, nor any of the Norman priests whose livings lay in his gift. Further, though aware of Remigius's private opinion of Ranulf, they would not gainsay the wife of the powerful right hand of a dangerous king, a hand already felt by an insecure clergy.

Ranulf persisted. "Would *any* man in his conscience doubt what we have heard?''

"That would be difficult," Father Alric allowed, rising to come forward, his Lincolnshire accent flattening the well-studied French. "But allow me a certain reluctance to accept without some inquiry. There are a few questions I would put to the witness arising from her own statements. Goodwife Elfled, on that night in Rouen, you left your chamber to fetch a pot of herb tea?''

"I did.''

"You said the hour was late. Why did you not send one of your women?''

"I had brought no servants with me.''

"I see. But the palace has ample servants. Why not one of them?''

"I looked about. There were none at hand.''

"So you went down to the hall and there the accused trapped you, thrust you against a wall, rendered you helpless.''

"As God is my—''

306

"And there against that wall he took you, is that what you maintain?"

"No, he—he carried me to his chamber."

"Where was that?"

"As I said, on the lower level of the palace."

"Ah, yes. I have been there in His Grace's train. Rather dank, as I recall. Hard to sleep with the guard rooms so close by. And that is where Denby had his pleasure of you?"

"It is true, Father. I beg you to believe me."

"Lady, I want to," Alric assured her with sudden gentleness. "I am nearly convinced. You must have been so frightened."

"I was. I am."

"And he hurt you."

"He was without mercy." Elfled's response rang with a new depth of conviction. "Before God, I have never felt such pain."

"You need not dwell on that. How long did he subject you so?"

"I could not tell."

"Some minutes? An hour? Was there no marked candle to tell the time?"

"It seemed forever."

"And all that time in agony, yes. Did you plead with him, beg him to stop?"

"Oh, I did, I—"

"Begged him to stop, yes?"

"With every breath, I swear to you."

"Object!" Ranulf sprang up, a lean fury confronting Alric. "Where is this leading you?"

Alric answered the challenge with a benign smile. He turned to the bishop. "Your Grace, since Denby must be tried in absentia, I only sought to know the whole truth, considering what may be the outcome. All of us have been in Rouen palace, some of us quartered on that very level. Stone corridors where every sound echoes annoyingly, and very close to the guard rooms. This woman, pleading with Denby, must have *whispered* her anguish—for if she could weep and beg with every breath, could she not cry out as well? Howl, scream for someone to help her? If I must weigh a man's soul for all eternity, may I not weigh a reasonable doubt? And I doubt this woman."

"You call my wife a liar? This is not a civil court!" Ranulf shouted. "You will not bully her like a felon in the dock."

"Why not? You've done it yourself often enough!"

"Be silent!" Remigius rose, stern in his authority. "This is unseemly.

Father Alric, I will assume you have concluded."

"I have, yes." With a contemptuous glance at Elfled. "Save to remind the lady not only of the flames for perjury, but those for murderers. Your husband is the lawyer and a Norman. Neither of you need bother to blush."

"The witness knows well the dangers of perjury before God," Remigius said. "And you, Father Ranulf"—a clear reproach to the man who had so often mocked at his own holy cloth, to say nothing of the vows of celibacy—"do you know how this peril hovers closer over our heads than those of laity? Over yours?"

"His Grace poses aptly," Alric remarked from his place, taking up a quill and jabbing it at the inkpot. "The Church is universal, yet in England—at least at one time—a man was not damned without defense."

"No defense?" Ranulf returned. "Was he not summoned in good time, his name called out thrice tonight? Does not his absence proclaim his guilt? Father Alric, I would send no man to that end on the words of one witness alone. I warrant ample others whom I will call presently. But bear with me, Your Grace, brothers. I beg you all, if you have no more questions of my lady, that she be spared the remainder of these proceedings and allowed to go. As you can see, she is far from well."

Readily granted. Remigius enjoined Elfled to pray and meditate, promising his speedy blessing when her cleansed soul was fit to receive it. Pallid, shaken by Alric's attack, Elfled left the church on Ranulf's arm. He saw her to the waiting groom and helped her mount.

"That priest," Elfled said. "How could he doubt me?"

Ranulf smiled up at his wife through the dark of the spring evening drawing toward Compline. "You would know best, my love. He is of your race."

"Will it be concluded tonight?"

"Of course. Despite Alric, they could not but believe you; I watched their faces. Do not stay from bed for me. I will be late."

Ranulf waved the groom on, then conferred briefly with a group of shabbily dressed men who had loitered by the church door since the trial began, housed for days before that in Steep Hill at Ranulf's expense. These were his ferrets and moles, burrowing for years through Sherwood, storing up what he would now expend.

The trial resumed. The plain men came forward one by one as called, worn Phrygian caps in their hands, their testimony having the ring of truth because, as Ranulf skillfully shaped his questions to the biddable men, most of it was just that.

The tale of Guntrada was put forth as common knowledge in Sherwood, and that since the first plow broke fallow down at Denby, their hides yielded better harvests than any other local steadings. As well known was the fact that a witch named Wytha had set wards about the hall and fields on the founding of the house.

"This was known to the priest of Blidworth, Beorn, who refused to speak of the matter—or to deny it," Ranulf interpreted silkenly. "A priest defrocked once and excommunicated with Robin Hood, a matter of record I submit without enlargement. Next, we have the statement of Baron Richard de Guilbert of Buckden." Ranulf laid the signed deposition before the court scribe who handed it up to Remigius. "This speaks of the clearly demonic behavior of Denby during the siege of Norwich fourteen years ago, when the accused wrenched the head from the body of a Christian knight already slain, as well as the conduct of Fitz-Gerald, then and now Sheriff of Nottingham, now married to Denby's cousin and a known intimate of the accused. *Robin,* I say! Ponder the name and its meaning."

For what did *Robin* signify? A harmless bird? Not so in northern England, but Robin Goodfellow, one of the many nicknames for the Devil himself—horned, hooved, and believed to range Sherwood yet. "A name deliberately bestowed on the man by the woman who bore him. All Christians know that when one pacts with the Devil, he or she takes a secret name in mockery of the sacrament of baptism. And now that you more readily perceive the honesty of my arguments, I must show myself as flawed but a vessel as my poor wife."

This aside, too, Ranulf had planned and rehearsed, his voice gone soft and not quite steady. "I have put aside the Church's rule of celibacy, true. My wife has given me two daughters whom I cherish as any father would. They have Christian names. Would I call them 'bastard' without cause? Would any parent name a child so without reason?"

Ranulf's agents had already testified to the custom of blood sacrifice in Denby marriages. As the suspect name, so the customary scar by which the Devil marked his own, scars plainly to be seen on the hands of Robin, his wife, and his mother.

In the tower above them, the Compline bell began to ring. Ranulf waited until the last note shivered away, tolling the last of Denby with its ordinary office. *Ring the bell,* Ranulf thought, *close his book, snuff his life.*

"Lastly, Your Grace, there is the statement of our liege William, in whose personal retinue the accused served four years. The king spoke the truth in my own ear and I penned his words."

Truth turned different ways had varying shapes. Ranulf had not hoped for such a large nail as the last in Denby's coffin lid, but the king said it. Said it in anger, no doubt, but he said the words. Despite his affection for the accused, the king admitted that Denby could never long remain inside a church; that on the first day of their acquaintance at Fécamp, William, then a plain knight, saw Robin quit the abbey church well before Mass was done, emerging from that place as if fleeing the curse of God.

"This from our king." Ranulf laid the final evidence before the scribe. "And thus I demonstrate. " 'When I asked him of this later in time, he said only that *he could not abide our churches.*' "

Little doubt of the verdict. Edward of Denby, significantly known as Robin Hood, was found guilty of pernicious sorcery, once more excommunicated from the Body of Christ and His Church, and sentenced to death at the will of the crown. The candles were extinguished, the tower bell rung, the book closed. Normally the verdict would have gone directly to Osmund, but Ranulf would take particular pleasure in laying it before the royal custodian thereof whose signature would be the ax on Robin's neck.

Father Alric alone dissented. Let His Grace interpret the vote as he would; the woman did not ring true in Alric's ear. Her story left too wide a margin for doubt. More, not a soul in the Midlands had not sung and spoken Robin's name proudly when Saxons needed to find some pride left. The Church was infallible and must be preserved, true, but there were other truths to nag at Alric's conscience. This Ranulf did not serve the Church, he used it.

I was a laborer when your lords first rode through Lincoln. I stood in Ermine Street and felt a thing break in my heart. Then the shabby little men like you followed, Bayeux, as they always do. I hope you got a good price for what you have sold.

Then Father Alric turned his back on the king's assassin and would not look at him again.

Ranulf procured an extra copy of the writ of excommunication and rode up Ermine Street into Steep Hill. At this hour, he did not expect anyone in his household to be awake. He called one of his porters nodding inside the door to light his way through the hall.

"No need, sir," the sleepy porter told him. "The mistress hasn't gone to bed yet."

Nor even night-dressed, still in the white gown, drinking alone at one of the low tables in the hall, close to the still-smoldering firepit. One wall sconce eddied dim light and shadow over Elfled where she sat with a cup of wine. Ranulf thought for a moment—a brief impression, no more—that she might have been weeping. No, she was dry-eyed and composed.

"Good evening, husband."

"Wife." Ranulf set the writ before her. "Sentence death at the will of our sovereign liege, God direct his hand."

"Amen." Elfled bent over the writing she could not read. Her hand passed over the parchment as if to take the words physically into her body. "Let me hear it."

Ranulf accommodated her. She savored every word, attentive as when she did household accounts with her steward. "God's justice."

Ranulf rolled and tied the parchment. "Someone's, in all events."

"The king will execute him?"

"In time." Ranulf sat beside her, his feet in their fine doeskin boots stretched out to the fire's last warmth. "William loves him, you see. When a degenerate has the misfortune to love deeply, there's the emotional extravagance of a sinner finding God, all rather tremulous. The love is unrequited . . . yes, William will kill him. Eventually."

"Good."

The force in the word was a death in itself. The merchant's vindictive daughter collecting the last penny of her due. "Bless me," Ranulf admired. "You are formidable after all. You're enjoying this."

Elfled accepted that with the justice done. "And you do not?"

"Oh, quite. Especially the ease with which you broke the court's collective heart."

"What do you mean?"

Ranulf winced, able to tolerate vengeance hard as his own but not facile innocence. "Please. Spare me, Elfled."

"You don't believe me. Don't deny it, you *never* believed me."

Ranulf wet his lips from Elfled's wine cup. "If we must be bald, no. Only in your profound capacity for making yourself believe. To watch you at your mirror was ever an education. You could see yourself as a fascinatingly fallen woman in one breath and the Virgin Mary in the next—and believe both, because you will never question that lovely surface or seek the motives beneath. I at least have never deluded myself as to what I held in my arms. I can't afford to.''

Yes, she understood him. He saw no hurt in her face, only tacit recognition, in the downsweep of the long lashes, of a buyer and seller on equal terms. For a little time Elfled had been lured by glamor away from the tidy shop stall of her life, and in that fancy deluded herself as she convinced the court. Now she was back to business and profit as usual with a sharp eye to shaved pennies. He perceived the rest with a surprising absence of regret. *Yes, I will leave you when I must, though I would not have suspected until now how easy it will be.*

Elfled might have guessed his thought. Perhaps it dovetailed with one of her own. She finished the wine and dabbed her lips with an embroidered napkin. ''Whatever you hold, never make the mistake of underestimating me.''

''Never.'' He leaned over to kiss her soft mouth; she answered his caress coolly. ''I am enormously fond of you.''

''And I of you, Ranulf.''

''Your dragon is slain, Princess. You may sleep in peace.''

''Amen, and well done.'' Elfled rose and moved toward the stairs. ''Will you come to bed?''

''No, not yet.'' As always, the heedless king needed a tidy servant following close and profitably in his headlong wake. ''There is work to do.''

The dragon was not slain; down but still breathing. The death stroke must come from the king. Ranulf would guide it surely, not directly at Robin, but through the see of Nottingham.

39

THAT year, far to the north where fire contended with frost and the vast, deep bones of the earth ground against each other, a new wound opened hurling up smoke and flame to darken the sky and rain black ash on the Norse settlements of Iceland. Men there, while praying to Christ, swore that Odin slept while Loki stole Thor's hammer to strike down the gates of Asgard. The wind caught the upflung ash and daubed it southeast in a lengthening stain across the light of day.

The unusual blood-red sunsets were first noticed by sheepherders on the Isle of Lewis. The shadow spread steadily south over Cumberland and Northumbria, hiding the sun from York, flecking the city walls with ash. Farther south in the green Kentish Weald, Wytha felt the tremors from that agony deep in the earth. She had come here through a need for change; if that meant what men called death, no matter. She would come again, but now she pondered this sickness in the earth.

"Earandel, Morning Star, I bid thee come of my need."

She cast and recast the runes. They told her nothing of the ailing earth or festered sky, only of loss and ending.

Sherwood went dark as twilight at midday. Thinking of the barley, Robin weighed the equal risks of planting too early or late. In the last days of March, he plowed and harrowed his fields. His folk were leading ox-drawn brush hurdles across one field, Robin and Marian watching from the saddle, when they saw Father Beorn's mule bobbing toward them.

Years a carl-knight before taking orders, Beorn's long body bent no more with time than a vital tree through seasons, not quite so straight

313

as before or the shoulders so square, but never frail. Past sixty now, age had overtaken but hardly overwhelmed Denby's priest. He appreciated a nap in the afternoon, rode a little more stiffly, but the voice was firm as ever in blessing or conviction, now sharp with disgust as he handed Robin the writ passed to him by messenger from Nottingham not an hour before.

"You are excommunicated." Beorn said no more while Robin scanned the writ.

"I don't understand this. Sorcery? Demon aid?"

"What?" Marian stared at the words she couldn't read. "Who says that?"

Beorn added tactfully, "The specifications are set forth."

Indeed, fully explicit. Elfled, the time and place, what she charged.

"Why was I not summoned? I received no—Good God, Beorn, they've damned me without any defense."

Binding enough in an ecclesiastical court constrained only by God. Beorn lowered his head over his hand on the reins. "A copy has gone to every church in the shire. The filthy thing's done. Marian, there's that I must say to Robin alone."

"No, Father." Out of a growing fury, Marian spoke candidly. "I knew. Robin has no secrets from me, nor it ent meet he should. It's that little Chancery rat and his wife. She came here with him, you know. By God, *that* was why."

Marian sprang down from her horse with a thump that raised dust. "The bitch." She lunged away for a few strides, arms folded tight under her breasts. "That overpainted goddamned *cow*. She had the brazen— forgive me, Father. Nay, don't trouble, for there's more coomin."

Marian spun around, pointing to her husband. "Rob's never lied to me, or me to him or you. What should he do? They banished my husband for life, so why should he play the monk when he never hoped to see me again? That was a hurt, Rob, though I hid it. You were only a man and a pitiful lost one then. What hurt was her. I'll tell you flat, you could have found better in my stead."

Mickle truth in that. "I thought that was the end of it. I am sorry, love."

"And you mark me, Father Beorn," she said deliberately. "If he bewitched that woman into bed, by Dunstan, no bitch ever so begged shame of the Devil."

Robin never hated Elfled until this moment, more for the pain to

Marian than any spite against him. He took Marian's arm and brought her back to their priest. "Then Ralf knows."

"Or will that soon." Robin tried to make light of it for her sake. "Eh well, Beorn and I have been excommunicated before."

But that was years ago when they hid in the forest and Beorn went on saying Mass, not sure God heeded or not. Now his priest must forbid him any holy comfort, even burial in sanctified ground. Robin made the decision for his old friend. "You won't have to bar me the church."

"Thank you." Troubled, divided against himself, Beorn couldn't look at him.

"They never leave us alone," Marian mourned. "All from her. But the king's your friend."

"Was."

"For sure he'll do summ'at about this."

No. Like the bridge at Gisors, that one was down. "He testified against me."

"Oh, no." The defiance wilted out of Marian with the hope. "God, he didn't."

No matter there; for now, think on future safety. "Father Beorn, you will have to read this out in church. Just do it; do all as you must. We must all be careful."

"Don't I know that?" Beorn growled. "A priest should not be confused, but I am that now. My heart's not caught up with my duty in this. Christ's love!" He lifted his grey head as if, from behind the unclean sky, God might somehow volunteer an answer. "It is enough to turn a man heretic."

His eye suddenly squeezed shut about something lodged in it. Marian wiped at the black cinders on her sleeve; they left a dirty smear. Now the workers leading the hurdles across the field stopped, looked up, swiping at hands and faces themselves. One, then another hurried toward Robin, piping thin over the distance, then louder and full of fear as the sky darkened overhead.

"Lord Robin! The rain is black and dry. *The rain is black!*"

The sooty ash spread southward over Sherwood while Marian feared for Robin and worried over new calves and milk. The meager spring grass this year was not sufficient graze. Cows were fed on the last stored fodder, while churches filled with terrified people. The dirt falling from the sky blackened the muddy streets and alleyways of Nottingham, soiling high and low alike, fell unheeded on Judith, spurring her palfrey home from Mass in a white rage, the mare's hooves spattering mud in every direction. Beggars, urchins, and peddlers dodged nimbly out of her way and swore they could hear the Lady of Nottingham cursing like a fishwife.

"Lord! She ent half boiling."

A thorough high dudgeon that swung Judith down from the saddle and swept her into her house, flinging the ash-grimed cloak to a bowing servant—"Where is my lord husband?"—and on to the small privy chamber where Ralf and Osmund once acknowledged the danger of Robin as being greater within law than without. Judith burst into the room without her usual polite knock, startling her husband in conference with half a dozen deacons. "My lord, masters, pray you pardon me, but there is a matter that cannot stand on courtesy."

Ralf read his wife's mood by her stance in the doorway, but his own business was graver than she knew. "Lady, we are occupied. Please—"

"I beg my lord to indulge me," Judith requested in a tone that clearly signified he should. "Goodmen, if you please."

The imperative flashing in her eyes decided Ralf. "Gentles, refresh yourselves in my hall; I will join you presently." He saw them out, closed the door, and leaned against it. "Now, what is so important?"

"This."

"They are here on a serious matter."

Judith thrust the writ at him. "This was read just now at Mass. In my own city! The priest choked on reading it; you could hear the gasp go throughout the nave." Judith flung herself back and forth across the chamber, unable to remain still. "Ranulf's wife. Is that little slut sane at all?"

Ralf read the writ of excommunication and charge, dropped it on the table, and sat down. "She actually went so far."

"You don't look surprised."

"At this? No." Certain facts shared with him by Robin Judith had not needed to know, though the time for that discretion was past. "She was besotted with him ever since they met; even chased after him in Rouen."

"What of that?" In her anger, Judith was a riptide swirling about the rock of her husband. "What did Robin have to do with her?"

"Too much, I'm afraid."

"You're joking."

316

"He bedded her."

The absurdity halted Judith. *"That?"*

"He said he was drunk."

"He would have to be." After Elfled's brief stay as her own guest, there was that about the woman that urged Judith to count the silver. "But witchcraft? Ralf, we must do something. You know many honest churchmen. English clerics."

"And every one of them frightened of a king whose own testimony— wait. Let me read this again." Ralf snatched up the damning writ and examined it closely. "As I thought. No order for his arrest, and I've received none. The less I need do now, the better for all of us. This is Rossel's message to Robin. He doesn't want him dead, not yet; just limed and helpless."

Judith searched his face. "For how long?"

"Such orders, when they are meant, come with a warrant of arrest. There's none."

"Yet. I see."

Quite. Robin was now completely at bay, dead when the king raised one finger, like a bird pinned under the paw of a cat. And today, notification had been received—and protested by the horrified delegation awaiting Ralf in the hall—that the king himself would presently confiscate the valuables of Osmund's church in royal stewardship. Nottingham would wait indefinitely for a new bishop and much longer, Ralf feared, for the return of their holiest treasures.

When the plowing and harrowing were done, Robin called the folk to sow his barley and their own. Too few of them answered his summons.

"They're in Blidworth church half the day," Will Scatloch reported. "Crying out the end of the world and shriving themselves. Poor Father Beorn, he does what he can, but—"

"Do not speak of the end," Angharad quavered as they stood in Denby courtyard. "Well it might be."

Will turned on her, savage with his own fear. "Daft woman! If God is minded to end the world, look you, there will be signs as in Revelations, will there not? He will roll up the heavens like to a shade, not turn day into night. Flock of sheep they are, too frighted to sow their own fields."

Marian kept counsel with her own bitter truth. In their fear, some of the folk believed the charges against Robin, or were simply afraid to help. There would be difficulty collecting the summer quarterly rents.

The loyal, Marian trusted, would pay them indirectly to Blidworth where Mauger would collect; others would protest they were not bound to obey a cast-out man and even forbidden by Holy Church to do so.

"Damn them all," Will scowled at the grimy, lowering sky. "Damn, I say!"

"Wipe your face; there's dirty it is." Anxiously Angharad looked about for Eddain and Gwaun, Marian gathered Moira close to her, and retreated into her bower. Now, in the too-chill evenings, she sat with Robin while he did the age-old reckoning of farmers. So many days from sowing to harvest, so many of likely rain and needed sun, and both of them knew how little and pitiful grain the land would yield that year.

Returning one evening from south Sherwood, Edward slung one gawky, long-boned leg over the bench by his father. "Da, there's men talking in the taverns. They say the blight on us is this king, not you."

Other men whispered as well, though not in Edward's hearing, standing ale liberally and attesting piously that the darkness was God's displeasure at the disobedience of men.

"Look, then, the truth is there. Is not Denby convicted, cut off from the Church, condemned, and yet living free? Nay, it's clear: If the king won't rid us of him, men might have to do it themselves."

Some turned their backs on such talk, but many listened.

Undaunted by a little shadow, Rossel, who had thumbed his nose at France and stood them off at Gisors, jibed at the witless cowardice of laity and clergy alike, sending a second reminder through his Chancery to Nottingham. The treasures of their see would be taken by the crown early in May. To this end the king commanded the full support of Vicomte Fitz-Gerald.

40

▶▶▶▶▶

O
N a Sunday morning late in April, the ill-set bones of the earth
beneath the Norse island of fire and ice twisted and ruptured.
As tremors from that wrenching shuddered through the earth,
English folk rocked with the spasms and feared the end portended by
the evil-hued sky had indeed come.

Earlier that morning, before his first Mass of the day, Father Beorn
stood in the road outside his church, counting his flock as they came
to Mass. They trudged up the hill from Blidworth and across the dale
from Denby and the western crofts. There were Will and Angharad
working up the last rise toward him, Eddain and Gwaun flanking them.
A few minutes behind the Welsh family, Robin's son in Lincoln green
led his gran Maud on a shambling black mare. The boy carried his
unbraced bow, the quiver slung; he'd be hunting later, skilled as his
father by now. The old priest's eyes lifted to the small woman in the
saddle. She rode less firmly these late years, not always certain where
or when she was, confused as a child spun round and round in blind
man's bluff until she knew no direction anywhere. Beorn's fond memory
reached back many years to a half-forgotten picture.

*You rode beside Aelred the first day I set eye on you. He was so
proud, presenting you with a flourish. "Here is the lady of my hall,
Beorn. Give her welcome." My vows were new as your marriage then,
my heart still more carl-warrior than priest, and how it squeezed tight
at the sight of you. Welcome, Maud? I fell in love with you that day.
So beautiful, so alive, and such a capacity for joy. You never knew or
will. I watched you who were made for joy fill with sorrow, saw you*

hide your pain. If there are shadows over you now, at least they have been kind.

In the church tower, sexton Seaxwulf hauled on the bell rope to call the folk to worship. Angharad bobbed a curtsey to her priest and followed her husband and sons into the church. Beorn waited to greet Maud as he always did. Robin had not been near the church or Beorn himself since learning of the writ. Nor Marian. She was not cast out; she should come but she'd likely go to hell with her husband rather than let him suffer alone.

Edward led the mare into the churchyard, helping Maud down. She peered uncertainly at Beorn, then brightened in recognition. Edward laid his bow and quiver on the church porch before taking her inside. The boy scarcely acknowledged Beorn, seething with something that must boil over.

The edict, surely. Edward couldn't accept it. *Does he think I can?* The day after receiving the shameful writ, Beorn had read it out at Mass as he was bound to do. Bit off the words coldly to let his parishioners know what he thought of the deed and any man involved in its making, then handed it to his sexton for removal like something unclean. From Denby that day only Edward appeared at Mass, standing far back toward the door, arms folded, eyes blazing. After that Mass he'd not bid Beorn good-bye, only walked out of the church with a face dark as the skies over him.

But not this day. Edward gave his grandmother a leg up, handed the reins to Eddain—"Take Lady Maud home. Father, we'll have a word in private."—and stood apart, waiting while Beorn bade good-bye to this or that villager. To the priest there was something poignantly reminiscent in the boy's barely patient stance. *We'll have a word.* Not request but command, the manner of a lord to his tenant. Already the arrogance of another callow boy remembered. Beorn reproved and checked his own irritation.

"Well, then," he said pleasantly when they stood alone on the porch. "What would your lordship?"

The irony eluded dead-serious Edward. "I'll know your mind."

"Will you? In what?"

"The Church has cut my father from its body. He's been there before and you with him."

"That is true."

"How say you now?" Edward challenged. "Not the Church or God, but Beorn."

320

Beorn censored his answer carefully. "Your father, who has better manners than his snip of a son, would not ask that of me."

"*I* am asking. Manners be damned."

"Oh, peace, Edward." Too young to be kind, the boy cut to the quick of Beorn's own dilemma. He was Denby's tenant, now in the impossible position of having to deny any sacrament to his lord and lifelong friend. How to say this to an angry, outraged boy? Between man and God was one thing, between friends another. Robin did not blame him for what he must do, but the son had not lived that long.

Edward said, "I won't have it, you know."

Father Beorn sighed. "You will not?"

"I will give you the benefit of a doubt, Father—"

"That is kind of you."

"But this ent from God. What? A Norman clergy informs a Roman Church full of Germans and Eye-talians that an Englishman may not receive Christ on his own lands from a church whose livings come from him? Doesn't that stick in your gullet?"

Defiance, pure contention, quivered in every taut line of the young body. "Edward, you are halfway to a fine education that will someday imply wisdom as well as learning—but not yet. I've written whatever letters wherever I could for what good they may do, since we have no bishop of our own. We must accept the—"

"Bishops." Edward spat in disgust and did not trouble to excuse himself to the priest. He braced his bow and slung it over one shoulder. "Mauger and Da have taught me, aye. Taught me to question what other men just accept. I question a Church that's more of money-minded foreigners than of God."

"That's enough, now. I need not listen to a fool. Enough, I say."

"No, you hear me!" Edward lashed back. "If such a Church kills my da, when I am Denby there will *be* no such church, not on my land, if I must pull it down stone by stone."

Beorn turned away from him to quell his own anger, unable to add to the boy's pain already too great to bear by himself. Boy-brave mouthing boy oaths and no doubt terrified as the rest. He had Marian's eyes, warm and dark, but the set of his face as it firmed toward manhood was much like Maud's, something intractable that declared to all: This is Denby. Like the roots of the World Tree of old, we go deep and you will heed the warning at our gate.

"Father, I had to say that." Softer now, the respect firmly in place again, but the injustice unresolved. "The love my house bears you, I bear you. But I won't have it. Give you good day, sir.''

Edward strode away downhill toward the dale, veering north into the forest. Beorn turned sadly into his church.

Edward thinks it honor to become what his father's laid aside, to be Robin Hood and all that stood for, serving notice to God and men alike that he won't have it.

And you, "Father" Beorn, who went into outlawry with a brave man because he was right? Twenty-odd years of Normans, have they tamed the English out of you?

Step by deliberate step Beorn made his way down the flagstoned nave, mounted the single rise, and stood before his altar, asking the final question of Him to whom it was consecrated. "And what of You who prompt the baby's heart to beat and see into it all his life, who move the very heavens: are You so parochial that You read only Remigius's Latin? Help me.''

Wystan was alone in the kitchen house when he felt the first tremor, heard the knives and spoons rattle on Minna's worktable. Blind but sure of touch, he guided himself swiftly to the door as the tremors increased. A clay cup shattered on the floor.

"Name of God." Wystan groped for the latch, fearful for Minna outside in the kitchen garden.

"Husband!" The terror in his wife's wail went through Wystan as her footsteps pounded closer. He thrust out his arms, felt Minna clasp tightly to him. If this was the Last Day, they must go to Judgment together.

The first shock caught Maud between a dim dream and the absent plying of her needle, wrenching her back to the present. She rose, steadying herself as the floor of her bower groaned and warped under her.

Where are the children?

Maud wrenched open the door, searching the courtyard. "Moira? Where are you?''

Alone in his church and still asking questions of a God who had not answered, Beorn thought the first deep shudder through him the hand of Heaven laid on His house; then the heavy lectern began to teeter on its base. The silver cross rocked and fell over on the altar, the heavy reliquary bearing the lock of Saint Dunstan's hair jittered across the white wool altar cloth. A sharp *crack!* spun the priest about to see a fissure tear across the nave flagstones like a bolt of dark lightning.

"Is that You?" he whispered under the growing roar. "Is this Your anger?"

Halfway home from the near field with broken harness to replace, Robin halted, puzzled and then frightened at the feeling beneath his feet. He turned to see the field-workers look down, drop their tools, and run for whatever safety they could find. Robin dashed toward his hall as the earth rebelled under him.

Marian raced across the courtyard toward her daughter. Moira huddled against the well, white with terror at the invisible thing writhing under her like the shapeless fears in her worst dreams. Marian snatched her up and turned full of terror to see Robin vault the low steading wall.

"Quick." He dragged Marian toward their bower with one fear-shot glimpse of his barn and stable swaying on their foundations before he tore the bower door open and pushed wife and child inside. Marian fell across the bed soothing Moira, who clung whimpering to her. Robin covered them with his own body, his soul a fist shut tight around sick fear. He'd seen men die, cities burned, and his own death come too close, but nothing in life like this, which could only come from God.

"Keep Moira covered." His next incoherent thought was for his folk; *must get to the church*. God was shaking the world in huge, violent hands; Robin himself could flee or crouch and endure but never hope for the safety of the church. The very spirit of Christ would bar him entrance. Kneeling over his wife and child, Robin loosed an arrow question at the God who gave and took away. *Is it me who offends You? What must I do?*

His head jerked up at the sound of splintering wood.

"It's the roof beam," Marian quavered. "Where's Edward? Where's my son."

"Lie still, the beam will hold. Edward was hunting."

"In the forest? Oh God, please *no*."

Huddled in her mother's arms, Moira screamed and held on to all the safety left in the world.

He'd meant to hunt, but only halfheartedly followed the doe's trail north toward Holy Pool. Her hoof marks were delicately placed and left no more disturbance than need. Moving in a straight line, a long trail for this time of year when deer need not go so far for water or food. Well, he got her or he did not; Edward could not care that much today. She might well be carrying a fawn anyway. Robin's son stretched out in the clearing just inside the circle of bordering oaks where yellow grass bordered the rill, still grimed with the black ash from the skies. He lay on his stomach, chin resting moodily on his arms, bleak as the clouds overhead.

Some of it was shame and good manners remembered too late. The sun rose and set in his father, who earned the honor of thane every day. No mind that the old king stripped away the title; the folk would always call Da *lord,* for so he was. *Hlaeford,* bread-giver. He took the ills and cares of their folk on himself just as Christ took the sins of the world. If Jesus felt a mite godly in that, what wonder Denby went a bit stiffish about their own place? That was clear enough, but not the meat of the thing troubling Edward. No, he'd taken too much on himself with Father Beorn. Eh now, there was bluster; there'd be a blistering sure if Da got wind of the matter. But the Church was flatly unjust in condemning him and the man not there to defend himself. Oh, Da would've shook them summ'at and no mistake. Sorcery, indeed! Norman bastards wouldn't know a *wicce* man if one walked up and gave them good day. For himself, Edward had received Christ but would never question the wisdom of someone like Wytha, who was no less of a comfort to Denby.

"They ent right," he glowered to the rill gurgling past him. Well, he would say extra prayers each night for a week and send his next kill to Father Beorn's table with an apology—but damned if he didn't shake inside yet with the wrong of it; he could feel his belly trembling—

No, not in himself that deep shuddering. His body tensed. Animal terror flooded through him. The ground under his belly quaked impossibly and the trees began to writhe with the strain on the deep roots. Edward's bow danced impossibly over the grass, arrows rattling in the quiver. He would have crossed himself, but a different warning bred from a lifetime in the forest told him he was not alone. Amid the rising rumble of the earth, Edward sprang up.

The old doe stood at ease midway between the bargain oak and the wattle hut, the clean lines of her youth and prime long worn away, grey shimmering in her dull red coat. She swayed slightly with the anguish of the earth. Other animals of every kind would be fleeing the forest by now, birds deserting their trees, but she held her ground, and it seemed to Edward that the dark liquid eyes spoke to him, quieted and gave him courage in the calm example of her own.

He took a step toward her. She did not move.

"You?"

He hardly dared believe, taking another step and another over the heaving earth, touched by something as old and deep. Fear drained away. Edward thrust out joyful arms to the doe.

"Guntrada, is it you?"

Will hurried his family down the hill, making for the church atop the far rise where the tower bell clanged of itself with the convulsions of the earth. Eddain and Gwaun led, Angharad holding tight to her husband's hand. They were crossing the dale when Gwaun cried out and pointed.

"Look, it is Edward." He waved and bawled lustily at the boy running toward them. "To the church with us! Jesus, what's taken him?"

Not running at all. Edward danced over the ground, jigging and skipping, bow brandished high like a magician's wand of power as he caught them up.

"I saw her, Will. *I* saw her at last."

"There's no time, boy. Hurry on now."

Edward capered about them like a hound pup too full of life to be still. "Not today. I saw her by the bargain oak."

"Saw who, for Christ's sake?"

"Guntrada!"

Eddain grabbed at the boy's arm. "Is this a time for vision? Come on."

"To church? Nay, I've been. My da's at home and I'll be with him."

Edward broke into a rapid trot west toward Denby. Angharad cried after him. "Your father would be *wanting* you to—"

"Enough, I say!" Edward spun like a dancer, wheeling about to face Will and his family. Robin's son suddenly thrust his grasping hands to Heaven. From the air or his own heart, Will could never say afterward, but the reaching fingers touched and held something, closed on that and came down as if he'd caught Heaven itself by the scruff of eternity and brought it to heel on Denby ground.

"I—say—*enough!*"

Thirty years gone another boy had turned just so to Will Scatloch, singing out that *he* would lead the two of them home. Then, Will remembered, a shadow fell over Robin's face in open sunlight where none should be. That was the day Robin himself saw the old doe for the first time. Edward stood planted now as his father then, solid on his own earth, willing the roots of him down to grip the earth and still its pain—while the spasms lessened, weakened, faded away. The tower bell clanged twice more with the last tremor and went silent.

"Go on, then." Edward scooped up his bow and ran on, taking the hill in long, tireless strides.

* * *

The earth had quaked with mortal sickness but not succumbed. All England crept out of hiding, felt at bones and limbs to make sure they were whole. Denby and Blidworth breathed deep, and in the church where new fissures scarred nave and bell tower, the bones of Father Beorn's soul warred much as those of the earth and told the priest to choose and act.

There was no such war in Edward. Guntrada had passed something to him. "As she came to you once, Da. Now to me. Ask Will, then: I'd just damned well had enough and said so, and the shaking stopped. The land accepts me."

If Robin and Marian heard him with more somber acceptance than joy, they listened with ears tuned to a music different from Beorn's. Edward was young, but neither vain nor a fool. They did not question why or toward what future the bargain passed to their son, but talked far into the night before sleeping close in each other's arms. So entwined from the day they met, they would be one in whatever came.

And coming that soon. The king himself would be in Nottingham after May Day to confiscate the treasures of the episcopal see. If rage in Heaven shook the earth, neither God nor certain folk of Sherwood could turn aside and let that happen. Fitz-Gerald would not hear a hint or whisper until the thing was done, but for the doing, excommunicant or not, the man they turned to was Robin Hood.

To Will Scatloch and his family, mystic and musical in their emotions, Robin was now a man between two fires: what he should not do, for safety's sake, and what he must. The whiskey went round. Eddain and Gwaun drank silently and let their parents speak.

Angharad grieved over her cup. "He cannot and he must. Will not Marian try to stop him?"

"In this? Not her, lass. She'll be with him. She said that was why the earth heaved like to a poisoned stomach, to rid us of this king."

Will and Morgan would ride with Robin, though each heard the sad music of the inevitable run through the coming danger. That was the difference between them and their English masters. Robin simply said, "This has to be," and got on with it. God had answered his question.

41

►►►►►

ON the morning of the third of May, Robin, Will, Morgan, and
Edward began a wide sweep through Sherwood—north to Edwinstowe and Thoresby, southwest to the crofts outlying Mansfield and on to Annersley, Linby, and Papplewick, north again through
Southwell. The rain of black ash had thinned out, but sunlight was still
meager. Mud lingered on the heath and forest tracks. Edward worried
over the trail they left in the soft earth.

"We'll be that easy to stalk tomorrow."

"No fear of that," Will laughed. "Your father and I will be followed
when we wish and not before."

"There's boasting," Morgan jeered. "You could not hide from a
blind man at midnight."

They joked to cover their tension. Once begun, the venture could
easily fail but not be stopped. Marian would be committed as would
every woman and older child in Sherwood able to bear a load. From
Denby, only Angharad, Minna, and Maud would be left at home. Certain
old rebels came forward from the start. Wulf Edricson and his near-
grown son. Lady Algive, the widow of Alan of Linby Dale, and a
number of her own tenants. Algive volunteered with a vindictive ring
to her willingness and went to ready her sturdiest shoes and oldest clothes
for the task, with only one adornment: the gold chain she had worn on
feast days in Alan's hall. If she were caught or killed, she was *Lady*
Algive, and God forever damn all Normans and their king. Fiery Father
Ayulf of Papplewick, a mainstay in the enterprise, challenged his folk

from the pulpit, daring any man to look him in the face ever after who did not make one with them in this.

Not many came forth so willingly. Robin himself did the asking in doorways up and down the length of Sherwood. They all knew his cause; who would ride with him on the morrow? A hard choice for common men. He had been a hero to them all, no man forgot that, but Holy Church was a different matter. Wives kept silent and turned away as conscience-torn husbands evaded the urgency of the aging man once a legend and a pride. They themselves did not cast him out, he must believe that, but they had their own to think of and not much of a crop to count on this hard year. They had so little; the king could take all . . . do not lay this on them.

"We pray God be with you if He will, Robin, but we cannot."

So the wheel comes round, Robin mused as he rode the shadowed forest paths. *Why do I pursue this except I must? Rossel pushes this on me, but the act was ordained from the day old William came to England. Does Rossel push then or merely stumble forward, impelled by that father to dislodge me? And Ralf in turn, sure as a touch launches the crossbolt. Old friend, old enemy, I'm not the angry boy who dared you long ago in the forest. I would not do this thing and can do nothing else.*

Fate often spared the brave, so the old poem went, but sparing or not, the wheel turned forward. All of them moved toward this from the day they were born.

Early on the morning of the fourth, just after Prime, all Blidworth gathered for Mass in the church. As he had done for more years than he cared to count, Father Beorn bade farewell to each old friend, generations of them now, gave instructions for the care of the church to Seaxwulf, and went home to remove the cloth that symbolized his vows. He dressed in plain tunic and trousers and buckled on the old sword with the new-set edge.

That morning at Denby, the entire household remained at table after breakfasting. Robin read from the great iron-bound Bible as his family and servants bowed their heads over folded hands. For this day he chose his text with care: " 'All that the Father gives me shall come to me; no one who comes will I reject . . . it is the will of Him who sent me that I should lose nothing of what He has given me; rather that I should raise it up on the last day.' "

And from Revelations, a passage Maud had read so often that Robin knew it by heart: " 'God will wipe away every tear from our eyes; there will be no more death.' "

A smothered sound from someone near him. Robin wondered was it wife or mother. " 'No more weeping or pain, for the old order has passed away.' "

And Mauger, standing behind his lord in best robe, white staff of office in his hand and stiffness in his aging back, perceived beyond Saint John's meaning to a nearer one. The old order was gone. Young Edward with his fierce loyalty and love would most like be the last generation to remember anything of the old Saxon ways or feeling, already used to Norman overlords for all the injustice of them throbbed in him like pain in a tooth. Counts and barons held sway in place of earls and thanes. The aged English officials of Chancery and mint, cogs in the civil engine of a system the Conqueror viewed in awe but never understood, were giving place to Norman clerks who comprehended little of the workings of that machinery and none of its spirit. Harold's old standard, the Fighting Man, carried by Little John at Norwich, was John's winding sheet in Tombland there, a shroud to them all. As with old Arthur of the Welsh, Beowulf and Holger of the Danes, Englishmen might drink deep and dream, while they remembered, of Harold, Hereward, and men like Robin, but the sun had passed over, night fell on yesterday. Any greatness to come would be, like Mauger himself, of a mixed strain.

The little steward looked down at Robin's back as his lord bent over the Bible, satisfied these fourteen years to have left a Church he served with half a heart for a master who claimed the whole. Like Robin, Mauger could not see the world static while it shifted, changed, and moved under him. He prayed earnestly before bed each night, and between one sleep and another, tried to live in the ideal of a faith while the fact of history roared in the cellar of his soul.

I know in fact what men will sing in their cups and bad memory. You are almost yesterday, Robin Hood, and not God to still the sun or time in their passing. A dear, valiant impossibility whom men will fable and recall for all the wrong reasons.

Now with the saddled horses waiting, Marian fussed with Moira to turn the child out in her best kirtle. She hugged her daughter with a narrowing of her eyes at Angharad to deny the woman's brimming tears. *Not here, not now.* "There, sweeting, and you mind what Angharad

329

tells you while your mum's away. Well, then, I'm off.''

Straight-backed and crisp, Lady Maud kissed her son and Marian good-bye as if they were merely off to Nottingham Goose Fair. "I will see to dinner and supper today. When may we look to see you back?"

"Tomorrow for sure." Robin looked away toward the dale, surprised and unhappy to see Father Beorn in lay clothing and armed, working up the rise on his mule. Maud drew Angharad aside, stern at the woman's tears. "Leave off, you old silly. They will be home."

"Yes, Lady."

When Beorn's mule ambled up to him, Robin put a hand on the bridle. "Is this what it appears?"

"It is that," Beorn said.

"No, Father. You're of the Church. I can't allow this."

"He won't allow." Beorn's thin smile held more memory than mirth. "Have I not heard that from Aelred and you and Edward in turn? Still playing God."

They faced each other, each with his truth. "What can I say to you, Beorn?"

"Nothing easily, I suppose. The king is mad and the Church is wrong."

"I can't let you."

"I'm not asking, Robin. I will be there. I've made my peace, such as can be found, and I know my mind."

Will Scatloch handed the throwing ax to Robin. "The good father was a comfort and no burden when there was a price on his head. Have done, boyo. We might need a priest."

"Right." Robin tucked the ax in his belt and slung his quiver. "But do me the courtesy to stay clear of trouble. Move when I say and run like flamin' hell when I tell you. And you, Edward, never mind the old songs or any new ones you might be thinking to shape. There'll be trouble enough; don't go seeking more."

"No, Da." Edward had spent an hour honing his arrowheads and placing each shaft with care in the quiver so they wouldn't snag coming out. He was eager but nervous, troubled by an inevitability his father omitted to speak of, one a man couldn't get round. Uncle Ralf would be coming after them surely, not as kin this time but sheriff. Some of them might be dead by this hour tomorrow.

Perhaps Robin sensed part of his thought. "Stay close to me and don't waste arrows. To horse."

All through the misty morning, men, women, and wind-browned boys and girls trooped through Sherwood toward Papplewick. Before noon, they began to trickle in twos and threes into the square, where the village women had set out a cold dinner with ale and cider served on tables before the church. Father Ayulf beamed at them, hands on black-robed hips, glowing with pugnacious pride and the numbers swelling his square.

"We are a people and we will prevail," he whispered fervently. "By Jesus' Blood we will."

Hours after midnight, the streets of the Norman section of Nottingham lay drowned in moonless dark. In a short time, as Robin estimated, the church bell would call the yawning, sleepy monks to Matins. They slept yet, and the king's guard mounted over the church and the adjacent house of Osmund nodded at their posts. Mousing cats roaming the alleys off St. Mary's Gate to hunt and fight for love were the only creatures to hear the sackcloth-muffled hooves of horses slip down the narrow street ridden by men in dark clothing, their faces stained with soot to blend into night. The men spoke in whispers, continually quieting the horses. Robin led the first column with Edward, Will, and Morgan close behind, the rear contingent commanded by Wulf Edricson. At Robin's signal, both sections halted.

On his last few visits to Nottingham, Robin gleaned an accurate estimate of the royal guard force. Ten to a watch on each building day and night. Long enough by now to have gone a little slack. What trouble they might expect, if any, they assumed would come in daylight. But the months came and went. After the catastrophes of black ash rain and earthquake, the only mob to descend on St. Mary's came to babble prayers and be shriven sometimes twice a day. By now the guards would complacently believe the whole shire still cowering behind locked doors.

The present watch had come on duty at Compline, three hours before midnight, not due to be relieved until about six of the morning. Robin's raiders numbered two dozen of the best-mounted bowmen in Sherwood. Most of his people waited close by the fork in the cart track north of the city, where he'd once relieved Osmund of some of that wealth he now planned to deny Rossel. Oh, Osmund was furious and what a day that was—and what a turnabout from then to now. Where he once robbed a bishop to help the poor, he now stole from the same institution for its own benefit. God would judge if the whole were worthwhile, year for year, but none could ever call his a dull life. Robin leaned from the saddle and tapped Edward's shoulder. The boy signaled the first section to dismount and move forward on foot.

The two Norman soldiers posted before the door of St. Mary's church were fairly alert. Curfew kept all men indoors after a certain hour. They would stop and question anyone abroad. Even wobbling drunks, tedious as they were.

The soldiers heard the voices before the pair emerged from the gloom of St. Mary's Gate. Norman by the sound of them: a stripling boy doing his best to support a father too drunk to walk but obstinate in his effort to proceed.

"*Non, Père, il est beaucoup trop tard*. It is far too late. Go to church tomorrow."

They were challenged as they approached the church. "You there! What do you out after curfew? Come here."

Struggling to hold his father up, the boy appealed to them. "*Aidez-moi, braves gens. Mon père a trop bu*. He's drunk too much and nothing will do but he has to confess himself to a priest now in the middle of the night."

Drunk indeed. The older man listed on unsteady legs and wilted over his son's arms, sliding to the ground. The two soldiers shook their heads ruefully at the ruin stretched before them. They were still amused over his predicament when the two small Welshmen whipped the throttling cords about their throats. The process took only a moment. Robin sprang to his feet.

"Edward and Will, hide them. Morgan, give the call."

The soft, fluttering cry of a barn owl rose over the churchyard. Silent men flowed out of the dark.

Ralf Fitz-Gerald woke instantly at the ringing of the alarm bell, needing only a moment to realize the bell was not Matins, not that furious clamoring. He groped for his clothes in the dark, blowing the rushlight to a glow and lighting a candle end from it. Judith sat up, rubbing her eyes. "What is it?"

"I don't know. Trouble." Ralf slithered into the tunic, thrust his feet into shoes. Beyond the open casement he could already hear loud voices and feet pounding closer. Judith slipped into a robe as Ralf snatched an unlit taper from a sconce, fired it with the candle, and hurried out. Loud knocking at the hall door below.

"Who's awake?" Ralf called down. "Someone bring light to the hall."

The serjeant of the king's guard, a stocky Breton with a florid countenance, darkened no doubt with knowledge of the trouble he was now in, waited for Ralf in his hall with five men, two of them bearing lit torches. Ralf thrust his taper into a sconce.

"Now, what's amiss?"

"My lord, everything."

"What happened?"

"They were just too quick," the serjeant rumbled. "Too many of them."

"Dozens," one soldier blurted, staunching blood from a wound in his scalp with a white rag. "They were everywhere. I barely got out."

More hammering at the door as Judith appeared like a wraith in the hall entrance. Barré, one of Ralf's own lieutenants, nodded respectfully past her and hurried to the sheriff. "The bishop's house has been ransacked."

"And the church," the serjeant added bitterly. "Some of my men wounded."

"Some dead," Barré corrected. "Five we found so far."

Ralf asked: "The treasures?"

"Cleaned out," Barré told him. "The great jeweled cross, gold plate, the bishop's own crozier, vestments, chalices. Everything."

The red-faced serjeant glared at Ralf as if he were an accomplice. "I *said* we needed more men on watch."

"Yes, yes." Ralf turned away impatiently as another of his own men ran into the hall, panting. "They scattered, my lord. Some up one street, some another, but they're moving north."

North into the forest; that would follow. Ralf and Judith exchanged a look that guessed more than either wanted to know.

The Breton serjeant was single-minded in his concern. "Lord Sheriff, I will not be alone responsible for this."

"Be still. We'll get them."

"Get who?" the Breton challenged. "Who would dare such an act within hours of the king's arrival? Madmen."

"No, they are quite sane and obviously well prepared. Return to your duties. Barré!" Ralf issued rapid orders to his man. "I'll need you and forty men ready to ride in half an hour. Light by then, lighter by the time we reach the forest. And you"—Ralf rounded on the florid serjeant—"you may tell the king that if he'd given us a new bishop when we asked, this would never have happened."

"Me? I'll tell him no such—I am not a fool."

"No, I imagine not, though it will occur to the king and possibly even to you why this happened today of all days. Say to William that

333

we will meet him on the north trail hard by the Papplewick fork. Now let's be about it.''

When the last of them had gone, Ralf climbed the stairs to change clothes. Following after, Judith saw her husband sag down slowly on their bed, face in his hands.

"Do you have time for breakfast?" she asked.

"No, have them wrap me something cold." He looked up at her, and Judith saw his despair. "I prayed for years this wouldn't—I warned him, Judith." Ralf flung his arms around her waist, burying his face in the comfort of her. "I love you. I love our boys."

Judith stroked the thick, greying hair. "And if it is Robin?"

He didn't answer. They let the question go begging in silence. Like a timid afterthought, a church in the old Danish quarter of the city rang Matins.

42

▶▶▶▶▶

R IDING at the head of his column, Ralf cleared the northern outskirts of Nottingham as the first dingy light streaked the sky. When he could distinguish tracks on the road, he slowed the pace to read the hoofprints in the damp mud. Just here . . . some riders veered off across the heath while others moved on. A mile north of Nottingham, the horse tracks mingled with too many human feet to count. Women and even children among them from the footprints, all sharing the divided loads. The smallest prints pressed deep into the mud under far more than normal weight. None of them careless, no matter how encumbered. Wherever possible, the carriers chose the firmest ground before vanishing into the forest. Farther up the cart road no more tracks could be found at all. Barré cursed, but had to admire the execution. "For a peasant mob, they move like a disciplined company. No time wasted, thus far no mistakes. Whoever planned this knows what he's about."

"Yes." Ralf swung up into the saddle. "We'll ride on to the Papplewick fork. Shields up! Stay awake! From here on, you're all targets."

He pushed on at a brisk trot, wanting to be wrong, but with lessening doubt as to whom he followed. Only Robin would dare this out of principle alone; only he could so cleanly plan the audacious strike and neat withdrawal. He would disperse the carriers, some this way, some that, but peasants carrying heavy loads could move only so fast. And moving where? Sherwood afforded a number of ideal hiding places for men or loot. The king and Ranulf might never regain what they coveted. The notion pleased Ralf Fitz-Gerald in spite of his duty.

Full light now, cloudy, but no fog. Faint under the jingle and clop of harness, mail, and hooves, Ralf told the time by the distant church bells of Nottingham. The king would be in the city by now. Alert for any sound or movement in the surrounding thickets, Ralf speculated on which Rossel would want more, the master thief or the prize he made off with.

Careful, stay alert. They were not being watched, not yet. Robin had taught him that much of Sherwood: to listen for unnatural silence or the telltale thrashing of a flushed animal through underbrush, the drumming wings of a frightened pheasant, a certain kind of caw from disturbed rooks. . . .

Lucky there's no mist. Wouldn't have a chance if he wanted to kill me. There'd been fog near Ancaster that day he and Robin grappled and near killed each other, but they were young then and both had the Devil's own luck. Puck-Robin wasn't that nimble anymore, or himself, all but the last of their cat lives gone. No pardon or exile this time. Rossel would not have it so.

If it is you, then death will be a mercy, because you've no more time. If it is you, take Marian and run, run with the last of your luck far from Sherwood.

They had just passed the Papplewick turning, approaching the broad stretch of open heath where Robin once ambushed Osmund and his retinue. Ralf wheeled about to his men.

"Some of them were here. Dismount, search any paths for tracks. We'll wait on the king."

No long wait: While Ralf's men rooted about for recent tracks, a mounted knight dashed onto the heath from the south, leaping from the saddle to confront the sheriff. "From the king, my lord."

"Oh?" Ralf acknowledged without enthusiasm. "He will join us?"

"A quarter hour behind me, no more. He stayed only to inspect the looted house and church and to relieve the guard serjeant of his duties. And his rank," the knight concluded with some emphasis.

"A pity."

The knight's manner was gravid with Rossel's own anger. "He will have words with you."

"Responsibility of the royal guard. I had no orders to assist their detail."

"But your men guard the city. My lord, the king is very unhappy."

* * *

Marian trudged along the swine track under a sack that weighed two stone or more in gold and silver holy ornaments. Father Beorn labored close in her wake, past his second wind, but refusing to halt. Behind them a human ant chain toiled under equal loads, children bearing what they could. A fat fifteen-year-old boy puffed up to Marian to tug at her sleeve. She glared from under sweat-matted eyebrows, little breath to spare on talk. "What? Where's your bundle?"

"Left it," he panted. "The folk've stopped back there, say they've got to rest."

"Rest? Mary and Joseph!" Marian swung down her own load. "Father, you breathe now while you can." Her lowering eye swept dangerously along the way they had come. "Stopped, have they? Boy, come with me."

Skirts tucked up in her apron, Marian hurried back along the narrow trail. She passed some people pushing gamely along, but farther back many had fallen out and sprawled, sweating and breathing hard amid bracken and their burdens. Marian fell on them like the wrath of God, pulling women and children to their feet, booting at irritable men—aye, she knew they were spent and some too old for this—"But so is my priest up yonder and a better man than any I see here. Up, I say! We're all but there. You don't know where your son is or your man? Neither do I, woman. They may be dead. Get up and move. Yes, you. All of you. Push on, it's not far now."

One by one the people groaned and rose with every muscle protesting, shouldered their loads, and plodded on. Marian retied the damp kerchief about her matted hair and hurried back to prod the hindmost stragglers, knowing their pursuers would be close now. *They could be dead. Is it Ralf following? Where are you, Robin? Edward, be close to your father. . . .*

Robin, Edward, and their mounted contingent clattered into the village square at Papplewick, where Father Ayulf and a few older women came hurrying out of the church with water for the horses, bread and pots of ale for the men. Robin drained half a mug and passed it to Edward, shouting to his riders, "Five minutes' rest, then we go. Ayulf, are the pits ready?"

"They are that," the priest warranted.

"You men for the pits, go with Ayulf now."

"You said five minutes," one of the riders complained. "Give us that much. I've not slept since yesternight and nigh got killed back at the bishop's house."

Edward almost screamed at him. "You don't bloody *have* five minutes. Ride!"

"And then scatter, get rid of the horses," Robin called after the departing men. "You men for the cave, follow me."

In a moment, the swirl of men and horses were gone, leaving Papplewick near empty and tranquil as before. South of the village, the small animals and birds crouched silent and still as the forest about them trembled with approaching danger.

"Unbelievable, Sheriff."

Ralf Fitz-Gerald faced a king whose rage blazed from his eyes and all but oozed through the fingertips of jeweled gauntlets. About them on the heath under a sky the color of grime on white wood, a hundred men waited the order to ride.

Rossel dealt with his sheriff with barely contained savagery. "Your own watch could not detect so many riders?"

"Saint Mary's Gate is within the royal guard's perimeter, sire. And these are forest folk, quite used to eluding notice when they must."

"And I know who leads them."

Of course, but Ralf would not name him until he had to. "We are not sure."

"*Merde,* are you dim? Or do you protect him?"

"I do not, my lord. Not in this."

"He did this to me." Rossel glared at the two scouts riding toward him out of the wood to the north. "To *me*."

"My lord—"

"*What?*" Rossel coiled, then checked the urge to violence and willed himself to control. "What, Sheriff? You can shed some light on this disgrace?"

If no illumination, perhaps a remedy. "Let the king send us a bishop."

"That will solve everything," Rossel noted acerbically. "Anything else?"

"When that happens, it is more than possible the treasures will be returned."

"The office is not the issue."

"By your leave, it has been the issue for months."

Rossel's calm was lethal. "Do you gainsay me, Vicomte?"

338

Damn the man. Not even simple honesty. "Do you think these are common thieves, that common theft was their motive?"

The two scouts ranged by the king and dismounted to report. They'd found the trail—*a* trail at least, no more than a pig run through thicket and bramble. Riders moving single file along it toward Papplewick not less than an hour past. Rossel pounded one fist into the other gloved palm.

"To me, Robin." He mounted and rode off with the scouts. "Alive, you hear? I want Robin Hood alive!"

Yes, he would want that, Ralf thought sickly, following his king. *You want him to kneel before you and know himself helpless under your thumb. You want revenge like a jilted woman.*

Their pursuit was slowed by the narrow swine track that sometimes disappeared altogether into thick brambles, costing more delay and fouling Rossel's already vicious mood. When the king's company entered the village with imperious horns blaring, only a frightened Father Ayulf crept forth from his church to greet them, bobbing and bowing to the king, Ralf observed, with twice the servility the feisty priest usually gave to anyone.

Yes, Father Ayulf admitted, a rude company had galloped in demanding food and drink and water for their laden horses. The village folk were terrified they would take more, but they rode on.

"Who led them?" Rossel demanded. "Robin, no?"

"Yes, sire." Ayulf hung his head. "A pride to us once, but now a shame."

Rossel grinned coldly at his sheriff. "You see?"

Ralf saw a great deal he would not reveal to this king more interested in revenge than lost revenue. Ayulf's cringing was a sham; the man was in this thick as Robin. That was unimportant now. "Where did they go?"

"North, my lord. I heard one of them speak of Ollerton."

As the company clattered out of Papplewick, Ralf weighed appearances against his long experience of Robin. Something he said once after they'd become friends, when Robin first set up the chess pieces on the board between them.

"If you'd learn the habit of a man's mind, the *way* he thinks, play chess with him."

They both played well, but Robin won more often through his ability to think so many moves ahead. All planned, nothing careless. Robin

339

was no longer hiding his trail or identity but putting his clear seal to this action—and Ollerton, if the priest spoke true, could well mean the natural cave two miles north of the village on the east bank of River Maun. Displaced folk from the forest enclosures had often sheltered there.

And where was Marian in all of this?

Their quarry now moved across open heath whenever possible, choosing speed over concealment, but the gap closed. From the horse droppings, they were no more than half an hour ahead of Ralf. The heath ended in thicker wood, and some time was again lost moving through underbrush before gaining the cart track to Ollerton. As Ralf expected, the trail led down to the banks of Maun into the water and up the opposite bank. Rossel peered across the narrow stream, shading his eyes.

"They've turned west."

"No." Ralf indicated the muddied waters along the bank stretching north of them. "Most of them are still on this side. Using the shallows. I think I know where they've gone. If my lord will follow." He swung north along the shoreline, waving the others after him.

Rossel had given their horses little rest since leaving Papplewick, hating any lost time. No more than three hours after leaving Ayulf's village, Rossel and Ralf stood at the mouth of the cave on the banks of Maun while foragers sent inside cried out their exultant discovery of silver cups and plates freshly buried, only a little earth flung over them. "Here! It is here! Bring light and something to dig with."

Unable to wait, Rossel shoved his way into the cave, calling for a makeshift pick. Only a few cups and items of plate had been unearthed, but surely there were more. With mattocks improvised from dead branches, scooping out dirt by hand, the men dug furiously, deeper and wider around the area of the first find, Rossel goading them on. Faster! More torches in here!

Their horses needed rest. Some of the men led them down to the river to drink while Ralf scoured the area minutely with Barré. His lieutenant had been with him for ten years, still relatively young, but an experienced tracker. Barré scrutinized the confusion of hoofprints and footprints, worrying back and forth over them like a puzzled hound on a scent gone cold where it should not. "Somewhere, we've lost most of them. Some crossed the river as diversion . . . but the rest? Where?"

"And no tracks leading away, none we've seen anyway." Ralf wouldn't expect any less of Robin. Lulled them into confidence and vanished. Were they meant to come this far and no farther? Barré threw a prophetic glance toward the cave. "Won't the king love this. What now?"

"Now we search. There are tracks somewhere." Ralf swept his sight about the area in a full circle. Stopped. Narrowed on the thickest underbrush and gorse close at hand. "There."

A quarter hour later, Rossel emerged from the cave bellowing for the sheriff of Nottingham. All within earshot took warning. The king was in a dangerous mood. "Nothing, you hear? Nothing. A few pieces to make us waste time digging, that's all. He will pay. He heaps insult on insult." Rossel slung his improvised mattock into the cave. "His lands are forfeit, Fitz-Gerald. Everything. Raze Blidworth, burn his hall, slaughter his stock, turn his people out to beg. I'm sick of this!"

Ralf did not move. "My lord, I beg you reconsider."

Rossel blinked at the quiet strength denying him. "What did you say?"

Ralf answered respectfully, but his mind raced. He and Barré had found something, possibly the key to Robin's strategy. Whatever the man risked, his own life was the least of it. There were Marian and the children; for them, Ralf would risk as much out of love. "You should not, *mon roi*."

"Everything, you hear? His lands come from me—"

"From your royal father, who then put Denby within my honors. Robin is my vassal."

Rossel descended on the smaller man like a Channel storm about to break. Barré flinched at that fury hovering over his lord and quite ready to strike him down. "Little man, do not tempt me."

"If my liege will?" Ralf invited the king aside from the others and spoke in a low tone. "The king will appreciate privacy in my reasons." He led Rossel to the thickets he had studied earlier. Rossel indulged him with the thinnest patience, arms akimbo, blue eyes icy and flat with anger. "Well? What?"

Ralf chose his words with care, knowing he dare not retreat an inch. Rossel was capable of anything now. Years Robin spent with this fine soldier and ruinous king, yet never learned to think *like* him. "Sire, there are measures, extremes a king cannot afford. Your father knew this."

"Speak plainly. We're wasting time."

"I speak of fealty, the very mortar to our strength. Denby is to me what I am to you, sworn on his oath and receiving mine before God.

Whatever men believe privately, they form a natural chain of loyalties through this wise custom. Break that chain, and what officers, what lords will feel secure in their lands or titles?''

Rossel turned away, seething to be gone, to close and end it. ''You don't understand.''

''My liege, I do. You cannot afford to put anger before your oath.''

''You presume—you dare to tell me of limits to my place?''

''No, sire. The crown you wear warns against that abuse.''

Something suspicious and sly flitted across Rossel's open anger. ''Are you looking to his lands for yourself?''

Ralf quelled the urge to scream at the stupidity. *Name of a saint, are you human at all? Take from Marian and the children? Their guts are in this land. You never paid that price for anything.* ''His son is my wife's cousin. If Edward is leagued with Robin in this, I will give you both their lives if I must; that's my duty and their lot. But I will *not* confiscate Denby nor pauper his blood.'' Ralf met the king eye for eye to emphasize every word. ''My vassal, sire. My decision.''

For all the spleen eating at him, Rossel could admire this aging knight whose virtue, as old William remarked, was that he was easily satisfied with a little place and a loving wife. ''Fitz-Gerald . . . have you gone Saxon on me?''

Ralf beckoned him behind the stand of gorse, pointing to a bare patch of muddy earth. Clear in the yard-wide stretch, a single bootprint was imbedded. ''Robin.''

''You are sure?''

All his life Robin threw his weight to the outside of his foot in walking, wearing down the boot heel unevenly; its impression slanted so in the mud. Barré had found the tracks of five horses north of the cave, but only one set deep enough for a ridden mount. One last trick and a dangerous one considering how little time Robin had to bury the plate in this cave and get away. ''Forget the horses, my lord. Robin's afoot and moving south again.''

Ralf would not share the rest of the premonition with Rossel. One last unexpected twist, as Robin so often bested him at chess. A feigned retreat, sacrificing pieces all the way, Ralf slashing across the board after him; then, as he prepared to checkmate—mated himself. Robin meant Rossel to lose the others, lose all but him. If there must be sacrifice, Robin would expend himself. *Follow,* his footprint summoned them. *Spend yourself on me, Rossel.*

Rossel went down on one knee over the bootprint. "You are absolutely sure it is him?"

"No question."

"And the treasure?"

Ralf could only shrug. "God knows. But you will have him."

"Well enough. We are not ignorant of our oaths, Sheriff. Or our fealty. Or the verdict of Holy Church that condemns him." Crouched over the signature in the mud, the whole unhealable wound of his life in one upraised fist: "Witness me, Fitz-Gerald! We, William, by the Grace of God, King of the English, decree that the sentence of death passed in Lincoln be presently executed on Edward of Denby, known as Robin Hood. Done this fifth day of May in the year 1089. *Done!*"

The fist slammed down, pressing Rossel's seal into the footprint. He hunched there, frozen over his act. "I'll settle for Robin. Find him."

Then Barré was with them, reporting a trail picked up along a swine track deep in the brush, so seldom used he found it only by blind luck. Three men moving south, perhaps four. "No more than—they must have had us in sight when they slipped away. Not far ahead now."

43

LADY Maud slipped out of Denby gate, only dimly aware of closing it behind her. There were more and more gaps like that in her memory of late, but she remembered Robin telling her she must do something today, go somewhere if . . .

She tried to recall as her wandering way led toward the forest. If something happened, there was that she must do with Mauger. Yes, she clearly remembered that much. Maud skirted the dale, turning north toward the heart of Denby, the bargain oak. Aelred would—Mauger would—be waiting for her. She must hurry.

Three miles north of Blidworth in the ancient virgin stand of beech and oak not far from the bargain tree, Marian and Beorn scattered leaves and deadwood over the last traces of burial. The exhausted folk had angled their pit in under the roots of a bramble bush, pulling the thorny stems forward to cover their work completely. As each group finished their stint they were sent home with Marian's thanks and the blessing of Father Beorn.

"Nip along now," Marian sped the last of them on their way. "Wash the dirt well from your hands. Mind, you've not stirred from your hearths this day."

Beorn rested his weary, overtaxed body against a tree, one hand on his sword hilt. "Done, Marian. Now back to your hall with you."

She tucked her skirts up into the soiled apron where they'd loosened in digging. "Go you on, Father."

"You must go. You know Robin's orders."

344

"Aye, and you?"

"I will be that close behind you." Beorn's sudden grin for a moment wiped away his age. "In the event of trolls."

Marian understood and loved him fiercely just then, futile as he might be. "One sword, Father? Don't be foolish."

"Woman, don't tell a man what to do."

"Rob always knew the difference between brave and stupid. Your church needs you." She kissed his lean cheek. "We will meet soon again. We will all be together."

Beorn looked after her as she moved away through the trees. Tired as he was, he didn't comprehend until Marian was almost out of sight, not toward Denby, but going north. "Marian!"

Beorn jogged after her, cursing himself for crying out. No telling how close the king's men were now. He caught her up, shaking a stern finger in her face. "Don't talk fool to me and then be one. What are you doing? The plan—"

"Enough." Marian laid a finger on his lips. "Mauger knows what to do. He'll see to Mum and Moira and the rest."

"You know what Robin wanted. You promised."

"Promised nowt. I said I understood his wishes. By now they're done at the cave. Whatever comes, I'll be with him."

"Then I'm going with you. No, don't argue, girl. And be quiet. They might have heard me call out just now."

They moved away, north through the thickest brush, not trusting even the swine trails now. The sound of a hunting horn froze them both still.

"Norman horn," Beorn whispered.

"But Robin's call. Signal to Will and Morgan should they be parted from him. King will think it one of his own." Marian lifted her head. "Aye, love, I'm coming and you'll just have to put up with that."

Less than a quarter mile behind them, the five royal huntsmen milled about, frustrated at the impossibility of so many people just vanished or taken wing. Then they'd heard someone call a name and moved on after the sound, crossbows cocked. One of them found a barely visible but fresh trail: two people moving carefully but unable to avoid a bit of crushed bracken or part of a footprint.

"One is a woman."

A man and a woman. Possibly *him* and his wife. Then, farther off than the cry that set them on but from the same direction, two short notes on a silver hunting horn. King William was near. The huntsmen stepped along swiftly as caution permitted. Between themselves and the approaching king, for all the vanished thieves and treasure gone, they had *someone* nearly brought to bay.

From strike to escape, Robin's plan was conceived like an icicle: solid but melting away as each group of folk completed its tasks. While his picked group lured Rossel to the cave, the bulk of the treasures were buried in three previously dug pits scattered through Sherwood. Robin's family was to disappear into the thinly populated vastness of Northumbria, where he and Edward, Will, and Morgan would join them. If possible. If not, Robin counted on Ralf to do anything else before confiscating Edward's heritage. Edward would get out regardless of what happened. Time would pass, Rossel—stung but neither constant nor implacable as his father—would turn away and forget, or even die young. For the rest, Robin took his chances and reckoned at least some of his old luck left to see them through. The last game and a splendid one, the best of all. Ralf would say he need not have played and folly to try. No, this had to be. Denby would not live with a sword over its head, but no need yet to sing requiems while Robin could still call the turn.

After two near-encounters with Rossel's men, the four of them had separated. Within minutes of the horn signal, the two Welshmen slid soundlessly out of the thickets to rejoin Robin and Edward. The older men felt the strain now, tension and lack of sleep, all the way from Ollerton on foot. Ralf would be as spent, Robin calculated, and the king's men too at the pace Rossel set for them. Edward bounded along, eager as when they set out. Robin had forgotten how it felt to be fifteen, proud as he was of the boy. As well as he could reckon, none of the folk had been caught. Done neat as a pin . . . when it was done. Rossel and Ralf would be that close now.

Then Edward touched his shoulder, pointing into the thick tangle of underbrush to their south. Arrows already set to their bows, Will and Morgan stanced, ready. They heard the soft rustle of movement where Edward had pointed. Robin hooked his bowstring—then heard Will's low warning.

"Hold, it is Marian."

Relieved and frightened at once, Robin hurried toward the two figures emerging from the thicket. "Jesus, I almost—and you, Beorn. What is this?"

Beorn spread his hands. "She would not go without you, and there it is."

"Fine! Damn it, girl, do you have no respect for my wishes? D'you know how close they are? Didn't I tell you to ride with Mauger?"

"The world's in God's hands, not yours." Marian beamed imperturbably at her husband. "And we're wasting time."

Robin felt rattled and confused. She'd changed everything. Concern for her safety blotted out his ability to think. He hesitated; sensing that uncertainty in him, Morgan spared Robin the decision.

"I'll be asking a few shafts of you, Scatloch." As Morgan placed them in the quiver, his head came up, alert. "I hear them. Close."

He strode out toward the hazel thicket from which Beorn and Marian had come. Not the best cover, but fair concealment. "Go on, all of you. I'll give them that much to think on."

"We both will." Beorn drew his sword and discarded the scabbard, taking his stand beside Morgan. "Regrets, Lord Robin, but I am flat run out."

Robin shook his head, incoherent. No time to argue or stay. The thing was turning beyond his control. "I'd expect better sense out of my priest."

Morgan hissed a last warning at him. "Away!"

To his priest Robin made one last entreaty. "God knows—"

"He does." Beorn signed the Cross over them as they padded away through the forest. Morgan methodically stuck arrows in the earth before him. He plucked up a bit of grass, kissed it, and let it fall. Himself here he might understand, but not Beorn and his old sword and no cloth of his calling about the man. "Not that you need reminding, but the saints will be asking weighty questions of you."

Beorn heard the rustling in the bush not many yards in front of them. Coming nearer. "And I have seen better Christians than you."

"What will you do with just a sword?"

"They will come that close."

"So close I cannot miss," Morgan agreed with a hint of relish. "Father, there are two matters that may go hard with me."

Beorn gripped the sword tighter. "I am not hearing confessions today."

"There's pity, for I have lived uncharitably."

"Easy, think I see 'em."

"Two things I could never abide." Morgan hooked his string. "A woman in the house longer than it took to bed her, and foreigners. So." Morgan's stance and press were one silken movement. The arrow whistled, ended in a grunt of shock.

347

"*Prenez garde!* They are here!"

Morgan loosed again. He bent for a third arrow as the answering crossbolts whistled wide of him. Before he could stop the priest, Beorn lifted his sword and charged out into the open, blade swinging high over his head.

Beorn could see two of them; they were enough. The prayer or curse tore out of him as he picked his man, almost within sword length when the bolt took him full in the chest. Beorn jerked with the force of the missile, crumpled to one knee, and fell over on his side.

The three Norman huntsmen were momentarily too startled for caution. They stared down at the body of an old man who'd roared out of the bush at them like a part of the forest itself come to lethal life. "Just an old grandfa—"

The long cloth-yard arrow took the man in the middle of the word, expelling the last of it in an explosive rush of air. The other two dove behind a fallen log, too shaken to move. Cautiously, they signaled their remaining companions to set and loose with them.

Morgan shifted to his right. Two down; the others would have a good sense of his position now. He shook the hazel bush to his left, ducking away as three bolts ripped through it. Three out there, at least three. He pursed his lips, breathing an old Powys tune as he drew and loosed for the last time. He would be going now. Robin was a good lord and one to sing of, but Morgan was not minded to die for any Saxon this day.

Time lost, maddening delay, and Robin must be laughing through it all. In the wilderness of northern Sherwood, exasperated but driven, Rossel left the useless, exhausted horses with most of his equally played-out company and pressed on afoot with Ralf and twenty of his hardiest men. Barré found the fresh tracks. Here five or six of them had paused. Four went on, a woman among them.

So Ralf and Rossel found the two dead huntsmen and three frightened others who had declined to go on without help. Rossel kicked them to their feet contemptuously. As for the other body—"A crazy old man, my lord. Came screaming out from just there where the other devil waited, the one with the bow. Swinging his sword at us as if he could make a difference. He might have," the man considered, "but we were wound and ready. Is he the one the Saxons called Robin Hood?"

"No." Ralf was weary with the long chase, slumping under the weight of the mail coat over his sweat-sodden clothes. Pointless to tell these indifferent hinds who had come at them or why. He knelt by Beorn's body, drew the bolt from the still-warm flesh, and straightened the limbs. Will Scatloch always said Beorn had the look of a hunting hawk; the open eyes were still those of a defiant raptor. Ralf pressed the lids down over them as Rossel snatched up the crossbow and quiver from one of the dead huntsmen.

"He's moving west, but still close." Rossel wound the bow and set a bolt. "Now I'll have him."

Something in the man's face Ralf did not want to look on.

With no time to cover their tracks, Robin chose his way through the thickest brambles and undergrowth, Marian behind him, Will and Edward trailing to cover them. At times they had to belly under hazel and thorn, snagged and scratched as they crawled forward.

Robin helped his wife to her feet. "Not far now. Just—" He broke off, catching Will's hand signal. Edward pointed to his ear, then back at the broad stand of bramble they'd just crept through. Robin listened for the sounds no town folk would hear: the rustle of a bush thrust aside, the faint clink of metal or *tick* of a twig snapped under a man's weight. He pulled Marian close, beckoning the others. "Behind and to our left."

"And right," Will made it.

"At least we've the clear way out," Robin whispered. "You two go on with Marian. I can hold them up long enough. Get to Wulf Edricson."

Edward nocked an arrow to his string. "No, let me."

"No time to argue, son. And no fear. You don't think those sods will get *me*, do you?"

"Or me," his son protested fiercely. "I'm faster than you."

"Louder, too." Robin shoved him forward, but Edward rebelled, turning on him with love angry as his pride. "I'm not a boy."

A memory flared bright in Robin's mind: Aelred at York, ordering him home for the same reasons he now denied Edward, the same imperative love. "There needn't be me anymore, but there will be you."

Marian understood. She kissed her son quickly. "We'd task no boy with this. It is a man we ask. Go."

Robin put out a hand to his son—then flinched as the crossbolt whined close enough to fan the air across his cheek. "Down!"

Flattened on the ground, he heard the familiar voice that defied Philip at Gisors, the reckless love that raised him up at Rouen, warned him at Grantham when love tore down the middle. "Robin, you hear me?"

Robin snaked an arrow from his quiver. "Get them gone, Will. *Now.*"

"I didn't have to miss, Robin. *C'est fini.* Surrender. I'll let the others go."

"Robin, there's no chance." Ralf's voice, reluctant, pleading. "Let the others go and come out."

For all of them, hunters and hunted, time stilled and hovered, then rushed into the vacuum of that one moment, all creation shrunk to this patch of forest under a dirty grey sky. Robin weighed odds. No cover and little concealment, but enough for a swift fox like Edward. He grasped the boy's arm, started to pull him to his feet—only to be pushed sharply off balance from behind.

Edward cried out: "Mum, *no!*"

Marian darted off through the thickets toward the Normans, bending low but thrashing loudly through the brush to divert attention. Robin sprinted after her, forgetting Rossel, forgetting all except that this could not happen. Only a stride behind her, reaching to pull her down out of danger as he heard Rossel's barked command to loose. Robin leaped and bore Marian to the ground as the wasp-flight of missiles converged on them both.

44

THEY riddled the bramble patch with more than thirty bolts. They couldn't all have missed. Robin wasn't that lucky. Rossel's hands shook as he braced the crosspiece to wind the bow again. *Was it me got you? I didn't want this—*

His thought cut off in shock and pain as the grey-feathered arrow tore through mail, cloth, and the flesh of his upper arm. Rossel went white, sagging back against the tree as Ralf hurried to him. "The king is hurt!"

Rossel pushed him away with a snarl. "To hell with that. Get Robin."

But the men dragged him back behind the tree to better cover. Ralf snapped the long shaft and pulled the arrowhead through. Barré cut away the torn mail and sleeve. The arrow had missed bone but pierced through the thick muscle. "You cannot continue, *mon roi.*"

As Rossel glared at the man, the new voice lanced across the yards of bracken and thicket. "Norman!"

Rossel's head jerked around, eager though pale with shock. "Robin? I told you I needn't miss."

"Nor I." Not Robin, not that young voice high-pitched with tension and hatred. "Stay down, Norman. Or try against me."

Rossel pushed the men away from him. "Move out. You know where Robin is. Get him."

"There are others out there," Ralf cautioned.

"I've given the order. Spread out. Take him!"

A few of the men began to creep forward warily, using every inch of cover, toward the stand of bramble where their quarry had gone to ground. Behind the tree with his king, Ralf heard the quick *thum! thum!* of longbow strings—*God, they're close. No more than thirty yards. Get out, Edward!*—then the strangled cry as one of Rossel's men jerked and rolled over.

"Come, lord king," Edward taunted Rossel over the hostile ground between them. "You try this time."

Ralf cursed the desperate recklessness of the boy. *For the love of all of them, Edward, go! Your father's done, you can't help him more.*

Rossel peered cautiously out of cover, ascertaining the deployment of his huntsmen. One was down, the others not moving. "That's not Robin," he told them. "Just a boy out there. Can't you tell a boy from a man? Go on!"

One of the men slithered quickly over the fallen log that covered him and rolled twice, three times toward a tangle of fallen branches. Encouraged by his action, a second man tried a rush, broke from cover in three long running strides before the two arrows struck him. The rest of the men froze, hugging the ground.

"Name of Lucca!" Rossel roared at them. "He'll slip away. Must I show you how?"

"Stay down," Ralf hissed at him. "They've got your range."

"Get away. All of you, follow me!"

The crossbow clutched in his good hand, Rossel lurched forward, seeing only that patch of bush. *"Robin—"*

Bow at the ready, he charged at the bramble patch, not caring who followed. The long arrow barely missed his back, driving into the ground beyond. With a raw cry, Rossel disappeared around the bramble patch, leaving a silence in his wake. Ralf held his breath. The silence drew out. Several of the men called to the king but heard no answer.

Barré looked at Ralf fatalistically. "Perhaps it is over."

One way or another. In the instant before the first bolts flew at Robin, Ralf had glimpsed the smaller figure, a dun blur against green. They might both be dead, or perhaps Robin had tricked the hounds one last time. *Let it be so. Let Edward go, let Rossel bleed to death or mortify, I don't care now.* But he could not help caring, unable to conceive beyond those few yards between him and Robin.

Then Rossel's voice called him sharply from the thicket. "Fitz-Gerald!"

Barré started to rise, but Ralf stopped him. "No. Follow me. Keep kissing the ground, we'll live longer."

They bellied forward, flattened to the earth.

352

* * *

Ralf was first to reach Rossel. The king stood motionless, the still-cocked bow dangling at his side. All about the trampled fern and bracken the short bolts protruded from the ground thick as flowers in a meadow. Robin's bow and quiver lay at Rossel's feet. The rest was easily read. Here, someone fell in the growth of fern and left the dark blood of a deep wound. Then a broad, crushed path where one had dragged the other for a few yards before the deeper bootprints began, too heavily pressed down for Robin's weight alone.

Barré's lips moved, silently counting the bolts about him. "We made a sieve out of . . . impossible."

Rossel's wound bled freely now; he ignored it, bent over the drag marks. "I told you he'd get out. *C'est impossible,* but so is he."

The huntsmen retrieving bolts from the ground believed with no difficulty at all. They stalked a witch, and the Devil looked after his own. This hunt became an unnatural thing, showed them deeds beyond human men, but not warlocks. They would tell of this day for years.

Ralf held up the two snapped-off bolt ends. "He will not be hard to follow. My lord, we must dress that wound before you go on."

"Never should have left me. . . . " Rossel brushed his fingers over the blood-stained ferns. "Yes, wrap me and be quick. We finish this now."

Above, the ravens gathered, wheeling in the sky to the north of them. Ralf knew there need be no hurry now. He felt old.

Through the thinning stand of silver birch as they hurried along, Edward could see Wulf Edricson waiting with four fresh horses beside his own. Two more than they would need now, perhaps ever. Wanting to cry or be sick, his voice caught on the edge of a sob. "I was on him clean, I had him. How did I miss?"

"You hurried the loose." Will pushed him on toward the horses and safety. "But you marked the man, and your father and mother had time to slip out. You did your best, Edward-fach."

Edward's merciless young doom on himself would not allow that much comfort. No, not well done, not near his best. Failed them in their greatest need, plain as that. Pressing bow on the Norman king, he hated the man too much to loose clean. *There will be no haste next time, William, I promise. Next time I'll do it easy and smiling.*

Edward swallowed back the sob and broke into a trot toward the horses and the future before him.

353

* * *

Robin struggled toward the faint sound of the rill. Weak now, spent with the weight of Marian in his arms. Not much farther, just across the stream to the bargain oak—but too far without rest. He had to stop. No use trying to draw the bolt from his right shoulder; it had driven in at too deep an angle, he'd only lose blood the faster. Nothing to be done for Marian. The missile was too close to her heart. Nothing for either of them but where he carried her. He couldn't risk setting her down, not sure he could lift her again, or himself. Robin rested against the ancient beech trunk, sucking air into his lungs, fighting dizziness. Full circle they'd come. Met in a forest nineteen years ago, running from Normans and in trouble even then. All their married life had been shadowed by these men, but grew and throve despite them like flowers that prospered on Sherwood's floor with what little sun they could find.

Marian's eyes fluttered open. They had been dull with shock when he dragged her from the thicket, shadowed with coming night now. "They hurt you, Robin."

"Easy, love. They ent got us yet."

But she knew the truth, felt it coming more swiftly for her. "To our tree, Robin?"

"Yes." He tightened his failing grip on her body. An enormous effort to push himself away from the beech and move forward. The rill ran only a few strides beyond, and then their clearing and the bargain oak. He'd never have reached Denby. Better this way.

Marian whispered against his chest. "Don't want to leave you."

"You'll never leave me again."

"Does it hurt much?"

"No," he lied. "Not much now."

"I can't feel anything."

Only a few more steps to the rill. "Eh, girl, we gave 'em a good run, didn't we?"

Marian's head tilted back. She sought his eyes with her own and wanted truth. "Moira and Edward . . . ?"

"Got clean away."

"Don't lie."

"Could I ever lie to you? They're safe, Marian."

Robin stumbled and caught himself. Marian's arm crept up his back to stroke his neck and hair. "Look at me."

A man wouldn't think to find eyes so dark in a woman fair as Marian. Dark and deep and honest. They had never aged, clear and direct now

354

as the day he first found her lost and grieving for her family and her cat Biddy, but still able to cut his arrow from a dead Norman.

Her lips barely moved. "Oh, Robin. Oh, love. . . . "

He didn't feel her hand fall away from his back. The bargain tree and the hut blurred together in Robin's vision, but something moved in the blur.

"It's Mum," he said to his burden as he bore her the last few yards. He set Marian down by their oak, pausing to catch his breath that came so shallowly now. The world seemed to shrink in on him, denying time and space. Robin lay against the bargain oak. What was Maud doing here? She should have gone with Mauger. Oh, she forgot, that was her way.

Or perhaps Maud chose this place clearly as himself. No matter, reasons were unimportant now. Robin undid the kerchief and buried his fingers in Marian's hair: faded through the years, but the hints of gold were still there when Angharad washed and brushed it out.

Rossel wouldn't have either one of them; they'd get out together. Fair enough and passing fair. God didn't let Marian suffer too much in her wounding, nor would He now in her passage. For his own case— well, there was a tangled matter for any lawyer, what with the Church edict to complicate prosecution. No, let God look through his deed to the intent, as in that old story Father Beorn once told. *Let the Angel write on us: Inasmuch.* For the rest, give him a few English for jury and he just might win.

"Aelred."

The old woman bent close over Robin, cradling his head. So tired, he let it rest in her arms.

"I knew you would come," she murmured.

Robin tried to see her face. "Take my knife, Mum."

"We were here, remember. Even here we conceived Robin."

"Hurry." He pressed the blade into her grip. "The king's coming and there's that yet to do."

She was clearer to him now. She had removed her veil and unbound her hair so that it fell in white waves about her face. She whispered to him and through him to another reality. "This is where we made the pact."

Maud let the knife dangle in her hand, only part of her here and now, most with Aelred and a time the sinking sun could never steal from her. Then her grip firmed on the handle. Her eyes knew him and the still woman beside him. "Marian, too?"

355

"She's gone on." Robin stretched out his bared wrists to her. "I'd be with her. Haste now. And bless you, Mum."

A little sting, nothing beside the other wound, though even that pain was ebbing now. When the thing was done, Robin pressed his wrists overhead to the oak, pouring and setting his last seal to the ancient bargain. When he could hold his arms up no longer, he laced his fingers again in Marian's hair and watched with no interest the foolish men coming too late out of the forest toward the rill. So far away and moving so slowly. They called to him, but they didn't matter. He was drowsy, bent for sleep and Marian and their forest closing tenderly about them both.

At the rill's edge Rossel warned his men back. "He is mine. He belongs to me."

"My vassal, sire," Ralf reminded him. "And my friend as once he was yours. Do not deny me. Let's go together."

Rossel glared at the still figures by the oak. "How did you know he would come here?"

"The ravens. And because he is Robin."

The black scavenger birds circled slowly over the clearing. Rossel jumped the stream and closed the last distance, Ralf at his side, until they stood by the old woman bowed low over her knees by her son.

"Damn you," Rossel accused the still figure propped against the tree. "All you had to do was follow me. Why did you make me do this? Why?"

No answer and far past answering. Robin's gaze was fixed on Rossel, the edges of his mouth curled in the beginning of familiar laughter, an expression Ralf had known through half his life: gentled with age now, more humorous than arrogant, but never so far from that failing a man couldn't smart beneath its scathing. I've beaten you, that smile said to Rossel: ran you out of horses and men and now you'll never catch me again.

That is you, Robin, Ralf thought by way of elegy. *The world's wrong and you were always right. But the world is Rossel and always will be.*

"Did I ask so much?" Rossel challenged the unmoving figure. "Was it so hard to be loyal? You—just like my mother. We could have done so much, been so much together. But no. Just like her, you made me beg and then walked away."

Ralf's fatigue was an increasing burden under the galling weight of his mail coat, yet he felt a savage urge to take Rossel by his neck, turn him about, and kick him. Tiresome man. That such a great soldier could be so small a king. *Be still, you fool.* Ralf moved past him, bending to close Robin's eyes.

"He does not listen, *mon roi.*"

Rossel pointed to Marian. "This one? His woman?"

"His wife. Lady Marian." Ralf had spared himself that sight, too aware of the cost. Now he impaled his heart on a knife and knelt by her. She could not have lived with such a wound, but her eyes were closed in peace and there was no mark of suffering in her face.

Robin was rich in you, nor was I a fool to love you all those years ago. I knew him and yet never fathomed him. What more did he want, Marian? What did he reach for that was not offered him in your arms?

"This one's alive." With vindictive energy, Rossel made to pull Maud erect. Without thinking what he did, Ralf could not allow it. He caught the king's arm in a stern grip.

"Gently, sire. She is old. Let me." Not a request but a statement. Ralf took the bowed old woman by the shoulders to help her up. As she rose, Ralf was behind her. He didn't see the knife flash out of her sleeve. Rossel cried out in warning as Maud turned on Ralf, thrusting up and in with Robin's knife. He caught her wrists but not before the blade found the old rent in his mail. Ralf flinched at the sudden burning sear. Not a deep wound, she had not strength enough left to kill. They hung there together, Ralf's hands slippery with the blood flowing too swiftly from Maud's own wrists, facing a determination unteachable as Rossel's before the king tore her away and she fell on her side next to Robin. Her head moved and her eyes sought Ralf.

"Little bastard, do not trouble me now."

Rossel waved his men to join them. "Quickly, Barré. Look to the sheriff. How is it, Fitz-Gerald? The old bitch was too quick."

"No . . . no. It is nothing." The blade had only broken his skin, no more. "She surprised me, that is all. Leave me alone." He shoved Barré away from him. "It is not deep."

Deep enough for him to feel the blood seeping through the linen under his tunic. One more wound for Judith to tend, one more mark this England and this family left on him. Ralf stripped off his gauntlets and fumbled at the buckles of the mail coat. His hands didn't work right. "Help me, Barré. I am very tired."

"All of them mad," Rossel despaired. "Or witches. Was he a witch, Fitz-Gerald?"

"No."

357

"Then why was it so difficult for him, for any of them, to understand?"

Ralf dropped the armor and sat down awkward as a sack. The Norman huntsmen stood about, waiting the will of their king, uncaring as the ravens overhead. His own voice sounded alien and hoarse. He was weeping. "William," he said, "take it on trust. You will understand before ever they do. As the old woman said, do not trouble them now."

SOUTHWEST AIRLINES®

TSA PRE

LAUDERDALE/LESLIE

LESLIE LAUDERDALE

Flight 5220   Gate E18

Apr 14, 2019

BOARDING PASS

Confirmation Number: SV8AY3

FROM	TO	FLT#	TIME	FB	BOARDING
STL	MDW	5220	07:20PM	O	08:30PM

EARLY BIRD

Boarding Group **A**

Position **39**

WNE22854   SV8AY3

39R

SOUTHWEST AIRLINES

OPEN SEATING

39

LAUDERDALE/LES

Conf.   SV8AY3

Apr 14, 2019

5220   ST LOUIS LAMBERT
to   CHICAGO MIDWA

47826225

RR ERBD

A
39

45

> ⮞⮞⮞⮞⮞

AUGUST A.D. 1100: this Lammastide, England's future hinged on recent and unforeseen events. Turbulent, gusty Rossel was dead at forty, accidentally killed by his hunting companion Tirel, Count of Poix—or so men said. The circumstances left room for suspicion. Tirel did quit the scene on the instant, galloping out of New Forest to take ship for France. Henry, the Conqueror's youngest son and a member of the hunting party, rode immediately to secure the treasury at Winchester and three days later, on the fifth of August 1100, became Henry I of England. Of Rossel's death, Edward Edwardson and close-mouthed others knew what they knew. The grave and the questions were closed, Henry crowned two days later.

Edward waited with Ralf Fitz-Gerald in the babel of crowded, echoing Westminster Hall. His eye roved about the vast space, marking this baron or bishop, that royal sheriff. The two white-haired old Welshmen, one amused, the other wary, stayed close to Edward like good hounds at heel. This day would be Henry's first working court. He and Ralf would be called forth soon, nor did they imagine that summons would be couched in generous goodwill. Edward took shrewd measure of the new king: thirty-two, thoughtful and reserved in contrast to his flamboyant brother, Henry retained that watchful manner Robin had marked in the half-grown boy. No easy informality about him; like the Conqueror himself, that eye missed nothing and drew a circle about Henry that kept men at a distance. The mind was far sharper than Rossel's, if darker. Henry dealt with men and orders without raising his voice, as one who expected to be obeyed without question.

"About Ranulf," Ralf spoke close in Edward's ear. "D'Abetot of Worcester confirmed what we heard. The dear bishop's been taken to the Tower."

"There's progress," said Edward.

"I think few will weep." Neither of them by now deluded himself about Ranulf's prodigious talent for survival. Such men were to a kingdom what scullions were to a kitchen. Meanwhile, Henry came to his throne under unusual circumstances, formally acknowledging a clear debt to his realm. Part of that bill had been presented yesterday by Vicomte Ralf in the name of the barons and lords of Nottinghamshire, the written articles informed by Norman self-interest and Saxon shrewdness.

Stationed on the dais by Henry's chair of state, Walter Giffard consulted his schedule and whispered to the king. Henry rose, having just dismissed the delegation from Norfolk. Giffard rapped his staff on the flagstones and cried out over echoing Westminster, "Fitz-Gerald, Vicomte of Nottingham."

The four shire men shouldered forward through the press of nobles and officers to kneel before their king. Henry bade them rise. A tall, spare man with the length of leg that would mark his Plantagenet descendants. He had received from Giffard another parchment before speaking to the hall at large. "Let all attend! Our honor, impawned at our coronation, requires that the pledges spoken then be writ in charter as binding on ourself and our successors."

Henry spoke directly to Ralf. Edward's guess had been right. There was no cordiality, even a hint of acid. "We have noted the wishes of the men of your shire, particularly in abolishing the abuses of our—of the previous reign." Henry allowed the old sheriff a measured smile, more of resignation than anything else. "They are prudently framed. Might have been writ by a lawyer."

"My liege, they were." Ralf nudged Edward forward. "By my vassal, Edward of Denby."

"Denby? Ah . . . yes. You are the lawyer from Sherwood?"

"Yes, sir."

"Let us be candid." Henry lowered his voice to be heard by these few alone. "It is royal custom to take oath, and that of subjects to accept it in fealty—and trust." The last word was emphasized rather heavily. "While doubting not of our subjects' good will, we consider the demand for writ impertinent."

Edward at twenty-seven was sensible enough to say nothing, hearing the warning in Henry's inflection. This noble impertinence conceived by his own father under Henry's had infected with its spirit every lord sworn to fealty this week. The new king had no choice but to accede, if with ill grace. A promise constituted a contract; written thus it became precedent for other promises, the cornerstone of law. If the reality of royal government implied the Ranulfs, so its spirit needed the Robins.

"But let all hear our royal pledge. These articles shall be executed in a hundred copies, signed and witnessed and published to our bishops and sheriffs throughout the realm."

The promise sounded a mite forced to Edward's ear. The Conqueror's son acknowledged the mass of the law before it fell on him.

"Of Denby, you say?" The king regarded Edward with no warmth but perhaps a certain *déjà vu.* "Were you ever called Robin?"

"Sometimes, sir. By my folk in Sherwood."

"We did think the name familiar . . . no matter. But mark you, Denby." Henry laid a hand on the younger man's shoulder. "Take care henceforth how you hedge a crown or the king who wears it. Go in peace. Let you all keep that peace," he added to Ralf and the old foresters in Lincoln green. "Farewell."

Their embassy done, the four men of Sherwood rode straight away from Westminster toward Ermine Street that led north and home.

"Did you hear?" Ralf exulted. "A hundred copies throughout England. Clear victory, Edward."

"When I see it in writing, Uncle."

"Careful as his da," Will Scatloch approved.

To Morgan of Powys, kings were as kings did. "This one speaks English fair enough. When he learns Welsh, then I will listen."

Edward now gave his concern to these three old men who had become pillars of his life in the absence of his father. Though fit for their years, Morgan and Will would be saddle-weary in a few hours. Uncle Ralf rode now with a cane tied to his pommel. The old knight's pride would not permit him to use it in front of Henry, but Edward knew what the vanity cost him. He decided to break their journey at the first inn along Ermine, claiming his own fatigue as reason.

A hundred copies of the coronation charter: a fine royal flourish, but royal memories were known to be brief. An extra copy tucked away at Denby had been good legal foresight. *One hundred and one, Henry. Da would call that mere good sense. In case my liege forgets.*

*　*　*

Some say Henry had grave misgivings about the charter he never wanted to sign, and made a nearly successful effort to recover all copies. Certainly they became so rare as to be completely forgotten over the next century. In another August, in the reign of Henry's great-grandson John, Stephen Langton, Archbishop of Canterbury, read from the pulpit of St. Paul's the contents of a parchment brittle and brown with age. Under the lamentable rule of John, Langton's purpose was to remind Englishmen of rights granted and then conveniently forgotten by anointed kings. Who inspired or wrote these articles was not known or important; the words and the idea behind them closed and locked about a crown that, whatever its wearer fancied, would never afterward be absolute in fact.

Henry, King of the English to all his barons and faithful men in Nottinghamshire, both French and English, greeting . . . I henceforth remove all the bad customs through which the kingdom of England has been unjustly oppressed; which bad customs I here in part set down. . . .

" 'Henceforth,' 'd' you mark that?'' Edward chortled to Ralf, spearing the written word with his finger like a cloth-yard arrow flying true to its mark. " 'Henceforth remove.' Forth from this time and for all time, there's the mark Da shot for. The precise words, the *precedent*. There'll be more words, Uncle, and more precise. Poor Henry: Must have flamin' nigh killed him to sign.''

Most shrewdly conceived and written, nor was Henry the last to feel the sting. When King John signed Magna Charta in the meadow at Runnymede, he learned like his ancestor how costly to kingship to sign anything framed by an English lawyer.

Afterword

▶▶▶▶▶

S INCE Anglo-Norman royal itineraries for 1083–1089 are specifically known, I have followed them closely as framework for this story. The accident at Mantes that resulted in William's death, when described to a modern physician, was estimated to be a ruptured spleen. If this was the case, no contemporary medical procedure could have saved him. The king's last hours at St. Gervais are minutely described in David C. Douglas's *William the Conqueror* based on eye-witness and later accounts. In the latter, William supposedly made a long confession stating that he had no right to the English crown. Beyond the tendency of apologists to adorn the life of a great king, this is highly questionable. What William may have privately confessed before receiving extreme unction would have made little difference, his son William (Rossel) already named to succeed him. Douglas puts forth Norman custom to explain why William passed over Robert for the English crown: that the practice was to bequeath lands of inheritance (Normandy) to the first son, those of conquest to the next. But since the Conqueror's every move was toward consolidated personal rule, it is much more likely that he took Robert's repeated defections and unreliable character into account in making his choice.

The shabby abandonment of the king's body by nobles and prelates and the looting of his chamber by menials is also a matter of record. Rossel cannot be personally blamed for this, since his father ordered him to make for Winchester to secure the royal treasury, a standard first step on succession in that age.

William II, designated "Rufus" by history, was apparently not so called in his lifetime (circa 1060–1100). Frank Barlow in *William Rufus* suggests that his family nickname was Rosel which might mean "little bird." I've called him "Rossel" because the added *s* seems stronger in narrative use and to avoid reader confusion with his father and the plethora of contemporary Williams.

Rossel has come down to us as one of England's more disastrous monarchs. The Church viewed him with horror, which he amply repaid in contempt, looting the riches of vacant bishoprics under his right of royal stewardship. Margaret Murray in *God of the Witches* argues that Rossel was a secret follower of the surviving Old Religion and that his death in New Forest, accidentally shot with an arrow by a companion, was actually a ritual sacrifice to which Rossel gave himself willingly. This would indicate a devotion which hardly goes with his rough, flippant, and wholly irreverent character. Very likely he gave no thought to any religion until the brief but alarming illness of his mid-reign, when he promised to amend his dissolute life and rule if spared, then promptly resumed them on recovery. More than one man has become a deathbed devout out of fear, only to renege later.

"A king can't keep all of his promises," he said afterward when Anselm reproached him. That *is* like the man.

What was Rossel then? From the prosecution: a catamite, a bisexual whose household was a licentious scandal from which women were conspicuously absent. A royal bandit who blithely looted the Church with Ranulf as his lockpick. A crude boor who loved to humiliate more dignified men. A cynic who, from one alleged remark, put no more credence in witches than in psalters and saints. A thoroughly secular soldier king.

From the defense: a loving, loyal son who toiled years for his father as an impecunious bachelor knight; who took a wound at Gerberoi defending William from Robert's own sword. Warm toward those few close to him and of unquestioned personal courage. Playful, profane, friendly toward his brother Henry, eight years his junior, though the hostility between Rossel and Robert appears to date from their youth. If riotous and dissolute, able to turn wholly to business when necessary and—a trait of critical importance, I think—with the shrewdness never to mix royal policy with pleasure or personal leanings. Barlow points out that his personal favorites in dalliance were never elevated to important posts.

Rossel's yearning for his mother Matilda's affection is my own interpolation, though her revulsion at his life is certainly consonant with the attitudes of the time. Rossel was a third son; until the death of Richard, he never expected to succeed to anything beyond a minor title or a cash settlement such as was bequeathed to Prince Henry. He slogged through William's wars as a younger son while Robert was spoiled and titled, young Richard doted on by his mother. The miserly William paid Rossel no more than any other bachelor knight in the royal employ. His later rapacity might have stemmed in part from this. To inherit a crown and a fortune after years of relative penury, it would be natural for him to go *nouveau riche,* flaunting and spending like a prodigal, which Rossel did. As for the flippancy always noted in him, this trait may have masked a number of deep personal wounds.

Ranulf of Bayeux (circa 1060–1124) was known as Flambard or "Torch" much later in his interesting life. Rising from obscurity, he became Rossel's *de facto* justiciar in the manipulation of vacant bishoprics before rising to the see of Durham in which he proved very capable. Later imprisoned by Henry I, he escaped to Normandy and lived to the then ripe age of sixty-four. I have followed the known facts of his character, appearance, and marriage, departing only in making him keeper of the Chancery seal perhaps a few years earlier than he actually assumed that post. In the last two years of the Conqueror's reign (1086–87), Ranulf's seal appears in witness to a number of writs, verifying that he was definitely important in the Chancery at that time. Apparently he was as aggressive and ruthless a lawyer as he was personally flamboyant and abrasive. Not surprising, given his origins. Competence may suffer fools graciously but never gladly. Ranulf had enough ego and vindictiveness to rub their noses in their own mediocrity, a trait no more endearing to men of his age than now.

His English wife was the daughter of a merchant, though nothing is known of her or the two children she bore him, except that Ranulf made generous provision for their living when he put them aside. For a priest to have a wife and children was not uncommon at the time. Only later did the Church achieve (relative) celibacy throughout its ranks.

Elfled's character and motivations are entirely my own invention, the sort of person (gender incidental) who will fixate on a fantasy with bottomless self-delusion. Her interpretation of what the seer read in her stars is typical of her self-dramatizing nature. Astrologers were universally condemned by the Church then, and universally consulted as they are today. Elfled's obsessive fears of possession by Robin would be taken quite seriously by the orthodox, her "evidence" accepted without serious question by an ecclesiastical court.

The darkened summer sky and the earthquake of 1089 are recorded in the *Anglo-Saxon Chronicle* for that year. Feeling that readers would be as skeptical as myself, a look at plate tectonics in an encyclopedia yielded one logical answer. The Mid-Atlantic Ridge, a line of plate tension, neatly bisects Iceland, one of the most active volcanic areas in the world today. With the right wind conditions, volcanic ash could have blotted out the sun for weeks, even months. The earthquake would have been of considerable magnitude to be felt in England—but the record is there.